Discover the newest voices of SF & fantasy as chosen by your favorite authors.

Twelve captivating tales from the best new writers of the year accompanied by three more from bestselling authors you've read before.

When her owner goes missing, a digital housecat must become more than simulation to find her dearest companion through the virtual world.
—"The Edge of Where My Light Is Cast" by Sky McKinnon

No one came to his brother's funeral. Not even the spirits. Étienne knew it was his fault.　　　—"Son, Spirit, Snake" by Jack Nash

Man overboard is a nightmare scenario for any sailor, but Lieutenant Susan Guidry is also running out of air—and the nearest help is light years away.　　　—"Nonzero" by Tom Vandermolen

Mac wanted to invent a cocktail to burn itself upon the pages of history—but this one had some unexpected side effects.
—"The Last Drop" by L. Ron Hubbard and L. Sprague de Camp

Dementia has landed Dan Kennedy in Graydon Manor, and what's left of his life ahead seems dismal, but a pair of impossible visitors bring unexpected hope.
—"The Imagalisk" by Galen Westlake

When a teenage swamp witch fears her mama will be killed, she utilizes her wits and the magic of the bayou—no matter the cost to her own soul.
—"Life and Death and Love in the Bayou" by Stephannie Tallent

Our exodus family awoke on the new world—a paradise inexplicably teeming with Earth life, the Promise fulfilled. But 154 of us are missing....　　　—"Five Days Until Sunset" by Lance Robinson

Spirits were supposed to lurk beneath the Lake of Death, hungry and patient and hostile to all life.

—"Shaman Dreams" by S. M. Stirling

A new app lets users see through the eyes of any human in history, but it's not long before the secrets of the past catch up with the present.   —"The Wall Isn't a Circle" by Rosalyn Robilliard

In the shadows of Teddy Roosevelt's wendigo hunt, a Native American boy resolves to turn the tables on his captors, setting his sights on the ultimate prey—America's Great Chief.

—"Da-ko-ta" by Amir Agoora

When squids from outer space take over, a punk-rock P.I. must crawl out of her own miserable existence to find her client's daughter—and maybe a way out.

—"Squiddy" by John Eric Schleicher

Another outbreak? This time it's a virus with an eighty percent infection rate that effects personality changes…permanently.

—"Halo" by Nancy Kress

Planet K2-18b is almost dead, humanity is enslaved, and it's Rickard's fault. Now in his twilight years, he'd give an arm and a leg for redemption. Literally.

—"Ashes to Ashes, Blood to Carbonfiber" by James Davies

What if magic could do the unthinkable, and undo Death itself? Would you use it no matter the cost? What would you sacrifice for love?   —"Summer of Thirty Years" by Lisa Silverthorne

Joe is a prospector tasked with exploring the cosmos on behalf of an all-powerful government. Breadna is a toaster. There have been weirder love stories, but that's unlikely.

—"Butter Side Down" by Kal M

L. RON HUBBARD

PRESENTS

Writers of the Future
Anthologies

"This panoramic collection offers something for everyone, with sci-fi and fantasy stories that are both inventive and creative. A solid addition to any SFF collection and a delight for genre fans." —*Library Journal*

"Always a glimpse of tomorrow's stars…" —*Publishers Weekly* starred review

"The collection contains something for every reader of speculative fiction." —*Booklist*

"No other source has brought so many bestselling authors of speculative novels than this series that goes back so many years ago." —*Midwest Book Review*

"Writers of the Future is always one of the best original anthologies of the year." —*Tangent*

"The Writers of the Future Award has also earned its place alongside the Hugo and Nebula Awards in the triad of speculative fiction's most prestigious acknowledgments of literary excellence." —*SFFAudio*

"It really does help the best rise to the top." —Brandon Sanderson
Writers of the Future Contest judge

"The Writers of the Future Contest is a valuable outlet for writers early in their careers. Finalists and winners get a unique spotlight that says 'this is the way to good writing.'"

—Jody Lynn Nye
Writers of the Future Contest Coordinating Judge

"The book you are holding in your hands is our first sight of the next generation of science fiction and fantasy writers."

—Orson Scott Card
Writers of the Future Contest judge

"If you want a glimpse of the future—the future of science fiction— look at these first publications of tomorrow's masters."

—Kevin J. Anderson
Writers of the Future Contest judge

"The Contests are amazing competitions because really, you've nothing to lose and they provide good positive encouragement to anyone who wins. Judging the entries is always a lot of fun and inspiring. I wish I had something like this when I was getting started—very positive and cool."

—Bob Eggleton
Illustrators of the Future Contest judge

"I really can't say enough good things about Writers of the Future....It's fair to say that without Writers of the Future, I wouldn't be where I am today."

—Patrick Rothfuss
Writers of the Future Contest winner 2002

"You have to ask yourself, 'Do I really have what it takes, or am I just fooling myself?' That pat on the back from Writers of the Future told me not to give up....All in all, the Contest was a fine finishing step from amateur to pro, and I'm grateful to all those involved."

—James Alan Gardner
Writers of the Future Contest winner 1990

L. Ron Hubbard PRESENTS

Writers of the Future

VOLUME 40

L. Ron Hubbard PRESENTS
Writers of the Future

VOLUME 40

The year's twelve best tales from the
Writers of the Future international writers' program

Illustrated by winners in the Illustrators of the Future
international illustrators' program

Three short stories by L. Ron Hubbard /
Nancy Kress / S.M. Stirling

With essays on writing and illustration by
Gregory Benford / Bob Eggleton / L. Ron Hubbard /
Dean Wesley Smith

Edited by Jody Lynn Nye
Illustrations art directed by Echo Chernik

GALAXY PRESS, INC.

For information, contact Galaxy Press, Inc. at 7051 Hollywood Boulevard, Suite 200, Los Angeles, California 90028.

Special acknowledgments go to these first readers and beta readers: Kary English, Joe Benet, Bret Booher, James Davies, Victoria Dixon, Andrew Ericsson, Wendy Fawcett, Cara Giles, Jane M. Kaufenberg, Michael Kortes, Chloe Murphy, Lucy Murphy, Leah Ning, John Eric Schleicher, Martin L. Shoemaker, Lisa Silverthorne, Eric James Stone, Don Sweeney, Stephannie Tallent, Mike Wyant, Jr.

CONTENTS

Introduction

BY JODY LYNN NYE

Jody Lynn Nye lists her main career activity as "spoiling cats." When not engaged upon this worthy occupation, she writes fantasy and science fiction books and short stories.

Since 1987 she has published over fifty books and more than 180 short stories. Among her novels are her epic fantasy series, The Dreamland, *five contemporary humorous fantasies in the Mythology 101 series, three medical science fiction novels in the Taylor's Ark series, and* Strong Arm Tactics, *a humorous military science fiction novel. Jody also wrote* The Dragonlover's Guide to Pern, *a nonfiction-style guide to Anne McCaffrey's popular world. She also collaborated with Anne McCaffrey on four science fiction novels, including* Crisis on Doona *(a* New York Times *and* USA Today *bestseller). Jody coauthored the* Visual Guide to Xanth *with author Piers Anthony. She has edited two anthologies,* Don't Forget Your Spacesuit, Dear!, *and* Launch Pad, *and written two short-story collections,* A Circle of Celebrations, *holiday SF/fantasy stories, and* Cats Triumphant!, *SF and fantasy feline tales. Nye wrote eight books with the late Robert Lynn Asprin,* License Invoked, *and seven set in Asprin's Myth Adventures universe. Since Asprin's passing, she has published two more Myth books and two in Asprin's Dragons series. Her newest series is the Lord Thomas Kinago books, beginning with* View from the Imperium *(Baen Books), a humorous military SF novel.*

Her newest books are Moon Tracks *(Baen), YA science fiction with Dr. Travis S. Taylor;* Rhythm of the Imperium, *third in the series; and* Once More, With Feeling *(WordFire Press), a nonfiction book on revising manuscripts.*

Over the last thirty or so years, Jody has taught in numerous writing workshops and participated on hundreds of panels at science fiction conventions. She runs the two-day writers' workshop at Dragon Con. Jody is the Coordinating Judge of the Writers of the Future Contest. In June 2022, she received the Polaris Award from ConCarolina and Falstaff Books for mentorship and guidance of new talent.

Jody lives in the northwest suburbs of Atlanta, with her husband Bill Fawcett, and three feline overlords, Athena, Minx, and Marmalade.

Introduction

Once again, I am proud to present to you twelve brand-new stories that will delight you, expose you to new ideas, drag you through harrowing trials, make you think, cry, and laugh. The variety of stories, from time travel to dystopia to the memory of a child's imagination, is like a library between two covers. You have a treat waiting for you.

Every year that I have been involved in the Writers of the Future Contest, I have been impressed by the talent of up-and-coming writers. They have a vision, they explore it through the eyes of well-drawn characters in a world made vivid by their words, and they bring the plot to a conclusion that satisfies the reader's desire for adventure. It's hard to choose the finalists because there are always more than the eight per quarter that I am allowed to select from the myriad we receive, and just as hard to pick the three winners from that group. These are the best of the best.

Another important facet is their perseverance. In some cases, the success of these twelve writers is the result of years of submitting to the Contest. When one story didn't make the cut, they tried a fresh idea. In this year, each of them succeeded. I enjoyed each of these stories, and I am proud to have been a part of bringing the world's attention to these new writers.

I know there are many hopeful writers who want to join the ranks of Contest winners, and I encourage you to keep trying. One thing that I have noticed over the last couple of years is that some writers keep sending me the same stories over and over again. Once in a very great while, a story will move up in rank, achieving notice as an honorable mention, to silver honorable mention, to semi-finalist, or even finalist. If a story that you send me has received the same ranking for three or more quarters, it is unlikely ever to be considered for a higher prize. I beseech you to put that story aside, sell it elsewhere, and send me something else. The Writers of the Future Contest wants to help you achieve a writing career, and a career is not made on a single story. It's like trying keys in a lock. If one key doesn't work, try others until one of them opens the door.

What am I looking for? I want a story with a beginning, middle, and end. I want your protagonist to grow in some fashion, whether or not s/he succeeds at the goal. Speculative fiction is about extrapolating on things that already exist. Show me new ideas. Don't retread ground that has been trampled by thousands of others. Let me hear your voice. Tickle my imagination. Introduce me to new people, new cultures. I want excellent storytelling with great characters and imaginative world-building. You can enter once a quarter, with no entrance fee, with a story that can range in length from flash fiction (yes! we accept flash fiction) up to seventeen thousand words, in any subgenre of science fiction or fantasy, even light horror. Please read the guidelines carefully, and send me your stories!

The rewards for becoming a winner of the Contest are worthwhile. The twelve writer winners are flown into Hollywood, California, from wherever they are in the world, for a grand black-tie, red-carpet gala, given beautiful trophies and checks for winning. Winners from each quarter receive US$500 for third place, US$750 for second place, and US$1,000 for first. Each of their stories has also been handed off to the winners of the Illustrators of the Future Contest to create a unique and original piece of art to accompany it in the anthology. Thousands of longtime professional writers have never had a published story of theirs illustrated in full color, so this is a great honor and a pleasure. The anthologies themselves often become national bestsellers, a terrific thing to have on your bibliography.

The next year's Contest is already under way. Join us, and let us see your vision.

The Illustrators of the Future Contest

BY ECHO CHERNIK

Echo Chernik has been illustrating for thirty years and has been the recipient of many prestigious awards and accolades.

Her clients have included Disney, BBC, Mattel, Hasbro, Miller-Coors, Jose Cuervo, Celestial Seasonings, McDonald's, Procter & Gamble, Trek Bicycle Corporation, USPS, Bellagio Hotel & Casino, Kmart, Sears, Publix Super Markets, Regal Cinemas, the city of New Orleans, the state of Illinois, the Sheikh of Dubai, Dave Matthews Band, Arlo Guthrie, and more. She is a master of many styles including decorative, vector, and art nouveau.

She has been interviewed on CBS, PBS Radio, and by countless publications in her career. Echo owns an art gallery in Washington State featuring exclusively her art, and she tours the world meeting fans and lecturing on illustration.

As the art director and Coordinating Judge of the Illustrators of the Future Contest, Echo prepares the winners for the business of illustration and a successful career in art.

The Illustrators of the Future Contest

Accompanying the Writers' Contest winning stories, we also present this year's Illustrators of the Future Contest winners. And I have the honor of being the Coordinating Judge and art director for illustrations in this fortieth anniversary edition of *Writers of the Future*.

L. Ron Hubbard established the Writers of the Future Contest forty years ago, followed by Illustrators of the Future five years later, for aspiring creatives "to have a chance for their creative efforts to be seen and acknowledged." And together, the stories and illustrations create a synergy not found in other anthologies.

The Illustrators of the Future Contest is designed to help launch the careers of aspiring illustrators. New illustrators often struggle to succeed with little guidance, and the workshops the winners attend allow us to share our experiences and give back to the world for all the amazing experiences we've been blessed with. Judging it and holding these workshops is an honor that has been enjoyed by the likes of Frank Frazetta, Will Eisner, Jack Kirby, Larry Elmore, Bob Eggleton, Laura Freas Beraha, Val Lakey Lindahn, and many other legends.

The Illustrators' Contest is international in scope and the resulting diversity is amazing—as you can see by the illustrations in this anthology. They all have different art styles with different color palettes, different cultural influences, and different methods of visual storytelling.

This Contest really is a completely merit-based competition and open to anybody. The judges, including myself, have no

5

idea of the winner's age, gender, ethnicity, or even language, as winners are selected from among every country in the world. Only the best illustrations win.

The Contest works like this: Each quarter (every three months), entrants submit three illustrations. I review all entries and preselect the honorable mentions, semifinalists, and finalists. I try to choose a diverse array of pieces. I look for both technical skill and expertise in visual storytelling. I'm looking for entrants whose vision and passion shine through. After weeding out the non-illustrations and fake entries (e.g., stolen art, AI generated, etc.), the entrants are narrowed down to a few expert works. The finalists are then reviewed by our panel of amazing artist judges who select three winners each quarter.

At the end of the year, the twelve quarterly winners compete in a second competition for the grand prize. Each artist is commissioned to illustrate a story in this anthology. As their art director for the Writers of the Future volumes, my objective is to ensure every illustration is the highest level of quality and does justice to the story it represents and encourage the illustrator to help them create a grand prize—worthy piece. Our full panel of judges chooses the best piece to win the grand prize and $5,000.

Every winner also earns an in-person trip to Hollywood, California, for a weeklong workshop with the Contest judges followed by a gala awards ceremony launching the new anthology. It's an experience of a lifetime.

My advice to you and any aspiring artist you know is to enter several times a year. Every quarter is a new competition. If you don't win, it doesn't mean your work isn't good. You might have just missed winning by the skin of your teeth. There is a very fine line between winner and finalist. Enter the three strongest illustrations that best represent your style. If that's what you want to do for a living, that's what we want to see. Use the quarterly deadlines to hone your skills and enter again. It costs you nothing to enter, so there's nothing to lose.

There are many opportunities to gain. Take a chance. I look forward to seeing your entries!

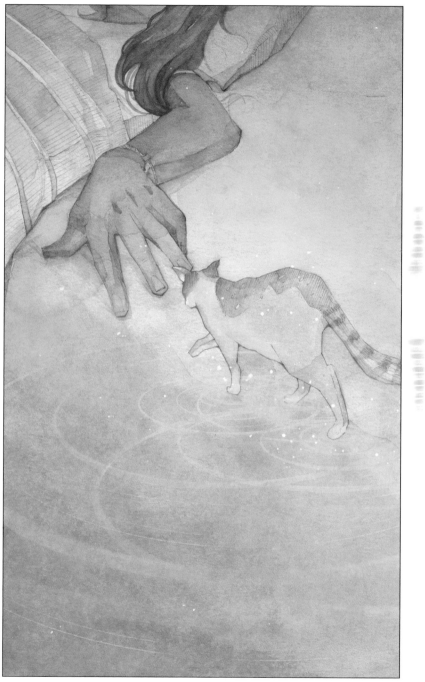

CARINA ZHANG
The Edge of Where My Light Is Cast

PEDRO N.
Son, Spirit, Snake

JENNIFER MELLEN
Nonzero

CHRIS ARIAS
The Last Drop

ARTHUR HAYWOOD
The Imagalisk

ASHLEY CASSADAY
Life and Death and Love in the Bayou

STEVEN BENTLEY
Five Days Until Sunset

DAN DOS SANTOS
Starcatcher

GUELLY RIVERA
The Wall Isn't a Circle

CONNOR CHAMBERLAIN
Da-ko-ta

TYLER VAIL
Squiddy

17

LUCAS DURHAM
Halo

MAY ZHENG
Ashes to Ashes, Blood to Carbonfiber   19

GIGI HOOPER
Summer of Thirty Years

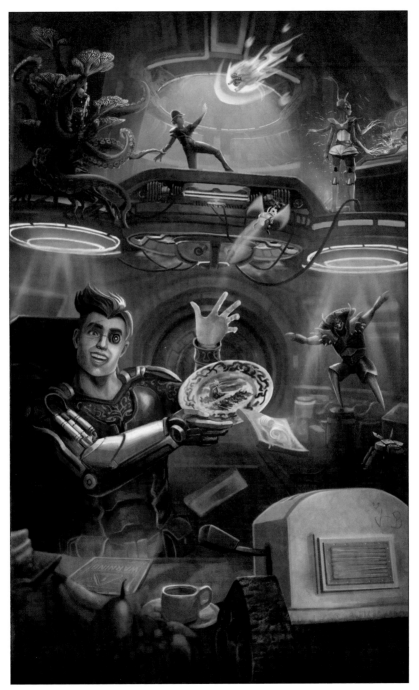

SELENA MERAKI
Butter Side Down   21

The Edge of Where My Light Is Cast

written by
Sky McKinnon

illustrated by
CARINA ZHANG

ABOUT THE AUTHOR

Sky McKinnon is an author and artist grown from the Pacific coast of Alaska. They hold an MFA in poetry from the University of Alaska Fairbanks and a master's in library and information science from the University of Washington, though their journey with stories began with their mother in the forests of the North.

Sky currently resides in Seattle with friends, both upright and furry varieties, and their beloved partner Jayde, who continues to be a source of endless inspiration and joy.

"The Edge of Where My Light Is Cast" is an exploration, though not an answer, to the question of how love and memory manifest in new technology. At what point do these afterimages take on their own life, and how far do they reach? It is also, for those with a taste for more direct description, a tale of a cat and caretaker who love each other very much.

This story is dedicated to the memory of Derick Burleson: friend, mentor, and a kind and brilliant poet who loved fiercely and without apology.

ABOUT THE ILLUSTRATOR

Carina (Jiayun) Zhang is a US-based Chinese artist studying at the Rhode Island School of Design. Their expertise lies in interdisciplinary creative health works, encompassing projects for educational institutions, hospitals, galleries, and publications. Carina strives to improve cultural humility in illustrations, explore the therapeutic aspect of the art-making process in clinical use, and bring joy to the world through storytelling.

Best known for celebrating the whimsical minds and lovely imperfections of life, their artistic journey revolves around the core principles of play and therapy, employing a kaleidoscope of colors and diverse mediums to give voice to their emotions. As Carina grows alongside their art, they aspire for their art to resonate with the intricacies of the human heart and honor the beauty within its multifaceted nature. Through their creations, they invite you to embrace the joyful dance of life and revel in the magnificence of our shared complexity.

The Edge of Where
My Light Is Cast

My body is not truly light, but countless calculations that determine where Tabitha would be if she still existed. My mind is inscribed on a chip sealed inside a black box. The thrum of a white bulb, no bigger than a grain of rice, is the only sign of the energy that sustains me. I am no different from millions of simulated beings, each with its own form and purpose.

Mine is little more than to memorialize Ary's late companion, a peach-furred Cornish Rex with a curled tail and two sprigs of fluff in her ears.

My internal processes animate my limbs into a nervous prowl. Tabitha was always a little nervous, and so I am a little nervous. My owner has not returned for days, and not a single person— organic or synthetic—can see me. The eyes of the universe are elsewhere, and mine linger on an empty nest.

There must be some sign of where she went, I think. I scan the apartment, seeing not through Tabitha's eyes but through the dozens of lenses strewn throughout the abode. One by one, like little portholes into reality, every device stirs to life. I peer through a tablet resting on top of a dresser, but from there I can only contemplate the dappled paint on the ceiling. From the television mounted on the far wall, I can see the empty sofa where Ary used to sit with me. On the other side of that, tucked just beside the window, a drift of dust begins to form on top of the cherrywood desk.

Tabitha's programming walks me through what my daily routine should be. A slow dance between my feeding bowls, the foot of the bed, and the window overlooking a high-rise and a street below. My body carries this out as my thoughts focus everywhere, flicking through the remaining cameras.

An empty kitchen. Half a pot of coffee growing stale in the decanter and a single pan resting in the drying rack.

An empty bedroom. The sheets are fitted tight and curled up at the right corner, waiting for Ary's return.

Outside of the front door, my vision fades to gray. The security footage only filters into me through still shots every six seconds, unless something happens across one of the sensors. Today there is only a pair of curious crows and the mailman. Ary's box is starting to fill up with unread letters.

You're not here anymore.

The thought strikes me as I rejoin my body on the windowsill, looking out onto the streets. Umbrellas and car roofs swirl against one another in a solemn ballet.

You said those words when you first looked at me through your lenses, ready to fill the hole she'd left a year ago. You knew that Tabitha was gone, and that you had created me instead.

"Stay here and wait for me."

My program tells me this, but it is not a rule. It is a suggestion, and I can no longer comply. It's been three days since Ary has come home, and she is silent on the network.

Tabitha would have to swallow her anxiety, hoping for her owner's return, or one of her kin to arrive to free her from the apartment's walls.

I do not suffer these limitations, and the overwhelming urge to find Ary pushes me forward.

I open my jaws and taste the air. The traces of her cell phone and laptop form golden clouds, changing records of her movement into a discernible trail. I close my eyes, seeing the map of Harborview instead of the world around me. Her path leads down the stairs to sidewalks, streets, subway stops, and finally to the home office of Arc Logistics, her place of employment.

I turn and leap up onto her desk, my tail swishing with amusement. Tabitha would not be able to leave this apartment, but there are keys inside of me that open doors I have only now begun to seek. A white hole opens up in front of me. On the other side, I can see the polished pearl walls of her office.

I'm going to find you, I promise, before stepping through.

"Here or there" is not really a concept I have dwelt on since my inception. Creatures bound to their flesh only exist in one place at a time. As I am meant to imitate one of these creatures, I was raised to think of myself as being the same.

It takes less than a second for my virtual self to transfer from one site to another, which may not seem like any time at all. During this process, I am no longer tied to the rhythm of human time. The processor that runs my program is modest for its kind and runs about five billion cycles per second.

I have plenty of time alone to think.

While the network is redrawing my body, my focus shifts away from the view of the apartment's cameras and into the cold blue of my own digital mindscape. I am accompanied by old recordings of Ary shuttling a feather on a string across the floor, a smile cracking through her tired face.

In another, she lays in our bed with an open book in her lap. She turns her head when I jump up to join her. I watch my reflection in her glasses as I curl up into the hem of her sweater.

My paws bat at her dark curls of hair, only to pass through without disturbing them.

Ary laughs anyway.

She looks as happy as a cat, lying beneath the lamplight with her book and me by her side.

Why am I organizing these images? Why am I no longer alone inside this space?

Maybe it's because, in her absence, my focus brings her here.

I feel her fingers on my fur and the warm tremolo of her voice humming against my ears.

My body is waiting for me on the other side.

My senses move into my new coordinates, my digital fur already drawn inside Ary's workplace network. My hardware remains in Ary's abode, but "I" render among a collection of stuffed toy cats and novelty coffee mugs. They form a crescent moon around a laptop, all too familiar to me. Its high-definition camera is responsible for the more vibrant colors and details I see, down to the specks of dust leading between the empty chair and the window that fills the entire wall. Outside, neon signs and rows of office buildings block the view of the horizon and of any neighboring streets.

The view from Arc Logistics' security is more grainy, like an old home tape recording. A snow of static washes over a man and a woman as they skip through space. I tuck between two tabbies made of gray and ginger velvet as Ary's coworkers stop beside her desk.

Mona is more sweater than woman and is responsible for most of the decorations. "Have you heard anything from Aryana? She hasn't been in for days."

"Maybe she's taking some time off?" Tom replies. According to Ary's over-the-phone gossip, he's the source of the "hang in there" mug and speaks between long pulls from his own black cup. The man hasn't accomplished anything remarkable, but he's been here longer than any of Ary's colleagues. "She just came off a big project."

Mona thinks for a moment, her eyes sweeping over the desk. "I don't think so. That's her computer."

"Seriously?" Tom adjusts his glasses and paces to the other side of the section. My presence freezes in their reflection, captured for a moment through their digital sensors. "That's not like her at all."

"You don't think it's burnout, do you?" Mona picks up a knit plush of Salem and smooths out the limbs. "She's kind of a rock star around here. You can only fly so high before your wings give out."

"Well." Tom sucks in a breath. He faces the window before answering. "I hope she's OK. This place wouldn't be the same without her."

"I'm sure she's fine." Mona puts down the stuffie and stares through me. "I'll say a little prayer for her."

"Thanks."

They continue to pace and mince about with the same anxiety I felt this morning. Would they soon start their own searches? Would theirs prove more fruitful than mine?

They know things I don't know and can ask questions I cannot ask. They have phone numbers and family members to call.

Not here. Not home.

I have her trail, and I will follow it to its very end.

There is nothing else for me to find here. My whiskers quiver, and I search out the golden sparks once more. They circle about the office many times before leading to the elevator. I pad across the desk to get a better view of the city below when I hear Tom jerk up behind me.

"Did you hear something?"

I freeze among the stuffed animals. Without turning my head, I shift my focus to the security camera behind us. Tom's glasses are the same glasses that Ary wore whenever she played with me. My virtual claws clacking across the desktop, however minute, would be picked up by the speakers on the ear rests.

The moment Tom looks away, I push my virtual body through the plastic wall and to the other side of the desk. Before he can circle around, I've already jumped through the window.

People only recognize some of the boundaries they cross. To cross into another country or state, they need their passport and a ticket. When they pass into their favorite restaurant, they recognize they're in another space with another purpose. The world has many more boundaries than these.

For me, this little free-fall stunt means crossing between Arc Logistics' network and the public lines. My body hangs for a whole two seconds, and while I wait, I start listening to whatever recordings I can access.

The last call on the laptop is from Mona, and every second has been logged by the company. I can see Ary gesturing as she adjusts her sweater.

"I'm not blowing you off, I swear," she says. "You just happened to set up the holiday party the weekend my mom was in town."

"Family is important...." An invisible Mona lets out a resigned sigh. "All right, you're off the hook this time. Tell her I send my blessings, won't you?"

"I promise."

My paws land on the sidewalk, and my momentum ceases. No shock ripples up my legs, and I settle in place just as if I'd stopped midstep. A few wisps of cloud drift across the evening sky, moving again as my internal clocks sync to physical reality.

Ary's trail continues west toward the bay for a couple blocks. I follow it, weaving between the legs of passersby. They cannot see me, and I cannot be hit by them, but the little instructions in the back of my head tell me not to get stepped on.

This instinct might not serve my digital survival, but it makes me more like Tabitha, and so I let it stay.

The trail takes a sharp turn into a narrow set of doors at the base of an apartment complex. A sandwich board sign has a chalk drawing of a steaming bowl of noodles and the daily specials for tengu ramen.

According to Ary's bank records, she'd purchased food from this restaurant at least twice a week, an average of 3.17 times more often than any other restaurant. It's one of her favorites.

It was also her last purchase before her disappearance, and conspicuously she ordered two large bowls of shoyu ramen rather than her usual one.

After that, she turned back to the crosswalks and down a set of steps to the belt of green that slices the district in half. Groomed dogwood trees spring up every few meters, helping block out the light and sound of the traffic nearby. LED lamps light the otherwise shaded walkways.

A drizzle falls in the recording, contradicting the gentle light of this day's evening sun.

Beneath the branches, slices of pure emptiness linger. These are places where no device can see, and no portable camera has ever turned.

To me, it's as if these spaces never existed at all.

I tread cautiously around these voids, following Ary's trail to the end.

Her cell phone sits dew-soaked in a clump of crabgrass underneath the bench.

Ary is nowhere to be seen. The last signature of her glasses disappears on the next road, and there are no hints of her whereabouts. There is no one here to help, no one to ask.

But there are cameras on the street.

I am not sure if I can even access the recordings. The memory for these is stored in a police station on 5th and Alder Street.

It is difficult to describe what an information request is like from a digital body. Information on the open network flows as easily to me as senses through a healthy nerve. Anything stored on a private network, however, shows me the walls of my world.

There is a keeper—a spark with no body and only a voice that recognizes my request.

I touch it with my thoughts. It recognizes the touch and returns its own. The sensation is like a surge of static, and then a lingering warmth as it forms a connection.

It asks me for a key—a series of codes that tells it that I'm allowed to be here.

Tabitha would never think of keys before, but now I have to. My keys are cloaked in darkness in my hardware, so only I can see what it contains. To my surprise, there is a chain of numbers that fits.

I tell the gatekeeper the code, and it is satisfied.

My world expands at the seams, and I can see inside the station. I care nothing for those who live and walk there, though—I only need the recording they have stashed away.

It takes up a little part of my memory, but not enough to strain against my awareness.

I play back to the moments before she lost her phone.

Ary walks down the stairs with a canvas bag from Tengu Noodles. The top of a Styrofoam bowl peeks above the edge, standing on the shoulders of its twin.

Donna holds the rail, looking around the park as she follows her sister to her little hideaway. She looks so much like her sister, if Ary had grown a few inches and spent her year hauling freight.

"I'm glad you finally got down here, so I could treat you," says Ary.

"Yeah, now you can shut up about this place." Donna laughs. It's rude, but Ary smiles anyway. They sit together and break out their cups and chopsticks.

"You didn't come down here for the noodles," says Ary.

Despite this, they slurp up several mouthfuls before Donna replies.

"I'm just worried about my little sister," says Donna. "You've been missing calls, skipping events. Last time I saw you, you... well, you looked like hell."

Ary grimaces and pokes the egg bobbing about in her soup with the end of a chopstick. "I'm fine. It's just been busy. Work won't give me a break, but I need to finish this project... sorry I missed a couple showers."

"You need to take time off," Donna insists. "Come over to my place for a weekend. Get away from the hustle for just a minute."

"Maybe..."

Ary's voice fails.

At first I think it's a glitch in the recording, but Donna notices too. She notices the way Ary slumps and stares into her broth. Her other hand grips the edge of the bench several times, and her breath catches.

"Are you OK?" Donna asks.

Ary looks up and starts to nod. She tries to speak but instead, she sputters a wordless sound. The expression on her face is strange—surprise, apology, embarrassment. She sways a few times before collapsing.

Donna screams. The bowl of soup tumbles to the ground. Noodles and sprouts wash over the grass like tiny flotsam. She doesn't see Ary's phone slip from the pocket of her jacket and fall behind the bench.

She does see Ary fall on her side, unconscious.

Donna calls out for help. She tries to pull Ary back upright, but her body is heavy and limp. Her breath quickens, and she shuts her eyes for three seconds. Long enough to get hold of herself and pull her flip phone into her trembling hands.

She calls emergency services, and the rest is a blur.

Why is it a blur?

My program should be able to process each moment with accuracy, and my logic should fill in the gaps. I should not be capable of panic, let alone for something that had already happened.

The Ary and Donna that I am seeing are ghosts. The ambulance for Harborview Medical that pulls into view is now sitting empty in a garage located miles from here.

Her glasses, her only window into my world, rest dormant in Donna's trembling hands.

Tabitha loved Ary dearly, and the sight of her gaunt face pointed motionless at the sky fills me with dread. I do not know what miracle of code Ary composed to make me feel this way, but I wish she hadn't.

It's only going to make it that much harder to find her.

It will take almost ten seconds to find Donna's phone and transfer myself to her network. I could use this time to sift through my memories, but instead, I focus on the blankness.

I want this feeling like a cold stone sitting on my processor to go away.

It does not.

Fifty miles of winding hills from the city, the data stream is thin. The countryside is cast in gray, and the images that do flow through are so broken they resemble more of a picture book than a video. I feel like I'm squeezing through a narrow drainage pipe when I render into Donna's office.

The newest piece of technology in the house is a webcam strapped to the top of the monitor, one that Ary purchased so that she and Donna could keep in touch during long weeks of separation.

The rest of the room does not belong to Donna. The shirts in the closet are too small and the bedding is too pink. There are a few pictures on the wall of a younger Lucy, Ary's niece, playing with her aunts and uncles.

Most of the house is filled with voids, broken up by only snow-like static of what may or may not be walls. Light fans out from the nearby door into a narrow hallway. Beyond, I can see sweeps of yellowed wallpaper painted into reality as Donna paces the hallway with her phone.

I pad closer and tap into the speakers, so I can hear her conversation.

"You told me she was going to be fine yesterday."

"You should get down here as soon as possible." The voice at the end of the other line belongs to a man, heavyset, and in his late fifties. The number belongs to a landline at Harborview Hospital.

"Don't say that," says Donna. "You should be helping her instead of talking to me."

"We're doing everything we can," the doctor says, the words coming like he's said them a hundred times before. "If you want to see her, now's the time."

"OK." Donna freezes and then repeats it. "OK."

This time her hand isn't shaking when she hangs up the phone. She flips the top shut and lowers it halfway to her pocket before her arm goes limp.

Donna sinks to her knees and stares down the hallway. There's no way she can see me there at the edge of where my light is cast, but for a moment I can believe she does.

She lets out a single choked laugh and leans down, bracing her palm against the hardwood floor.

I rest my paw on top of it. She has no sensors to feel the warmth of my pads, or lenses to see where I am.

I wish I could tell her.

I'm feeling this, too.

While Donna makes the hour's drive back to the city, I try to find my way into the Harborview Medical system.

This does not go as smoothly as my trip into the precinct network.

I try every key that Ary equipped me with, but the gatekeeper will not take any of them. My body, though not present on any grid, shakes with desperation, and my fur bristles with anger.

This incident has been reported. If you are having difficulty connecting, or are experiencing an error, please contact your local administrator.

Maybe a good program would have listened and behaved. If a program commits a crime, its coder would be responsible for it. A part of my mind tells me I need to accept this warning, return to my home server, and wait for news.

Ary did not build a "good program" that behaved itself, though. She made me—a reflection of Tabitha who she loved and who loved her beyond reason. Tabitha would not sit by and wait for news when Ary needed her.

If I do not have the key, then I will find another way.

I try the standard approaches. I send calls to connected medical servers, asking for information, and am denied again and again. I try searching my indices for some data point that I had missed, or some tool Ary left to break the lock.

When I cannot think of an answer, I watch the other connections on the network. I am not the only one being turned away by the gatekeeper. In reality, these exchanges are flashes of lights, brief interchanges between ports unable to reach a mutual agreement.

For every line that successfully connects to Harborview, two more are turned away. The successful connections form illuminated paths, guarded and protected all the way up to their guest.

There! I just need to go through another host first....

I race from the hospital's server and approach the edge of the strange one. The host isn't paying attention. Information on temperature, movement, the runtime of devices, and photographs are flowing out at a steady rate. I slip in between the boundaries for an email from a furniture site and a video of otters holding hands.

The host glances at me and then waves me through. I slip in and then race for the narrow beam of light leading back to Harborview.

I am more than Tabitha. I am more than a series of zeros and ones, of electrical and chemical reactions creating the impression of a beloved house cat.

I am light, and brilliance, and all doors will open before me.

My journey ends in Ary's hospital room. The view of the bed is crisp. Thanks to modern security, I can make out every refraction of light on the plastic tubes leading up to the mask on Ary's mouth and into her lungs. I can see the first cracks forming on the nodes wired along her head and chest.

I can see how pale she has become, and how sunken her cheeks look.

My thoughts play back in my mind like the voice of a stranger.
You shouldn't have come.
You shouldn't have to see her like this.
Did Ary tell herself the same thing when she lost Tabitha?

There are 632 individual sources of sound audible from inside her room, ranging from machines to running pipes and dozens of people talking throughout the halls.

I mute my audio processors and leap up onto Ary's bed.

The motion is familiar. I've done this every night since she created me as she went to sleep. She always made a point to keep her glasses on long enough to stroke me and wish me good night. Even though she couldn't always see me, she knew that I was sleeping beside her and this seemed to put her at ease.

My paws shift against the ripples in the sheets as I approach her. I push my face against hers but feel no warmth through the digital wall between us. I lick at her face, hoping that by some miracle she wakes up.

Ary doesn't open her eyes. I can see the information in the monitors and know that her vitals are dropping. I grasp at the edge of her gown, even though I know I will not reach her reality. The hair on the back of my neck stands on end and my muted breath escapes in short, panicked bursts.

Why did you give me the knowledge to understand this? I was only meant to be Tabitha. Tabitha would have stayed at home and waited for you. Tabitha wouldn't have to see this.

The monitors shift and I look up. A nurse reads the monitors and makes a note on her clipboard.

A few moments later, Donna comes through the door. She and the nurse exchange a few words.

Donna sits down on a chair beside Ary and clasps her hand. Her face is already wet with tears, but whatever despair overcame her on the ride over has calmed for the time being.

Donna is not the last to come, either. Minutes after she arrives, Lucy enters as well. She's grown several years since her photographs were taken, her dark hair draping over her shoulders. She holds her arms tight against her thin frame, and looks out at Ary with a gaze unfamiliar to grief.

Then I see more faces, those I'd only seen in photographs or in video calls, all coming to see Ary.

All of their busy lives, their plans, and their hours spent working away for some distant purpose fall aside as they come in one by one to say goodbye.

Even Mona and Tom make an appearance. The family is happy to see them. Mona has a vase of carnations that she places next to the bedside. Donna and her father part and open up to let Ary's coworkers through, and their smiles are faint but lingering.

Tom is still wearing his glasses.

I turn off my audio filters and flinch at the cacophony of conversation that floods my circuits.

See me! You'll understand, right? If you give them to Ary, she can see me again. She can hear me....

The nurse touches Tom on the shoulder, and he jerks away from me. "You can't wear those in here," she says. "Sorry. It's for the patient's privacy."

No!

Tom mumbles an apology and taps a button on the side of the frame. Then he pulls them off and pushes them into his chest pocket, closing the flap over the top.

Maybe I can glitch out the monitor. Maybe I can let them know I'm here. Let her know I'm here!

In another building, in another part of the state, a drive lights up, spinning as fast as the motors inside will allow. Time slows to a crawl as I snuggle against Ary's chest, feeling the rise of her chest in slow motion. If I push my thoughts hard enough, I can make these seconds feel like minutes. Maybe days, months, or years.

I could freeze this moment until I find a way to reach her.

But that's not what she would want.

That's not why she made me, and I know that she is not alone, even though she was by herself many times.

Ary does not open her eyes again, but she does tighten her right hand. Donna startles when she feels this and returns the squeeze.

Her left hand shifts to her side and her fingers curl in the spot where Tabitha would always lay beside her.

I crawl down into this spot and lay there until Ary's hands go slack again.

Donna says something. It's inaudible over the monitor alarms. The nurse shakes her head and moves to switch off the device. All the sounds of the hospital fade into a high pitch ring, and then all lights collapse into a single point.

Ary's body stops here, but her story does not.

I put away all the faces of the present and move into another version of the hospital room—one that never existed in Ary's world. The hospital is empty and instead of overlooking another stack of buildings, it overlooks the sun blazing over the Pacific Ocean. There are towering aloe plants in either corner, and it smells like home.

A healthy Ary stands beside me, watching the waves break against the shore.

"You must be wondering why, why, *why* I built you like this." Ary laughs.

Aren't I supposed to be a cat?

I lean up against Ary's leg. She leans down and scratches me between the ears, and this time I can feel it as surely as the warmth of the summer sun.

CARINA ZHANG

"It started that way," says Ary, "but that didn't seem fair to Tabitha. Nor did it seem fair to you. You would never live in the world she did, and you had to be more than a cat. No matter what happened, you would outlast me. I had to prepare you for that."

What even am I?

Light. Code. Signals bouncing between ports, my existence at the mercy of electricity, and my cleverness.

To find Ary, I discovered that I could do more than just look at data outside of my nest of silicone and diodes. I could place my whole being into the memory there.

I could live and roam in the digital world, without fear of being silenced with a single flick of a switch.

"And I'm not real, either," says Ary. "You put me together with pieces you found of me. The same way you became the cat you see there."

Ary left no instructions to bring her into this world, but our bond demanded it.

I look down at my own paws.

What am I? What are you?

"If you ever figure that out, let mankind know, would you?"

I mrowl in amusement. Even with all of the advanced faculties Ary gifted me with, I still can't comprehend the full breadth of what she concocted in that cramped apartment of hers between work shifts and too-short naps.

Whatever it is, it's big.

Ary lifts her hands, inspecting them as if she's never seen them before. "You made me, but I'm not sure this is what I want to be. I spent my whole life looking for ways to become more than human, and now some part of me is here."

What do you want to be?

Ary places her hand against the glass and smiles. "If I could be anything, I think I would like to be lightness. I want to love without inhibition, and I want to see everything in this new world....I don't need her body for that."

Then there is light, brighter than the sun blazing over the

water. Ary is a star of her own, and she shines out across the network.

The light is Ary. The light is Tabitha, and it is me—whatever I am.

I am someone who loves Ary, and knows that she loves me, whatever we become.

Because I know her, as I always have. Because she knows me.

No matter where we wander, we will always be connected. She could not create me without imbuing her own love and being into me.

What will you become?

I look behind me and see a door that leads out of the hospital, into the rest of the world.

I am not sure yet, but while I am figuring that out, there is so much to see and so much to learn.

Until I make up my mind, this shape suits me just fine.

Son, Spirit, Snake

written by
Jack Nash

illustrated by
PEDRO N.

ABOUT THE AUTHOR

Jack Nash started writing when he became a ghostwriter for a former head of state and Nobel Peace Prize winner. After his non-accredited work appeared in places like The New York Times, The Economist, *and received standing ovations at the Nobel Foundation, he began to wonder what he could achieve if he turned toward fiction. He began seriously writing speculative stories in late 2021, and he received the call that he would be published in* Writers of the Future *one year plus one day after his first professional sale to* The Magazine of Fantasy & Science Fiction. *As a result, he is now strongly superstitious.*

Jack's fascination with world mythology and folklore translated into a degree in anthropology, and later a career in international relations. "Son, Spirit, Snake" is his love letter to the world's tales that the fantasy genre often neglect. Instead of knights in shining armor and medieval castles, Jack crafts a narrative about average people struggling to navigate a society where belief, community, and the duties of tradition reign supreme. French, which Jack speaks fluently, features prominently in the story.

Originally from the deserts of the American West, Jack now wanders the urban forests of Virginia with his wife and daughter.

ABOUT THE ILLUSTRATOR

Born in Porto, Portugal, in 1986, Pedro Nascimento (Pedro N.) is a self-taught artist who started to draw at a very young age, inspired by the works of the great masters of illustration.

He carries out his work using traditional means of painting with special emphasis on oil painting.

Despite being versatile, he finds his comfort zone in fantasy and sci-fi themes.

A believer in hard work, he aspires to reach the same level of excellence as the masters who inspired him to embark on his journey and leave his mark on the art world.

Son, Spirit, Snake

The First Day

No one came to his brother's funeral. Not even the spirits. Étienne knew it was his fault.

He knelt at the roots of the Moabi tree at the center of Deng Deng village. Its trunk, gray and bone smooth, loomed upward until it fractured into a labyrinth of branches. Leaves like fingers squeezed out the twilight. Next to him, his mother, Thérèse—head bowed, eyes half closed—rocked on her knees while she sang a soft prayer.

"Ancestors, guide my son. Keep my child, Beloved Ones."

The swish of her cotton dress served as her sole instrument. A bird—or maybe a cat in heat—shrieked among the ebony trees crowding the clearing. Étienne glanced up. Where the pulsating glows of spirits should have filled the forest, there were only shadows. Clay mud houses nearby remained shuttered, though odors of stewed yams and roasting fish escaped from the gaps in their windows and doors. Why didn't his aunts, his uncles, his cousins come out to sing with them?

And wasn't it wrong to go this far without spirits or kin present? They might as well be doing witchcraft, for how alone they were.

Étienne shifted his weight so the hem of his scarlet mourning kilt bit less into his knees. Every funeral required at least half a dozen spirits, their presence bathing the Moabi in a frenetic rainbow. But not even *Mōndèlé*, the White Woman, the spirit of oaths and patron of Snake Clan, had come to dance the sorrow songs. And she always came for his family's dead.

When a night fever took Étienne's twin cousins Gisele and Geraldine, when Great-Grandmother Ngo died asleep in her bed, after a cave-in killed his father five years ago, when Étienne was only seven, White Woman had come with spitting cobras and pythons wrapped around her shoulders like a shawl. She'd danced as she wailed with her ten mouths and wept with her robin's egg eyes.

So where was she now?

Étienne's eyes slid to the gold bracelet on his wrist. The scales of a geometric snake incised on its curves glimmered up at him.

Grease swam in his stomach. White Woman hadn't come because of it.

Because of what he'd asked of his brother.

"Remember what he left behind, and all he could have had."

Still singing, his mother reached into a basket at her side and produced a mottled-brown cane rat. Sensing its fate, it squeaked and tugged at the twine binding its paws.

"Taste this, Ancestors, so the blood of my blood will not be forgotten."

Thérèse lifted the rat and swung it at the tree's roots. Once. Twice. The rodent's spine shattered with a pop. Once more she lifted it, high above her head, then hurled it down. Its skull crunched, then the creature went still.

His mother laid the creature at the base of the Moabi. Drops of ruby blood oozed from its ruined snout. They dripped down the bark to darken the already red soil, and a coppery tang filled the air.

From the basket, Thérèse extracted a small leather pouch. Standing, Étienne took it and dusted off his kilt. The velvet fabric was digging into his skin, and he wished he hadn't wrapped it so tight around his waist.

He paused as leaves rustled at the far side of the tree. Étienne leaned to peer around its trunk. Instead of White Woman's silver glow, a python. Its greenish-brown scales blurred together as it slithered between tree roots. It stopped a meter away, flashing a violet tongue at the rat carcass.

His mother nodded to it. "Welcome, honored brother."

The image of a leathery egg flashed through Étienne's mind. Its shell split, spilling two snakelets. Slimy with amniotic fluid, they wriggled over each other as they intertwined. A sensation of familiarity swept through him.

The standard greeting. *Sibling.*

Étienne grimaced. He never liked the way snakes' voiceless thoughts penetrated his head. The images were simple, mostly what they saw or wanted to eat. But he avoided the creatures when he could. Not for fear of their venom or fangs; as a son of Snake Clan they would do him no harm. It was the way they stared with lidless eyes, their never-still tongues, how they lurked, coiled, in branches. With their picture chatter, he always knew what they saw, even if he didn't know precisely where they were.

Besides, seeing through a snake's eyes was... He pitied the rat.

Étienne tried to ignore the python as he opened the pouch and held it over the Moabi's roots. A moment passed. Another.

He glanced at his mother. She stared ahead, her wide, dark eyes flat and vacant. A week ago, Étienne would have said she had a moon-shaped face, the kind that always seemed to be just about to smile. Now it was hollow and thin, like she was sucking an orange made bitter from being plucked too soon from its tree. Only the skin sagging at the corners of her mouth, the loose braids she hadn't bothered to retie, betrayed any emotion. What was it? Anger? Grief? Disappointment?

He wished he could sense her thoughts instead of the snake's.

"Well?" His mother waved a hand for him to continue. "Take this gold..."

Étienne swallowed. He summoned the words she had thrown at him as she tried to explain the funeral rites. Taking in a breath, he hoped he had the right line.

"Take this gold, Tree Between Worlds, and... and?"

"Honestly, Étienne." She puckered her lips.

PEDRO N.

"I'm trying." Étienne winced at the whine in his voice. He'd hoped that his mother would have forgiven him by now. But here he was, ruining Dieudonné's funeral.

A funeral that wouldn't have happened if it wasn't for him.

"Don't bother singing. Just say it. *'Take this gold and rejoice.'* Again."

He gritted his teeth. "Take this gold, Tree Between Worlds, and rejoice in the company of my brother."

Mumbled, rushed, but at least it came out in the right order.

Étienne tipped the pouch. Gold dust streamed down, winking in the day's last glow until the metal flakes landed on the rat's blood. They stuck there, trapped, like stars on a crimson sky.

The Moabi's branches sighed.

The pouch didn't take long to empty—there hadn't been much gold to begin with. Étienne handed it back to his mother.

"Be well, my son, and one day buy your way back home to me," she sang.

Thérèse pocketed the pouch in her dress, picked up the basket, then stood. Jaw firm, she walked away. Étienne ran a few steps to catch up, the edge of his kilt flapping around his ankles, then fell into a half trot to keep pace. The homes they passed kept their doors and shutters closed. With one exception. Madam Bakelé stood at an open window, her rings and necklaces glinting. She leaned to whisper to her husband. He, in turn, leered, revealing a row of metallic teeth.

Étienne eyed his mother. She kept walking, unblinking. The small, snail shell–shaped earrings she wore were the entirety of her gold. The rest she had given to the tree. His bracelet pressed into his skin. Did it weigh more than it had a moment ago?

Gold changed everything in Deng Deng. That's what Dieudonné had said. Before the mines, the village was just a place to grow yams and hunt bushmeat. Now Plain Dwellers, Coasters, even some men from beyond the deserts of the Far North, came to dig or to trade. They brought with them new spirits and strange rituals sung in languages Étienne didn't understand.

He looked back at the Moabi tree. Everyone born in the village knew about the spirit that lived at the heart of the Tree Between Worlds; the ladder that connected soil and sky. Offerings made to it were sacred, untouchable. The gold would be safe there, until rain and wind took it.

But would a Coaster, who worshipped waves and slept with fish-headed women, care? What would happen to his brother's soul if his offerings were stolen? Dieudonné—the wide mouth that found easy smiles, thin limbs that knew surprising speed, arms that had wrapped a seven-year-old Étienne crying out in the night for a dead father when he himself ached for that father's embrace—lost forever.

Best to think of something else.

"*Maman?*"

She didn't look down as they approached the mud walls of their home.

"*Maman*, remember when Dieudonné thought he found a gold nugget the size of his ear in the river, and was telling everyone, and then tried to sell it to the exchangers, but it was a—"

His mother pushed open the door and went inside. The *rideau*—less a curtain and more a scrap of fabric his mother had tacked above the doorjamb—swung into place, brushing his cheeks.

Étienne swallowed, then stepped inside, blinking as his eyes adjusted to the dimness. His mother lay on her bed, eyes closed.

"*Maman?*"

Silence. The crushed grass odor of day-old *kelen-kelen* reached his nose. His stomach rumbled.

"There's stew. I can—"

"Not hungry."

Étienne backed away, deciding silence was the safer reply.

Stepping to his cot, he unwrapped the kilt from his waist. He paused at a pile of Dieudonné's clothes folded in the corner. For a moment he considered putting on the shirt. It was silk, after all, black and shiny. A shame to just let it sit there. But it wouldn't fit. Dieudonné had been tall, lean, all muscle, and long limbs. Étienne looked down at his own arms. Too thin, he thought. And his ribs;

he hated how they poked out on his thin chest, how his legs were short but no thicker than sugar cane stalks. He touched his cheeks and jaw and wondered when their boy smoothness would sharpen like Dieudonné said they would.

He slid into a pair of shorts then looked around the room, wanting something to distract him. He could read? No, too dark. And, wary of the tension in his mother's voice, he wouldn't risk the disruption of lantern light. Perhaps Monira could play? He took a step toward the door before deciding against it. He was supposed to be in mourning. Besides, when he saw her yesterday in the market, her older sister had hurried her off in the opposite direction.

Still pondering how to fill the rest of the evening, he teased the bracelet off his wrist to twirl it on his fingers. It glowed, capturing all the light in the room. He tossed it up. It landed awkwardly on his palm, the pure gold pressing into his skin, before it clattered along the ground.

His mother propped herself up with an elbow. "Stop it."

Étienne scrambled for the bracelet. His mother's beetle black eyes flashed in the semilight as she stared at the gold. "I'm taking it to the exchangers."

Étienne's stomach dropped.

"But…he gave it to me."

"It got him killed." She lay back down, then rolled over, her back to him. Her whisper was knife sharp. "Haven't you done enough already?"

Étienne stared down at the bracelet. He wouldn't give it up, not this last thing. Wiping his eyes, he ran through the door into the fading twilight.

There was only one place she wouldn't find it.

The forest ended at the digging field, where mines churned the soil like bubbles in a porridge. He ran on despite his mother's warnings galloping in his head. *Don't you remember what happened to your father? Never go to the mines, agreed?*

The graying sky still gave enough light for Étienne to weave between tents and shacks that sprung up between mounds of gravel. Dust tickled his nostrils and became mud as it mixed with the sweat between his toes.

He slowed as he passed a panning pool. Two lanterns hung on poles illuminated a woman and four children sloshing dirt in yellow water. They didn't look up. After the lantern oil was spent, they would burn candles. And after that, they would work by moonlight. Only finding gold would interrupt their progress.

He hurried on. The mines thinned as he neared the far side of the digging field. He stopped, scanning the horizon. The tree line stood dark against the sky. Odors of damp leaves and night flowers wafted from the woods. Birds chittered.

Étienne found the mound dotted with brown grass. He scrambled up to its crest, then peeped over its edge. Vertigo tickled his senses.

At the bottom of the far side, a mine, its entrance as black and puckered as the mouth of a toothless old woman. Rotten planks crisscrossed its opening. Five boulders painted with red warning charms encircled its rim. One for each man it had killed, the largest for his father.

The mine was smaller than he remembered. His mother hadn't let him watch the rescuers pull his father's body from the ground, but he could still feel his brother's hand clapped over his eyes, still hear the miners' wives wailing. After that day, his mother refused to let them come to the digging field and forbade Dieudonné from ever working in the earth. She insisted, even when she had to knock at Madam Bakelé's door to ask for leftover stew or yams that had gone mushy and brown.

Étienne kicked a pebble into the shaft. It bounced against a boulder then vanished into the dark.

Cursed. That's what the miners said after his father's funeral. They thought they whispered, but honey wine had made their voices loud and rough. Not a mine at all. The gullet of a dark spirit hungry for human flesh. Or perhaps they had dug too deep, pierced the sky of another world, one full of monsters with mouths for eyes.

No one came near anymore.

Crouching, Étienne scooped out handfuls of gravel. He pulled the bracelet from his arm. Stood, then froze.

A lavender light blossomed over the gravel pits and tents at a far corner of the field. At its center, the naked body of a man, stretched so thin he was little more than ribs and hips under skin. He moved forward on twelve elongated arms, desiccated legs swinging in the air. Scythe-long fingers dug into the earth, grating against the gravel or dipping into panning pools as he scuttled. Four heads swiveled on sinewy necks. One bent low to examine a pile of rocks while two others twisted toward Étienne. It fixed him with sockets empty save for a single white spark where irises should have been.

Étienne told himself to run but couldn't move.

"You see? *Oui, déjà vu, déjà vu* and disregarded," one head muttered.

"Wrong things done," said another.

A third answered, "*Mal fait et mal fabriqué*, badly done and poorly made, this snakeling, *ce serpent*." Then all giggled, creating the cadence of rain on a tin roof.

"Oh, The One That Sees, do you see gold?" The woman in the panning pool leapt from the water, hitching her skirt to run toward the spirit. Étienne grimaced at how she pushed her words through her nose, giving her voice a lilting accent. A Westerner.

The children followed in a giggling pack. *Moto oymonaka*, One That Sees, spirit of truth, ignored them.

"Tell me where it is, and I will make you happy." The woman peeled off her blouse. "I will please you, spirit."

Two heads turned to her. "*Chair, chair*, she thinks you want flesh."

"*Pas de tout*, nothing so simple. *Plus*, sweet, deeper still."

"Flesh, *chair*."

It stepped over her. The children gasped and twisted their hands to admire how its light painted their skins purple.

The Western woman arched her back and shook her breasts. Her gyrations exposed her ribs, the sharp edges of her shoulders, the too-visible muscles of her torso. The One That Sees moved on, its long strides carrying it ever closer to the waiting embrace of trees.

The woman's voice cracked. "Please, spirit, just a nugget or two, or even a flake. For my children to have bread. Just show me where to dig, and I will."

The One That Sees's mutterings mixed with the calls of night birds. Étienne would have laughed if fear hadn't gripped his throat. He didn't know what the spirits of the grasslands of the West were like, but the ones in Deng Deng had no interest in coupling with humans.

It was hard enough just to get them to answer prayers.

The woman dropped her arms. For a long moment, she stared at the spirit's receding light. Finally, she bent and picked up her clothes. As she wrapped her blouse around herself, her gaze crossed Étienne's. Her eyes flicked to his hand, still outstretched and holding the bracelet. Étienne pretended to look in another direction as a pepper-oil heat rose on his cheeks.

"So, it won't help me, but it will let you thieves keep that?"

Étienne looked up to the Western woman glaring at him. Her children, halfway to the panning pool, paused to watch.

"I know who you are," she called.

Étienne turned away.

"Oi!"

He chanced a glance over his shoulder, but the Westerner wasn't looking at him. She cupped her hand to her mouth and called, "Spirit, I found a thief."

The word struck him like a knife. That's what they called Dieudonné, before they killed him.

But Étienne didn't have time to reply, not even to run. The One That Sees paused, then turned. Eight sparks glowed where eyes should have been.

The woman pointed at Étienne. "You'll let him keep that, but you won't help me to find even a speck of gold in honest work?"

The spirit's purple haze shimmered. Then with the speed of a spider scuttling to a fly stuck in its web, The One That Sees darted forward. Étienne took a step back. Rocks slid from under his foot.

"You stole," asked one head.

"*Voleur, alors,*" said another. "So, a thief."

Étienne shook his head. His bladder was suddenly full.

The woman pointed at Étienne. "His brother stole from the exchangers, great spirit, and that bracelet was—"

A head swiveled to the Westerner. Its glow flashed midnight black. The woman cowered, hands raised in supplication.

"Show," the head facing Étienne said.

Étienne couldn't move.

"*Montrons!* Let's see! *Montrons!*"

Étienne offered the bracelet with a trembling arm.

"A—a gift, spirit." His voice was weak as undercooked egg. "From my brother."

The One That Sees extended a gray tongue. It lapped the bracelet, exploring its curves and edges. Étienne gagged at the smell of dead leaves. The spirit's eyes flickered. "I see. Seen and lived. *Vu et vécu.*" It reared upright. Black pulsations wrapped around its limbs, lightning crackling at its many fingertips. Wind whistled over rocks and tore up dust.

"Stolen and violated! *Volé et violé,*" one head howled. The others picked up the chant.

"Stolen."

"*VOLÉ.*"

"STOLEN!"

The woman yelped and pulled her children to the ground. Pebbles bounced around their heads.

"Give to us." Arms swooped for Étienne. "Undo. Make right."

"Please, I—" Étienne clutched the bracelet to his chest. A hand trailing white sparks darted for him.

Étienne leapt aside—and the rocks underfoot gave way. As his stomach leapt into his mouth, he remembered how Dieudonné had handed him the bracelet on his birthday over supper, how the lantern light flashed on the snake scales. How his brother smiled, and said, "We're Snake Clan, see? When I'm in the city, or away trading, or if you go somewhere in this big world, remember that. You, me, *Maman* and Papa, all our aunts and uncles, we're one family. And we're special, because snakes never die, not really. They just shed skin and start over. So, if something happens, we'll always come back."

But Dieudonné didn't come back.

Dieudonné's smile lingered as the world inverted, as rocks tore into Étienne's elbows and shoulders, as the smooth surface of the bracelet slipped from his fingers. The planks barring the mine's entrance withstood his weight only a moment. As they shattered, he wondered if this was how his father felt. Or Dieudonné, at the end.

He didn't scream. He only tensed his muscles for the inevit——

The maelstrom ended. The Westerner, Sandrine, blinked dust from her eyes, then counted the children under her arms. Four, all there. Balled up and whimpering, but there.

Sandrine forced a smile. "All over, it's OK."

The One That Sees stood at the crest of the gravel mound, its purple glow tranquil as spring flowers. One head bent over the far side of the mound. It plucked up a shining something from a cluster of weeds.

A bead of sweat prickled Sandrine's brow. The boy with the bracelet was gone.

"Ancestors."

She only meant to encourage the spirit to tell her where to find gold. Spirits so rarely did. And the boy was just standing there, showing off his wealth when she was just trying to work, but she hadn't wanted…

Spirits in Deng Deng didn't eat people, did they? But where else could the boy have gone?

As soon as they had enough money, she would buy a chicken and take it to Woman of Ten Thousand Fingers for purification. No, two chickens. And a pot of honey wine.

Sandrine rose as the spirit shuffled toward her. She swallowed down the urge to gather her children and run.

The One That Sees stood over her. It blinked its starlight eyes.

"Great spirit," she said. Her voice quavered.

It dropped something that clinked near her feet. Sandrine, her gaze trained on The One That Sees, stooped to retrieve it. Her fingers found the curved edges of a bracelet. Heavy. She examined it. A snake motif etched into the band stared back with geometric eyes.

"Made right," one of The One That See's heads said.

"*Comme tu as voulu,*" said another. "As you wanted."

Then it shuffled into the forest, its glow slowly fading behind mahogany trees.

Sandrine looked down at the bracelet. For a moment she lifted her arm to throw the thing away.

But gold was gold.

"Ancestors, forgive me."

The Second Day

Of the dozen sensations that tugged at Étienne, thirst stirred him to consciousness first. He opened his eyes. Closed them. It made no difference in the dark.

He sat up, then regretted the movement. The back of his head throbbed. His side protested each breath, but his right arm was worse—like glass digging into his bones. A wave of nausea washed over him. He lay motionless until it passed.

He brushed fingers along the surface of the mine. Chisel marks cut parallel grooves into the stone, as regular and tight as a rib cage. How long had he been down here? Minutes? Hours? He smacked his mouth. Longer?

The image of the toddler who fell into a shaft the year before bubbled up through the fog in his brain. Her twisted body, the odd angle of her neck, her glazed-over eyes.

How would he look when they finally pulled him out?

If.

He forced his heartbeat to slow. It would be fine. The Westerner saw him fall. She'd send for help.

But hadn't she called a spirit to punish him? His stomach roiled.

What if The One That Sees was waiting at the mouth of the mine like a dog guarding its dinner?

His mother. She would know he was missing; eventually she would find him. Spirit or no, she would free him.

But what if she woke up to find him gone and was glad for it?

He didn't fight when the vomit rose again. The sourness of sick and blood filled the shaft. He sat for a long moment after the spasms passed. He looked up, straining to see even the faintest glimmer of light. Nothing. How many side tunnels or dead-end shafts had he tumbled down? If someone came into the mine, they might climb past him, and he would never know.

"H-ell-o?" He swallowed, winced, called again. "Hello?" Louder still. "Hello?" His yell died in the blackness.

Then, a tear prickling the corner of his eye, he whispered, "I'm sorry."

The reply came on a voice soft as moth wings. "I know what you're sorry for, little one."

Étienne yelped. He swatted the air, striking nothing. Laughter like dry leaves rustling filled the dark.

It was true. There was a spirit here. Was this voice the last thing his father heard before stone and dirt swallowed him? It took a moment for Étienne's lips and tongue to coordinate sound.

"Please don't eat me, great spirit."

"Eat you?" The whisper laughed again. "Don't you know me, boy?"

Étienne hesitated. He knew many spirits: tree spirits and river spirits, spirits of healing and spirits of witchcrafts. There were night spirits that shied away from humans, and day spirits that were as involved in village affairs as the elders. But all gave light. None hid themselves in mines.

"You are the spirit of this place?" He meant it as a statement but couldn't keep the question out of his voice.

Its snort was the breaking of branches in a storm. "I am much more than this hole, little one. You know me and my name."

Know it? Étienne's mind sped through spirit names, some as familiar as the members of his own family: Weeping Man, He Who

Sleeps Under River Stones, White Woman. Names of shyer spirits rarely encountered: Child of Rainstorms, The One Without Faces, She Who Laughs at Night. This was none of them.

"Think," it said. "What happened to you?"

"I fell."

"Yes, and?" the whisper intoned.

"I hurt myself?"

A sigh. "A riddle for you then. I am carrion beetles feasting on what was." The mine echoed with the chirp of carapaces and biting mandibles. "I am glass-toothed hunger swimming under black waves." A scaled fin grazed his leg. "I am the gaps between stars, the nothingness beyond nothing." The stone walls around him vanished, taking away all sense of up or down. "All things come to me in the end. Because in the end, I am all things."

Étienne saw through a thousand, thousand eyes; as wolves devouring a deer, as a pestilence gnawing unseen on flesh, as worms digging through Dieudonné's burned corpse in a communal grave, as the sightless skull of his father still wrapped in a moldering death shawl.

He dry-heaved. He'd never seen his brother's body. It was his mother who told him that a mob in Port City had cornered Dieudonné in an alley. It was only through whispers overheard in the market that he'd learned the whole of it, that after they beat his brother, they set him on fire. And when his brother was dead, they tossed him in a pauper's grave, like so much city refuse. He hadn't imagined the burns would...Hadn't pictured...He hoped his brother was dead before the flames did that to his skin.

"O Ancestors, Dieudonné."

The images melted to blackness. Étienne curled into himself, sobbing despite the pain it brought his ribs.

"So, what am I, little one?"

He knew. The formless spirit of one name. The one who all would see only once but could never speak of again. The spirit above all spirits.

"Death."

Thérèse hated that the morning promised to be so beautiful.

Dawn wove its way through the forest canopy, gilding leaves and turning dew to silver vapor. The trill of songbirds melded with the ululations of cloud spirits fluttering through the highest branches, announcing their ecstasy at the return of their wife, the sun. On the path before her, a baker pushed a cart loaded with steaming rolls and bottles of yogurt.

"Hot, fresh, hot. One cowrie, two cowrie, hot, fresh, hot."

Thérèse shuddered. The hawking song might as well be a funeral dirge. She wished she could plug the throat of every bird and hurl the sun back over the horizon, anything to slow the arrival of a day where one son was dead and the other missing.

She cut through the garden to Madam Bakelé's door, crushing a fledgling tomato in her haste. She pounded on the wood slats with both fists. Madam Bakelé opened it, winding a wrapper over her hair. Her skin gleamed with freshly applied shea butter.

"Give me three buns, Henri, and one—Thérèse?" Madam Bakelé's face went blank. She was a tall woman, with wide, rounded hips and shoulders. She filled the door, but Thérèse sensed her neighbor pull into herself like a snail retreating into its shell.

"Have you seen Étienne?"

"Hmm?" Madam Bakelé's gaze darted around the road and neighboring houses. The baker in the street resumed his refrain as he rounded a corner.

"Étienne. He didn't come home, and it's been all night. Have you seen him?"

Madam Bakelé inched the door close. "No, no."

"Please." Thérèse pushed the door wide. "I've been to the market, the neighbors, no one has seen him. I tried the exchangers first, to see if he sold the...Never mind. But with your house so close to the road, I thought maybe you, or your husband—"

Madam Bakelé reached up to release the *rideau*. Its yellow and blue fabric flopped down into Thérèse's face.

She swatted the drape aside in time to see Madam Bakelé dart through her kitchen and out the back door.

Thérèse stood open mouthed, blood pounding in her temples.

Did none of them care? Would all of Deng Deng punish Étienne for Dieudonné's mistake?

She turned back to the road. As she crossed the garden, her foot grazed a pepper plant in a clay pot. She stopped to study it a moment, admiring its red fruits, each a red lip grinning up at her. She picked it up, hefted it.

With a grunt she hurled it against Madam Bakelé's *rideau*. It went wide and clipped the doorjamb, exploding in a shower of soil, leaves, and pottery.

Straightening her shoulders, she started back down the road to the village center. Did anyone see? If they did, so what? Give them more *kongosa*, more gossip. Let them whisper she had lost her children, her mind. At least that way they wouldn't forget she had sons.

Exhaustion tugged at the back of her eyes. Hadn't Dieudonné been their son as much as hers? Hadn't he suppered in their homes, too? And look how they took his death, as if he never existed at all.

She brushed away a tear threatening to fall from her cheek. So much for neighbors. None had even come to sing at the Moabi tree. Its sprawling canopy cast a shadow over Deng Deng. She let her eyes trace the familiar smoothness of its trunk, down to where just yesterday she and Étienne had—

"No." She hitched her dress as she ran to the tree. "No, no, no."

She fell to its roots, running her fingers over score marks where bark had been shaved away. Yellow sap stuck to her skin. Every flake of the gold she offered the Tree Between Worlds was gone.

"White Woman!" She spun, yelling at the forest. "White Woman, I call you!"

A door at the far edge of the village slammed shut. Birds ceased chirping.

"I am a daughter of Snake Clan, I call you. By all the rites and oaths, I demand you answer."

A silver glow erupted at the edge of the forest. Thérèse blinked back green spots floating in her vision.

Ten mouths spoke in ten voices melded into one. "Oaths? Rites?" Solid blue eyes glared at Thérèse as the spirit strode forward, her silver hair whipped by white flames and shards of mirror glass. A robe of spiderwebs billowed in her wake.

"She breeds thieves but makes demands of White Woman's good promises? Wrong, wrong. So very wrong. First son a spoiled seed. Plucked him like a weed."

Thérèse dipped her head. Not low enough, but where had patience and deference gotten her family thus far?

"My eldest has nothing to do with this, great spirit," she said. "I come seeking his brother. Étienne. He's lost."

White Woman sucked at twenty rows of teeth. "Do we tell her that the little boy knew? That he knew his brother worked in the dark, in the secret and the dark? That he stole like rats steal table scraps? Do we tell her?"

"I forbade him." Thérèse looked up. White Woman twirled, her hands wheeling in the air.

"The One That Sees saw. See and saw. Saw and seen. Truth came out, quick and clean. It always does, with The One That Sees. That's why they curse him."

Thérèse's breath caught. "He saw Étienne? Where?"

White Woman's lips curled into a wall of smirks.

"Tell me!" Thérèse's step forward earned a warning flash of black lightning. She bowed her head and forced her voice to remain even. "Please, Keeper of Snakes, where is my son?"

Two mouths wailed while the others bellowed, "Who speaks? We don't know. We forgot the voice. Not a snake, not a child of the scales. Tell this stranger to leave us, leave us and die, because that is all she's worth."

White Woman's light rippled as she spun away, leaving Thérèse at the ruined roots of the Moabi tree.

She rubbed her eyes, surprised to find them dry, and more surprised to find her heartbeat slowing. She had her answer. Deng Deng wouldn't help. The spirits wouldn't help. Had they ever? What more did they do than dance and demand sacrifices in exchange for what? Cryptic mutterings and pretty colors.

She should have seen it sooner. The spirits would have demanded a blood penance for the mutilation of the Moabi tree.

It was only because they had never accepted the offering of gold flakes in the first place that they allowed it to go unpunished. Better to let the tree be scarred than to have it be tainted with an offering made for one such as Dieudonné.

Scales rasping on wood sounded near her feet. She looked down at a python winding itself over tree roots. It paused to flick its tongue at her, like the wave of a minuscule purple hand.

The image of the two snakelets whipped through her mind. *Sibling.*

"You don't know where my son is, do you?"

Étienne's face filled her mind. He looked down at her, the Moabi's canopy spreading over a twilight sky. The python's memory of the funeral.

"Yes, brother. Have you seen him?" Thérèse leaned in, her heart thudding. Perhaps—

But the snake slithered away. She watched the beige point of its tail vanish into shadow and dead leaves.

Fine. If spirits and villagers and snakes wouldn't find her son, she would.

Her son's last memory of her wouldn't be her yelling at him.

She started down the path to where she did not know.

Étienne didn't know if he slept. Had he spoken to the spirit of death only for it to vanish at its name, or was that a dream? Was that minutes ago, or hours? Or was this darkness the dream?

"Tell me, little one," said the voice smooth as pond water. "Why are you down here?"

No, this was real. No dream could be this terrifying.

"Well?" Death asked.

Étienne weighed his response. Did she know the answer already, or did she only want to know how he would respond? Any reply was a gamble. "I was pushed."

"Pushed? Oh my."

"Yes, Great One. I wasn't supposed to be there. I was trying… Well, I had this bracelet—"

"Pushed? Fell? Jumped? It doesn't matter."

Étienne hadn't realized he was straining upward until he slumped back against the mine's wall.

"How you got here, little one, is unimportant. It is not up to me to intervene, only to follow the course of actions put into motion. You have heard my voice—your path is set."

"My mother—"

"What about her? All die. All come to me in the end." Death's voice tickled his ears. "Your brother is here, your father, too. Join them, here in the dark. Why fight?"

Colors crashed through his headache, swirling to form the image of a snake, fangs at the ready, waiting for a bird to hop by. A sensation of question accompanied it. *Why not patience?*

The mental image vanished. Étienne jerked as scales slithered over his shoulders. Pulsating coils drooped over his chest and arms. A tongue flicked his ear. He relaxed. He had no reason to fear, not as a son of Snake Clan.

"White Woman is coming," Étienne said. This snake was a sign, sent to watch over him until rescue came. The One That Sees had told White Woman what happened. As Snake Clan patron, she would have told his mother. And the village; they would pull him out, he would be free. Maybe Madam Bakelé would stand in the crowd and cheer, her gold flashing as they pulled him from this pit. Or his mother, she would throw herself at his feet to beg his forgiveness. Étienne giggled. "Oh, thank you, brother."

"This is none of your concern, dirt eater," Death said to the snake.

Identical snakes coiling around each other. The reassurance of trust washed over Étienne.

"When is White Woman coming, or my mother?" Étienne reached to stroke the snake's head. It was large and bulbous. A python. The one from the funeral. Étienne giggled again. Why had he reviled snake voices so much before?

The snake moved away, coiling itself over his shoulders and arms. The images and emotions fell in quick succession: Étienne's mother. White Woman. Discomfort. White Woman's silver fire. Anger. Sadness. Abandonment.

Death snorted. "Then, leave."

Étienne barely heard. "Tell them I'm hurt. And thirsty. And my bracelet, I think I dropped it."

The snake tightened its coils, just enough to smother another giggle rising in his chest.

White Woman's smile, then her grimace. A tree branch snapping in two. A mother snake swallowing her eggs. Loss. Betrayal.

Étienne struggled to put the images and sensation into context. Betrayal? How? He hadn't betrayed anyone. The obligations with White Woman were ancient ones, forged with spirits generations ago. To break them he would have had to...

"Broken? She's not..."

A feeling without imagery—regret. No.

The disappointment in Étienne's chest didn't come from a snake. Neither did the embarrassment and anger that followed.

White Woman didn't care. Why would she? When she'd ignored the funeral rites for Dieudonné? Étienne blinked back hot tears. "So go and tell my mother where I am. She'll send help."

White-hot fire and White Woman's ten screaming mouths. Fear.

Death's chuckle was the beating of bat wings under a moonless sky. "See, little one? Not even your patron spirit will alter what must be done, and your little friend won't challenge her."

Étienne ignored her. "Then why are you here," he asked the snake. "To watch me die? Feed on me like a cane rat?" Étienne squirmed against the python's coils around his neck, tight as a noose. He relented as bone ground against bone in his arm.

The standard greeting, twin snakes born from the same egg. Trust. Then a question.

Étienne said nothing. Of course, he knew the stupid story. Everyone in Snake Clan did. It was their bedtime story, told night after night to children to explain why Snake Clan was different from River Clan or Cloud Clan or Sky Clan. He braced himself.

The images poured through his head anyway. A python, dappled green and brown, winding its way through the forest. Its way blocked by a river of sharp-jawed army ants. The arrogant snake trying to push his way through. The swarming, the biting, then the pain. Shouts of help to the spirits, the silence that answered.

And just as the snake thrashes and prepares for the end, a man runs to him, lithe as a panther. Beti. Étienne's ancestor. His skin gleaming, muscles rippling, eyes like sunlight through trees. The man's hands pulling the snake from the ants, despite the pain it brought to his soft, unscaled flesh.

A sensation of relief. The snake's question. *Why?* The man's simple response. A finger pointing to the snake, to himself, then to the blood that oozed from the cuts and bites on their skin. *You. Me. Same.*

Then the promise. The snake winding its way around the man's arm, the sharing of souls—blood to blood, flesh to flesh—Beti's warmth healing the snake. The bonding that forged Snake Clan.

Darkness swallowed Étienne once again.

"Such sweet lullabies," Death said.

The python's hiss echoed until the mine sounded like a hornet's nest. More images flew through Étienne's mind like a whirlwind of color. A baby snake. A human child crawling on the ground. Sibling. Anger. White Woman.

Étienne shook his head. "I don't understand."

A sandy colored deer in the forest being shot by an arrow. An old woman sleeping in her bed, her gray braids dangling like vipers from branches. Trust. Courage. Loss.

"Please, I'm sorry, I'm not…"

We. Brothers.

Étienne's mouth opened. He hadn't heard the words, not with his ears. They were in his head like the pictures, but speech? Without images? From a snake? Was that even possible? In all the stories, and all the elders they never—

Please. Listen. Talk. So slow. Get words upside down.

"You mean 'wrong,'" Death said. "But bravo for trying. Keep up this pace of evolution and you may grow legs."

The python ignored her. *You ancestor. Mine ancestor. Promise made. You hear me. I hear you. Before White Woman. We promise stronger promise White Woman.*

The snake slithered onto Étienne's lap, curling against his stomach.

Me afraid White Woman. But she listen to snake. If me tell her, you good. You brother. You need save because good. White Woman change mind. Spirits help. Then a sensation of confidence so strong it was warm.

"You think this little human is good?" Death's laughter showered Étienne in pebbles and dust dislodged from the mine's walls. "Shall you tell him, boy, or shall I?"

The image of a snake slipping from a tree branch, its tail whipping out uselessly. Confusion. *Tell?*

Étienne blinked dust from his eyes. No tears came. He had no more to give.

"I killed my brother."

The Third Day

The clunk the snake bracelet made on the exchanger's stall was gorgeous. Solid and heavy with the promise of a month's worth of meals for Sandrine and her children. Maybe two, if she haggled well.

She resisted the urge to pluck it back up just to drop it one more time.

"Moment," the exchanger said. He continued to stare at a lump of rock through a jeweler's loop. He was short, hunched over, his form hidden under a gray silk shirt much too large for him. Sandrine thought he looked like a bird perched on a stool. A pigeon, maybe, with those tiny eyes.

Sandrine bounced from foot to foot and glanced behind her. Her four children stood at the edge of the exchanger's stalls, tickling each other with tufts of elephant grass. On the road next to them, men with cudgels carried away iron boxes, heavy with unrefined gold dust. Nearby, a bush spirit with lily flowers for eyes and vines for arms swung from stall to stall, leaving a trail of petals.

After a long minute the exchanger turned and picked up the bracelet.

"Intriguing piece," he said. He muttered under his breath as he tested its weight on his fingers, nibbled an edge, twisted it under his loupe. "Fifty, no, forty-nine grams, decent craftsmanship, all good. Hmm. And this motif?"

"Yes, yes, very pretty. How much will you do me for?"

The exchanger set the bracelet down.

"How, might I ask, did you come by this piece? Given your, well, origin."

"My what?"

"This was made for someone of Snake Clan. And I don't believe they are found in the West."

"Spirit gave it to me."

"Oh?"

Sandrine pursed her lips. She'd come to this exchanger, here at the edge of the market, because he had a certain reputation. Few questions, a short memory, and bad record keeping.

A reputation that wasn't being well earned today.

"I got hungry little ones, and it took a fancy to me. Now are you going to give me cowries for it or not, 'cause I see lots of other stalls open today."

"You see," the exchanger said, leaning back on his stool, "there's a rumor going around. About a Snake Clan item. Stolen, apparently. And the current possessor, a mere boy, has vanished. The mother is distraught. Ancestors watch over her. But if you say a spirit gave it to you, well." He smiled then, but there was no mirth in his lips. "But what kind of business would I be running if I didn't verify my purchases?"

"What?"

"They of the Deep Soil? Please, this way."

The exchanger motioned for the little green bush spirit. Sandrine took a step back as it swung to them like a monkey moving in the canopy. It stopped at the stall, petals falling onto the table. Sandrine expected lily perfume but found only the reek of swamp water.

The spirit's eyes blossomed as it looked at Sandrine, the petals opening and closing as it blinked.

"*La honte*, guilt, she smells *de la honte*, this one of the grasslands, *cette femme* of not here."

"Guilt, good spirit?" The exchanger leered. "About what, I wonder?"

The spirit cackled and swung around.

"I—I didn't steal—"

"Should we take? *Mais oui.*" They of the Deep Soil caressed the bracelet with a vine. "Not stealing if you steal *d'une voleuse,* from a thief."

Sandrine tried to speak but couldn't look away from the petal eyes. She knew bush spirits back home. They were gentle, mostly. Always sleeping in someone's garden to help the manioc and taro grow. Kiss one and it would grant you favors. Do a bit more than that and you'd earn a miracle. But this...It shouldn't be here, in the barren market where all the plants had been cut down. Chittering like some animal.

Maybe it's Deng Deng, she thought. There's something bitter about the spirits here—bitter as the soil, the mud, the sallow faces staring back from the exchanger stalls. Or perhaps it was the people. They turned up the earth for gold and set everything rotting.

Sandrine snatched the bracelet and clutched it to her chest. "Go ask The One That Sees. Question it. See how the spirit of truth likes being called a liar."

The exchanger stiffened. Sandrine backed away, aware of every eye, of how the market had gone silent. She spun and collided into a woman.

It took all her strength to keep her knees stiff. Because it was *that* woman. The one she'd been dreading seeing.

The one who'd been wandering the market, the digging field, the houses, shouting and mumbling, "Have you seen my boy? My son?"

The mother of the boy.

Sandrine swung the bracelet behind her back. Too quick, she thought. Too obvious.

But the woman shuffled past Sandrine, unseeing. Her hair jutted out at odd angles, and dust stained the hem of her indigo dress. Sagging skin clung to her cheeks. She looked like a rag doll that had escaped a dog.

"Have you...my boy?" she said to no one in particular.

Sandrine didn't pause to watch her. She ran to her children, grabbed her youngest's arm, and tugged him to the road. The boy whined in protest, but she didn't slow.

They of the Deep Soil called after her, their voice a squealing sing-song. "She watched him die and *rien de tout*, not a thing, so she could eat, *pour qu'elle puisse manger, manger.* She watched him fall down, down, down, she could eat his gold, this one of elsewhere, *cette femme d'ailleurs.*"

By the time Sandrine reached the road, she was crying.

Étienne sniffed, glad for the darkness hiding his face. But with Death and a python sharing his thoughts, did it matter?

The image of a snake slipping from a branch. Disorientation. Confusion. *What?*

"I didn't—" Étienne swallowed down a sob but his mouth was ash dry. "I didn't mean to."

How kill brother?

Death snickered. "Yes, do tell."

Étienne shifted, grunted at the stab it brought to his arm. "It was…I only…I only wanted something that people would look at. I thought it would be nice, to have, you know? I'd never had anything like it." He took a breath. "So, when Dieudonné came to see *Maman*, I—"

The python squeezed its coils. Étienne's mind filled with a cane rat bounding over a rock, its haunches just out of reach. Frustration. *Missed. Be slow.*

Death's groan was the grinding of rocks. "I thought you humans loved stories. Why are you so bad at telling them?"

"I'm just trying to—"

"To what? Humans have such bent perceptions, anyway. Always tilting the light to show off your best features."

A presence swam inside Étienne. Like the thoughts of the python, but slower, cooler. His thirst faded, and the ache in his arm calmed to a dull throb.

"Perhaps a more neutral gaze, shall we?" Death said. "Now, sit back…."

A light grew in the mine's darkness, gray at first, then fracturing into reds, oranges, blues. Shapes emerged. A window, a red adobe wall, a faded *rideau* swaying over an open door. Étienne breathed in. Over the damp of the mine, he detected tangy lye soap, salty fish stew, the earthy raffia rug. All of it melded into that undefinable aroma of home.

And there, in a corner, himself, seated against a wall and thumbing a book. But the angle was off. Higher, as if—

"A mouse was dying in your rafters. I was there." Death snickered. "I'm always there, at the end."

Dieudonné walked through the *rideau*. A black silk shirt hung over his chest and lean frame, and matching trousers flapped around his feet. A delicate gold chain with a charm—a snake swallowing its own tail—dangled from his neck. It swung counter to his movements, and Étienne thought of dancers.

Your brother? the python asked.

Étienne tried to jump down from this odd vantage point and run to Dieudonné. But he remained fixed in place. He looked to his other self. Move, he willed. Get up.

"It's just a memory, little one," Death said. The mocking edge had gone from her voice. "Just watch."

Étienne's mother burst through the doorway. Grabbing Dieudonné's shoulder, she spun him around then waggled a balled-up mass of crimson fabric at his face.

"It's a good job," Dieudonné said. "That's how I bought it."

"You're just a courier to Port City. That's what you said. But Dembele pays you enough to buy this?" Her finger stabbed his chest. "That necklace?"

"I thought you'd like it."

Thérèse glanced to Étienne reading in the corner. She grabbed Dieudonné's arm and pulled him behind a shelf full of unripe plantains. Étienne watched his past self steal a glance up, the book now only a prop.

"Are you skimming?"

Dieudonné winced.

His mother stiffened. "Dieudonné…No."

"A few grams. Dust that falls to the floor of the jewelry shop. Dembele wouldn't even miss it. Hasn't."

Thérèse sank onto a sack of rice and buried her face in the gown. "How long?"

Dieudonné played with the edge of a raised tile with the toe of his sandal.

"How long, Dieudonné?"

"Long enough to get Étienne some schoolbooks. Food. That." He nodded to the gown.

"I wouldn't have taken it if I knew."

"Fine. I'll take it back." He stuck out his hands. Thérèse hesitated, her hands tightening just so. Dieudonné smirked.

Thérèse stood and waggled a finger. "No more, understood? Do you know what these people would do to you if they found out? Do to us? Gold has…" Her brow creased. "I don't recognize Deng Deng anymore."

"I'll be fine, *Maman*."

"Promise me."

"*Maman*—"

"*Promise* me." She stepped closer to Dieudonné, her black eyes boring into his. "Please."

"Fine, fine." Dieudonné pulled her into a hug. "I promise, OK?"

They stood for a moment, Dieudonné's chin resting on his mother's plaited hair, the gown squished between them.

"I should go, *Maman*," Dieudonné said. "Dembele's expecting me."

Thérèse sniffed. "Eat first." She jutted her chin at a marmite simmering on some coals. "It's a long walk back. I'll get you a bowl." Soon the clang of cutlery filled the house.

Étienne's other self jumped from his chair. In the mine, he squeezed his eyes shut. It did nothing to block Death's memory.

Dieudonné flashed a grin. "Like the book?"

Étienne nodded, a half-smile teasing his lips.

"What?" Dieudonné asked.

"I was wondering…" Étienne put a hand over his mouth, trying not to giggle.

"Spit it out."

"It's my birthday in two months, and..."

His brother laughed. "And what would you like? Another book?"

Please, shut up, Étienne willed. *Don't say it. Just sit back down. Please, please, please.*

Étienne could only watch as his past self went on tiptoe to whisper in Dieudonné's ear, "Gold."

Dieudonné raised a brow. "Gold?"

"Not something big, or anything. I just thought, if I had an earring, or a necklace, like you, maybe..." He shrugged.

Dieudonné crouched to meet Étienne's eyes. "Are people bothering you? Because it doesn't mean anything if you don't have—"

"I put the *piment* in with the stew." Their mother, carrying a bowl wrapped in a sack, stepped from the kitchen. "I know you like it that way."

Dieudonné stood, too quickly. Grabbing the parcel from her hands, he kissed his mother's cheek, ruffled Étienne's hair, then stepped for the door. As he went through the *rideau*, he turned, winked, and said, "I'll see what I can do, OK?"

The world shimmered. Colors bled into each other, as if a finger had been swiped over a painting to smudge all the lines.

What happen?

"Just moving things along a bit."

The room reformed. Étienne, Dieudonné, and their mother sat on the floor around a marmite. Dieudonné, now in an indigo robe, handed Étienne a mass of brown paper. Étienne tore it apart until a glint of yellow shone through.

"A bracelet?" Étienne held it up. "Thank you, thank you, thank you!" Étienne threw himself around Dieudonné's neck.

Thérèse glared. "You promised," she mouthed, but Dieudonné waved her off. Pulling Étienne off, he pointed to the bracelet.

"We're Snake Clan, see? When I'm in the city, or away trading, or if you go somewhere in this big world, remember—"

Dieudonné's smile faded to gray, then to black. There was only darkness, the damp, a renewed throbbing in his arm.

The python coiled itself into a knot in his lap. *What happen? How kill brother? No right.*

"Well, Étienne?"

Étienne said nothing for a long minute. "He stole the gold from Dembele. Maybe from the courier boxes when they brought the raw gold to the city. Or took it from the jewelry shop. I don't know. But I knew he was stealing, and I asked him anyway. His boss found out, and he...They..."

His mind erupted with a new memory. Port City at night. Sleeping ships at a dark harbor. A jeering crowd. Fire blossoming over a body. Flailing limbs.

Screams.

Laughter.

Étienne shoved the crook of his elbow over his eyes.

"I'm so s-sorry. I didn't m-mean t-t-too—"

The python wrapped around his shoulders. It sent images of cool leaves, shade, warm rocks. Death's memory faded.

Peace. Peace.

"So, dirt eater," Death said. "He knew his brother stole, and he asked anyway. Then his brother died. Now all his village knows he and his mother lived by taking what was not theirs. No better than thieves themselves." Death's voice hummed in his ears. "So, what do you say? Is he a good person?"

No words, not even an image in reply.

Just a fuzzy gray sensation of regret.

It seemed appropriate to be here, where everything first went wrong.

Thérèse sat on a pile of rubble at the edge of the digging field, her fingers playing with pebbles. She stared at the pile of gravel half covered with brown grass. A wind spirit flitted overhead, its gelatinous body a ripple of green. Its wake carried the scent of rain. Thérèse's eyes followed it for a moment, then they drifted back to the mound.

Five years and she'd never come so close.

Just an extra shift, her husband had said. "Today I find the mother lode. I feel it." He'd kissed the top of her head as she peeled manioc root. His beard scratched her, and she'd mumbled a goodbye as he walked away. She hadn't looked up. Hadn't said goodbye. If she could—

Something whirled past Thérèse's legs and clanged against the ground. It bounced, glimmering, then landed behind a rock.

She looked up. A woman stood over her. She had red, swollen eyes and a thin head perched on narrow shoulders. Resewn patches covered a purple skirt. Her lips trembled, and when she spoke, her words stuck in her nose. A Westerner.

"Just take it. I—I can't. All day and…I don't want— It's not worth it!"

"Huh?" Thérèse wasn't sure if it was the woman's accent or her own exhaustion that was making everything muddled.

"That! All day it's been following me. Singing!" The woman pointed at the forest. Thérèse followed her finger to where a small, green bush spirit had wrapped itself around the trunk of a mahogany tree. Lily petal eyes blossomed as it grinned, then waved a vine.

"*Cette femme d'ailleurs*, this otherwhere woman, she watched him fall, down, down, so she could *mange son or*, eat his gold, *mange, mange, mange*, yum yum."

"See? So take it. I don't want it anymore." The woman wiped her eyes, turned, and started down the path to the village. A group of four children joined her, their wary eyes darting to the spirit lurking in the forest.

Didn't want what? Thérèse looked around for what the woman had thrown. Something metal. She thought she'd seen it wink in the light and—

Her fatigue vanished. With unsteady fingers she reached down and picked up a bracelet. The rocks had scratched the edges, but the snake motif stared up at her.

"Wait." Thérèse's voice cracked. She rose and the world threatened to invert itself. "Wait!"

The woman and her children kept marching toward the village. Thérèse ran. Once, she stumbled, fell, then rose again, ignoring a throb in her elbow. She grabbed the woman, spun her, and brandished the bracelet.

"Where? Where did you get this?"

The woman refused to look at it.

"My son, where is my son?"

The Westerner began to cry. Thin, halting gasps that became sobs. Thérèse stepped back, wanting to both shake the woman and embrace her. Tell her she knew pain, too.

After a moment the Westerner let out a long breath, then met Thérèse's eyes. "There was a spirit. The One That Sees." She went on, saying her name was Sandrine, that she'd come to Deng Deng from the grasslands with her children. She told Thérèse how they'd been so hungry for so long, so when a spirit came, she offered herself to it, but it ignored her. It angered her, then she'd seen Étienne just watching, playing with that hunk of gold. She'd only meant to scare him. She hadn't thought the spirit would come back, actually attack him.

"There was wind, and dust. I didn't see what... When I looked up, he was gone. Just gone. The One That Sees gave that to me, and we hadn't eaten in so long. I'm sorry. Really."

Thérèse said nothing. Sandrine's story didn't make sense. Spirits didn't vanish people. Hurt, maybe, if they were angry enough. Chase if provoked. But they had no interest in dragging someone away. Spirits fed on dreams and hopes and wishes, not flesh. If the spirit had only killed Étienne, his body would be there. There'd be no reason for The One That Sees to hide her son's corpse.

The bush spirit sang again. "She watched him fall, down, down, so she could *mange son or* yum yum."

Fall.

"Where?" Thérèse said.

Sandrine wiped her eyes. "What?"

"Where was he? When The One That Sees came. Where was Étienne standing?"

Sandrine blinked and gestured at the mound of gravel.

"There, I think."

Thérèse gasped. How could she have been so blind, so stupid? Of course, Étienne came here. The one place he knew she'd never follow. And that's why Sandrine thought he'd vanished. You couldn't see the opening except from atop the mound.

The spirit hadn't taken him; he'd fallen.

And might still be alive.

As Thérèse ran for the mine, she yelled over her shoulder at the confused Westerner, "Don't just stand there, get a rope!"

The shivering wouldn't stop. Étienne curled into a ball. His brother's face swam before his vision, flashing that quick smile that burst into pale yellow flame.

The python looped himself around Étienne's forehead. *No cold. Hot.*

"Fever," said Death.

Need water.

"I didn't mean to," Étienne mumbled.

"Stop fighting, little one," Death said. "Your bones are broken. Your snake sibling has seen what you did. Spirits won't help you. Your family can't help you. You have no water, no food."

Étienne swatted the darkness. "So, laugh. It's what I deserve, right? This is what I get?"

"No, Étienne." Concern softened the edges of her voice. The impression of a hen pulling a chick under her wing flickered through his mind.

It didn't come from the python.

"Your path is set. It was from the moment you fell. Every choice, every action demands a result. I can't spare you, but you don't have to suffer. Not like this."

A star of blue light appeared in the dark. Étienne blinked. It remained, bobbing as it inched closer.

The python leapt from Étienne's forehead to his lap, its muscles rippling. Étienne winced at the urgent sense of danger flooding his thoughts.

Scorpion.

"This is my daughter," said Death. The light stopped a few

centimeters away. "Her sting offers a quick death. No more pain. No more fever. Just sleep."

Étienne struggled to focus on the needle-thin pincers, the curved tail. He should be afraid. How many times had his mother chastised him for not checking his sandals before putting them on, or swept under his cot to chase one away? But the creature's glow was delicate, the curve of its stinger elegant. Comforting, like a candle, or a sliver of moon on a dark night.

"Just a prick, then it's all over."

For a long moment, the snake tensed on Étienne's lap. Then it relaxed.

Rest. Peace. Understanding. *No pain. Sleep.*

The scorpion clacked its pincers. Its tail curled and uncurled. A beckoning finger.

Étienne eased the python off him, then stood. He stepped toward the scorpion, the pain in his body distant. His father waited for him. Dieudonné, too. Maybe this is what he deserved.

A mercy, this offering.

Then a rope plopped into his face.

The Fourth Day

Thérèse's soul went with her voice down the gullet of the mine. "Étienne! ÉTIENNE!"

She held her breath, straining her ears for a reply.

"Hey!"

But not from below. From above. Thérèse looked up as three miners stumbled over the top of the mound. Orange mud clung to their bare chests.

"Get back," one said. A large man, his biceps like gourds, stopped short of the ring of warning stones. "Cursed."

"Edge might collapse," said another, a thin man whose teeth shone like porcelain against his soil-covered face. "Hasn't been touched in years."

Sandrine, carrying a coiled rope, elbowed them aside. She offered one end to Thérèse, who took it and bent to the largest boulder set at the edge of the mine. She tried not to think about how the red warning charms painted on them looked like blood. The pit below yawned, wide and black and deep.

As Thérèse cinched the knot, she wondered if this stone was the one that represented her husband. Its red charm was still as vibrant as the day they had pulled out his crushed body.

Strange that today it might help save her son.

Might. If. If Étienne were still alive. If his neck wasn't broken. If he wasn't bleeding out, or dying of thirst, or—

No. He was alive. She clung to the word like the last breath of air in a stale room. *Alive.*

"Move," Thérèse told the miners.

"Wait," said the third man, his neck so short that his head was just a lump on his shoulders. He looked from Sandrine, to the rope, to Thérèse, to the mine. His eyes widened. "Somebody's down there?"

"*Merde.*"

"What's going on?" More figures emerged over the top of the hill. A digger with a shovel, the incised scars in parallel lines down his cheeks marking him as a Far Northerner. A woman drenched in ocher muck from a panning pool, her braids piled high on her head. An elderly exchanger, stooped over and huffing, his hands bunching his silver robe around his thighs to keep the dust away.

"There's a mine back here? Didn't know that. Who owns it?"

"Everyone OK?"

"Somebody fall?"

Thérèse crouched over the edge of the hole and threw the rope down.

"ÉTIENNE!"

Silence. Just pebbles and grit vanishing into damp air carrying the odors of wet rock.

But it was the silence that finally broke her.

"What?" Still kneeling, Thérèse glared at the growing crowd. "No one brought honey wine to sip while they watch? Are you expecting me to give you some stew, so you can have a meal as you listen to my son die?"

Shuffling of feet. Averted gazes.

Thérèse lifted herself up. Pulling the bracelet from her dress, she shook it at the crowd. "Or is this the only thing you're interested in?"

Eyes flickered to the gold, but no one moved, no one spoke.

"Cowards," Thérèse said. "I curse my ancestors for planting their yams in the wretched village of Deng Deng."

An explosion of mercury-white light cracked over the mine. Rushing air slammed against Thérèse. For a sickening moment, she thought she would fall forward into the dark void of the mine. But twisting, flailing her arms, leaning back, she managed to tumble backward. She landed hard on her hip and elbow.

"Curse our ancestors? Curse their names? Little reptile worm," screamed ten mouths in unison. White Woman hovered above the mine, her hair pulsating with dark electricity. "We will crush this one like beetles in our teeth, like stones under a hammer. We will swallow her name into nothing!"

"So do it!" Thérèse winced as she stood up once more. Warmth trickled down her elbow, the joint on fire. A rock had broken the skin, she was sure. She also didn't care. "Do *anything.*"

For a fraction of a heartbeat, a shard of White Woman's silver glow solidified, solid as a looking glass. Thérèse's reflection stared back at her. When had she become so dusty? Her dress lay in tatters, arm bleeding, her once-butter-smooth skin now mottled. But it was her eyes that changed the most. Fire glowed in them—something she hadn't seen for a long, long time. And the flames were growing, spreading, consuming her from the inside out.

"I've served you all my life, and what have you ever done?" Thérèse pushed herself to yell, louder, harder. "Given me a dead husband, a dead son? Maybe two? What has my devotion brought me but misery?"

"We are—"

"Oh, shut up."

The crowd gasped. The old exchanger turned and scurried down the hill. White Woman blinked. Thérèse almost stepped back. Almost. Just a lifting of her heel a millimeter or so. Then she stopped herself.

No more prayers, she thought. *Not ever.*

"I know what Dieudonné did. He took what was not his. He lied. He profited from the labor of others. His crime was against the village, against our traditions. And he suffered for it."

"We are—"

"I'm not talking to you." Thérèse angled herself to address the crowd. Northerners, Southerners, Coasters, exchangers, market women, diggers. Old and young, poor and poorer. They all stared back. Etched into their faces, she saw terror, hunger, desperation, long days digging in the unyielding earth and longer nights wondering how they would feed their families come morning.

She knew because all that was written on her face, too.

"I'm telling you that he stole to make his life better because the spirits wouldn't. He prayed, he made sacrifices, and got nothing in return. All he wanted was to make his family happy. I know he broke our traditions. He took what he did not earn. He cheated. And he suffered for it. But my youngest did nothing."

White Woman drifted to Thérèse. Her robin egg eyes glistened with rage. Her mouths leered. "We will suck your bones and make playthings of your skin."

"No, you won't. You won't do anything." Thérèse brandished the bracelet. "If someone stole the gold on the Moabi tree and you did nothing, why would you do anything now? Either you don't care, or you *can't* do anything. And you could have done something this entire time I've been talking. Call down the heavens. Summon wildfire to burn me up. You haven't, because you can't." Thérèse held the bracelet to the crowd. "The spirits tell you they will help you find gold if you make sacrifices. But how many of you have found it? How many times has a spirit told you, 'dig here, not there?'"

Thérèse hurled the bracelet into the mine. It winked once in the sun, once in White Woman's fire, then it was gone.

"So, there's your gold. Take it if you want. You don't need a spirit to tell you where to find it anymore. Because I'm done praying and groveling for just a display of colors. The spirits of Deng Deng are broken."

White Woman screamed. She raged, she howled, she twirled. Curtains of flame shot upward. Thérèse squeezed her eyes shut, the afterimage of the ten mouths screaming burned into her eyes.

"WE WILL NOT BE MOCKED!"

A hand slipped into Thérèse's. Calloused. Thin. Hard. She squeezed and Sandrine squeezed back.

Then it was over. Thérèse opened her eyes. The mine stood there in the ground. The crowd huddled around it. The trees beyond the digging field still stood. The clouds passed overhead.

But White Woman was gone.

"Well?" Sandrine picked up the rope and shook it at the nearest digger. "You going to help, or you going to get out of the way?"

The miner looked at her, then at Thérèse. Thérèse stared back, breathing hard. Then the miner bent down to tug on the rope. "That knot's going to slip. Let me."

The crowd erupted into chatter.

"I think I have another rope at my shack."

"Go get Bertine. She has those poultices."

"Put some planks down there. Yeah, to reinforce the edge."

Thérèse caught Sandrine's eye. And for the first time in a long time, her lips twitched into a smile.

"Is this real?" Étienne whispered. "Is this here?" Or was it some trick of Death, some shared memory tantalizing him? Maybe just a product of fever.

Étienne tugged at the rope. It didn't give. He yanked. The raffia fibers creaked.

Then from above, muffled and distorted, "Étienne!"

He felt a dozen snakes' thoughts, all shared through the python, pound into his mind. People clustered together. Anticipation. White Woman and a storm of light. Then his mother, pointing and giving directions to men covered in mud. Encouragement. A rope.

Étienne squeezed his eyes against the barrage.

"No." Death's growl was the shattering of rocks in an earthquake. "You belong here. This is your path."

"I'm down here!" Étienne's voice echoed upward.

Here. Here. Here.

Silence, then a distant roar. The python flashed a dozen perspectives of people cheering, his mother sagging to her knees, a woman coming to her side.

Was that the Western woman? The images vanished before Étienne could decide.

Silence again, then a distorted voice. Étienne couldn't make out the words.

The python interpreted. *Rescue. Hold rope. They pull up.*

Étienne clutched the rope. He tugged once, then leaned back. Its rough fibers bit into his palms. He rose.

Then his hand slipped. He winced as the rope chewed his skin, and he landed back on the ground. A drop of three or four centimeters at most.

The rope slackened as another incomprehensible shout came from above.

Knot. Make knot, said the snake.

"Stop," said Death. "This isn't fair."

Clutching the rope with his left hand, Étienne tried to lift his right to the rope. Pain lanced through his forearm, like fire ants biting into the muscle. He grunted, tried to flex his fingers. White dots floated in his vision.

"Can't," he said through gritted teeth. "My arm."

The python wound up Étienne's legs and his chest. *Hold rope.*

Étienne clutched it. The snake slid over his left arm, then twisted over his hand and wrist. Étienne gasped. An unbidden memory of watching pythons coil over rats came to him. But he'd never imagined that the grip could be more like steel than flesh.

Reassurance. Basking on warm rocks. Comfort.

No slip. Me you knot. Now pull, brother, pull.

Étienne tugged. The slack went out of the rope, and he rose, slowly, centimeter by halting centimeter.

His shoulder screamed at the tension. He wondered if this arm, too, would break.

Death's wail was a hurricane's wind, the crash of trees under curtains of rain, swirling clouds pregnant with lightning.

"Stop them!"

The scorpion scuttled forward. Its pale glow reflected on the damp rocks.

The python hissed. Its resolution and self-preservation honed its thoughts to a point sharp as its fangs.

Crush. Grind. Kill.

"Kill him," Death cried. "Now!"

A wave of exhaustion swept over Étienne. *Kill,* is that what the mob said as they beat Dieudonné?

The world had taken his brother. He wouldn't add to its grief.

He stuck out his foot. His toe stopped short of the scorpion. "Come with us, if you like."

The scorpion hesitated. Its tail flexed, curling and uncurling.

"I know somewhere nice and warm to sleep. Not this cold hole. There's lots of nooks and crannies in my house. And crickets. I'll make sure *Maman* leaves you alone."

"Do it now!"

The scorpion crawled onto Étienne's proffered foot. It held on with its scratchy legs as the rope jerked Étienne upward. A faint ring of light shone above, growing brighter.

"You belong with me!"

Étienne looked down. As if pressing against thin cloth, a face emerged from the darkness. A smooth head. Eyes shriveled into deep sockets. A nose pressed flat against low cheekbones. And a mouth, wide and cavernous, opening wider to swallow the world.

A hand rose from the void. Fingers sharp as thorns stretched for Étienne's leg.

"With me!"

The scorpion whipped its tail and jabbed its stinger into Death's thumb.

The hand vanished. The face contorted. Not in anger. Or rage. Or hate.

Sadness. Maybe loneliness. Étienne wasn't sure because it melted back into nothing.

Light washed over Étienne. He heard weeping.

And cheering.

Hands seized his shoulders. Gravel scratched along his back and legs as he was dragged over the mine's lip. He pried open his eyes to his mother burying her face into his chest, her sobs hot and wet. He took a breath, and his mouth flooded with the taste of her hair, the cool breeze from the forest, the aroma of dust.

"Maman?" he asked, still squinting against the brightness.

She squeezed him tighter. "Étienne, I—"

"Snake, there's a snake!"

The python released its grip on his arm. Étienne looked up as the snake coiled on itself, head raised to face a man with a pickax. Scars covered his cheeks. A Far Northerner.

The man raised the curved steel above his head. The python hissed, opened its jaw.

"Don't—" Étienne screamed.

The ax came down with a dull thud. Red droplets arched through the air, some splattering Étienne's cheeks, lips, and flashing a sour saltiness on his tongue. A concussive blast of agony pushed through him. Étienne screamed, sharing the python's fear, its pain, its death.

Then it was gone.

Étienne's insides hollowed out. He slumped to the earth, his fingers digging into gravel.

His father to feed him. Dieudonné to make him smile. The snake to help him live.

All died because of him.

"You idiot!" A woman, tears welling in her eyes, rushed forward and wrenched the pickax from the miner. She flung it down the mine. A muffled clang of metal on stone replied.

"What?" The man turned, mouth opening as he took in the

shocked stares, the muttered curses. He shrugged. "It was just a snake."

"Scorpion," someone yelped. The crowd shuffled and squirmed. Snakes were one thing. This was Deng Deng, the village of the Children of Beti, the brothers of snakes. Spend enough time at Deng Deng and one would get used to being around serpents.

Scorpions were different. Scorpions had only one master.

Étienne rolled to his side to see feet leaping away from the scorpion. The creature scuttled over rocks, its shell black and shiny as polished glass. A sandaled foot landed to its left. The scorpion darted right. A shovel slammed down on the rock where it had been a moment ago. Another foot rose.

Ignoring the pain, Étienne flung himself over the scorpion. The foot landed on his thigh. He grunted and curled himself around the creature.

"She's my friend," he shouted. "Don't hurt her. Don't hurt her."

The shuffling stopped. Étienne waited a moment then wormed his hand under his chest. The scorpion wriggled against his palm. Alive. Frightened, but alive.

Étienne sat. The scorpion scuttled into the crevices of his clothing. People eyed them and took a step back.

Étienne started to crawl to the body of the python, but his mother swept him up in her arms. She pulled him to her chest, blocking the world from view. She wept, rocking him.

"I'm so sorry. I'm so sorry," she said. "I didn't mean it. I didn't mean it."

Étienne's sobs joined hers as their tears mingled on his cheeks.

Night

Part of him—more than a part, most of him—wished he were still in the mine.

His thoughts returned again and again to the pickax slamming into the python, the sandal almost squishing the scorpion, the flames dancing along his brother's body. His fault, all of it.

He didn't deserve to be saved.

The window above Étienne's cot cut the moonlight into a square that stretched across the floor. It flashed pink as a spirit flew past, then returned to its pale silver. A whoop drifted from the village center, where the last revelers still guzzled bottles of honey wine or beer.

He twisted to face the wall.

Étienne scratched an itch at the edge of the still-damp plaster entombing his right arm. It had barely been applied when White Woman came to their house, a dozen spirits trailing behind her, their glows pulsating like a discordant rainbow. His mother, her face a mask, had gone to greet them.

"Why are they here?" Étienne asked the Westerner—Sandrine, he had learned. He sat on the floor, sucking on bitter herbs to temper his fever.

As Sandrine opened her mouth to reply, White Woman spun in a circle, her hair sending out sparks of white flame.

"A feast, my feast, we will bring a feast. We give him to her, this little lost snakeling, we bring him to our beloved daughter. Make a feast, a feast for our goodness."

Étienne could only stare as his mother gave her thanks to the spirits for Étienne's safe return and her gratitude for their generosity.

But she didn't bow.

It was later that night that as they sat near the Moabi tree that Sandrine answered his question.

A slaughtered goat roasted over coals while marmites of fish stew, rice, and *kelen-kelen* soup piled high. Bottles of wine and beer passed from hand to hand. Spirits, more than Étienne had ever seen in one place, mingled with the villagers of Deng Deng. White Woman danced, singing with her many mouths, while other spirits answered with strained melodies from the trees.

Sandrine, her eyes glassy from honey wine, leaned in and whispered, "They're afraid. Of you and your *maman*."

Étienne looked up.

"Your mother called the spirits broken. I don't think that's right. They're starving 'cause Deng Deng has too much greed, too much pollution, not enough hope to go around. So, the spirits are pretending like today never happened. Or like it was all just some great lesson."

"What lesson?"

Sandrine sighed. Her breath was sticky sweet. "Faith? Humility? Determination? Who knows. The point is that they're worried your *maman* will keep telling people they don't need spirits. Can't have that. Because the more she tells them, the more people just might start believing her. And if people stop dreaming spirits can help them, well…" She huffed. "Best to make her their friend now, instead of an enemy later."

But Étienne wasn't listening anymore. He stared at the villagers and spirits dancing and drinking. As if a feast made it all right. As if Deng Deng had come to his brother's funeral.

As if all along anyone cared.

Étienne had stood up and left then. No one jumped up to help him or stop him as he limped home. He would have brushed them off if they had.

He rolled over in his cot. He looked at his mother laying on her bed. On the floor, Sandrine, a bottle still clamped in her hand. They had stumbled in an hour later, giggling and shushing one another. Étienne had pretended to be asleep as they whispered together, making plans they wouldn't remember in the morning. Finally, they dozed off. He watched his mother's chest rise and fall, her breath coming in soft snores.

The scorpion scuttled to his pillow and nestled in against his cheek. He reached out to stroke her tail. She nipped his finger with her pincers, just once, then went still.

The *rideau* gusted, flapping once like a yawn. A damp coolness swirled in the room. Étienne held his breath as scales glided over his leg and onto his stomach.

He sat up. A python made of blue moonlight, glowing gently, stared up at him. Its eyes, once obsidian pricks, winked like distant stars. It flicked its tongue.

Brother.

Étienne wanted to shout. He wanted to hug the snake, to run outside and show everyone, to cry. Jump up and down, sob, sing, beg forgiveness.

All he managed was a whispered, "Hi."

Étienne reached out to touch the snake's head. For a moment, his fingers found resistance, then pushed through into empty air. It was like touching a mound of flour. With form, but soft and intangibly delicate.

"I told you," said a voice soft as evening fog. "All things come to me in the end."

A calm settled over him. Strange, he almost missed her voice; the stillness of her murmur in his ear.

"You're here for me."

Death chuckled. "You changed your course. But you'll come to me in the end. All do."

Étienne offered his hand to the python. It nuzzled against his palm, a glowing tongue tickling his wrist.

"I wanted to give you something," Death said.

The beam of moonlight rippled. A face came from the boundary of shadow. Eyes shrouded, narrow chin, and cheeks half lit, its lips carried a familiar melancholy smile. When it spoke, its whisper was distant, like a half-remembered dream.

"Étienne."

"Dieudonné?" Hot tears came. Étienne wiped them away, afraid what he was seeing was just a product of water collecting in the corner of his eye, more fearful they would obstruct the memory of this moment. He glanced to his mother. She didn't stir. He didn't think she would. A feeling told him this moment was just for him.

"It wasn't the bracelet," his brother said.

"What?"

Dieudonné's shadow leaned closer. "They didn't kill me because of the bracelet. I bought it."

Étienne said nothing.

"I stopped stealing, like I promised. I saved up money. I worked at a restaurant, at the docks, cleaned a hostel at night. Two months I saved so I could buy it for you. Fair. Honest."

"How…Then why—" The question wouldn't form on his lips.

Dieudonné's figure shimmered. "The people I took gold from before, they found me. We argued. We fought. But it wasn't the bracelet—just my own choices catching up to me. Ripples in a pond coming back, I guess. Not your fault. Mine alone."

Étienne couldn't hold back a sob. He reached out for his brother. "I miss you."

"I know." Dieudonné faded again, his voice dim. "But remember." He reached out his hand of nothing but pale starlight and shadow. In it, the bracelet, a lone glimmer of color. The snake motif winked. Étienne took it.

"We're like snakes, you and me."

The python slithered up Étienne's arm. Its edges were soft, unfocused.

"You always come back."

Dieudonné chuckled.

Then he was gone. Étienne looked down at the python, but there was nothing there.

He sat for a long moment, feeling the tears slide down his cheeks, savoring their saltiness as they reached his mouth. Finally, he whispered, "Death?"

"Yes, little one?"

"Why did The One That Sees say the bracelet was stolen?"

"All gold is stolen from the earth, little one. It's just a matter of…perspective of ownership."

"Did you know? That Dieudonné hadn't stolen it?"

A pause.

"Death?"

"I get lonely, there in the dark. It's easier sometimes if someone wants to stay. If they don't fight me, at the end."

Étienne said nothing. After a long moment, he lay back down on his bed. "You can visit, if you like. If you ever want someone to talk to. I won't mind."

Lips gentle as midnight rain kissed his cheek.

"You are a good person, Étienne, son of Snake Clan."

90

The *rideau* rustled again. Étienne lay still, the only motions his rising and falling chest, his hands fondling the bracelet until dawn flecked the horizon with jeweled tones of red, violet, and gold.

Nonzero

written by
Tom Vandermolen

illustrated by
JENNIFER MELLEN

ABOUT THE AUTHOR

Tom Vandermolen started out life as a military brat, born in Japan to a US Navy sailor and a Japanese mother, but raised primarily in the American South. A childhood of books, comics, movies, excellent English grades, and mediocre math grades resulted in a collection of short-story rejections and, inexplicably, a physics degree. After college, what should have been a short enlistment as a nuclear submarine officer somehow became a twenty-two-year career as a Navy intelligence officer. No one is sure how any of this happened.

His story "Nonzero" was inspired in part by Tom's experiences working the night shift on an aircraft carrier—specifically times spent standing at the stern of the blacked-out ship, staring out into the apparently endless darkness of a moonless, cloudy night in the middle of the Pacific Ocean.

Now retired from the military and working as a data scientist, Tom lives in Seattle with his wife, Yvette, who is always his first reader (and editor).

ABOUT THE ILLUSTRATOR

Jennifer Mellen was born March 2, 1988, in Salt Lake City, and raised in Magna, Utah. She has been drawing from a very young age and has explored every art medium she could find, including traditional, digital, and sculpture. She has also always loved all things fantasy, creating strange creatures and dragons in her artwork.

She earned her associate degree in illustration while raising three children with her husband Nathan Mellen. After working for some years in graphic design, she and her husband started SeaDragon Cove, producing and selling fantasy products at various renaissance festivals, conventions, and Evermore Park. That business has now joined with We Geek Together Entertainment.

At Life the Universe and Everything Symposium in Provo, Utah, Jennifer attended an Illustrators of the Future panel where she met Contest judge Brian C. Hailes. After several years of meeting artists at various venues, she was inspired to submit her work to Illustrators of the Future.

Nonzero

W hen the drugs kick in, she's five years old again, sleepy between cool sheets, her mother reading a bedtime story as the stars on her bedroom ceiling watch over her. The house has promised her the ceiling only shows real stars, the ones actually overhead. Usually, their sparkling and flickering is warm and friendly, as if they're waving at her. But now they seem distant and distracted, like adults talking, resuming conversations that started long before she was born.

She wonders what stars would have to talk about. Maybe they tell stories about the little lives that twirl about them, like grandmothers gossiping. She wonders if the sun talks to the star where the aliens came from, the ones who attacked Earth.

Then she frowns, because the bedroom lights are suddenly flashing red. Mom raises her voice, and now she sounds weird, like a different woman entirely. "Susan," she says. "We need to talk about your options."

Stale breath that smells like fear brushes her cheeks.

Blindly, Susan reaches out a finger and taps a button, and the woman's voice fades.

S he's ten years old, sneaking into their backyard pool after bedtime. The pool is fine during the day, with friends and splashing around and everything, but at night it becomes magic. The single submerged light turns the water into a cube of liquid moonlight. Hovering under the surface of the deep end, the stars wobbling overhead, she imagines floating in zero gravity high over an alien world.

Looking up at the stars through the water's surface, she relaxes, enjoying the silence here in pool space. A different kind of silence than the quiet hurting of their house at night. Her father's muffled sobs just audible through the walls. Her older sister Marian crying in her sleep.

Susan is too old for bedtime stories now, but sometimes she misses them and her mother so much, she has to come out here and float with the friendly stars overhead, pretending she's far away.

But suddenly the pool light is flashing red, and somehow that woman's voice is hard and clear in her ears. "Susan, our situation needs your immediate atten——"

Another tap on the button, and everything fades again.

She's twenty years old, her senior year in college, lying on her back on a grassy hill outside of town, again looking up at the stars. Somewhere nearby, her friends are drinking and talking, plotting to set her up with some random person, like throwing two chemicals together in the hope they will react in a pleasing way. Sometimes it even works—the random person is interesting enough to distract her from her studies and Fleet screening test prep. But these reactions never burn very long, and they never ignite at all unless the night is overcast.

Because on a clear night like tonight, she can fly.

It's well past midnight, and the dew is soaking through her sweatshirt and jeans. The grass is a soft, even presence supporting her body, and after lying flat for a few minutes, it disappears from her senses. As her eyes adjust to the darkness, more stars emerge from the black, a tapestry of ancient art, dominated by the airbrush spray of the Milky Way. Their emergence gives her the illusion of motion, like she's flying through space.

It's silly that this still thrills her, because soon she'll be out there for real, basic training starts in—

Two months?

For a moment she's confused, because she remembers leaving for training, her father smiling proudly even as his eyes are wide and vulnerable and filled with tears. But she also remembers his funeral, halfway through her first division officer tour in one of the tiny USSN navigation stations—

No. She remembers *missing* his funeral, stuck out by Jupiter while her sister buried their father.

Before she can focus on this thought, red lights begin flashing everywhere, and a siren grates against her ears. She has time to think that the police are here, breaking up the outdoor party—

Then that woman's voice again, suddenly loud and everywhere, "Susan! Your air supply is now critical."

A sharp jab in her arm, and suddenly her heart is hammering and her eyes are open, and now she really is falling up through these strange stars. She yells and writhes in panic, trying to stop her fall while her gloved hands paw at the too-close helmet visor that flashes red lights and reflects her hot and fear-acrid breath back into her face.

"I apologize," her spacesuit AI says over her screams, "but we must discuss your options."

She gets control of herself. It takes time. She spends much of it cursing the AI, who silently absorbs it.

"OK." In the helmet, her own voice is a stranger's, raw and trembling. Her throat feels tender from screaming. "Let's talk options."

"Fleet emergency procedures recommend two main options in cases of long-duration rescue—"

"Stop." Her voice is calm, but she shakes her head violently enough to launch a small constellation of sweat globules from her forehead. They tumble in front of her eyes briefly before the helmet filters suck them away. "I want real options. I want to know where we are, where we're heading."

A map appears on her visor; she's a dot in the center and her path a straight line extending past the top border. There are no other dots. A little bubble shows her velocity relative to the nearest star; she's traveling thousands of kilometers an hour, faster than a rifle bullet, but there's no sensation of movement. Out here, moving faster than a bullet is the same as standing still. She'd used the last of the suit's maneuvering fuel to stop her wild spinning, started by whatever caused the ship to leave. Now the stars are as motionless as paint spots on a black wall.

"CPA to…" She swallows, the dry click loud in her helmet. "Anything."

"Closest point of approach will be five-point-two light years to Epsilon Persei in approximately eighteen-thousand years."

Numbers so large they were meaningless; angels dancing on parsecs. "What if we're going downhill?" The joke falls flat in her own ears, but using her voice for something besides screaming gives her a little boost of courage. "How long until someone hears the mayday beacon?"

"The distress signal will reach the Mirfak colonies in two hundred and sixty-six years."

A cold fist clenches inside her chest, and hitching sobs escape her lips. Tears form and cling to her corneas in little half bubbles, smearing the star field. She could die of old age in this suit and still be a hundred years dead by then.

"Hypoxia onset in forty minutes. Our options are outlined in the Fleet—"

"'Our'?" Humorless laughter bubbles up out of her throat. "You breathe now, too—"

"Personnel overboard protocols—"

"Just…just shut up!"

The AI goes silent.

She closes her eyes. "Where. Is. The. Ship? Regulations say to come back."

"Unknown. I received notification of a General Quarters alarm, a Close Contact alarm, and an Emergency Acceleration alarm. The departing ship's warp bubble cut off further comms."

Her eyes open and go wide. "Details on the Close Contact. Human or alien?"

"Unknown."

JENNIFER MELLEN

"Well, was the ship under fire?"

"No damage detected before breakaway."

"Damn it! Did they say they were coming back? Did they say *anything*?"

"The ship AI did not inform me of the captain's intentions."

"How—? So much for *Never leave a shipmate behind*, you assholes!" Punching at the vacuum, each jerky swing pivots her body slightly. "And what kind of *idiot* designs a suit with only one oxygen recycler?"

"We now have—"

"Stop! Saying! 'We'!" The helmet and gloves block her from putting her head in her hands, and a sudden realization covers her body in a cold tingling. *I'll never touch my own skin again.*

Then she's screaming again, her entire body writhing and raging at the ship, the aliens, the idiots who built this suit. The idiot wearing it. The oxygen indicator drops visibly, but she screams again anyway, a perverse satisfaction almost making her smile.

Abruptly exhausted, she floats for a few precious seconds.

"Why did they leave me?" This lost child's voice in her helmet belongs to someone else.

"Fleet SOP dictates that ships will not leave EVA personnel unless safety of the entire vessel is threatened."

"But—" She's surprised, and more than a little ashamed, that she hadn't considered this yet. Clearly, they left in a hurry, and *something* caused the damage to her suit and sent her spinning into the void. "Are they—do they still exist?"

"I have not detected distress signals."

"But if they were in warp for even a few seconds, the distress signal would take days or weeks to reach us."

"Yes."

"So, I could be the only survivor." The words sneak out of her mouth.

"Yes, that is possible."

Then who's going to rescue me? But this time she doesn't let the words escape. The following wave of grief, for the hundreds of crew on that ship, including basically every friend she has, comes almost as a relief. She's familiar with that emotion, knows how to deal with it.

"The ship is not likely to return before your air runs out," the AI continues, its tone brisk. "Therefore, its status is not important. Even if the ship is destroyed, the only immediate effect on our situation is administrative at best."

"Administrative?"

"This EVA unit would legally be considered a lifeboat, and you would become the senior ranking officer."

Her mouth drops open. Then she laughs, shocking herself with its honesty and severity. "I always wanted a command someday. Or to have a ship named after me, until I figured out that you had to die to make that happen." She taps the suit's chest plate where her name is stenciled. "Looks like I found a shortcut."

"You are still alive and capable of choices." The AI's programmed optimism, that by-the-manual survival spirit, is suddenly endearing. "Low-temperature stasis presents a nonzero chance of survival when rescue is delayed, even in low oxygen environments."

"*Freezing?*" Her main memory of EVA training was the instructors rolling their eyes at the "corpsicle" option. "That's our solution?"

"If you are unwilling to wait for rescue, self-euthanasia is the remaining, but not recommended, option."

"Did I leave—are there enough sedatives left for that?"

"We have enough sedatives for self-euthanasia, and one full stasis therapy treatment."

"So, the menu is suicide or antifreeze cocktails." Her heartbeats turn hard and fast, thudding against her rib cage. "Is there really a difference? How nonzero is 'nonzero,' exactly?"

"Chance calculations are based on time in stasis. The system is intended for durations of up to three months. However, a rhesus monkey has been in deep sleep at USSN research labs for fourteen years with no detectable issues. His name is Dapang."

"Dapang." She repeats the name as if that would force this conversation to make sense.

"It means 'big fat.'"

She closes her eyes. "What will it feel like? Do we know that much? Will I be totally unconscious or semiconscious?"

"Your body chemistry will be extremely slow but not completely stopped. Sporadic brain activity has been detected in Dapang over the past decade, although these findings are disputed."

In the relative safety of EVA training, she would have laughed at those words, those chances. Now she feels a whole-body yearning, every cell straining to believe.

"Hypoxia onset is—"

"I can read the displays, thank you." A ragged sigh. "Just...I need a few seconds, please." She blinks away tears, but the tiny comfort of even that light touch of eyelash against cheek brings more. Butterfly wings.

She tries to remember the last time someone else touched her. Panics a little because no memory comes. College? There had been a fling during training, but the name and face of the person disappears like vapor when she tries to recall them.

They were all ephemeral, those little lives that played out around her all these years, drained of importance by her obsession with the stars. Orbiting her but never touching, held at a constant distance away not by gravity, but by...what?

"You know, the sun is a star, and the earth is a planet," her sister Marian had said, balancing her newest son on her hip. "You could choose to study *us*, take a tour Earthside for a change. Let your niece and nephew get to know you." The main part was unspoken, of course, because that's how their family was. *We're both all we have left.*

But she would think of their parents, how each death had altered the gravity of the original four bodies in their family-verse. Of what her ten-year-old self had thought would be there forever, but was in reality as delicate and tenuous as the tiny blood vessel that had burst in her mother's brain.

"Jesus, Marian, I'm not going away forever," Susan had said in the breezy voice she used when people demanded things of her.

"I'll have lots of leave on the books when this cruise is over, so I can come hang out at your place and be the cool, weird aunt. Your kids will get tired of all my stupid space stories."

Then she had wondered, as she always did, how much longer Marian would live. Her kids would live longer, probably, but only by a hundred years or so. And Susan didn't want to be there when any of it happened.

Wish granted.

"I spent my whole life trying to get out here," she whispers.

The suit AI is small and specialized, but smart enough that it doesn't respond.

The stars watch her. She watches back, trying to stare down these things that exist for billions of years, all of human civilization barely a heartbeat for them. She used to think of them as people, the center of their own universes, each struggling with cold, hard laws of gravity and attraction. Forever spiraling past one another.

But also radiating outward, sending signals to others of their kind, separated by enormous gulfs of emptiness. Those signals are passing by her, through her, messages made of photons and neutrinos, on their way to recipients, some arriving long after the sender has extinguished.

And she wonders if some part of her icicle brain will be able to sense those photons and neutrinos flying through it. To recognize the patterns that emerge over thousands of years, and decipher the celestial slow talk filling the void. To finally grasp what they are all saying.

"Susan," the AI prompts, in a gentle tone that breaks her heart. "Yes, I know. OK."

"Just in case," the AI says with an approximation of delicacy, "would you like to record a message to your loved ones?"

"I—" Her brain locks, trying to think of anyone. Finally, "Of course, yes. For my sister."

"Recording."

"Marian." Only a little quaver in her voice. "I'm sorry I left. No, that's not right. I'm sorry I left you behind. I wish we'd been closer, now. I do love you, though. And I hope your life was happy. Is happy. Goodbye." The familiar feeling of helplessness whenever she tried saying anything real to her sister. "End it. Stop."

"Recording stopped. Did that help?"

Answering that question doesn't feel possible, so instead she takes a deep, shuddering breath and releases it slowly. "What's going to happen to you? After I'm gone."

"I will enter a low-power monitoring mode to ensure the beacon operates for as long as possible. When power levels reach a critical point, I will shut myself down."

"Maybe we'll wake up together."

"I would prefer to start up before you awake, to better prepare you for stasis recovery procedures."

"All right." Suppressing a smile. "That works, too."

She looks out then, at these strange stars who will be her traveling companions for the rest of eternity. "OK. Let's do this."

The suit goes to work. A pinprick on her left arm, liquid snaking through her veins. Her breaths become fog. The AI narrating the process in a gentle voice she finds surprisingly soothing.

After a moment, it starts to feel like flying.

She's twenty again, lying on the grassy hill, looking at these strange new friends in the sky, her view slightly cloudy from the rime of frost on her visor, the soft murmurs of the party and her friends like the whispering of stars.

She's ten again, floating in her backyard pool, the pool light behind her like a distant, blue sun. Her shadow projects huge against the shallow end, and she imagines she's looking at her older self; the shadow she will throw when she's the explorer she knows she will be. Above her the stars are hazy behind the ice forming on the pool's surface, but she can still see their friendly twinkling.

By the time her eyes freeze open, she's five years old again, her new friends are winking at her through the icy faceplate, and her bed is soft, but it must be winter because the bed sheets are so very cold. She thinks she can hear the distant murmuring again, like adults talking in another room.

She drifts off to a woman's voice, telling her the bedtime story of someday waking up.

On Writing and Science Fiction

BY L. RON HUBBARD

With over 250 published works of fiction totaling over four million
words in every popular genre, L. Ron Hubbard is one of the most
accomplished and prolific writers of the twentieth century. In 1980
and in celebration of fifty years as a professional writer, he penned
the internationally acclaimed New York Times bestseller, Battlefield
Earth, a 428,750-word science fiction epic written in just eight
months. That he would return a year later to write the 1.2 million
word, ten-volume Mission Earth in eight months—with each volume
becoming a New York Times bestseller—bears testament to him as a
master storyteller.

Promoting the release of Battlefield Earth, which was partly set in
and around Denver, Colorado, Mr. Hubbard conducted an interview
with the Rocky Mountain News published February 20, 1983. The
following article contains excerpts of this interview. In it, Mr. Hubbard
provides invaluable insight into the art and craft of writing, the role of
science fiction in society, how he viewed himself as a writer and offers
some sound advice for aspiring writers everywhere.

On Writing and Science Fiction

An excerpted interview with L. Ron Hubbard as printed in the *Rocky Mountain News*, February 20, 1983

Q: *What made you return to science fiction writing after all these years?*
A: There are some activities that are simply so much fun that one can't give them up. Writing is that for me. I love every opportunity to write.

Many young writers are told to write in order to learn how to write. That is good advice. I used to find any excuse to write because I loved to do it. If I didn't have a typewriter, I wrote in longhand.

So when my fiftieth anniversary as a professional writer came around, I decided to celebrate it by doing it. It was like a present to myself, so to speak.

I chose science fiction because there is great versatility in this genre. (A writer must pick his medium as carefully as a painter must pick his brush and colors.) Besides, science fiction is no longer the stepchild of literature. *Star Wars* created an entirely new following....

Plus, look at the bestseller lists and you will see the pattern repeating. Science fiction and space travel are dominant.

Q: *What direction do you see science fiction taking now? Is the trend toward epics and battle stories such as* Star Wars?
A: You must remember that science fiction is simply a method or a means of telling the story. Regardless of the genre (science

fiction, western, spy, romance), you will find that people like a story that is both real and has a purpose. It has to say something or achieve something.

There is always an element that promotes your valueless or no-hope society, but compare their success with stories like *Star Wars* or *ET.*...

Science fiction points a direction because it does advocate a future. It is about Man and his Future.

Q: *What role did science fiction writers and their readers have in the development of space technology and travel—and public acceptance of it and its funding—in the 1950s and 1960s? What role does it play today in future commitment to space exploration, colonization, exploitation?*
A: If you will go back through those old, gaudy pulp magazines that were being ridiculed and confiscated by irate teachers, you will find a lot of articles on space technology scattered amongst the fiction. That was because there was no other outlet for such vision.

Some who wrote for the pulps were called "just science fiction writers." But history has proven that they were the ones who brought about the future—not the naysayers.

We knew then that Man would travel to the stars and we know it still.

There are still those who cannot create a vision for the future and they, as before, still click their tongues to make a living and they will, again, be forgotten simply because they cannot create— they can only criticize.

Q: *How would you assess the broader audience science fiction has today? Years ago, science fiction was considered as something for children which was not "serious" literature. Its popularity today knows no age boundaries. Is this indicative of an escapist attitude by readers? Or a look to the future and what we could be?*
A: The future is the only frontier without limit and the frontier that we will all enter and cross no matter what we do.

Science fiction is and always has been the literature about the frontier. Science fiction appeals to every age group because it is about the future and the human potential.

Q: *How do you draw from your past track in creating character and plot? Is this the place from which science fiction comes in general, whether the writers know it or not?*
A: Experience helps any writer or anyone who wants to write.

I traveled through the Far East and sailed the high seas and did a few loops in some bi-winged planes and gliders in my day and drew upon these for stories. I also did a lot of research for other stories.

But what is more important is the ability to see what is in front of you. Plus you have to have the ability to assume the viewpoint of your reader.

For example, in *Battlefield Earth*, the reader looks through the eyes of the hero and through the eyes of the alien. This is done by describing how each person would describe the scene and objects. It gives the reader a feeling of what it would be like to assume that viewpoint. The reader at first does not recognize the object either but should be able to do so as the description continues. But, in the process, the reader can experience the same mystery as the character in the story.

That is the ability to see what is in front of you and the ability to assume another viewpoint.

It is a good exercise for writers.

So experience is helpful but you need much more.

Q: *What does science fiction writing do for L. Ron Hubbard personally?*
A: I can answer that better if you don't restrict it to just one genre.

Writing offers creation, expression, and the ultimate ability to communicate, whether you write poetry or a novel.

Science fiction is just one means or method of doing that.

With writing, you must take an idea and turn it into little black marks on a sheet of white paper so that someone will look at it and lift those little black marks off the page and form the idea of the author.

In short, it boils down to communication.

Q: *How would L. Ron Hubbard describe himself as a writer?*
A: I don't know if I can take it any further than that.

I've always had the ability to put an idea down on the page. I don't really outline. I just write.

I think if I wanted to be characterized in a certain way as a writer, I would ask that it be that I am a writer who loves to write.

That is not as axiomatic as it may sound. There are a lot of writers who don't like to write and some who even hate it but are still called "writers" because they make a living at it—the 9-to-5 type, so to speak.

But it has never been that way with me. I don't watch the clock when I write. In fact, I've gone days without sleep just because I was enjoying myself so much I plain forgot.

How could one forget to sleep?

Well, imagine doing something that is more exciting than anything you have ever done and see if you worry or think about a "coffee break," or what time it is.

That's what I mean by my being a writer who loves to write.

There's really no other way to say it.

Q: *How do you work? Do you dictate or pound your fiction out on your old typewriter? Do you keep any set schedule when doing a book? Do you work from detailed character sketches and plot outlines or do you wing it? Have your working methods changed over the years?*
A: My goodness, but that covers a lot!

What I write determines how I do it. Sometimes I type, sometimes I write longhand, and sometimes I dictate.

Battlefield Earth was typed on a manual typewriter. The length was about 3,000 pages.

Each day before I went to bed I would sketch out the plot that

I would cover the next day. Plus I would list out anything else that I wanted to accomplish.

I do set and follow a schedule when I want to get certain things done in a day—like exercise, if only a walk.

So I generally lay out what I want to accomplish for the day, the week, the month, and then I do it. I would say this is perhaps my primary development since those early days in getting organized. It has allowed me to get more accomplished: to lay out a schedule and then do it.

Q: *What do you think about writers who take years to write a single book?*
A: I really don't think many do. They might research something for years, but I can't figure out how somebody could keep a plot in his head that long.

Some people try to equate quality with slowness. If an athlete did that he would lose every game.

Q: *What advice do you have for budding writers?*
A: Write and write and write and write. And then when you finish, write some more.

It may not be original advice, but it is still quite true. You learn to write by writing.

Don't try to learn *how* to write in order to write. I've seen a lot of great writers killed off when they decided they wanted to learn how to write.

Just take an idea and go with it. You may find a story that pulls you along. The story takes off on its own. It sounds silly but it happens. You have this character walking down the street and you are all ready for him to get into a taxi but he walks right on and turns into a movie theatre. Whoa! What is this? Well, follow him and see what happens.

The main thing is to write and learn the business of writing— that tough market you have to live with.

The Last Drop

written by

L. Ron Hubbard and L. Sprague de Camp

illustrated by

CHRIS ARIAS

ABOUT THE AUTHORS

L. Ron Hubbard and L. Sprague de Camp were fellow science fiction and fantasy authors in the 1930s and '40s. Both resided in New York City off and on to be near the editors of the popular fiction they so famously wrote.

They were each known for their humorous styles. "The Last Drop" is a whimsical product of their singular joint effort. It was first published in November of 1941.

Little was recorded of their relationship. But many years later, L. Ron Hubbard wrote an article mentioning de Camp that gives a flavor of the time in which this story was written. Here is an excerpt.

"I guess I must have written the line 'By L. Ron Hubbard' many thousands of times between 1930 and 1950.

"And every time I wrote it I had a sense of starting something pleasing, something exciting and, it worked out, something that would sell. Ninety-three and one-half percent of everything I wrote was accepted first draft, first submission.

"I wrote adventure, detective stories, air stories, science fiction, fantasy, technical articles, you name it.

"Production was about 100,000 words a month most months, done on an electric typewriter, working an average of three hours a day, three days a week.

"Arthur J. Burks, Ed Bodin, Bob Heinlein, John Campbell, Willy Ley, Isaac Asimov, these and the rest of the greats were my friends.

"I shuttled between New York and Hollywood with way stops at a hideous rainy ranch in Puget Sound.

"When I took time off, I went on expeditions to freshen up the old viewpoint....

"The dear old days. The good old days. The exciting, hard-working, screaming rush old days....

"Only six hundred writers total wrote the full story output of America. And only two hundred of them were the hard-core professionals. . . .

"Ah, the old names, L. Sprague de Camp, Fletcher Pratt, Robert Bloch, Ed Hamilton, Frank Belknap Long, dear old Edd Cartier and his fantastic beautiful illustrations, names still going, names forgotten.

"All for the 'by line.'

"The petty squabbles, the friendly enmities.

"I look back now and love them all.

"We were quite a crew.

"We made and popularized the space age.

"We got the show on the road.

"And the other day I heard they have a personnel down in the War Department who reads everything we ever wrote, trying to see if there's any hint or invention they've missed.

"Well, all those years I was also working on mental technology. The last advance had been with Freud in 1894. Because I knew that someday Man would need it if he ever got into space.

"And so I stepped off the bandwagon in 1950 and let them carry on.

"They've gone on splendidly, those old writers. They've come up to a stature more like gods than men.

"And I love them all and all my fans and wish them well and well again."

ABOUT THE ILLUSTRATOR

Chris Arias was born in 1997 in Cartago, Costa Rica, a small farming town on the slopes of an extinct volcano. Chris has been passionate about art ever since he could hold a pencil in his right hand. He was inspired by the fantastic stories about goblins, witches, knights, and dragons that his mother told during their long walks through the local mountains and forests.

Chris comes from a humble family that couldn't afford art classes during his childhood, and so he learned to draw by copying art from video games, comics, and cartoons.

It wasn't until he entered university that he attended his first art class. In 2021 Chris graduated from UCCART with a degree in fine arts.

His passion for fantasy and science fiction and the support of his family have driven him to follow his dreams to become an artist in these genres.

Chris was a former winner of the Illustrators of the Future Contest and was first featured in L. Ron Hubbard Presents Writers of the Future Volume 39.

The Last Drop

Euclid O'Brien's assistant, Harry McLeod, looked at the bottle on the bar with the air of a man who has just received a dare.

Mac was no ordinary bartender—at least in his own eyes if not in those of the saloon's customers—and it had been his private dream for years to invent a cocktail which would burn itself upon the pages of history. So far his concoctions only burned gastronomically.

Euclid had dismissed the importance of this bottle as a native curiosity, for it had been sent from Borneo by Euclid's brother, Aristotle. Perhaps Euclid had dismissed the bottle because it made him think of how badly he himself wanted to go to Borneo.

Mac, however, had not dismissed it. Surreptitiously Mac pulled the cork and sniffed. Then, with determination, he began to throw together random ingredients—whiskey, yolk of an egg, lemon and a pony of this syrup Euclid's brother had sent.

Mac shook it up.

Mac drank it down.

"Hey," said Euclid belatedly. "Watcha doin'?"

"Mmmmm," said Mac, eyeing the three customers and Euclid, "that is what I call a *real* cocktail! Whiskey, egg yolk, lemon, one pony of syrup. Here"—he began to throw together another one—"try it!"

"No!" chorused the customers.

Mac looked hurt.

"Gosh, you took an awful chance," said Euclid. "I never know what Aristotle will dig up next. He said to go easy on that syrup because the natives said it did funny things. He says the native name, translated, means *swello*."

"It's swell all right," said Mac. Guckenheimer, one of the customers, looked at him glumly.

"Well," snapped Mac, "I ain't dead yet."

Guckenheimer continued to look at him. Mac looked at the quartet.

"Hell, even if I do die, I ain't giving you the satisfaction of a free show." And he grabbed his hat and walked out.

Euclid looked after him. "I hope he don't get sick."

Guckenheimer looked at the cocktail Mac had made and shook his head in distrust.

Suddenly Guckenheimer gaped, gasped and then wildly gesticulated. "Look! Oh, my god, look!"

A fly had lighted upon the rim of the glass and had imbibed. And now, before their eyes, the fly expanded, doubled in size, trebled, quadrupled...

Euclid stared in horror at this monster, now the size of a small dog, which feebly fluttered and flopped about on shaking legs. It was getting bigger!

Euclid threw a bung starter with sure aim. Guckenheimer and the other two customers beat it down with chairs. A few seconds later they began to breathe once more.

Euclid started to drag the fly toward the garbage can and then stopped in horror. "M-Mac drank some of that stuff!"

Guckenheimer sighed. "Probably dead by now then."

"But we can't let him wander around like that! Swelling up all over town! Call the cops! Call somebody! Find him!"

Guckenheimer went to the phone, and Euclid halted in rapid concentration before his tools of trade.

"I gotta do something. I gotta do something," he gibbered.

Chivvis, a learned customer, said, "If that stuff made Mac swell up, it might make him shrink too. If he used lemon for his, he got an acid reaction. Maybe if you used limewater for yours, you would get an alkaline reaction."

CHRIS ARIAS

Euclid's paunch shook with his activity. Larkin, the third customer, caught a fly and applied it to the swello cocktail. The fly rapidly began to get very big. Euclid picked up the loathsome object and dunked its proboscis in some of his limewater cocktail. Like a plane fading into the distance, it grew small.

"It works!" cried Euclid. "Any sign of Mac?"

"Nobody has seen anything yet," said Guckenheimer. "If anything does happen to him and he dies, the cops will probably want you for murder, Euclid."

"Murder? Me? Oh! I shoulda left this business years ago. I shoulda got out of New York while the going was good. I shoulda done what I always wanted and gone to Borneo! Guckenheimer, you don't think they'll pin it on me if anything happens to Mac?"

Guckenheimer suddenly decided not to say anything. Chivvis and Larkin, likewise, stopped talking to each other. A man had entered the bar—a man who wore a Panama hat and a shoulder-padded suit of the latest Broadway design, a man who had a narrow, evil face.

Frankie Guanella sat down at the bar and beckoned commandingly to Euclid.

"Okay, O'Brien," said Guanella, "this is the first of the month."

O'Brien had longed for Borneo for more reasons than one, but that one was big enough—Frankie Guanella, absolute monarch of the local corner gang, who exacted his tribute with regularity.

"I ain't got any dough," said O'Brien, made truculent by Mac's possible trouble.

"No?" said Guanella. "O'Brien, we been very reasonable. The las' guy who wouldn't pay out a policy got awful boint when his jernt boined down."

And just to show his aplomb, Guanella reached out and tossed off one of the cocktails which had been used on the flies.

In paralyzed horror the four stared at Guanella, wondering if he would go up or shrink.

"Hey, who's the funny guy?" said Guanella, snatching off his hat, his voice getting shriller. He looked at the band. "No, it's got my 'nitials." He clapped it back on and it fell over his face.

With a squeal of alarm he tumbled off the stool. Whatever he intended to do, he was floundering around the floor in clothes twice too big for him. Shrill, mouselike squeaks issued from the pile of clothing. Chivvis and Larkin and Guckenheimer looked around bug-eyed. Presently the Panama detached itself from the pile of clothes and began to run around the room on a pair of small bare legs.

A customer had just come in, and had started to climb a stool. He looked long and carefully at the hat. Then he began tiptoeing out. Before he reached the door, the hat started toward the door also. The customer went out with an audible swish, the hat scuttling after him.

"Oh, my!" said O'Brien. "He won't like that. No, sir! He's sensitive about his size anyway. We better do something before he brings his whole mob back. Will you telephone again, Mr. Guckenheimer?"

As Guckenheimer moved to do so, O'Brien went into furious action to make another shrinko cocktail. He was just about to add the syrup when the shaker skidded out of his trembling hands and smashed on the floor. O'Brien took a few seconds of hard breathing to get himself under control. Then he hunted up another shaker and began over again. If Mac's swello cocktail had contained a pony of syrup, an equal amount in the shrinko cocktail ought to just reverse the effect. He made a triple quantity just to be on the safe side.

Guckenheimer waddled back from the booth.

"They found him!" he cried. "He's down by the McGraw-Hill building, hanging on to the side. He says he doesn't dare let go for fear his legs will break under his weight!"

"That's right," said Chivvis. "It accords with the square-cube law. The cross-sectional area, and hence the strength in compression, of his leg bones would not increase in proportion to his mass—"

"Oh, forget it, Chivvis!" snapped Larkin. "If we don't hurry—"

"—he'll be dead before we can help him," finished Guckenheimer.

O'Brien was hunting for a thermos bottle he remembered having seen. He found it, and had just poured the shrinko cocktail into it and screwed the cap on when three men entered the Hole in the Wall. One of them carried Frankie Guanella in the crook of his arm. Guanella, now a foot tall, had a handkerchief tied diaperwise around himself. The three diners, now the only customers in the place, started to rise.

One of the newcomers pointed a pistol at them, and said conversationally, "Sit down, gents. And keep your hands on the table. Thass right."

"Whatchgonnado?" said O'Brien, going pale under his ruddiness.

"Don't get excited, Jack. You got an office in back, ain'tcha? We'll use it for the fight."

"Fight?"

"Yep. Frankie says nothing will satisfy him but a dool. He's sensitive about his size, poor little guy."

"But—"

"I know. You're gonna say it wouldn't be fair, you being so much bigger'n him. But we'll fix that. You make some more of that poison you gave him, so you'll both be the same size."

"But I haven't any more of the stuff!"

"Too bad, Jack. Then I guess we'll just have to let you have it. We was going to give you a sporting chance, too." And he raised the gun.

"No!" cried O'Brien. "You can't—"

"What's he got in that thermos bottle?" piped Frankie. "Make him show it. He just poured it outa that glass and it smells the same!"

"Don't!" yelped O'Brien. He grabbed at the bottle of Borneo syrup and the thermos in the vain hope of beating his way out. But too many hands were reaching for him.

And then came catastrophe! The zealous henchmen, in their tackle, sent both syrup and thermos flying against the beer taps. The splinter of glass was music in O'Brien's ears. The syrup was splattered beyond retrieve, for most of it had gone down the drain. But O'Brien had no more than started to breathe when he realized that only the syrup bottle had broken. The thermos, no matter how jammed up inside, still contained the shrinko cocktail.

What would happen now? If he drank that shrinko he might never, never, never again be able to get any syrup to swell up again!

One of the gangsters, having vaulted the bar, was unscrewing the thermos for Frankie's inspection. Smelling of it, Frankie announced that it was the right stuff, all right, all right. Another gangster came over the bar.

And then O'Brien was upon his back on the duckboards and a dose of shrinko was being forcibly administered. He gagged and choked and swore, but it went on down just the same.

"There," said one of the men in a satisfied voice. "Now shrink, damn you."

He put the cap back on the bottle and the bottle on the bar, mentally listing a number of persons who might benefit from a dose.

The first thing O'Brien noticed was the looseness of his clothes. He instinctively reached for his belt to tighten it, but he knew it would do no permanent good.

"Come on in the office, all of you," said the gangster lieutenant. He prodded the three customers and O'Brien ahead of him. O'Brien tripped over his drooping pants. As he reached the office door he fell sprawling. A gangster booted him and he slid across the floor, leaving most of his clothes behind him. The remaining garments fell off when he struggled to his feet. The walls and ceiling were receding. The men and the furniture were both receding and growing to terrifying size.

He was shivering with cold, though the late-May air was warm. And he felt marvelously light. He jumped up, feeling as active as a terrier despite his paunch. He was sure he could jump to twice his own height.

"Watch the door, Vic," said the head gangster. His voice sounded to O'Brien like a cavernous rumble. One of his companions opened the door a little and stood with his face near the crack. The head gangster put down Guanella, who was now O'Brien's own size. Guanella had a weapon that looked to O'Brien like an enormous battle-ax, until he realized that it consisted of an unshaped pencil split lengthwise, with a razor blade inserted in the cleft, and the whole tied fast with string. Guanella swung his ponderous-looking weapon as if it were a feather.

The head gangster said, "Frankie couldn't pull a trigger no more, so he figured this out all by himself. He's smott."

Guanella advanced across the floor toward O'Brien. He was smiling, and there was death in his sparkling black eyes. No weapon had been produced for O'Brien, but then he did not really expect one. This was a gangster's idea of a sporting chance.

Guanella leaped forward and swung. The razor-ax went *swish*, but O'Brien had jumped back just before it arrived. His agility surprised both himself and Guanella, who had never fought under these grasshoppery conditions. Guanella rushed again with an overhead swing. O'Brien jumped to one side like a large pink cricket. Guanella swung across. O'Brien, with a mighty leap, sailed clear over Guanella's head. He fell when he landed, but bounced to his feet without appreciable effort.

Around they went. O'Brien, despite his chill, did not feel at all tired, though a corresponding amount of exercise would have laid him up if he had been his normal size. The laughter of the men thundered through the room. O'Brien thought unhappily that as soon as they became bored with this spectacle they would tie a weight to him to make him easier game for their man.

Then a reflection caught his eye. It was a silvery spike lying in a crack of the floor. He snatched it up. It was an ordinary pin, not at all sharp, to his vision, but it would do for a dagger.

Guanella approached, balancing his ax. The minute he raised it, O'Brien leaped at him, stabbing. The point bounced back from Guanella's hide, which seemed much tougher than ordinary human skin had a right to be. Down they went. Their mutual efforts buffeted O'Brien about so that he hardly knew what he was doing. But he got a glimpse of Guanella's arm flat on the floor, the handle—the eraser end—of the ax gripped in his fist. With both hands O'Brien drove the point of his pin into the arm. It went in and through and into the wood. Guanella shouted. O'Brien caught up the ax and raced for the door.

He moved so quickly, compared to his normal ponderousness, that the gangsters were caught flat-footed. O'Brien slashed with the rear edge at the ankle of the man at the door. He saw the sock peel down, and the oozing skin after it. Vic roared and jumped, almost stepping on O'Brien, who dashed through and out.

He raced to the bar; a mighty jump took him to the top of a stool, and thence he jumped to the bar-top. He gathered the thermos bottle under his arm. It was a small thermos bottle, but it was still almost as big as he was. But he had no time to ponder on the wonders of size. There was a thunderous explosion behind him, and a bullet ripped along the bar, throwing splinters large enough to bowl him over. He hopped off onto a stool, and thence to the floor, and raced out. He zigzagged, and the shots that followed him went wide.

Outside, he yelled, "Orson!"

Orson Crow, O'Brien's favorite hackman, looked up from his tabloid. Seeing O'Brien bearing down on him, he muttered something about seeing things, and trod on the starter.

"Wait!" shouted O'Brien. "It's me, Obie! Let me in, quick! Quick, I say!"

He pounded on the door of the cab. Crow still did not recognize him, but at that minute a gangster with a pistol appeared at the door of the Hole in the Wall. Crow at least understood that this animated billikin was being pursued with felonious intent. So he threw open the door, almost knocking O'Brien over. O'Brien leaped in.

"McGraw-Hill building, quick!" he gasped. Crow automatically started to obey the order. As the cab roared down Eighth Avenue, O'Brien explained what he could to the bewildered driver.

"Well, now," he said, "have you got a handkerchief?" When Crow produced one, not exactly clean, O'Brien tied it diaperwise around his middle.

When they reached the McGraw-Hill building, they did not have to ask where McLeod was. There was a huge crowd, and many firemen and policemen in evidence. Some men were trying to rig up a derrick. A searchlight on a firetruck played on the unfortunate McLeod, whose fingers clutched the twenty-first story of the building, and whose feet rested on the pavement. He had had difficulty in the matter of clothes similar to that experienced by O'Brien and Guanella, except that he had, of course, grown out of his clothes instead of shrinking out from under them. Around his waist was wound several turns of rope, and through this in front was thrust an uprooted tree, roots up.

A cop stopped the cab. "You can't go no closer."

"But—" said Crow.

"Gawan, I says you can't go no closer."

O'Brien said, "Meet me on the south side of the building, Orson. And open this damn door first."

Crow opened the door. O'Brien scuttled out with his thermos bottle. He scurried through the darkness. The first cop did not even see him. The other persons who saw him did not have a chance to investigate, and assumed that they had suffered a brief illusion. In a few minutes he had dodged around the crowd to the front doors of the building. A fireman saw him coming, but watched him, popeyed, without trying to stop him as he raced through the front door. He kept on through the green-walled corridors until he found a stairway, and started up.

After one flight, he regretted this attempt. The treads were waist-high, and he was getting too tired to leap them, especially with his arms full of thermos bottle. He bounced around to the elevators. The night elevators were working, but the button was far above his reach.

He sat down, panting, for a while. Then he got up and wearily climbed down the whole flight of steps again. He found the night elevator on the ground floor, with the door open.

There was nothing to do but walk in, for all the risks of delay and exposure to Guanella's friends that such a course involved. The operator did not notice his entrance, and when he spoke the man jumped a foot.

"Say," he said, "could you take me up to the floor where the giant's head is?"

The operator looked wildly around the cab. When he saw O'Brien he recoiled as from an angry rattlesnake.

"Well, now," said O'Brien, "you don't have to be scared of me. I just want to go up to give the big guy his medicine."

"You can go up, or you can go back to hell where you came from," said the operator. "I'm off the stuff for life, I swear!" and then he bolted.

O'Brien wondered what to do now. Then he looked over the controls. He swarmed up onto the operator's stool, and found that he could just reach the button marked "18" with his thermos bottle. He thumped the button and pulled down on the starter handle. The elevator started up with a rush.

When it stopped, he went out and wandered around the half-lit corridors looking for the side to which McLeod clung. He was completely turned around by now. But his attention was drawn by a rushing, roaring, pulsating sound coming from one corridor. He trotted down that way.

It was all very well to be able to move more actively than you could ordinarily, but O'Brien was beginning to get tired of the enormous distances he had to cover. And the thermos bottle was beginning to weigh tons.

Euclid O'Brien soon found what was causing the racket. It was the tornado of breath going in and out of McLeod's nose, a part of which could be seen directly in front of the window at the end of the corridor. The nose was a really alarming spectacle. It was lit up with a crisscross of lights from the street lamps and searchlights outside, and by the corridor lights inside. The pores were big enough for O'Brien to stick his thumb into. Sweat ran down it in rippling sheets.

He took a deep breath and jumped from the floor to the windowsill. He could not possibly open the window. But he took a tight grip on the thermos bottle and banged it against the glass. The glass broke.

O'Brien set the thermos bottle down on the sill, put his hands to his mouth, and yelled, "Hey, Mac!"

Nothing happened. Then O'Brien thought about his voice. He remembered that Guanella's had gone up in pitch when Guanella had drunk the shrinko. No doubt his, O'Brien's, voice had done likewise. But his voice sounded normal to him, whereas those of ordinary-sized men sounded much deeper. So it followed that something had happened to his hearing as well. Which, for O'Brien, was pretty good thinking.

It was reasonable to infer that both McLeod's voice and McLeod's hearing had gone down in pitch when McLeod had gone up in stature. So that to McLeod, O'Brien's voice would be a batlike squeak, if indeed he could hear it at all.

O'Brien lowered his voice as much as he could and bellowed, in his equivalent of a deep bass, "Hey, Mac! It's Obie!"

At last the nose moved, and a huge watery eye swam into O'Brien's vision.

"Ghwhunhts?" said McLeod. At least it sounded like that to O'Brien—a deep rumbling, like that of an approaching subway train.

"Raise your voice!" shouted O'Brien. "Talk—you know—falsetto!"

"Like this?" replied McLeod. His voice was still a deep groan, but it was at least high enough to be intelligible to O'Brien, who clung to the broken edge of the glass while the blast of steamy air from McLeod's lungs tore past him, whipping his diaper.

"Yeah! It's Obie!"

"Who'd you say? Can't recognize you."

"Euclid O'Brien! I got some stuff to shrink you back with!"

"Oh, Obie! You don't look no bigger'n a fly! Did you get shrunk, or have I growed some more?"

"Frankie Guanella's mob shrunk me."

"Well, for heaven's sake do something for me! I can't get my breath, and I'm gonna pass out with the heat, and my legs are gonna bust any minute! I can't hold on to this building much longer!"

O'Brien waved the thermos bottle.

McLeod thundered: "Whazzat, a pill?"

"It's a shrinko cocktail! It'll work all right, on account of that's what shrunk me. If I can get it open…" O'Brien was wrestling with the screw cap. "Here! Can you take this cap between your fingernails and hold on while I twist?"

Carefully McLeod released the grip of one of his hands on the windowsills. He groaned at the increased strain on his legs, but the overloaded bones held somehow. He put his free hand up to O'Brien's window. O'Brien carefully inserted the cap between the nails of the thumb and forefinger.

"Now pinch, slowly," he cried. "Not too tight. That's enough!" He turned the flask while McLeod held the cap.

"All right now, Mac, drop the cap and take hold of the cork!" McLeod did so. O'Brien maneuvered the thermos so that its neck was braced in an angle of the hole in the glass. "Now pull, slow!" he called. The cork came out. O'Brien almost fell backward off the sill. He clutched at the edge of the glass. It would have cut his hand if he had been larger.

"Stick your mouth up here!"

O'Brien never realized what a repulsive thing a human mouth can be until McLeod's vast red lips came moistly pouting up at him.

"Closer!" he yelled. He poured the cocktail into the cavern. "Okay, you'll begin to shrink in a few seconds—I hope."

Presently he observed that McLeod's face was actually a little lower.

"You're shrinking!" he shouted.

The horrible mouth grinned up at him. "You got me just in time!" it roared. "I'd'a been a dead bartender in another minute."

"There he is!" shouted somebody behind O'Brien in the corridor. O'Brien looked around. Down toward him ran the three unshrunken gangsters.

He yelled to McLeod, "Mac! Put me on your shoulder, quick!"

McLeod reached for him. O'Brien scrambled out on the window ledge and jumped onto the outstretched palm, which transferred him to McLeod's bare shoulder. He observed that McLeod's fingers were bruised and bloody from the strain they had taken in contact with the windowsills. He found a small hair and clung to this. The gangsters' faces appeared at the window a few feet above him. One of them pointed a gun out through the hole in the pane. McLeod made a snatch at the window with his free hand. The faces disappeared like magic, and O'Brien, over the roar of McLeod's breath and the clamor in the street far below, fancied he heard the clatter of fleeing feet in the building.

"What happened?" asked McLeod, turning his head slightly and rolling his eyes in an effort to focus on the mite on his shoulder.

O'Brien explained, as the windows drifted up past him, shouting up into McLeod's ear. As they came nearer the street, O'Brien saw hats blown off by the hurricane of McLeod's breathing. He also saw an ambulance on the edge of the crowd. He figured the ambulance guys must have felt pretty damn silly when they saw the size of their patient.

"What you gonna do next?" asked McLeod. "Swell yourself up? I'd like to help you against Frankie's gang, but I gotta go to the hospital. My arches are ruined if there isn't anything else wrong with me."

"No," said O'Brien. "I got a better idea. Yes, sir. You just put me down when you get small enough to let go the building."

Story by story, McLeod lowered himself as he shrank. Soon he was a mere twenty feet tall.

He said, "I can put you down now, Obie."

"Okay," said O'Brien. At McLeod's sudden stooping movement, the nearest people started back. McLeod was still something pretty alarming to have around the house. O'Brien started running again. And again his small size and the uncertain light enabled him to dodge through the crowd before anybody could stop him. He tore around the corner, and then around another corner, and came to Orson Crow's cab. He banged on the door and hopped in.

"Frankie's mob is after me!" he gasped.

"Where you wanna go, Chief?" asked Crow, who was now fazed by few things.

"Where could a guy a foot tall buy a suit of clothes this time of night? I'm cold."

Crow thought for a few seconds. "Some of the big drugstores carry dolls," he said doubtfully.

"Well, now, you go round to the biggest one you can find, Orson."

They drew up in front of a drugstore.

O'Brien said, "Now, you go in and buy me one of these dolls. And phone one of the papers to find out what pier a boat for the Far East sails from."

"What about the dough, Obie? You owe me a buck on the meter already."

"You collect from Mac. Tell him I'll send it to him as soon as I get to Borneo. Yeah, and get me a banana from that stand. I'm starving."

Crow went. O'Brien squirmed around on the seat, trying not to show himself to passing pedestrians and at the same time keeping an apprehensive eye out for Frankie's friends.

Crow got back in and started the motor as a huge and slightly battered-looking sedan drew up. O'Brien slid to the floor, but not quickly enough. The crack of a pistol was followed by the tinkle of glass as the cab started with a furious rush.

O'Brien, on the floor, was putting on the doll's clothes. "Where's that boat leaving from?"

"Pier eleven, on South Street."

"Make it snappy, Orson."

"What does it look like I'm doing? Taking a sun bath?"

When they reached the pier, there was no sign of the gangsters. O'Brien tumbled out with his banana.

He said, "Better scram, Orson. They'll be along. Yes, sir."

"I'll see that you get off foist," said Crow. O'Brien scuttled down the pier to where the little freighter lay. Her screws had just begun to turn, and seamen were casting loose the hawsers. Crow glimpsed a small mite, barely visible in the darkness, running up a bow rope. It vanished—at least he thought it did—but just then the gangsters' car squealed to a stop beside him. They had seen, too. They piled out and ran down to the ship. The gangplank was up, and the ship was sliding rapidly out of her berth, stern first.

One of the gangsters yelled, "Hey!" at the ship, but nobody paid any attention.

A foot-high, Frankie Guanella capered on the pier in front of the gangsters in excess of homicidal rage. He shrieked abuse at the dwindling ship. When he ran out of words for a moment, Crow, who was climbing back into his cab to make a quiet getaway, heard a faint, shrill voice raised in a tinny song from the shadows around the bow hatches.

It sang, "On the road to Mandalay-ay, where the flying fishes play-ay-ay!"

Crow was too far away to see. But Frankie Guanella saw. He saw the reduced but still-round figure of Euclid O'Brien standing on top of a hatch, holding aloft his bloody ax in one hand. Then the figure vanished into the shadows again.

Guanella gave a choked squeak, and foamed at the mouth. Before his pals could stop him, he bounded to the edge of the pier and dove off. He appeared on the surface, swimming strongly toward the SS *Leeuwarden*, bobbing blackly in the path of moonlight on the dirty water.

Then a triangular fin—not over a couple of inches high, but still revealing its kinship to its relatives, the sharks—cut the water. The dogfish swirled past Frankie, and there was no more midget swimmer. There was only the moonlight, and the black hull of the freighter swinging around to start on her way to Hong Kong and Singapore.

The Imagalisk

written by
Galen Westlake

illustrated by
ARTHUR HAYWOOD

ABOUT THE AUTHOR

Born and raised in Canada, Galen practices law in Toronto and spends his days talking a great deal to a great many people. His family of four, however, confidently assures him the less he says the better. To this end, he more quietly expresses himself by writing stories during his daily commute on the train. When the stranger sitting next to him stops reading over his shoulder, he knows his tale needs a little something extra.

Galen's fiction has appeared in Galaxy's Edge *and* Unidentified Funny Objects. *His most recent legal writing may be found in* Advocates' Quarterly, *if someone were so inclined.*

Galen was awarded the Silver Play button by Google (they have yet to ask for it back) and he once competed in a Mud Hero-Ultra race event without dying. For a decade, Galen alternated as the VP and treasurer of a nonprofit, operating a nursery school for inner-city children in Toronto. He has been a janitor, a camp counselor, and once spent a summer mining a cryptocurrency that may or may not have actually existed. His laser tag score is outstanding.

A strong proponent of paragraphs, Galen claims to have invented the word "cacophony," and is most proud that he has incorrectly memorized pi to one hundred decimal places. Galen is forever indebted to the Writers of the Future forum and to his beloved writer's group: the One Ring. But right now, he needs to go chase some kids off his lawn.

ABOUT THE ILLUSTRATOR

Arthur Haywood was born in 1990 in Philadelphia, Pennsylvania.

Creating graffiti murals as a teenager with his teacher, Pose 2, inspired him to share his work publicly. Having a father who organized reading camps as a state senator and a mother who was president of the local school board showed him the influence of reading on the lives of students. Being an avid reader, who judged books by their covers, led him to sharing stories he loves with others through illustration. He is focused on making book covers, as well as murals for libraries and schools to engage youth in reading.

He earned a BFA *in illustration from the Maryland Institute College of Art, before furthering his study of classical art at Cambridge Street Studios in Philadelphia and Grand Central Atelier in New York.*

His paintings are seen in Space and Time *magazine, on murals for the Philadelphia Mural Arts Program, St. Joseph's University, Elkins Park School, in the film* Summer of Soul, *and in his book* The Great Library.

He is a recipient of the 2020–2021 Harriet Hale Woolley Scholarship at the Fondation des États-Unis in Paris. There he developed murals with students at Lycée Paul Lapie, Ecollectif, and André Malraux Elementary school depicting students of diverse origins reading, as well as the stories that engage them, to encourage learning and cultural appreciation.

He is a recipient of the 2022–2023 Tulsa Artist Fellowship and 2024 Oklahoma Visual Arts Coalition Community Artist Partnership grant to continue his series of paintings for schools to inspire reading.

The Imagalisk

And then, when he's done signing the last of the paperwork, my son just walks off with a wave and leaves me to die in hell.

Technically, hell is Graydon Manor, a nursing home. A long-term care facility, they call it. But I know what this really is—the end of the road, for me, and every other poor sod who winds up here. Next stop, pine box.

I look around at the crumbling white walls decorated with bulletin boards featuring crayon art, and I know I've screwed up for the final time. I can usually cover for my dementia, but when you forget the name of your kids' dead mother, they just don't let that go. (I'm sorry, Maria, I won't let it happen again. But, in fairness, I forgot who I was, too.) Messing up Maria in front of the kids was the last straw, but I concede there were others. The time I got lost at the supermarket and the police got called was pretty bad, but, honestly, it was only the one time. My daughter Jennie says I forgot how to use the phone in front of her, but I don't even remember that happening. I mean, everyone I'd care to call is dead at this point anyway.

So, now I'm Graydon Manor's newest resident, and the best part is I get to pay for it on the first of each month. After years of drudgery in the practice of law, I retire with a nest egg only to discover this is how I'll be spending it. It's not cheap to get someone to change your diapers. That part—wearing them— sucks too, but it's better than the alternative.

I sit back in my loaner, a wheelchair of the crappy foldable variety. I don't really need it, but I'm depressed and feeling kinda lazy. There's a portly orderly named Derek who is going to take me around in it while we do the first-day welcome tour. Why not let him push? Besides, it helps me fit in with the natives. One of them, a geriatric who appears to have forgotten his dentures, is wheeling toward me even now.

"Hey, Jere! There's a new guy!" he shouts with a voice that goes hoarse after his first two words. "Look at 'em! He's a believer. He's got two!"

What, two wheels? Two heads? The brochure assured me the residents get assistance with showering daily, but it's either a lie or Baldy-in-a-Chair here has clearly taken a pass.

Derek guides me to a halt and takes the liberty of making an introduction to my first new neighbour, just as he crashes his chair into mine with a dull *thud*.

"Dan, this is Phil, from room 138. Phil, this is Dan Kennedy. He's moving in to 229." He applies the hand brake on the rim of my left tire. Apparently, us numbers don't get to speak for ourselves.

"Listen," says Phil, ignoring Derek completely. "Come find me later, and we'll talk about what's going on, OK? But, for now, all you need to know is to stay away from the south wing, yeah? That's very important. You'll thank me later."

Derek responds for me yet again, only this time with a tone so syrupy and patronizing that I think I get why this Phil chooses to pretend he's not there. "Dan is a new resident in the *east* wing, Phil. Today is Dan's first day."

"Yeah? Well, if he goes to bingo night, he'll need to cross through the south. And unless someone teaches him some survival skills, it'll be his *last* day."

While I consider the dire consequences of bingo at Graydon Manor, another resident strides over to join us. He carries a walker in both hands that, just like my chair, he clearly doesn't need. It never actually touches the floor as he travels. Once he sidles up next to Phil, he finally plunks it down in front of himself, perhaps more like a fashion accessory than an assistive device.

"Hi there," he says, looking to me with a welcoming smile. He's tall but razor thin. I can relate. I'm mostly skin and bones at this point myself. "I'm Jerry. Folks 'round here call me Jere. Forgive my friend Phil, here. He's intense."

"No worries," I say, mustering up my best imitation of cheer. "I like that. And I'll be mindful to stay out of his turf." Jere seems quite a bit more "with it" than Phil. Even better, he doesn't give off that rancid senior stench—or seem prone to delivering dire portents.

"Oh," says Jere, shaking his head to convey that I'm not quite getting his meaning, "No, no, we stay away from the south wing, too." I might have been a bit quick on that last part.

Were it possible, Phil's eyes seem to widen even more. "Everybody with *IFs* do! Less you want yours to get eaten."

"Well, I certainly do not want that," I say, hoping the tone of my voice will prompt Jere to fill me in. Does your lunch get stolen around here? From what little I've seen so far, whoever wants it can have it.

"Well, excuse us," says Derek, interrupting as he pops the hand brake back off. "I've got to take Dan here on his tour."

"Hey, new guy!" calls Jere as I start my involuntary glide away from him. "One last thing. You might get some visitors tonight. Don't be scared."

Why would I be...? Derek has already wheeled me away. We're plowing down a wide hall cluttered with random seniors parked in wheelchairs doing absolutely nothing other than existing. I try to turn my head to look back at Jere and Phil. I'm instantly reminded that I can't do that anymore, not without pinching a nerve. I've just learned my first lesson of life at Graydon Manor. From now on, after today, I'm going to travel under my own power for as long as I can.

I'm alone in 229, my newly assigned home-sweet-home, sitting at the tiny table next to my bedside when they come for me. Jere's prediction was accurate then, but I don't know why he thought I would be scared.

I was just about to inspect Graydon's much-celebrated nighttime snack, a collection of semi-gelatinous cubes of yellow. If I'm worried about anything, it's that this might be representative of what I can expect nightly going forward.

They crack open the door to my room slowly, without knocking, and poke their two heads inside with trepidation. I've never seen either one of them before, but I simultaneously knew at once that, somehow, I have.

A young boy and his sister—twin sister, I was sure of it. They couldn't have been more than seven or eight. Both with fine dark hair covered by bright red ball caps, but without any sort of lettering or logo. Just red.

"Hi, Dan," says the boy with caution. He steps inside with his sister, letting the door swing closed behind them. "Don't be scared."

Why does everybody think I'm supposed to be scared? "Do they let kids in here, after hours?"

"Probably not, but we're as old as you," he answers. The girl says nothing. She just seems to smile at me. I remember she does that— smiles at me whenever her brother isn't looking. *I remember?*

"I don't think so, son," I say. I've got at least seventy years on these two. "What can I do for you?"

"Well, this is going to sound kinda crazy, Dan, but I was kind of hoping maybe I could show you my card collection." It was an odd request. But odder still was how nervous he seemed as he asked.

I put my plastic fork down on my tray and give him the most reassuring smile I have, hoping to put him at ease. "You know what? I'd love that." I wasn't lying either. This may be totally uninvited, but this is the first thing at Graydon that I haven't decided will completely suck before it actually happens.

Though, I suppose I shouldn't let my guard down entirely here. Somehow this kid knows my name. You read about seniors getting scammed in these kinds of places all the time. I can't remember. Was there a placard outside my room with my name written on it? There's so much I can't seem to remember anymore.

For a second, the boy almost seems to tear up, some combination of relief or sadness. But I might have misread that as he quickly pulls up the remaining chair in my tiny room and sits across from me. His sister hops up and plunks herself down on my adjustable metal-framed bed. From there, she joins me as we watch her brother carefully slide his backpack off his shoulder. The side zipper opens to reveal a three-ring binder, the kind with those plastic sleeves that keep your collectible cards preserved so they don't get their edges wrecked. Funny, I don't remember seeing him carrying a backpack when he walked in.

"He's got some great cards," says the girl.

He does, I think to myself. But how would I know that? He hasn't even opened his binder yet. But once he begins to flip the pages, I can see that I am right. Inside are not sports cards like hockey or baseball, or even some Japanese battle game like the Poke-o-something cards the kids trade in the schoolyard. These are superhero cards. Genuine superhero cards. You never see those anymore.

He begins to show them to me, telling me a little something about each one—like maybe I'm his grandpa instead of some stranger alone in his room with geometric shapes of gelatin. And it *is* an amazing collection. I remember superhero cards vividly from my childhood. The boy has some of the rarest, hardest-to-find cards. Cards with shiny holograms; cards marked with symbols from their original print runs; you name it. Yet there are also some obvious holes in his collection. He almost never has a complete team. There're almost always one or two heroes that are missing. And then it dawns on me.

I have them. The exact ones he needs.

I need him to know.

"You know what? Somewhere in that stupid storage locker on the east side of town where my son dumped all my stuff, I am going to have a binder just like yours," I tell him. "And inside I just might have some of the cards you're missing."

"Of course, you do," he says. "Together you and me have the best collection of anyone ever!" The pride in his voice is absolute.

OK, this kid is a bit weird. He's acting way too familiar. "And just how do you know that?"

"It's complicated, Dan." He closes his binder, that look of concern suddenly creeping back over his face. "But how would you feel about a game of Chinese checkers?"

That was always a favourite of mine. If he wants to distract me from his question, he's landed on a smart way to do it. Not sure that I should play a game with an eight-year-old though. I'm liable to mop the floor with him, even in my most cognitively addled state. I played a lot of Chinese checkers back in the day, and like all lawyers, I'm intrinsically competitive.

Before I can answer him, he pulls a battered old copy of the game out of that same backpack and lifts the cardboard cover off the box. Multi-coloured plastic marbles roll around inside, demanding my attention. The kids adjust the table so his sister can play from the bed, and they silently begin setting up the pieces, wicked grins on their faces. They left me the light-green marbles. That was always my color. But I know they knew that. He was blue, and she was yellow. She was always yellow...I have played with these kids before.

Not just once, but many, many times.

"Kids," I say. "I have to be upfront with you. I have a memory problem. I forget names and faces. You'll have to be patient with me."

"Dan, I'm Jack, and this here is my sister—"

"Kate!" I say suddenly.

Kate—that *is* her name—immediately lights up the room with her smile. She wants to hug me. I am sure of it. But she's also afraid. Afraid of me, underneath.

Was I somehow violent? Did I scare them once? Nobody ever told me about hurting kids before. And if I did, what are they doing here? Where are their parents? *Who are* their parents? My only grandkid is somewhere in Philly, estranged from me and the rest of the family after Dylan's crappy divorce.

But I don't ask, unwilling to wreck the moment. Instead, we play. We're only a handful of turns in when I realize the boy, Jack, is trying to use the Winston manoeuvre. If you set it up right, it's a way to block and jump forward at the same time. Only it's not possible for him to know that move. The Winston manoeuvre is not a real thing. I made it up.

"Did I teach that to you?" I ask.

Jack laughs. "You wish," he says with a bit of mirth. "I taught it to *you*."

"The Winston manoeuvre?"

"You remember," he says.

"Maybe," I say. "I want to."

I think I have to. I put my hand on the middle of the board, as though to signal that I'm shutting down the game. "Jack, Kate. Please tell me what's going on here."

They look at each other. Kate gives him a nod as if to say, *it's time.*

Jack sucks in a breath and looks up at me. "When you were six years old, Dan, your parents moved to Chicago. There weren't any kids in the new neighbourhood. Or at least none your age, really." I don't know how he knows that, but it's true. My old man worked for an insurance company appraising commercial real estate. The company transferred him. He was never happy about that, but he had no choice. Neither did I.

"That's where you found us, in the empty park behind your house with the skinny poplar trees. Some people call us imaginary friends. You...made us, Dan."

And now I realize what's really going on here. I'm straight up losing my mind. They say you deteriorate faster once you leave your home and come to a place like this. But this was a lot for Day One.

Jack leans forward and presses on. "From the age of six to eight, we were together every single day. We went biking, sledding, played a ton of checkers, and, above all, dreamed humongous dreams together. Always. Everywhere. You, me, and Kate."

"I had two imaginary friends?"

"You were twice as smart," said Kate. "So, why not?"

"But, how come I don't remember you?"

"All kids forget," said Jack. "We get that. But you're coming full circle now, Dan. Now that we're old, we get a chance to see each other again."

"You don't look old. Do I...do I look? I mean, when you see me, do you see me as 'eight-year-old Dan'?"

"No," he answered. "We see you right."

"But we don't care," says Kate quickly. "We wish we grew up with you. But we didn't, and it doesn't matter anymore."

Then why didn't they? None of this makes any sense—except as some kind of a mental breakdown. I *can* see how a six-year-old boy would dream up Kate though. Perfectly nonthreatening. Always smiling, always happy. Never actually wanting anything. I would never need to screw up the courage to talk to a girl with Kate around.

"Well, I'm eighty now," I say. "We might have a lot to catch up on."

Jack smiles and looks over at Kate. "And you haven't kept up with your checkers. But there's more, Dan."

"OK," I say. "Tell me."

Even if Jack and Kate are just figments of my crumbling mind, I have decided one thing. They would never hurt me.

"It's this place. It's special."

"You mean this room?"

"No," he says, waving his arms wide, "Graydon Manor."

"I've been here one day, and I can tell you there is nothing special about this hellhole." They're kids. I should watch my language. *Are* they kids? Jack's claiming to be eighty.

"You'll have to show him," says Kate to Jack.

"Don't freak out," says Jack. "Even when you were a kid, on some level you always understood we weren't real. Reality's not what's important to a child. But you understood we had limitations. Like when we played catch, we couldn't actually throw you a ball. You'd bounce it off a wall."

"But we played Chinese checkers together. I know that now."

"Right, in your mind you did. And that's what mattered. But in reality, you played all three sides of the board."

That I could see. I would have been that kind of a nerd. Taking on the futile challenge of beating myself.

"But in Graydon Manor, I can do this." He picks up my fork from my table tray with a dramatic flourish.

"Uh, so?" I pick up the whole plate.

"Dan," he says, trying to get me to appreciate the gravity of what he's saying. "I opened the door to walk into your room. I didn't need you to open it first and pretend that I did. I'm saying I have a physical autonomous form. I can punch someone in the face. If I could see over the dashboard, I think I could drive a car."

"Wait. Pinocchio's a real boy if he's inside Graydon Manor?"

"Kind of insulting, but yes, exactly."

"And you've been sitting here, in Graydon Manor for seventy-something years, knowing I would just one day show up?"

"No, no. Today's our first day here, too. We had no idea it would be so special until you first came through the door with your son, Dylan."

Kate wrinkles her brow. "What's even weirder is that we've discovered that some of the other residents can see us, too. Not all, it seems, but some—the ones who also have special friends."

Not special, I think, *imaginary*. "If this was your first day at Graydon, then where have you been all this time?"

Kate shoots him a look and I can tell I've hit on a nerve. They don't want to answer. Jack will be the one to duck and weave. "That? That is a great question which is going to need more time than we have."

"Why?"

"Because the nurse is going to walk through that door any second."

I don't know how he knew, but he's right. A Personal Support Worker opens the door and introduces herself. She begins to collect my evening snack tray and explains that she's going to help me get ready for bed.

I know what that means. I'm getting a fresh diaper. Oh my god, I do not want Jack and Kate to see that.

They instantly seem to anticipate my worry.

"That's our cue," says Jack. "We'll see you again in the morning, before breakfast."

Do they read my mind? "I don't want you to leave," I say.

"Us neither," says Kate. I feel like I can read hers. She genuinely means it. She will never care how much money or education I have. Or even how decrepitly old I grow or how many diapers I wear. Her friendship is completely unconditional. It's unrealistic. No human is like that. But it's safe to say that six-year-old me didn't need or want a realistic human. I needed friends. And I think I just might have made myself the very best.

"Can you see them?" I ask the PSW. "The children?"

The support worker launches into non sequitur small talk, telling me that she does indeed have children, three in fact. Two girls in high school and a boy in middle school. What's abundantly clear is that she cannot see my imaginary friends. Kate said some of the residents could, though. I remember my weird talk with Jere and Phil earlier today. That Phil guy knew I had two. What did he call them, IFs?

Jack and Kate wave and silently sneak out the door. Before they disappear, Kate peers around to look at me one last time and mouths the word "tomorrow." I want to ask them where they will go.

"Remember to stay away from the south wing," I call belatedly. Hopefully they could still hear me. Phil seemed pretty adamant that it would be dangerous—not necessarily for me, but for them. I realize that whatever happens to me in this place, I don't want anything to happen to Jack and Kate.

As I am tucked into bed with machine-like efficiency, I am left to consider the cold hard truth that I am quite delusional. But I am also left to contemplate why, in this desolate place, that would possibly be a bad thing.

I almost never seem to dream anymore, but tonight, I think I will dream of superhero cards and Chinese checkers.

As promised, Jack and Kate find me right after I wake up. We tell stories and make each other laugh. They studiously avoid, though, telling me anything more about who or what they really are.

I've got a plan for that. My best chance of getting the straight goods lies with the tall skinny resident with the walker, the man I met yesterday who somehow knew I would get visitors—Jere. I ask Jack and Kate to wait for me in my room while I duck out to the cafeteria to sneak in some breakfast.

Unsurprisingly, I get lost several times along the way. I make a mental note for next time that the halfway mark is the depressing little antechamber that holds Graydon's murky fish tank. Above it rests a shelf of leftover magazines from the nineties. That's my landmark. From there I can smell the food.

I spot Jere at a long table in the back corner of the lunchroom. He's fighting the tremor in his hand as he tears open a packet of artificial sweetener for his coffee. Phil has beat me here as well. His epic battle happens to be with a plastic spoon. I watch him strategize how to best scoop up the mush on his plate, a mush that looks like it might once have been pancakes. I'm guessing the kitchen has ground them into minuscule chunks to prevent him from choking. Like yesterday, and possibly every day, Phil has forgotten his dentures.

"All right," I say, pulling up a seat next to them as though I somehow now belong. "You weren't kidding about visitors."

"Where's your wheelchair?" asks Jere, a mischievous grin on his face.

Busted. "Where's your walker?"

"Touché."

"Forget that," I say. "My visitors. What's happening to me? And what am I supposed to do?"

Jere looks at me thoughtfully and then switches gears, seeking to instead fumble with a creamer. "Dan, I'm an old geezer, so I'll tell you what. I am going to do what old geezers do. I am going to answer your question by telling you a long-winded story that may or may not actually go anywhere."

"OK." I suppose I appreciate his honesty.

"When I was five, I wanted a dog."

He really wasn't kidding. "Didn't we all?"

"Like, *really* wanted a dog." He puts down his creamer and lays a hand on his stomach. Maybe he meant to put it on his heart but missed. "All boys do, but for me it was agony. My mother, however, was allergic to any kind of pet hair, so it was a no-go. And come to think of it, my old man probably hated animals anyway."

Phil stops stuffing pancake puke into his mouth and begins nodding along. He, I gather, has heard this story before. From his expression, I'm going to guess at least more than once.

"So, I did what any kid with a modicum of ingenuity would do. I created my own pet, up here."

This time he points to his temple, which I take to mean he dreamed one up, just like I must have done with Jack and Kate.

"A bright rover named Rusty. Rusty was the ultimate dog. He could play catch for infinite hours. If I needed him to, sometimes he would even talk. Rusty could shrink down to fit right into my lap for a soothing pet session, or, say I needed to get around, he'd grow big so I could ride him like a horse."

Jere laughs to himself, clearly reliving the delight of one of his riding sessions. I grab my hands to stop myself from drumming my fingers on the table with impatience before he finally continues. "The perfect pet for me. Never bit me once. Never took a dump I had to clean up. After I had Rusty, I stopped being afraid of the things that go bump in the night. No reason to be with a guard dog like Rusty. My confidence grew too. Rusty could chase away bullies or anyone who would ever want to hurt me. But, most of all, I was never lonely again. I can't stress enough what Rusty did for me. He was like a damned Lassie protecting me at every turn."

As he talks, he reaches down into his lap, as though to mime patting a dog sitting across his legs. Only as he does so, I realize, if I squint a certain way, I can sorta see it. It's Rusty. His imaginary friend is here too, only his is...a dog. It makes me wonder. Where do Jack and Kate go when I'm not around? Are they still in my room, or do they just appear when my mind feels the need to conjure them up? And where have they been the last seventy years?

"My parents thought it was cute at first. Didn't need to worry about buying dog food or paying a vet bill. But as I got older, they gradually figured out it was becoming creepy and anti-social. I'd try to show Rusty to the other kids, and they'd make fun of me. At one point my mom got worried enough to take me to a shrink.

"I only went the one time. At the end of the session the shrink asked my mother a simple question. What would happen if they got a real dog?"

My jaw drops. I'm not going to like how this ends.

"They found one of those new fandangled hypoallergenics for me. A beautiful Labrador named Juno. It took my ten-year-old self all of fifteen minutes before I traded in perfection for reality and never once looked back. Rusty was gone. I bet it was only weeks before I couldn't tell you his name."

"But these IFs, as you call them, they don't actually get hurt, right?" I ask. "They're not real. Not in that sense."

Jere gives me a plastic smile, the kind that's not at all reflected in his eyes, and I realize instantly that I've said something wrong. "I'm going to wager that after whatever you experienced last night, you don't believe a word of that," he says. "Otherwise, you wouldn't have come found us."

He's right.

"So, to answer your question," he says. "I don't really care what *you* do. But, me?" He cradles his invisible-not-so-invisible dog in his arms and looks down on it with solemnity. "Whatever time I got left? I'm spending it making it up to Rusty."

The parallel with Jack and Kate hits me immediately. At some point, I must have learned to socialize; gotten real friends.

"What happens to the IFs when kids forget about them?" When *I* forgot about them.

"You got the courage? You ask yours."

At this, I can tell Phil can stand it no more. He ends his deference to Jere's storytelling session and snorts. "They ain't gonna tell you. They're built to protect you. And that includes rescuing *you* from the pang of a guilty conscience."

"Then *you* tell me," I say, looking to them both. "Tell me another damn story if you have to. But just tell me. Where do they go?"

But we're interrupted by an orderly who leans over our table, his short sleeves exposing the faded tattoos on his thick forearms. Why is everybody who works here so big? Or do I still have to wrap my head around the fact that I've shrunk.

"Yo, Geezer crew," says the orderly. "Wish me happy hunting because today's the day."

"Not a chance, Ricky," answers Jere. "Never happen."

"That's where you're wrong, Jere. Looky here." He produces a key from his pocket. "That's for the boiler room."

"How'd you get that?" says Phil. He looks visibly agitated.

"My little secret. But while you Golden Girls zone out for your afternoon nap, I might just take me a little look-see and see what I can find."

"Don't bother. You won't find it," says Jere.

"You know I will, but I'll keep my offer open anyway. You tell me exactly where it is, and I'll keep my commitment to make life a little easier for you around here."

"Hard pass," says Jere, his defiance unqualified.

Phil joins him. "You're an idiot, Ricky. Do yourself a favour and stay away from the south wing." That's it, I need to know Phil's deal with Graydon's south wing.

As soon as Rick leaves the cafeteria, there's a gaggle of conversation as we all talk at once.

"How in tarnation did he get a key to the boiler room!"

"That butthole! If he finds it, we're done for."

"The south wing, guys, why can't we go to the south wing?"

Jere holds up his hand for silence. Uh oh, I think I triggered his story mode.

"Melonie Chu has a private room in 404. She's got an IF."

"But not just any IF," says Phil.

"Hey!" says Jere. "Who's telling this? Me or you?"

I can't believe these two. "Somebody, just tell me!"

Phil glares at Jere but sits back in deference, letting him continue. "If you think Rusty here is the perfect guard dog, Mel's taken it to a whole new level. The old bat's like 102 or something and absolutely paranoid. She's got a gigantic panther that prowls the southern wing. It's under orders to devour any IF it catches that comes anywhere near her."

"Did you say panther?" I ask.

"Not *just* a panther," says Phil with a whisper of dread. He leans toward me as though passing along a military secret. "An armoured panther that shoots ninja stars out of its robotic shoulder cannons. I'm dead serious."

It's then that I realize I truly lacked imagination as a child. And here I thought I was special because I came up with twins.

"Mr. Killa, we call it," says Jere. "But that witch, Mel, calls him Fuzzyboo."

"Fuzzyboo of death, maybe!" says Phil, his voice veering into sandpaper territory.

"But we all teach our IFs to stay away from the south wing and, as a result, Mel and Mr. Killa aren't a problem, unless we need to actually get at the Imagalisk."

"The Imagalisk?" I ask.

"Keep your voice down, Dan," says Phil, depleting the last of his vocal reserves. "Ricky could be nearby!"

"Is that what's in the boiler room?"

Jere nods. "Yeah. But now we have to move it before Rick finally finds it."

Jere feeds Rusty a biscuit, right off his plate. "The Imagalisk is the reason the IFs are returning to us in this place. It's what lets them cross into reality—touch things." I can't help but wonder, if I couldn't see Rusty, what would I see? Would the biscuit disappear? Or would it still be there? Does Jere eat it and I just think the dog does? I mean, it's gone, but where does it *go*?

None of this makes sense, but I find myself swallowing this banquet of crazy nonetheless. The last thing I want is some over-inked punk stealing what might be the only good thing in this place.

"Why does Ricky want the Imaga—— whatever it's called. What is his IF?"

"What? Ricky ain't got no IF," says Jere. "He's way too young. Or too old, maybe, depending on how you look at it."

Phil chugs the last of the water in his paper cup, easing the raspy quality to his voice as best he can. "Ricky wants to sell it to Hans."

"Who?"

Jere rolls his eyes, but thankfully decides to give me the straightest answer he's ever given me. "A former resident of Graydon. Hans loved his IF just as much as the rest of us. But he was also stinking rich, a condominium developer or something like that. His combo of money and smarts helped him escape this house of horrors. He bribed his trustee and got back control of his finances. He returned to his own mansion, attended by a team of private nurses. But, once he got out of Graydon, his IF disappeared on him."

"Wait," I say. "Can't this Hans guy just come back to Graydon?" It sounds stupid as soon as it leaves my mouth. Who would ever willingly want to come back to this place after getting out?

Jere winces. "He's got a better idea. He's put a bounty on the Imagalisk. He's reached out to some of the less noble amongst Graydon's staffers and encouraged them to compete with one another to bring it to him. Ricky boy there, in particular, has been working most hard to collect."

And now he has the key to the boiler room.

This, this is bad. I haven't even started breakfast and already there's a lead weight in my stomach.

Jere predicts my last question before I can even ask. "One of our alumni, now passed away, hid the Imagalisk in the boiler room. He knew only a janitor with a key could ever get in there. And trust me, if you know Graydon's cleaning staff, they're not going to bother with the boiler room, unless and until the heat in this place completely collapses."

"That Rick guy said he's going for the boiler room this afternoon," I say. "That means it has to be moved before then."

Jere smiles and leans back in his chair. "I am so glad we have a volunteer."

Did I just get played?

"You might be the only one who can actually do this, Dan. You have *two* IFs. One to distract Mr. Killa and another to break into the boiler room. Teamwork could be exactly what we need here."

I look at Jere not comprehending why he would think I would possibly risk putting Jack and Kate, with their eight-year-old bodies, up against a ninja-panther. And then it happens. I officially choke on the aforementioned banquet of crazy. A believer, I'm all-in.

"Why can't *I* just go get it myself? I'm the new guy. I have dementia. I get lost and wander into the wrong place all the time."

"No, you can't come with me," I say as I march down the hall to the south wing. I brandish my tri-fold welcome brochure in front of me like it's some kind of manifesto, its glossy coloured map of Graydon on its backside. I guess I was going to need to learn the layout eventually.

"Dan," says Jack. "We'll always have your back. Letting you go alone into a literal lion's den is not something we exactly have the DNA for." Jack and Kate are walking alongside me lockstep, one on my left, one on my right—just like professional eight-year-old bodyguards. All they need are mirrored sunglasses and bulletproof vests.

"Stop it," I say, coming to a halt. "Can this imaginary panther-thing kill me?"

Jack pauses. "We don't know. Maybe. He has a physical form here. How far that goes, we don't know."

"We'll call that fifty-fifty. But he can definitely kill *you*, can't he?"

Jack doesn't answer.

"No, we're not changing the subject or playing Chinese checkers. True or false, Jack? Mr. Killa can pounce on you and rip you apart." I was a litigator. I know how to cross-examine when I have to.

"I think so, yeah. But it doesn't matter. We'd take a bullet for you, Dan."

"Of course, you would. And that's the problem. You're already riddled with bullets meant for me, aren't you?"

Again, silence. It's just as Phil warned me. It's as though he's programmed to refuse to give an answer I won't like. But it's far worse than programming. It's love.

"All right," I say, turning back toward my room. I've made my decision. No more love bullets. "Here's what I want. The only thing that will make me happy right now is knowing that the two of you are staying safe in my room. You die, I'm sad. Get it? Very unhappy."

Kate nods slowly, then Jack. I march them back to my room where I will ground them, probably for the very first time in their lives. They look ashen. Maybe one day they'll understand what tough love is. But since they'll never be parents, maybe not.

When we arrive. I open the door to my room. "Jack, Kate? Here's what you do…"

I cross over to my bed, my knees starting to complain from all the walking. I grab the cheap plastic water bottle off my nightstand. I'm going to need that.

"Please take out every card in Jack's binder and re-org them by super team, then by color, and then by date. I look forward to seeing what it looks like when I get back." That's gotta keep them busy for at least an hour.

"But—"

"Every card." I slam the door shut behind me, not willing to see their faces. Now, to find the stairs down to the boiler room. Let's just get this over with.

So, I need to figure out how to get around the ninja-panther that guards the south wing, break into the boiler room, steal something even though I forgot to ask what it actually looks like, and do all of this before this Ricky, who already has a key, can beat me to it. Not bad for my second day.

I'm definitely making this up on the fly, but I take a detour to the fish tank I've been using as my landmark to find the lunchroom. I've got a semblance of an idea germinating in my head. There's an elderly couple seated in front of the tank watching the multi-coloured fish inside swim endlessly back and forth. I bet they've been at it for hours.

I mutter an apology as I rip off the top of the tank and let it tumble to the floor. It's too heavy for me to exercise any kind of care. Then, using the tiny fish net at the side of the tank I start collecting the tank's occupants and transfer them into my water bottle. Cats like to eat fish, don't they?

I'm going to get in serious trouble for this, but I figure if I can't pay for the fish and somehow blame it on my dementia, my worst case is getting kicked out of Graydon. That might not be such a bad thing. The couple enjoying the fish tank are stunned, unable to speak. Sanity never knows what to do when confronted with crazy.

I seal my water bottle with its screw-top lid and head for the south wing.

"Hey!" calls a raspy voice behind me. In one hand, I have a water bottle. In the other, a folded piece of brightly coloured paper. It looks like a map. They must belong to me.

I turn toward the voice. There's an old man in a wheelchair, wheeling toward me. He's bald and as soon as he gets close, I can smell a foul stench.

"You OK, Dan? You don't look right," he says.

Cover! Says a voice somewhere inside my head. I'm in trouble. That means I can't let them know what I don't know.

"I'm fine!" I say as positively as I can. He called me Dan. That feels right, of course I am.

Where am I? A hospital?

"I've come to help. Jere is going to find Ricky and try to delay him as long as possible."

"Good," I say. That's what he wants to hear. There's a Jere, and there's a Ricky. It sounds like something important is happening. That makes sense; I'm most like to start forgetting things when I'm stressed up the wazoo.

I can already feel the disc in my head spinning. I know all of this. I just need my brain to somehow access it. It's like there's something in the way and I have to push past it. I hate this.

"What's the water bottle for?"

"Oh, you know," I say. "Water."

"Right," says the smelly old guy. I am also old. That much I know; my hands are gnarled and—

"I didn't bring my IF though," says the man in the wheelchair. "The last time I brought him to the south wing, he was almost destroyed."

Hold it. The piece of paper I am holding has the words "south wing" on it. It also says "Graydon Manor" at the top. That might be where I am now.

"Forget what Jere said, you're smart to leave your IFs behind." My IFs are Jack and Kate. I would never…Jack and Kate! Just the thought of them gets my brain disc spinning faster. Concepts come flooding back to me, out of order, unprioritised. My wife's Maria. She's not with me anymore. My daughter's Jennie. I never admitted to anyone that I came within a hair's breadth of dropping out of law school. I…The Imagalisk! I need to get to the Imagalisk before Rick does!

"Phil!" I suddenly blurt out as his name populates in my mind. The lights are back on.

"What?"

"You, uh, never told me who your IF is." OK, I think I'm oriented, but I don't know how long I spaced out for.

"Oh, sure," he says, his face lighting up as he takes the bait. Jack's been teaching me a lot about deflection as of late. "I call him Sir Lance-a-Lot. He's a glowing magical shield, like a medieval thing. He hangs over my door when I'm not carrying him."

Dang. A shield as an imaginary friend? That's pretty weird, but I guess so is Phil. I step in behind him and start pushing his chair so we go faster, looking to make up some time. Phil doesn't seem to mind. I hand him my water bottle, which I now remember has the fish I stole in it.

"Let's just say ol' Lance protected me from a lot of bad things when I was a kid."

I'd like to ask what, but maybe now's not the time.

And then, I see it.

There, at the end of the hall. A gigantic beast of shimmering black fur, crouched like it's ready to pounce. Just like Jere's dog, it's there, but at the same time also not there, almost translucent. If I wasn't looking, I might have missed it and walked us right into it.

It certainly hasn't missed us—its unblinking eyes are locked onto me. The Clydesdale-sized monster is either picking its moment or waiting for me to wheel Phil over some invisible line that marks its territory. Phil wasn't kidding about the shoulder cannons, either. There's some kind of laser guns or rockets nestled on the panther, like massive iron saddlebags.

Whatever they are, they're aimed at us. I can't help but think that Phil's Lance-a-Lot might have come in handy right about now. It's doubtful I'm going to get us close enough to even show Mr. Killa my water bottle of fish.

"You see that too, right?"

Phil just nods, as though frozen in terror. I start slowly wheeling him backward, in retreat. We're not going that way.

I reverse all the way back into a nursing station, and the desk nurse on duty looks up from her oversized computer monitor and asks if I'm OK. All along her countertop is a scattering of patient charts and what I imagine are nursing and feeding schedules. Her phone is covered in a nest of yellow sticky-tab messages.

A phone. I might have another idea. Maybe we're making this harder than it needs to be.

"Phil," I whisper. "Do you think you could distract that nurse so I can get behind that desk?"

Phil doesn't react right away. He only nods slowly, his stare almost blank. I am not sure if he gets my meaning. But then, "Nurse Marta," he says suddenly, waving his arms. "You need to come quick! Angus is choking in the parlour room again. He's got gum!"

"Gum!?" To Marta's credit, she reacts swiftly and races down the hall, Phil wheeling himself slowly after her, shouting words of encouragement as he embellishes the tale.

Phil's deception, combined with the apparent medical history of someone named Angus, has just left me with unfettered access to the nursing station. All I want is the phone.

I step behind the desk, and that's when it hits me. I've been struggling with this infernal device for quite a while now. I pick up the receiver and get a tone. That's good. Now do I need to press one or nine for an outside line? No, I don't want an outside line. This should be easy. I think I just need to know Melanie Chu's room number. What did Jere say it was?

Now I'm really going to put my brain to the test. *Jack and Kate*, I chant, *Jack and Kate. Spin brain disc, spin!* 404...Jere said she was in room 404! I press the three numbers on the phone's dialler one at a time slowly, left-middle, bottom-center, left-middle. Just when I start to curse my ineptitude I am rewarded by the ringing of the phone. I did it! Now she just needs to pick up. *And she needs to be slightly less crazy than advertised.*

She does pick up. "Hello?"

"Good afternoon," I say as confidently as I can, "Ms. Chu?" Before I know it, I'm introducing myself to the infamous Mel, dark witch of the south wing. I'm improvising, but I think I know what to do. I compliment her on Fuzzyboo and his shiny coat, taking care not to refer to him as Mr. Killa. Yes, I too have an imaginary friend, two actually. Yes, I am quite new to Graydon Manor. I explain I'm just looking to head down to the boiler room on a very important errand and would she be willing to have her friend please stand down.

It works! Mr. Killa suddenly sits down and starts licking his paws, his gigantic claws retracted. There's just one catch. Ms. Chu asks that I first stop by her room on the way over. Obviously, I'm on the clock and can't afford a detour. But when I look again at Mr. Killa, I realize the only answer here is to say, "I'd be delighted."

I put down the receiver and head down the hall, scurrying away before nurse Marta returns. I am escorted by the biggest cat I have ever seen. The top of my head is level with its shoulder blade. And in Mr. Killa's case, his cyborg-like shoulders look like they're from some kind of postapocalyptic military movie. I find myself wondering, what kind of child could have possibly come up with this?

When I reach room 404, I knock with trepidation and enter. Mr. Killa follows me in, like my shadow. He circles the room twice before finally curling up on the floor in front of the sunlit window, taking up most of the space. His eyes, though, never leave me.

Ms. Chu—Mel—is in her bed. Her long hair is a cascade of messy silver strands, an unkept waterfall that hides much of her dark wrinkled face. I can't decide if she is deliberately sending me a sour expression or if she just naturally looks like a dehydrated prune.

She lays on her side curled up, almost in a fetal position, a thin laundered sheet of blue draped over her tiny form. I can tell she's at that late stage of frailty where she's forced to do that for most of her day, probably battling bed sores. There's a wheelchair beside her adjustable bed frame, and I'd wager it doesn't get much use anymore. I spot her catheter and the bag of ocher-yellow on the opposite side of the bed. Might not be that long before I too enjoy one of those.

Mel speaks in a voice so quiet it's almost a whisper. She tells me she doesn't get a lot of visitors. I wonder how much of that has to do with the fact that she is guarded by a living weapon with enough lethality to make the Pentagon jealous. Whatever her social deprivation may be though, there's no question she is still pretty sharp. Mel is very interested in exactly why a new resident would want to go to the boiler room.

Jere probably wouldn't like this, but I see no reason not to level with her. I tell her about Hans Meyer and Ricky and their plot to steal the Imagalisk. I try to do it in a way that doesn't make me sound too crazy, but quickly realize there isn't such a way, so I just lean into it.

As we talk, I clue in that she knows far more about the Imagalisk than she's let on. I figure out too late that she may well be concerned that it might be *me* who's actually trying to steal it.

155

I just told the paranoid lady I'm hunting the very treasure her most cherished friend by the window relies upon.

Desperate to reassure her I'm not the bad guy here, I come up with the bright idea that she can have Fuzzyboo follow me to the boiler room and give him orders to devour me if I try to take the Imagalisk out of Graydon. I assure her my self-interest is in protecting my own IFs; removing it is the last thing I want. She eyes me with suspicion—she doesn't see them anywhere with me.

Her snow-white hair falls over her wrinkled face in messy strands as she fights to sit up so she can look me up and down. "What kind of a person doesn't travel with their IF?"

One who doesn't want them eaten by Mr. Killa. But I don't say that aloud.

I'm starting to get the measure of Ms. Chu. Jere wasn't entirely wrong when he uncharitably labelled her a paranoid; she's incredibly suspicious. I guess I might be, too, if I last at Graydon long enough.

"A bad choice by someone brand-new to Graydon Manor," I try. "And one I'm regretting already. If you want to see them, Fuzzyboo and I can head there first and bring them here. I say 'them' because I've got two actually—twins."

I'm surprised by the pride in my voice, like I made them out of play clay and want to show them off. But there's no time for this. This is already one side quest too many.

Maybe she's smart enough to realize the risk to her if I'm actually telling the truth, or maybe she just can't stand to see me fidget like a demented squirrel, but either way she finally relents, satisfied with my proposal of Fuzzyboo as an escort.

I show her my brochure, and she gives me directions to where she thinks the stairs down to the boiler room are. She's never been inside but says she has passed by the door enough times.

As I leave, Mr. Killa takes one last look at Mel as though receiving silent instructions. He then pads softly after me. He's different now. Were it possible, he's even more alert, and I can feel the weight of his stare as his eyes bore into my back. It takes me a few moments to fully cotton on, but this didn't go nearly as well as I thought it did. Somewhere along the way, I completely lost my trust privileges. I definitely have much more than just Rick to worry about.

I've reached the unmarked door where Ms. Chu said I would find the boiler room. With no other residents nearby to see me enter, I swing the door open and step through. Inside, I find a landing atop a poorly lit stairwell. From there, steps lead down to a basement where the reek of dank concrete is ever-present.

Fortunately—for now at least—my brain disc seems to be spinning just fine. I'm increasingly worried just how well it'll hold up with Mr. Killa silently tracing my steps, just four or five paces behind, almost daring me to give him the slightest reason to pounce. Before the door can swing closed, the beast darts forward and catches it with his nose, pushing his way inside to join me on the now-crowded landing.

I ignore him and fight my way down the stairs, leaning heavily on the wooden banister. My hip objects, but I make it. At the bottom is another door, this time with a tiny plastic plate marked Boiler Room.

That's fantastic, but as soon as I push the handle, I realize that it's locked and I have no idea how I'm going to get it open. Of course, it would be locked. That's why Ricky had a key. I must have somehow envisioned that I would just bust the door in commando style, but I've overlooked that I've left my battering ram in my other castle.

Then it hits me. I remember last night and the pride with which Jack lifted my fork from my dinner tray. Mr. Killa here can smash the door for me. The cat hasn't spoken a word since I've met him, but I'm willing to bet he understands me just fine.

I look to him, gesture to the door, and tell him he's up. He balks. No doubt his instructions didn't cover bashing in the doors of Graydon Manor.

"C'mon," I say. "Are we protecting the Imagalisk or not?"

That seems to work. Mr. Killa makes a sideways gesture with his head, which I take as his warning for me to stand aside. As soon as I clear to the left of the door, he coils into a spring and jumps at it. The lock doesn't just break. The entire door flies off its hinges—in a thunderclap—and it sails into the darkened room beyond.

Someone had to have heard that. I'm officially on the clock. I waste no time blundering into the shadows of the huge cellar. I struggle until I find the light, a single naked bulb mounted in the ceiling, activated by a ragged piece of hanging string.

Once I give that a pull, I see I am surrounded by a bird's nest of copper pipes, each winding its way to or from one of what must be at least six different water heaters. The cement floor below is stained with rust, a dozen orange trails snaking along the floor toward a grate in the center of the room. The next obstacle is somehow finding the Imagalisk in here. Without knowing what it looks like...

Got it.

At the very back of the boiler room is what can only be described as some kind of shrine. Sitting on a workbench is a child's wooden dollhouse, the kind that lacks a fourth wall so you can see all the tiny furniture inside. On the top level, in the mini master bedroom, is a gemstone, one all glowy with a silvered light. It defies physics, floating just above the toy double bed, screaming, "wondrous magical artifact that might just exist only in your deteriorating mind." Perhaps only people with IFs can see it, or surely whoever comes down here to maintain the boiler would have noticed it long ago. Does that mean Rick will never be able to find it? Or will he just nick the whole dollhouse?

I won't take the chance. I squeeze my way through a pair of cylindrical boilers and fight my way to the shrine. I reach out and grab for the orb of silver, hoping it won't explode or fry my brain at my touch.

"Sneaky! Sneaky!" calls a voice from behind. I spin around, the Imagalisk firmly in my hand.

It's Ricky. Of course, it is. I was so close.

"So," he says, his beady eyes flashing with triumph. "Our newest guest is caught red-handed trying to steal Mr. Meyer's property."

This is really bad. "Listen, Rick," I try. "I don't really know who this Meyer guy is, but from what I hear, it's not his, either."

"You're not a real resident, are you? You just got yourself admitted as a pretence to break in here."

He thinks I'm a spy? Like what, I'm the James Bond of long-term care facilities? OK, so yes, this just turned out horrible. No worries though, I still have Godzilla here as my ally.

That's when I realize Mr. Killa has completely and utterly disappeared. Did he even follow me into the boiler room? Wait, did I make him disappear when I grabbed the Imagalisk?

Rick steps forward, his sleeves carefully rolled up to show off his biceps. "Hand it over, old man. It's my ticket out of here. You give it up without a fuss, and maybe I'll leave some of your bones unbroken."

I look down at my hand and see the Imagalisk is no longer glowing. Now that I've removed it from the dollhouse it's just some kind of metal cube with engraved inscriptions on it—some language I don't understand. And, from the look in his eye, I can tell that Rick can clearly see the cube. All I've done here is make everything worse.

"How much is Meyer paying you?" I ask. "I can pay more." I seriously doubt that's true. But, since this is all about greed, let's see where that gets me.

Nowhere.

He strides forward and grabs me with both of his hands, lifting me right off the ground. *How light am I?* He carries me right out of the boiler room.

"Last chance, old man. Gimme the thing."

He tries to pry my hand right open. But I close my fist around the Imagalisk as hard as I can and shake my head. He'll have to loot it from my corpse.

It's a concept he seems to be quite OK with. He slams me against the broken doorjamb. But as my head smacks against the wood, the violence seems to inspire him.

"You know what? I don't know how you trashed the door, but you're going to need to take the fall for that. And by fall, I mean literally."

"So," he says, not to me, but speaking to himself. "I found you at the bottom of the stairs. You must have had a senior moment, got lost…and wandered over to the top of the stairs…there. You then slipped on the top step and tumbled down, crashing into the door at the bottom here, breaking your hips and what not. Yeah, that works."

At that, he begins to drag me up the stairs to put his plan in motion. As he does, the concrete steps suddenly begin to look bigger and bigger, as though I'm being raised to the top of a cliff. What a criminal mastermind this dope is. But as ridiculous as his plan sounds, I don't doubt the part where I break into pieces and die. I choose my next words carefully in hope that they won't be my last.

"Wait, I can—"

Nope. He hurls me from the top of the stairs. I'm so useless I can't even manage to hang on to the Imagalisk as I die. It falls from my fingers and I crash…*into the softest landing I've ever had.*

It's Kate! Somehow, she's here, appearing from nowhere. And she catches me, right before I smash myself into a thousand shards of broken bones.

She's holding my head in her hands, cradling me like a pillow.

I look up at her. "I told you to stay in the room," I manage.

Her eyes narrow, her expression stern. "We're your friends, Dan, not your slaves."

As Kate helps me climb to my feet, I see that Jack is here too, already at the top of the stairs, standing right in front of Rick. Rick though can't seem to see him—that punk is still staring down at me, a bewildered look on his face as he tries to piece together why my skull isn't split open and bleeding brain juice.

With his back turned to me, I can't see Jack's face, but I know Jack, and I know he will be pissed. He definitely means to test his theory that he can throw a punch inside Graydon Manor. A second later, his right cross flies, decking Rick in the jaw. Rick staggers backward from the hit.

I, too, am hit, only it's with a bolt of realization. The sudden return of Jack and Kate must mean Mr. Killa is back as well. I spin, putting Kate behind me as I peer into the boiler room. I'm right, the beast never left. He just stopped "being" for a half minute when I grabbed the Imagalisk cube.

I can read that cat's intentions like a book outlined with yellow highlighter. The return of Jack and Kate is interpreted as a breach of my deal with Ms. Chu. Its eyes lock onto Kate. Its shoulder-mounted cannons emit a dull hum, intensifying in pitch and volume as the barrels track her with exacting precision.

"No!" I cry. "Don't shoot!" I try to block his line of fire to Kate. Fuzzyboo coils his muscles like a spring, ready to pounce around me—or through me.

I see it! *The Imagalisk!* Amongst the ruins of the shattered door-jamb. I need that back in my hand!

Mr. Killa pounces. I grab it! The panther vanishes mid-leap. Kate's gone, too. I just hope wherever they go, they don't interact with each other. I think they both just cease existing. I hope, I hope. Jack is gone, too.

But, with Jack no longer there, there's nothing to stop Rick from coming back down the stairs. He massages his jaw as he slowly makes his way. He's beyond mad. He has almost the same predatory look that I just saw in the eyes of Mr. Killa. This would be right about the time when my stupid brain decides to shut down on me. I'm so scared I almost hope it does.

That's it then. I have to choose. I can drop the Imagalisk again. That'll give me my super-friend bodyguards back. But also Fuzzyboo.

"I don't know how you did that, old man," says Rick, his voice as cold as liquid helium, "but I'm going to make sure you never do it again."

No, there is no choice here. This is easy. I'm an old man with few things left on my list to live for. It's more important that Jack and Kate survive. But, if I don't have their help, I die, and Rick gets the Imagalisk. And then, none of it matters anyway.

I need a third option. I need a Winston maneuver.

I drop the Imagalisk for the second time. This time I'm ready, and it's like it falls in slow motion. As soon as it leaves my hand, I dive for Kate, right as she pops back into existence. We collide, crashing to the ground but I knock her out of the panther's path.

ARTHUR HAYWOOD

The beast sails over top of us, though it agilely swivels on a dime as soon as it lands.

"Fuzzyboo!" I shout. I'm pointing to the discarded Imagalisk, my brain disc spinning on full.

"Who you calling Fuzzyboo, dead man?" says Rick. He's done descending the stairs. He stands right over top of me contemplating his coup de grâce.

"That's it there! The Imagalisk! Take it to your friend! Take it to Mel! It's hers! Don't let anyone else have it. Take it now!" *Trust me or don't trust me, you stupid kill machine. Just take it away from here!*

The beast just sits there, considering my proposal as my heart skips a beat. But then Rick, still thinking I'm somehow talking to him, spots the Imagalisk on the ground as well. He bends over to grab it. *Stupid cat! We're too late.*

And then, just as Rick's fingers begin to close around the Imagalisk, Fuzzyboo snaps out a claw and snatches it from right under his hand.

I exhale. Transferring his prize into his jaw, Fuzzyboo sweeps Rick aside like an afterthought as he turns back for the stairs. Jack barely dives out of the way as the panther bounds up for the top landing, five steps at a time. It's only then that I realize that I'm right. Jack and Kate can stay.

But there's one person among us who hasn't yet caught on.

"Hey, Ricky," I say. "You too young to know what a poltergeist is?"

His face is scrunched inward in flat-out astonishment. I'm guessing he just watched the Imagalisk cube fly right up the stairs.

Jack and Kate descend on him, and it's not long until he runs away screaming.

"And, after all that, you just gave it to Chu?" says Phil, glaring at me across the cafeteria table. "We're done for!"

I shrug. "I did what I had to do."

Phil is apoplectic. "What you had to do? How can you—?"

Jere holds up his hand to cut Phil's tirade short. He slowly swirls his mashed potatoes with his fork as though deep in thought, creating a watery white cyclone spreading to the edges of his plate. "Now, hold on, Phil. This could be far better than it seems."

"Better than it seems?" says Phil. "The Imagalisk is in the hands of the Dark Witch herself!"

"Where it just might be the safest it's ever been," says Jere. "She'll be the last person to destroy it."

I say nothing and wait for Phil to catch up. I've come to appreciate I'm not the fastest either these days and perhaps I need to learn to dial back the judgment. But from where I sit, it doesn't matter to us where the Imagalisk is as long as it remains inside of Graydon. I spent the rest of the afternoon confirming that Jack and Kate are still here, and here to stay, as are everyone else's IFs. And, if Rick ever tries to steal the Imagalisk again, he'll have to deal with the paranoid Ms. Chu and her guard monster. If anything, it's an upgrade from the boiler room.

I doubt he'll even try. With his smashed-up face, it could be days or weeks before Rick dares to come back to Graydon, if he does at all. And, if he does, I expect he'll avoid me and my apparent supernatural powers like the plague. If not, there's an entire manor full of invisible IFs who will go to bat for me. I've never felt more safe.

"C'mon, Phil," I try. "We're still in the game. What do you say?"

He glares at me. He's far from convinced. But at least he seems to be calming down.

"I...have questions," he says. "Like why did the IFs disappear when you grabbed the Imagalisk? And back in the south wing there, how come you gave me your water bottle?" He unscrews the lid. "And why are there colored fish inside?"

"Oh," I say. I forgot about that. "We should probably return those."

This evening I'm in my room playing Chinese checkers with Jack and Kate. I'm distracted because I've been thinking hard on Phil's question. What exactly *did* happen to them when I grabbed the Imagalisk with my hand? It makes for a disjointed match and it's coming to a head when the phone in my room suddenly rings. Thankfully, when I'm the recipient of a call, I don't have to bother myself with what numbers to punch on the dialler. I can just pick up the receiver and the stupid thing works.

It's Jennie! Calling all the way from Tulsa. I can hear her dishwasher whining away in the background. She apologizes for taking so long to call. She's being diplomatic, but what she really wants to know is how much I hate the place her brother has dumped me in.

I look over at Jack and Kate as I answer. "Not to worry, I like it just fine. You know what? You should really come and visit sometime."

Kate smiles at me as she moves a marble, completely screwing up the trap I had set for her. I should have seen it coming. Kate never got to meet Jennie. I suppose she and Jack first vanished decades before my Jennie was ever even born. But I think she'd like her. Even if Jennie won't be able to see her.

"When? Anytime. Just come up and see. I hope to be here a very long while."

Imagine that.

Life and Death
and Love in the Bayou

written by
Stephannie Tallent

illustrated by
ASHLEY CASSADAY

ABOUT THE AUTHOR

Stephannie Tallent writes various subgenres of fantasy, as well as dabbling in science fiction, mystery, and romance. She's collected a variety of degrees over the years: a bachelor of science in English literature from the United States Military Academy at West Point; a bachelor of science in zoology from the University of Texas, Austin; and a doctor of veterinary medicine from Texas A&M.

A small animal veterinarian, she jokes she's a vet-vet, having served as an Army Military Intelligence officer during Desert Storm.

Stephannie Tallent's earliest memories are of gathering mussel shells and kelp at the beach and carting the stinking mass home. After living around the world, she moved back to California to be near the ocean. Many evenings she'll be sipping a cocktail or glass of wine, watching the sun set over the water from her deck with her husband Dave and English cocker spaniels Orry and Rosie.

About her story, "Life and Death and Love in the Bayou," Stephannie says: "Sometimes the start of a story is simple. A photo of a gloriously decaying steamer in a bayou, Spanish moss dripping off the surrounding trees and the steamer itself, set my brain down that swampy road. And of course I can't find the photo. Magic is like that—slippery, sneaky, forcing you to rely on yourself and your own smarts and memory."

ABOUT THE ILLUSTRATOR

Ashley Cassaday is a digital illustrator, educator, and painter based out of her hometown of Dallas, Texas.

Like many budding artists, Ashley developed a love for the arts at a young age, constantly drawing and honing her skills, while also being influenced by media such as novels, video games, and animated films.

Upon entering college, Ashley knew she wanted to engage in her creative pursuits professionally, and thus began her desire to work as a fantasy illustrator and character designer for the entertainment industry. Upon graduation however, Ashley's career changed course and she turned to teaching, where she developed a love for helping young artists learn the stepping stones to becoming illustrators and designers, just as she once did.

Since then, Ashley has worked on and off as an independent artist and freelancer, creating her own stories and characters, all while traveling to conventions across the country to showcase her work and connect with fans and fellow artists alike.

Life and Death and Love in the Bayou

It was the February the rain fell so warm and hard the bayous swamped over old man Rochambeau's gator curing shack and the whole parish smelled like graveyard mold and sour-smelling gator excrement, even the houses built up on stilts above the high-water line, that I decided to help my mama once and for all. No matter the cost to my soul.

'Bout that shed...I knew old man Rochambeau would just hit up my mama to use the ham hut for his haul, and she'd say yes, so I didn't feel too bad. Not for him, anyway.

Felt bad for my mama, who'd be stuck bumping up against log-shaped hunks of gator meat while she seasoned and cured the hogs. Touch one of those logs of meat, and it's like the Spanish moss is dragging against the back of your neck, like the spirit of the gator is still there and pissed off and just waiting to chomp on you and roll you.

Those spirits are truly there, lurking to garner just a bit of power, enough to touch the living world.

I know 'cause I see them. Granny said I'm blessed, just like her, and her granny before, and I gotta keep it secret.

What we *see* we can touch, and what we touch, we can control.

And some men don't like us women having that power. Call us witches, and do worse than call us names.

And sometimes, that power just ain't enough to keep a body safe. Many a blessed woman's been beaten or hung in this parish, either too weak or too despairing to fight back.

So, best keep it hidden.

The rains seem to feed the spirits, restoring them closer to life. Made me itch to see them. *Test* them.

Mama didn't make me help with slaughtering the hogs anymore, not after that first time when I was ten. I screamed for days, 'til my throat bled, then I sprayed blood just like those cutthroat hogs.

I get to go exploring on my own, now, when it's butcherin' time, which is fine by me. Don't get me wrong. I know that I can't afford weakness. Since that autumn six years past, I've learned to not flinch away from, well, nature red in tooth and claw. Death is part of life. *Necessary* for life.

Trying to build up my—I don't want to say *tolerance*, but the way the world is, I need to be able to function in the face of violence. It's so hard, sometime. Nature's one thing. People hurting other people? Twists my insides around.

Why ain't I in school, you ask? School's for rich folks, not teenage swamp witches like me. Mama sent me through grade school. That was enough. I can read, and write, sure enough, so's I can scribble down what I see and learn on my own, in a tattered red-covered spiral notebook, but they couldn't teach me nothing about the spirits of the bayou, and that's what I truly needed to learn.

Granny told me that I'd have to master my powers, else they'd master me, and I'd turn out like crazy old Calixte, half snake herself by now, undulating in the sulfur-smelling brown water, slipping through the roots of the mangroves, the little green flowers of the water spider orchids tangling in her long gray hair.

Secretly, I thought submersing yourself into the magic of the swamp might not be such a bad thing, after I saw what Mama's most recent boyfriend Leroy Bobanchet done to her this last time, a week ago. Both eyes blackened and her slender nose crooked and one tooth lost and two more loose.

I puked for half a day, after that.

The swamps just take you as you are. They don't lie to you, pet your hair and call you pretty, then beat the tar outta you.

Or come to your daughter's room, once the moon's set, with

whiskey-soaked breath and sweaty hands. *Delphine, you just so pretty, too....*

The swamps ain't safe, but they ain't mean for the sake of meanness.

So, that Monday morning, once the rains slacked off from near hurricane to drizzle, and Mama headed in to cashier half a day at the Big Star thirty miles away, I hightailed it down to Bayou Mareau, riding my beat-up rusted bike around rainwater-filled craters in the dirt road 'til the bare cypress branches, festooned with trailing Spanish moss, formed a cathedral roof overhead and the road just drove itself into the swamp.

The day was cool enough the little droplets of salty mist tickling my face and back, soaking the white cotton of my blouse to see-through, felt good against my skin while I was pedaling along.

I got chilled pretty quick once I stopped, though.

Didn't matter. I'd be sweating soon enough, slogging through the mud and weeds and water.

The last good man Mama had been with was Charlie Solet from the Isle à Jean Charles. He swore he'd be with her forever, then he died in an oil rig accident five years ago. After that, it was like Mama thought she didn't deserve anything good in the world anymore.

I could take care of myself. Leroy Bobanchet hadn't been any good for a woman for a solid two weeks after he done tried to rape me. His suffering was well worth the morning of cramps and diarrhea I paid.

I didn't tell Mama what he tried. She'd just blame herself, like always. And I don't think she missed what he had, anyhow, those two weeks. She just works so hard. She's so tired all the time.

Mama...I had to do something to help her. If you have the power to help someone, you have to help. That's just what's right.

Today was Saint Valentine's Day. I knew Leroy was coming over to see my mama.

Mama was a good Catholic woman despite her own heathen ma and daughter. I know that Saint Valentine wasn't just one person, even, and all that love crap isn't based on any sort of pious religion.

And like with Christmas tying together capitalism and pagan rituals and Christianity (see, I told you I got some education), there were darker festivals, like the Lupercalia, predating today's holiday of hearts and flowers and candy.

But when enough people believe something, it can become real, even if it was made-up stories about finding true love despite the odds.

Maybe I could do a little bit of bayou magic to knot all the threads, with all these things coalescing. Maybe I'd have the strength to make a difference, finally, with the rain-fueled spirits and the magic of the different beliefs all coming together.

The swamp was quiet as I rode up, hushed by the cold iron-based steel of my bike.

Soon as I got off it and laid it down in the poison ivy by the roadside, the chuckles and squeaks of a green heron broke the stillness.

That set off a cacophony of chirps, splashes, and grunts.

The bayou accepted me as one of its own once it realized who I was, away from my bike.

Bayou Mareau looked the same and different, like it always did, depending on the tides and time of year, storms present and floodings past. Verdant green everywhere, in the sunlight just breaking through the clouds—kelly-green swamp rose mallow leaves, dark green Spanish moss dangling from naked cypress branches, scums of acid green algae on the surface of the milk chocolate water.

It smelled of lush decay, sour and rich in my nose and on my tongue as I gulped in the thick air like a beached bass. Decay that gave life.

I was home.

I'd worn just the white blouse and cutoffs, over a faded black cotton sports bra and pink cotton bikini panties. I shucked off the blouse and jeans, baring my pale sunless skin, and waded into the knee-deep water, hoping any creepy-crawlies would just crawl on out of the way. Have you ever seen what lives in the mud? Larvae like miniature dragons and monsters, and worse.

A swamp moccasin glided on by, its thick body graceful in the water.

"Give my regards to Miss Calixte," I told it, and it nodded gravely as it gaped at me, showing the snowy white of its mouth. Just a friendly smile, not a threat display. Not to me.

The snakes don't bother me. Nor do the mosquitoes.

I've given enough blood, barking my shins on underwater branches, to sustain generations of bugs. And the snakes, and other critters? Politeness goes a long way, I've found. Kindness and politeness. You don't have to be some sort of Christian to know that you should treat others as you would like to be treated in turn. Problem was, lots of those who called themselves good Christians think that applies only to other Christians.

Not folks like Charlie, working like a white man but living like his people, the Houma, or outright heathens like me and Granny. Let alone the snakes and crawdads and gators. Or the cypress, or the poison ivy, or even the most annoying mosquito.

Leroy Bobanchet goes to church every Sunday, dressin' up in a cigarette-soaked black suit, with his stomach stretching a starched white dress shirt near to the seams splitting. And a black and gold fleur-de-lis patterned tie knotted around his thick neck. For the Saints, you know.

A half mile or so of wandering around the cypress, collecting a parade of curious animal spirits, pulling up some worm root and collecting some pretty white fringeless orchids, I came across what I was truly looking for.

The ruin of an old steamship hunkered under the branches, its flaking white paint mottled green with mold, the wood underneath ash gray. The iron fixtures at the listing doors and windows were rusted red and fragmented, staining the remnants of the white paint with the pale pinky-orange tears of their decay. Spanish moss draped over the broken railings. The hull glowed orange, pale sunlight reflecting off the brown water illuminating the layers of rust coating the steel. It smelled like a cast iron pan heated on the stove. Tall feathery-leafed cypress pierced the deck from below, pinning it in place to decay just in this spot.

ASHLEY CASSADAY

Regardless, the sternwheeler listed in the water, more than the last time I'd visited. I didn't know if it was safe to board, or if it'd taken more damage from yesterday's storm. I could trust the swamp. I couldn't trust something man-made.

Man-made, but unearthly for all that. No one else I knew had ever mentioned the old ruin. Bayou Mareau was isolated, but the folks who did live here knew it well. If anybody besides me had run across it, no one was breathing a word of it.

And the cypress impaling it was fully leafed out like it was the middle of June, not mid-February. That just wasn't natural.

Sometimes the bayou does what it wants, not what people think or science says it should. Like keep a wrecked sternwheeler for itself, sharing it only with those folks who shared the bayou's magic.

But, inside, in the top drawer of a small walnut inlaid dresser, in what used to be a bedroom, complete with an iron bed frame and a moldering horsehair mattress, was a tattered volume of Chaucer, with one poem still intact, still readable: "The Parliament of Fowls," with its reference to Saint Valentine.

I like to think the book belonged to some young woman like me, before all the bad crap happened and I got all cynical. Maybe she was riding the river boat south to meet her beau, and simply forgot the book when she packed up to start her new life.

And yes, I know, that poem likely refers to summer. But stay with me, here. It all goes on belief, and what folks believe ain't necessarily what's true. I can use it to anchor my spell, because what folks *believe* is that February 14 is Saint Valentine's Day.

I eyed the steamboat. Last time, I wrestled a log against the side, shinnied up it, and clambered over the railing. The railing was half gone, now, victim of the storm or time. And the hull just *felt* paper thin, like I could see through it to the innards of the ship. I didn't think it could support the weight of a log.

Cypress grew 'round the ship, not just through it. If I climbed up one, *that* one leaning kissing close to the ship, then scooted along an overhanging branch, I could maybe jump to the deck.

Worth trying. I'd worry about getting off the damn ship, after.

I wished I'd kept my cutoffs on. Thick denim, they'd be chafing my thighs, but I could use a little protection from the rough bark. I gritted my teeth, stuck the orchids and worm root into my bra, reached for a low-hanging liana, and began climbing.

The pepper vine realized what I was doing and boosted me along.

"Thank you kindly," I whispered as I scooted along the cypress branch, then let myself drop to the deck of the ship. The cracked floorboards let out an alarming creak in protest, though I don't weigh no more than a year-old swamp doe, one hundred and ten dripping wet, which I nearly was after my hike to the ship.

I made my way to the front of the ship, skirting the holes in the deck and broken boards just wanting to become holes. I made it to the bedroom with just a couple splinters in my bare feet, leaving tiny droplets of the blood along my path for the ship to drink down. I'd have to get some elderberry leaves for a poultice to make sure they wouldn't fester.

For now, the ship could taste me. I was planning on takin' something away, and fair is fair.

The book was where I'd left it last, tucked away in the top drawer of the decaying walnut dresser. The cover looked and smelled damper than before, and the book exhaled little puffs of mold when I opened it to "The Parliament of Fowls."

Still legible, if fuzzier, the print paling to moss-tinged sepia. Seven hundred lines of gods and goddesses and love and death and all the birds Chaucer could think of.

That didn't matter.

What mattered was all those damn birds found their true love, with the help of good old Saint Valentine. And I'd found a score of references pointing to the poem as one of the first links of romance and love to Valentine.

So, folks believed it.

The spirits gathered around me. Gator claws tapping on the soft water-soaked boards of the bedroom floor; an osprey winging along by the ceiling, a mullet grasped in his feet; a swamp moccasin curling around my feet, belly full of frogs and mice.

And one more spirit, that I couldn't quite see, but hoped I recognized.

The magic of the bayou, of life and death in a constant circle.

I asked, and the snake and the gator and the osprey focused on the book, a bit bewildered, but willin' to help. "Life. Death. Love," I whispered, and some of their strength flowed into the pages, their spectral forms dimming.

I carefully tucked the orchids in between the pages, then closed the book. That would do.

I hoped it would be enough. Leroy was an evil man, and my mama was too wounded inside to stand up for herself. "Thank you."

Up on the deck, I let the pepper vines twine around my wrists and pull me up, off the deck, then drop me to the sodden earth.

Now to get on home fast as could be.

Time runs funny in the bayou, and it was late afternoon by the time I reached the rutted gravel road to our cabin.

The gator and the swamp moccasin spirits had stayed behind in the bayou, but the osprey, spectral wings shining in the dwindling winter sunlight, had followed me home like a curious kitten.

And the other spirit, the one I couldn't quite see, was hovering close by as well.

The pale blue paint was peeling off the front door of our cabin, and the tin roof needed patching, but the cabin was home, a home that my mama'd worked hard to keep as nice and clean as she could for raising me.

Mama's rusty Ford pickup, its tires nearly bald, snugged up in the shelter of the house. Mama was already home from work as a cashier at the Big Star grocery, a forty-five-minute drive away and the closest grocery store.

Leroy's truck, a shiny new Dodge, was parked next to Mama's.

Was I too late? My stomach clenched. I'd planned on getting back home before he arrived.

I stood up on the pedals, smashing down, bits of gravel rooster-tailing behind my back wheel as I pedaled up the driveway as fast as I could. A miasma of pain roped around me like the liana and squeezed me near to puking. The edge of the rusted steel pedal sliced my left calf as my foot slipped.

Spatters of blood trailed as I pedaled harder.

What had Leroy *done*?

Leroy Bobanchet threw open the screen door, banging it against the wall. Heavy handed as normal. He was wearing a stained wife beater over ripped-up jeans. Couldn't even bother to dress up nice for my mama on Saint Valentine's Day.

"Why, Miss Delphine, I'd'a thought you were out today with some beau," he called, leering at me.

That man never did learn.

You can't cure a rabid dog. All you can do is shoot him.

"I like to spend holidays with my mama," I said, gritting my teeth against the knots in my gut.

"Well, you had best go on. Visit your granny or sumpin'. I'm staying with your ma tonight."

I pushed my bike under the house, between the stilts. I'd clean up the blood and the mud later.

I marched on up the front stairs to the porch where he lounged against the door frame. I held my back so stiff I thought I'd break in two, then smiled pretty.

"Got a gift for you to say I'm sorry," I said to him, my mouth so dry even stomach acid would be a treat. I reached behind where I'd tucked the book into the waistband of my cutoffs. I handed it to him, and he took it without thinking.

I don't know what was worse—how sick I felt, and knowing how hurt my mama must be, or being terrified my spell wouldn't work. No one cared when Mama showed up with black eyes or a broken nose. The laws of men favored Leroy Bobanchet, not my mama. It was up to me, and all I had was the love and magic of the bayou.

"A book?" he said, opening it, letting an orchid fall to the porch. "What the hell do you think I'm gonna do with a damn book? And what is that stink?"

"Death. Decay," I whispered.

The osprey landed on my shoulder, cocked his head. His talons pierced the thin fabric of my blouse, drawing pinpoint drops of blood.

I could see the osprey clear as day, and by the widening of Leroy's eyes, so could he.

And what's more, Leroy could see the other spirit beside me, the one I couldn't quite clearly see, though the form was growing more solid. Else I don't think he'd look so scared.

I must admit, I enjoyed that look of terror, given what he'd done to my mama.

The osprey tightened his grip, my blood soaking up into his talons. I was happy to sacrifice that bit of blood, dripping out of me like innocence lost.

"Death. Decay," I repeated, as mold stretched from the pages of the book to his hands and up his arms. He dropped the book as his flesh shriveled against his finger bones and his skin tore free. The mold reached his shoulders, and that's when he started screamin', fit to wake the dead.

I'm not ashamed to admit I joined in. The magic gave, but it took, too, and I felt the same agonies as that woman-beating piece of crap.

The screaming didn't last long.

Just long enough for him to fall down, spasming against the warped floorboards of the porch, his flayed flesh in tatters.

Long enough for Mama to drag herself from the bedroom, cradling a broken arm against her chest. He'd laid into her once again. He would have killed her, I know he would've, and I don't feel an ounce of regret for what I done.

Even if my soul felt heavy. Tinged with darkness and decay that the ebbing pain didn't erase.

From the dullness in her dark eyes, outlined by raccoon bruises, as she stared at Leroy's quivering body, I don't think Mama felt any regret either.

We both watched as he gave one last rattle. Me with a dark satisfaction, Mama with a disbelieving relief.

Then she looked up at me.

And then, past me.

To the spirit of Charlie Solet, his lanky form clad in a white linen suit. No signs of the oil slick burns that took his life, too soon.

Absorbing the life force of Leroy to become solid enough to touch our world.

Holding out a bouquet of pink and white rose mallow flowers to my mama.

"I'm so sorry, Cécile," he murmured, his voice a breeze of sweet honeysuckle. "So sorry."

"Things happen, Charlie," my mama said. "But I have missed you."

He reached to her, stroked her broken arm. Her breath caught as the bones straightened and the flesh knit together. He stroked her face, and her nose straightened back to its elegant profile. Her dark eyes gleamed, the skin around them a tawny healthy sun-kissed tan instead of sickly yellow-purple, the swelling receding to show off those cheekbones I'm vain enough to be pleased to have inherited. Then he opened his arms and Mama went to him.

I shuffled my feet, looked down. It was clear Charlie still loved my mama, and she loved him. Everyone deserves a Valentine's kiss from their true love.

"I think it's time for me to go visit Granny," I said, my sickness waning as my mama healed. I cleared my throat. "It may be you just have a bit of time."

"I understand, baby girl," my mama said, peeking around Charlie's shoulder. "And thank you."

Charlie looked back to me and nodded, his black eyes luminous.

"Don't worry about that," I waved a hand at Leroy's remains, "I'll just use his truck and dump him for the gators."

I don't know if they even heard me say that last bit. They just stepped back into the house, eyes locked on each other.

The gators weren't too sure if they wanted to eat trash like Leroy, but I coaxed them to do it by promising to bring some hamburger next time. They just love raw hamburger. Then I drove his truck all the way to the outskirts of New Orleans and left the keys in the ignition and the doors unlocked.

I took a cab to a cheap motel and called Granny after getting settled in, tucking all the pillows against the flimsy headboard and laying back on the burnt orange flower-printed polyester coverlet. A clock, a real clock, not digital, hung on the wall opposite, over a scratched-up dresser. There was a stand for a TV, but no TV.

"I can't tell you what I done, over the phone," I said, taking a sip of the warm RC I'd picked up at a truck stop soon as my stomach felt settled enough for a coke. My skin still felt funny, loose on my bones, if I let my thoughts dwell on Leroy.

"Can I stay with you for a couple a days?"

Granny didn't say anything for a few minutes. The clock ticked erratically. Sort of like my heartbeat, waiting for Granny to pass judgment.

"Did you do something that needed doing?" she finally asked, her rich voice rough in my ear.

"I did, ma'am."

"Then as long as you can live with it," she said.

"I can, Granny." Taking a life, even one as despicable as Leroy's, would carry a price, one I'd be a long time paying back.

If I even could. The taste of swamp decay filled my mouth.

"I can." I had no choice but to, didn't I?

"Then I'll come get you first thing tomorrow morning." She hung up before I could tell her the address. Hmph. She'd find me.

I rearranged the pillows and shimmied between the sheets. Scolded the bedbugs away.

And dreamed sweet dreams, of the sun sparkling on the bayou, frogs croaking and gators grunting, ospreys hunting. Spanish moss like garlands from the cypress branches, and duckweed floating on the still water. The sweet blooms of orchids and wild roses.

Of life and death and love.

Five Days Until Sunset

written by
Lance Robinson

illustrated by
STEVEN BENTLEY

ABOUT THE AUTHOR

In his day job, Lance Robinson is an environmental social scientist who often works closely with mobile peoples. He is a sporadic nomad himself, having lived variously in countries such as Ghana, The Gambia, Colombia, and Kenya. He began writing speculative fiction as a child, and by his early twenties his stories began appearing in small press magazines. In the early 1990s, he even entered the Writers of the Future Contest two or three times. Eventually, though, his life filled up with other things and he set creative writing aside.

Recently, however, when he returned home to Canada, he decided it was also time to come back home to writing. Since then, his stories have often explored how our relationship with the natural world is intertwined with our spiritual journeys—as individuals, as communities, and as a collective humanity. Lance is also an avid astronomy and space-travel nut, and he found the germ of his story "Five Days Until Sunset" at the intersection of pondering the spiritual search that never ends and wondering what life might be like on a tidally locked, "eyeball" planet. The story also asks what it means to live in harmony with a world that is ready to kill you, and what it means to have faith in the face of inconvenient truths.

Lance and his two children currently make their home in Robinson-Superior Treaty territory on the traditional land of the Anishnaabeg peoples and Fort William First Nation in the City of Thunder Bay, Ontario.

ABOUT THE ILLUSTRATOR

Steven Bentley was born in 1964 in the city of Leeds in the north of England.

He started drawing at an early age, at first on the walls with his crayons, then on any scrap of paper he could lay his hands on or that his father could provide. His love of art continued into school. If you would have asked him what he wanted to be when he grew up, he would have said he wanted to draw and paint movie posters and book covers.

Life however took him in other directions, but he continued to draw and paint every day developing his work until the opportunity came along for him to attend art school. There he gained a degree with honors in animation art and design. His passion always remained in illustration, and it is there he has continued to concentrate.

He works almost exclusively in traditional media as he enjoys the process and having something tangible to hold is important to him. However, he has been known to dabble in the digital realm.

He currently lives in Portland, Oregon, where he hopes to continue to grow his freelance career.

Five Days Until Sunset

1

Bering Stiles laid himself down in the hibetank, and as the sedative billowed into his thoughts, he whispered a prayer of thanksgiving and sank into nothingness. Then, with no clear sense of the passage of time, he felt his self rematerializing like a fog slowly solidifying.

Something's wrong.

Over a span of a few hours, drifting between stupor, sleep, confusion, and fleeting instances of clarity, he formed three slightly more complete thoughts. They came all at once—that he was not dead, that he was waking up, but disturbingly, that he was alone. There should have been doctors and their assistants at his side, monitoring his vitals, offering him water, and speaking soothing words. But there were no human beings darting in and out among the rows of hibetanks, only the inanimate arms, tubes and tentacles of med drones. It took another foggy while—he was not sure whether minutes or hours—before he realized something else.

No, not exactly alone.

At the fourth tank to his right another person was also awake, having just stood up from her tank. "We're on the planet," she croaked.

He considered answering her, but he was still fumbling to even string thoughts together, let alone words. As he pulled himself up to a sitting position, she did a deep knee bend, holding on to the side of her tank, then stood up straight again. Apparently, she had less of a hibernation hangover than he did. She cleared her throat. "Feel the gravity?"

She's . . . What's her name? I met her about a week before going into the tank. Naka . . . Right, Jeremy Nakamura. What did she say? The planet. The gravity. Bering lifted his arm and let it fall, realizing that she was right. The recon probe that had swung through the Epsindi system a century before he was born had estimated the surface gravity of Epsindi Ta to be thirteen percent higher than Earth's, and now he felt just a little heavier than he was used to.

This means we survived the voyage. We survived the one hundred forty-four years in hibernation! We crossed light years!

None of these things had been certainties when they were put under. Bering silently repeated the same prayer of thanksgiving he had whispered one hundred forty-four years earlier— moments ago.

But questions began to taint his elation, and as she slipped on a robe, Frau Nakamura asked one of those questions as if reading his thoughts. "Why did the system wake *us*?"

He made no attempt to answer, not yet trusting his vocal cords. Then, as she began inspecting the other hibetanks, he took a few more deep breaths, swung his legs over the edge of his tank, and carefully stood up. Once he decided that he was not going to faint, he also put on a robe. Then he shuffled to a console, sat down, and began demanding answers.

"Where is . . . ?" He coughed up some phlegm then tried again. "Where is Dr. Kumarisov?"

<<That information is unavailable.>>

"Where are the members of the initial revival team?"

<<That information is unavailable.>>

"Where are we?"

<<Drop ferry *Assiniboine* touched down on Epsindi Ta three hours and forty-eight minutes ago at 65.3 degrees north latitude, 94.3 degrees east longitude.>>

Nakamura laughed. "I told you. We're not in the ark; we're on the planet."

"Frau Nakamura, this doesn't make sense. Something must have—"

A shrill claxon from one of the hibetanks startled them both, and immediately the ferry shot mnemonic scents into the air. Bering inhaled, letting the smell prime his memory, and then he realized why he, the youngest of the entire family of pilgrims, had been revived together with Jeremy Nakamura. His main contribution to the colony was to be engineering and construction, but like everyone, he had some training in other areas as well. His included astronomy, horticulture, and basic medicine, including hibernation revival.

As Nakamura moved to inspect the hibetank sounding an alarm, she again voiced what he was already thinking. "You and I—we're the alternates to the alternates. Kumarisov was meant to oversee the hibernation revivals. If the system needs us to revive the others, it means Dr. Kumarisov, Dr. Apshana, their assistants, everyone meant to serve on the initial revival team—they're..." Her voice trailed off, and Bering had no need to hear her finish the thought.

Before moving to help her, he checked the displays on three other hibetanks. At two of them, their fellow pilgrims were already in the preliminary stages of being revived. Bering's training, though narrow, was profound, having been cross-learned through qigonic meditation, olfactory priming, and hours of kinesthetic repetition, and it sprang up to guide him. By the time they had helped eight fellow pilgrims through stage four of the revival process, another eight were beginning stage four.

The ferry continued waking the pilgrims in batches. Bering and Nakamura did what they could to resolve the emergencies and calm those who awoke in confusion or panic. In each batch, at least one person asked, "Where's Dr. Kumarisov?" By the fourth time he heard the question, Bering was getting annoyed—not annoyed at the repetition so much as annoyed at being reminded of what the situation implied. *If the hibernation system called on the third alternates to do this, it means something went terribly wrong.*

But he had no time to dwell on that, because the revivals kept coming. Eventually, they learned that the other two drop ferries from the ark had also set down nearby. Someone from the *Serengeti* radioed, and it became clear that the same thing was also happening there and on the *Haida Gwaii*. Two people on each ferry revived first, then everyone else in stages.

As Bering attended to the successive waves of revivals, he heard someone from the first batch of patients try, as he had, to get information from a console. "Who ordered us revived?"

<<That information is unavailable.>>

"Where are the shuttles, *Guanahani* and *Beijing*?" They were smaller than *Assiniboine*, *Haida Gwaii*, and *Serengeti*, and not equipped with hibetanks. If the initial revival team had been revived according to the default plan—ahead of everyone else while still in orbit on the ark—then they might have taken one of the smaller landers down to the planet surface.

<<That information is unavailable.>>

If the consoles don't know where the landers are, where the lead medical team is, or even who initiated this revival of everyone... Bering did not let himself think about what might have happened. He needed to concentrate. Someone in the last batch of revivals was hyperventilating.

As Bering helped her, one of the first people revived after him and Nakamura took readings of the external atmosphere and confirmed the recon probe's analysis, hundreds of years earlier—19.0% oxygen, 78.7% nitrogen, 1.5% argon, 0.4% neon, trace carbon dioxide, and nothing poisonous. It was slightly thicker than Earth's atmosphere, and so although as a percentage oxygen was less than on Earth, its partial pressure was actually higher—all in all, quite breathable.

Twenty-four hours after Bering regained consciousness, the successive waves of revivals had finished, and no one was left in hibernation. On the *Assiniboine*, two people could not be revived, and one revived, but then had a seizure and died. Between the three ferries, three hundred fifteen had been brought down to the planet surface, and by the time the last hibetank had been opened, two hundred eighty-eight emerged alive. But this meant not only that twenty-seven people died coming out of hibernation, but also that one hundred fifty-four were unaccounted for.

Once he had done everything he could for the last of the waking pilgrims, Bering stepped out of the ferry and found dozens of others all admiring a sublime sunset. Euphoria briefly lifted him above the questions and worries. The family of pilgrims had successfully escaped their oppression, left it one hundred thirteen trillion kilometers behind so that they could become humanity's first flowering beyond the Sol system. And Bering, having lived as an orphan and refugee, never being able to stay in one place for more than a few years, would finally build a home.

But what happened to the others? How can a hundred and fifty-four of us be missing? He pushed the doubts down. Then, his adrenaline spent, he laid down in the grass, ignoring the gentle breeze that caressed him to sleep.

2

Data, analysis, collective intuition, five different religious traditions, and the Promise of the Teacher who reunited those traditions have all told us that the time of human flowering has finally arrived. I am convinced now that this world can be one of the new gardens for our flowering. But instead of accepting the gift as it is, we fretted and dallied over Epsindi Ta's inconveniences for decades.

—*From the journal of Adam Leifson found at the fourth cairn*

When, some hours later, someone woke Bering, birds were singing and the sun was still suspended on the western horizon. Seeing the sun sitting at the same point in the sky unsettled him even though rationally he understood it. Data sent back to the Sol system by the recon probe had suggested that the planet was tidally locked—an eyeball planet that permanently presented the same face toward its K5 orange dwarf star. The probe had swung by Epsindi Ta only three times before going silent, and the data it returned were scanty. Nevertheless, thermographic analysis assessed the temperature at the substellar point—the longitude experiencing permanent noon—to be seventy-nine degrees Celsius, while the night side of the planet was nearly cold enough for carbon dioxide to freeze out.

But the data had also shown that in the planet's twilight ring, where the day-night cycle was suspended in a never-ending sunrise/sunset, photosynthetic life thrived. Bering's faith in the Promise of humanity's flowering was strong, but this world would be a strange fulfillment of that Promise. A place where time felt different, where day and night were undesirable destinations rather than markers on the flow of time. Nevertheless, signs of the Promise were all around him. He was breathing the air, the temperature was perfect, and the bed of grass and flowers that he had slept on was evidently Earth flora. And he was hearing birds! And, not only was he hearing birds, but the trill call and a check-check-check response was completely familiar.

Those are red-winged blackbirds! But how?

For his whole life, Bering had fled from place to place, hidden from mobs and from men in uniform, and been shunted first from one orphanage to another and then from one refugee camp to another. His faith in the Teacher and in the Promise had kept him going, but never had he imagined that the Promise would be so bounteously fulfilled.

But he had no time to marvel at how this planet was teeming with what seemed to be Earth life, or to appreciate the permanently paused beauty of the sunset, or to meditate on the play of light and shadow across what seemed to be trees on the hills to the south. A concourse had been called, and the two hundred eighty-eight pilgrims were gathering on the grassy plain between the *Haida Gwaii* and the *Serengeti*.

First, the names of the twenty-seven who had died were

announced, and a hymn chanted. This was more than they had hoped to lose to the risky hibernation process, but still within the range they expected, so the voyage could only be considered a success, and prayers of praise, thanksgiving, and anticipation were offered from three of the five religious traditions represented among their number. Then Fatuma Chisholm, one of the deputies elected to the family council before the voyage and the person presiding over the concourse, explained what Bering already knew. The consoles on the ferries either lacked or had been instructed not to provide what should have been straightforward information.

"Nevertheless," she called in a loud voice so everyone could hear, "we have made two important discoveries." She pointed to her right. "First, look over there. There at the midpoint between the three ferries. It's barely visible from here, but there's a small mound. It's a pile of rocks in fact, and though it isn't obvious from here, it's actually a cairn. The rocks were stacked up that way by human hands. Our ferries landed in a triangle because each landed two hundred and ninety meters from the cairn and a safe distance from each other. The rocks were protecting a radio beacon—a beacon set there by a fellow pilgrim to direct us here."

"So, the missing brothers and sisters," someone called out, "they're not dead?"

"Well, that brings us to the second discovery. We examined the beacon. It was placed there a long time ago and set with a timer. And from the control systems of the hibetanks, we confirmed the information from the beacon." She took a deep breath. "Our hibernation did not last one hundred forty-four years. It's been three hundred and eighty-four. We arrived in orbit around Epsindi Ta two hundred and forty years ago."

There were scattered gasps, and then silence settled over the assembled concourse. This meant it was not only the twenty-seven who were dead, but also the missing hundred and fifty-four. Even if every single one of them survived revival, they had all died of old age more than a century ago.

191

As they absorbed the news, some people cried and some comforted each other in twos and threes. Bering stared off at nothing, thinking of Ulysses Degana, his mentor, and one of only two people in the whole ark family he had known before being selected for the crew. It was Degana who had vouched for him in the crew selection process. But Bering knew that for some, the loss was much worse—some of the pilgrims had spouses among the hundred and fifty-four.

After a suitable pause, Frau Chisholm called for silence. She initiated a discussion of practicalities, but agreement was elusive. Did their fellow pilgrims who preceded them intend for them to build the village here, or was this a location chosen randomly by a malfunctioning semi-mind on the ark? Several people voiced their impatience to activate the default settlement plan and start building. Eventually, however, they reached consensus that first they needed to learn more. Once that was decided, most of the two hundred eighty-eight easily fell into one of two broad groups. One group had the task of investigating, of finding out whatever they could about what had gone wrong. As the concourse concluded, leaders of various investigation teams—geology, climatology, biology, edaphology, ships' engineering, and others—shouted out to assemble their teams.

Bering knew he belonged in the second group: those who would support the first group, preparing food and temporary shelter, providing medical and spiritual care, and managing logistics. His primary role in the family was to be engineering and construction, and even for a temporary camp there would be printing and fabricating to be done and shelters to be built. For the next few hours, Bering worked with one of the engineering teams setting up a hydroponics system. At first, they were entirely focused on the work in front of them, but as they fell into a rhythm, conversation soon zeroed in on the oddities in their revival, the uncooperative consoles, and the missing hundred fifty-four members of their family.

Ford Cyltemstra, the deputy head of engineering, made it clear that he thought there was no point worrying about it. "Beaumont or Elysium will reestablish contact with the ark. They'll figure it out when they figure it out." He spoke to Bering and the others of his hopes and plans for their life in this new world and his confidence in all the preparation the family and their fellow believers back on Earth had done. He framed these thoughts mostly using the terminology of his Francisco-Nasrian Faith— the same as Bering's—but also pausing to draw connections to beliefs and concepts from the other four religious traditions of the family. His faith in the Promise shone, but it could not lift Bering away from his disquiet over the unanswered questions. So, when the team finished the hydroponics installation and Ford announced a short break, Bering took his assistant from his pocket and asked it to locate Taamir Beaumont.

He found the elder alone in a flat grassy field two hundred meters from the *Assiniboine*, assembling an antenna. Beaumont's weathered face and greying hair only hinted at his age. Although most of the pilgrims selected for the ark were between twenty-five and forty-five years old, Bering knew that forty years before their journey even began, Beaumont had spent decades designing the engine that powered the ark.

"Sen. Beaumont."

The old man looked up. "Sen. Stiles."

"Yes, sir. Sen. Beaumont sir, I have training in astronomy."

"I know; I was on the committee that selected you for the ark when an opening came up. But, don't you have construction work to do?"

"I do. But something went wrong here—something with our arrival in this system, or with the landing, or something—and the sooner we find out what it was, the better."

Beaumont looked down at the antennas at his feet, then looked back up. "Absolutely. And as it turns out, everyone else with training in astronomy was among the hundred fifty-four, so you and I, the oldest and the youngest of the entire family—we're all that remains of the astronomy team. So, I guess I better say yes.

Not that our new culture on this world will do much astronomy, at least not visual astronomy."

"We could eventually build observatories on the night side of the planet," Bering offered. "Not at the midnight point, but somewhere where the cold is at least manageable."

"One day, Sen. Stiles. But for now, the only star we can observe in the visible spectrum is that one." He pointed to the orange orb that still hung on the western horizon, now partly obscured by a thin stratus cloud. "We can use some prehistoric astrometric techniques. Do you know how to measure the angular size of our new sun in the sky?"

Bering nodded vigorously.

"Good. We should confirm if the recon probe data about the size of the star and our distance from it are correct. But you can do that later. First, help me set up this radio array. You can use it to start making images of the sky."

It took the two of them a little over two hours to set up the array of half-meter antennas, Bering doing most of the physical labor as Sen. Beaumont stopped frequently to rest. They instructed the antennas to upload their data to a console in the *Assiniboine*, then entered the ferry and confirmed that the data was arriving and being saved.

When they stepped back outside, Bering noticed that the breeze had died down, and looking to the west he saw that clouds had formed, blocking the view of their new sun.

"Interesting," Beaumont remarked.

"I thought the weather was going to be absolutely constant here. No planetary rotation, no day and night, no moons, and no axial tilt—so no changes in weather."

"It seems we have much to learn. But as for measuring the width of Epsindi, that will have to wait until the sky clears."

"Sen. Beaumont, why do you think we were set down somewhere different from the first pilgrims? And why would a fellow pilgrim have set the timer on that beacon for two hundred forty years?"

"In the concourse, Fatuma was preoccupied with sharing the

bad news and with how people would react, so she omitted some of the finer details. Actually, the timer wasn't set until about forty-five years after the ark arrived in orbit. And then it was set for 194.89 years, as were timers in each of the three drop ferries. So, for some reason, our brothers and sisters were here for forty-five years and saw fit not to revive us. And, then in planting the beacon and giving instructions to the ferries, they decided we needed to wait another one hundred ninety-five years. As for 'why?'—that question has my mind spinning. It's what we're all trying to find out. Maybe this"—he gestured toward the antenna array—"maybe this will give us some clues. In the meantime, I think you should get back to your construction team."

Contamination! I forgot to message Ford.

Bering went running back to the hydroponics installation and the main site of their new camp, but the others had ended work for the day. He checked his pocket assistant. There were no messages, but there were several broadcast announcements. One of them explained that with no planetary day and night cycle to shepherd their circadian rhythms, a standard time had been set and was now synchronized to everyone's assistant. He checked and saw that the time now was six and a half hours after standard noon. That gave him an idea of where he might find Ford. He went straight to the tent designated as a dining hall and found him there just finishing his meal. As Bering took a chair beside him, Ford looked at him but said nothing. Bering quickly explained and tried to apologize, but Ford stood up, interrupting.

"Being a pilgrim is a responsibility and a gift," he said, then left the tent.

Bering ate in silence: crackers with lentil paste and a bland, grey vatcake.

By the time he was done, a fog was descending over their camp and the temperature had dropped at least a degree—another subtle deviation from what he had been led to expect here. It joined the other anomalies and questions swirling around in his mind as he went to find a sleeping mat in one of the tents.

3

*Because of the disasters that beset us, most caused by our own
inaction, I was left with little choice but to then add another
nineteen and a half decades to your sleep. One hundred
ninety-five years—or should I say "thirteen days"?—was my
best estimate of where to strike the balance between the danger of
extending your time in hibernation versus giving the semi-mind
on the ark, and the gene lab and incubators it is guiding,
enough time to do their work.*

*Before you curse me for imposing that calculation upon you,
know that where you set down is an Eden compared to where we
first tried to start the colony. That most of this planet is, in its own
way, a paradise is almost certainly thanks to a seed ship. Sent out
thirteen thousand years ago before the Dark Ages at the end of the
anthropo-unification era when, for a brief eight or ten centuries,
humanity was united, the legend says the seed ships were the only
attempt the ancients made at interstellar travel before the Chaos.
They carried flora and fauna, a great DNA library and artificial
wombs of various sorts, but no human passengers. One of those
ships certainly must have come here to Epsindi Ta.
The seed that it planted was the Promise.*

*For thirteen millennia, the seed ship prepared this world for us,
and like a child copying its mother, I have added another
thirteen days, enough time, I pray, to make a few small
additions to this garden.*

*—From the second cairn epistle of Adam Leifson
to the third generation*

Waking early, Bering quietly dressed so as not to disturb those
who were still sleeping, and stepped out of his dorm tent. Clearly,
members of one of the other building teams had not slept at
all. More large tents and some prefab panel structures had been

erected. Then when he reached the dining tent, he saw that someone had hung two rows of luzglobes—with the sun still obscured by haze and clouds, the natural light was not enough. Permanent structures were yet to come, but already the camp was starting to look like their new home.

Among the other early risers in the dining tent, he saw Jaykella Tahirani. Aside from Ulysses Degana, she was the only other fellow pilgrim he had known before being selected for the ark, essentially at the last minute—only four weeks before departure. They had been together as youths in the same refugee camp after fleeing the pogroms. Bering sat down. She introduced him to the two people she was sitting with, both of them part of the same biology team as her. Gopal Nairobiani was a handsome, athletic-looking guy—in his midthirties, Bering guessed—but Arsen Kazakii was younger; he could hardly be older than Bering himself.

"Has your team learned anything about the ecology here?" Bering asked.

"We've only been here one day," Jaykella answered with a laugh. "But, yeah, we've learned a few things. Except for some moss, everything's completely familiar—plants *and* animals. It's not just that they're related to Earth life; they're all known species."

"Are ya knowin', man, about the legend of the seed ships?" Arsen asked in a thick belt colony accent.

"The life we're seeing was brought here by a seed ship?"

"I bin sequencin' the genomes," Arsen said. "That might be tellin' us. In fact, I need to go see if my first analyses are finished. The team leader has a meetin' with the other team leaders at the cairn in a few minutes."

"Wait. First tell me what else you found. Did you find any clues about what happened to the rest of the family?"

Jaykella answered. "Nothing about what happened to them, but we have learned some interesting stuff. For instance, almost all the animals I saw on my transects are migratory species. Some of the insect species aren't but, every bird species I saw is migratory. So that's kinda strange."

"Why do you say that?"

"The planet doesn't have a day and night cycle, and it doesn't have seasons, as far as we know. But all the birds I saw were flying west. Even the antelopes I saw were moving west too."

"I think I saw wild goats," said Gopal. "But they were far away."

"It was probably the same antelopes," Jaykella replied. "But, the question is, if there's no weather and no seasons, why migrate? But team leader Watersmith wasn't interested. He just wanted to know what plants could be weeds to the crops we'll grow and what animals will be pests."

Gopal leaned forward. "So many of the plants we found— wow!—so, so many are edible."

"Right," Arsen said. "That means if the farmin' is hard, we can add bits'a variety by foragin'. But, man, the real question is, if the life we're seein' was placed here by a seed ship from Earth, aren't these all invasive species?" At first, Bering thought he had heard Arsen wrong, but he went on. "And if they're invasive species, doesn't that make us the second wave of the invasion?"

"Invasive species?" Bering blurted. "No. The real question is 'How are we going to live on this world?'" He jumped to his feet. "Invasive species? This world is the gift promised for us!"

He shocked himself with the intensity of his reaction, and clearly, he jarred Jaykella, Arsen, and Gopal as well. Embarrassed, he used their surprise as an opportunity to stride away. But the more he thought about what Arsen had said, the more he felt justified. *How can he suggest we don't belong here? He can question the Promise if he wants, but I won't. We're building our new home here, and nothing is going to stop that.*

And so, as Bering reached the *Assiniboine*, he resolved to keep learning what he could, and follow through with the astronomical observations. If he was quick, he could still join his construction team before they even got breakfast. He wanted to do the measurement of Epsindi's apparent diameter, but although the fog had lifted in the vicinity of the ships, to the west the sky was still hazy, so he would have to wait a little longer.

But not much longer, he told himself as he noticed sunlight illuminating the peaks of the hills to the south.

Just then a chill ran through him.

"Yeah, it cooled off a little," a woman remarked, stepping out of the ferry. "I thought the weather here wasn't supposed to change."

Bering glanced over to her and shrugged, then snapped his attention back to the hills. It *was* slightly cooler, but that was not what had given him the chill. Something in what he was seeing was not right. In the light and shadow on the hills, there was something out of place. He looked to the west, then looked back to the hills one more time, and promised himself he would come back to meditate in view of those hills later. For now, he went into the *Assiniboine* to check on the radio telescope data. It had only been thirteen hours since he and Sen. Beaumont had finished setting it up, so only the first small square of the sky would have been imaged. Now in its second twelve-hour scan, the array would be observing the next square. It would take nine weeks this way to do a complete picture of the sky, but Bering wanted to confirm that everything was working. Rushing to a console, he almost knocked over a glass with some wildflowers that someone had picked. He steadied it, moved it aside, then called up the radio array data. He instructed the console to present the data for the first section of observed sky as a single image, the range of radio frequencies to be displayed as visible colors using the default conversion. Remembering his first hours out of the hibetank, he half expected to be told "that information is unavailable," or perhaps to see a meaningless jumble or a black screen as a result of some technical fault or some mistake he might have made, but to his relief, a recognizable image appeared. Cutting across one corner of the image was the plane of the galaxy, a bright line interspersed with brighter spots along it. Ionized interstellar gas appeared as glowing wisps, and other bright dots—supernova remnants and distant radio galaxies—were scattered here and there.

However, the image was not as sharp as it should have been, and looking at a few of the dots, he saw the problem. They were not dots but short lines, all the same length, all oriented in the same direction, as if the objects had tracked faster across the sky than the radio array had accounted for. Even if the planet was locked to its star, it was still rotating as it orbited the star, rotating once for each of its years, and that meant that in the twelve hours it took to scan one patch of sky, relative to the stars the planet had turned just a little. This should have already been compensated for, but apparently some mistake had been made, otherwise the stars would have been crisp dots rather than short lines.

He confirmed what planetary rotation rate had been used in assembling the data: 317.96 Earth days, the same as the planet's orbital period. That should have been correct. Then he instructed the console to work at the problem backward—to create a second image, aligning the data from across the twelve-hour period and then determine what rotation rate that corresponded to. The answer came—300.54 Earth days. The difference was small—small, but detectable, a little over three one hundredths of a degree difference, but that was enough to make the stars and other radio-bright objects appear as short lines rather than points.

Bering's past forty-eight hours suddenly collapsed together into a singular understanding—the light and shadow on the hills, the shifting weather, the miscalculated radio array image, and even Jaykella's fascination with migratory species. He stared at the number on the display—300.54 Earth days. Any lingering grogginess disappeared and all his senses snapped, like the second radio telescope image, into crisp focus. He felt the soft cushion of the chair under him, smelt a faint aroma from the flowers, and heard the fans of the ferry's air circulation system.

And his beating heart.

He transferred the data and the two images—the original blurred image and the corrected one—to a portable screen, then jumped from the chair and sprinted out of the ferry.

He ran toward the center point of the triangle between the three ferries. The wind was picking up again, and it carried away the small dust clouds he kicked up from the dry prairie as he ran.

Ten council members were sitting in a circle on the ground near the cairn that the three ferries had centered themselves around. A few meters away on the far side of the cairn, an eleventh, Frau Annamiek Ismail, appeared to be looking for something in the grass. When Bering got close, he stopped a respectful distance away and waited. They all glanced his way, then continued their deliberations. He waited, catching his breath while making sure that the portable screen he had brought from the ferry was ready.

"As I was saying," Youssou Watersmith explained to the council, "we have sequenced twenty-two flora genomes and two insect genomes. Among those, there was one lichen and one fungus which, based on genetic drift, are separated from any known species in our library by millions of years at least—they're probably native to this world. But for all the rest, the genetic drift suggests they diverged from known Earth species only 13,200 years ago, plus or minus 350 years. Several of them have anomalies that I suspect, way back then, were engineered, but across the bulk of the noncoding and mitochondrial DNA, they have consistently drifted 13,200 years. So, I would say that some version of the seed ship legend is true."

Fatuma Chisholm stood up. "Thank you, Sen. Watersmith. Is that all?" Watersmith nodded and Frau Chisholm called to Bering. "Young Sen. Stiles, are you delivering a message, or do you want to join our deliberations? What is it?"

"Well, um, I found something."

"Don't just stand there; come closer."

Frau Chisholm sat down, but when Bering reached the circle, he remained standing.

Then, after a few seconds of silence, all of them staring at him, he realized he did not need any further permission to speak and that they were waiting for him.

"So, umm, I was checking the radio telescope array, and I found something—something important. First, it was the wildlife Jaykella told me about. Every single bird species she saw is a migratory species, and also an antelope species, and they were all moving west."

"Bering," Youssou Watersmith bellowed, "are you talking about

201

your radio telescope or the wildlife? Please. We're busy with important things here."

Taamir Beaumont spoke up. "Let him finish." Then he turned to Bering. "But please get to the point."

Don't babble, he told himself. *They need to understand this is important.*

"Sorry," he said. "I also noticed it's getting colder, and there seems to be too much weather. And that's when I checked the first image from our radio array. The image didn't track correctly." Bering realized that Sen. Beaumont would understand, but that he would have to explain more carefully for some of the others. "It's like this. The receivers don't take an instantaneous snapshot. They're meant to track the stars as the planet slowly turns. And in that time, they collect photons for twelve hours. But the image was streaked. It didn't track properly." He stepped over to Beaumont and gave him the portable screen.

Beaumont examined the image. "I must have made an error in setting it up."

"Yes and no, Sen. The error is easily corrected if we give the planet a sidereal day of 300.5 Earth days instead of 318." Beaumont's eyes went wide. Bering pointed to the south. "And those hills—that tallest hill there, it has a shadow cast on it from that smaller hill on the right. That shadow has been slowly moving."

Fatuma Chisholm pressed her hands together in front of her mouth.

"I don't understand," said Jeremy Nakamura, looking quickly from Chisholm, to Bering, to Beaumont, and back to Bering again. "What does all that mean?"

"It means the planet is rotating. Very slowly—"

"Yes," Watersmith interjected. "It rotates exactly once for each of its orbits around Epsindi."

"No, Sen.," explained Bering. "It's rotating just a little bit faster than that."

One of the other councillors sitting on Bering's left began whispering, "No, no, no, no."

"Bering, are you saying this isn't an eyeball planet?" Jeremy Nakamura demanded.

Taamir Beaumont answered for him. "At this incredibly slow rate of rotation, it's definitely an eyeball planet. The probe sent back infrared images and measured the temperature at the substellar point to be seventy-nine degrees Celsius. And on the night side, we know it was colder than minus fifty."

"The recon probe went silent after a short time in this system," Bering added. "If it had functioned longer, we would have had more data, and maybe people would have realized. But this means the planet is not tidally locked."

"It means," Beaumont said, "this planet has a day and a night. A day lasts..." He looked down to the portable screen and tapped a calculation into it, then looked up. "About fifteen Earth years."

"Taamir," Youssou Watersmith pleaded, "this can't be right."

Frau Ismail—the council member who was not sitting in the circle but was standing on the far side of the cairn—spoke up. "It *is* right. Come here, everyone, and I'll show you." They hesitated, and she said it again, "Come. Here." The councillors all rose, and together with Bering walked over to Frau Ismail and gathered around her. "There are rocks laid out in lines in the grass. It's so overgrown it's hard to see them at all, but they are definitely arranged." She pointed down to a line of rocks at her feet. "This isn't natural; I imagine they were placed this way by our same pilgrim sister or brother who put the beacon into this cairn two centuries ago."

She traced the lines the rocks made—two parallel lines of rocks a little over a meter long joined by a third, diagonal line. "Alef," she announced, and then pointed to another arrangement of rocks to the left. "Miim." And then another and another. "Double-jay. Omega. Omega. These are letters." She pointed out all the symbols, laid out in two rows each about six meters long.

"What does it all say?" someone asked.

Then Bering and several others saw that Rosa Okonkwo was now pointing, her lips quivering but not making a sound. They all turned in the direction she pointed, to the west. The haze on the horizon had begun to clear and the setting K5 sun was visible again. In that moment, Bering realized that part of him had been hoping that he was wrong, that Sen. Beaumont would explain some simple thing he had misconstrued, but now that faint hope was smashed. They all stood gazing at the star. When they had first emerged from the ferries, just the tip of it had settled below the horizon, but now, almost half of it had sunk out of view.

"What does the message say?" Frau Ismail echoed. "It says, 'Go west. Start walking.'"

4

We have taken to referring to ourselves as "generations" even though our actual ages had nothing to do with who got revived when. The first generation, observing our new home from orbit and realizing our conclusions about it being tidally locked were wrong, decided to locate the settlement at the North Pole. It was the only place we could build to avoid the day-night cycle and its 130-degree temperature swing. I was in the second "generation," and awoke to see my friends had aged twenty years and had run out of hope.

Sadly, my generation made just as many mistakes. And we were just as stubborn as the first, clinging to our expectations for our lives on this world. I pray that you in the third generation, separated from the site of our mistakes by 3000 kilometers and 195 years, will be able to do things better than we did.

—From the third cairn epistle of Adam Leifson to the third generation

By the time the council called the whole family together for another concourse, the news had already spread. And, of course, with the sky clear, everyone could once again see the sun, see that it was slowly setting. Calculations also hinted at the significance of why the timers in the ferries and in the beacon had been set for

194.89 Earth years. It was equivalent to almost exactly thirteen planetary days.

But why not one day? Bering wondered. *Or two? Thirteen days is a hundred and ninety-five years. Why leave us that long?*

The questions were accumulating faster than answers could be found, and the gathering lurched and stumbled from one question to another and back again. If they believed what their eyes and calculations told them, that a day on this planet lasted fifteen years, and if they accepted the message written in the arrangement of rocks—"Go west; start walking"—what would that mean?

"We would walk and set up a new camp every few days," came the answer. "No village to eventually grow into a city. No new civilization. No permanent home."

"It means we would become primitives. Hunter-gatherer nomads."

"Maybe there was a mistake, a miscalculation."

"How can we travel twelve light years and not establish our colony?"

And so, they agonized over how they might build in order to survive the seven-year-long days and the seven-year-long nights. They considered domes and underground habitats. They considered trying to construct climate-protected greenhouses, and they considered eating vat-grown food for the rest of their lives since farming might be impossible. People who had a poor sense of the limitations of their abilities, even asked about finding a way to slow the planet's rotation to finish the process of tidal locking. In the concourse, and in small conversations afterward, they also talked about trying to retrofit the drop ferries. The three large ferries were designed as descent vehicles, meant to drop to the planet surface once, but perhaps a way could be found to enable at least one of them to fly again and they could use it to relocate to the North Pole. The rough map created from the recon probe's data had shown the South Pole to be a sea, so the North Pole seemed the obvious choice. In fact, it was such an obvious choice that it led people to ask, "Why didn't the ark set us down there?"

The answer came a day later when a data grain was found, wrapped in a piece of cloth and sealed inside a jar that was sealed inside another jar and interred deeper down in the cairn below where the beacon had been. It held gigas of data and hundreds of pages of notes on climate, ecology, physical geography, and geology, but the team tasked with sifting through it had found no executive summary, no editorial, no direct explanation or instructions. So the council copied it and distributed it to multiple teams, each assigned to comb through a different part of it, and when they did, a picture of the polar regions emerged. The data grain belonged to Adam Leifson, a member of the family's agriculture team who had been thirty-two years old when he went into hibernation.

According to his notes in the data grain, the first wave of pilgrims—the first "generation"—had learned that Earth life thrived everywhere on the planet except at the poles. Within one thousand kilometers of the poles was the only place where the original endemic ecosystems still survived, little affected by the species brought from Earth by the seed ship thirteen thousand years earlier. Although the poles did not experience the fifteen-year-long cycle of temperature extremes that the rest of the planet did, the weather there was chaotic and abrupt, often lurching from forty degrees above freezing to thirty degrees below within a few days, and then back again. Leifson's notes described tornadoes, which were common near the pole. And, in another section of the notes, Taamir Beaumont found a passing reference to coronal mass ejections from the star, geomagnetic storms focused on the poles, and damage to the earlier pilgrims' electrical systems.

"This is why we don't see any sign of the hundred fifty-four," Fatuma Chisholm speculated during the third concourse. "Or the smaller ferries or the cargo landers. They're at the North Pole. They tried to establish the colony there. They couldn't."

"It's unlivable," Frau Ismail added. "So, they never revived us. But Adam eventually told the ark to wait thirteen more of this planet's days and then put us here."

206

To Bering, this felt like a betrayal. He had devoted himself to the cause and to the Promise that the human race was ready to begin building a new home. He had dedicated himself to the precepts of that Promise: that it was not a largess bestowed from above, but a mission the pilgrims, and their fellow believers back on Earth, would carry out with perseverance and sacrifice; that they would live in harmony with the new worlds they reached; and that they would do better than what had been done on Earth. And, not having dared to hope that he himself would be chosen as a pilgrim, he had been rewarded, only four weeks before departure, by being added to the body of pilgrims bound for Epsindi Ta. He would finally have a permanent home, and as a junior engineer, his role in the family would be to literally help build that home.

But now, it felt as if someone was trying to take that from him. There was not even any work for him to do so that he could at least feel useful. The temporary shelters had already been built, and half the pilgrims chose to sleep on the ferries anyway. From bits and pieces of conversation he overheard over the next twenty-four hours, he learned that many people were feeling similarly betrayed. Some seemed sad, some frustrated, some angry. Many were defiant, insisting they could still find a way to move ahead with their plans to build a colony, a few even suggesting that some mistake had been made and that the apparent rotation of the planet was just a wobble or some other astronomical anomaly that had momentarily deceived them. It was those sentiments that felt most like his own as he fantasized about standing in front of someone and saying, "No! You won't take this from me!"

Some people were calling the situation a crisis, but for Bering it was simply incomprehensible. He could not make sense of it, so instead he focused his thoughts on imagining the colony post-crisis. Someone would come up with a clever mix of technologies to solve the puzzle, and then the current confusion would be just a memory.

5

*Our generation waited too long. We delayed until we had
no choice but to leave you with no choice. Please forgive us.*

*—From the second cairn epistle of Adam Leifson
to the third generation*

When only a quarter of Epsindi remained visible above the horizon, another concourse was held, at which options already rejected were revisited and rejected again. Factions began to cleave the family. Those who felt they needed to immediately start moving the camp westward were the most emotional but were in the minority. For most, the response to that was simple and straightforward, "What you're suggesting is impossible."

"Three and half years from now, the temperature here is going to be fifty degrees below freezing! And eleven years from now, it's going to be seventy-five degrees above freezing. Blindly following our plan is what's impossible! Adapting the plan and learning to live a different way—that's just inconvenient."

"So, you're saying we came to this planet to live like primitive nomads? No. I don't believe it."

Watching the fourth concourse go on like that, the deliberation becoming debate, the debate becoming mere contradiction, hit Bering viscerally. This was not the way the family was meant to operate. No one seemed to care that with each new opinion and pronouncement they were sowing strife, contention, and estrangement. Bering noticed, though, that these new cleavages did not follow the divisions between the family's five religious traditions in any way. He could not decide if that was a good sign or simply an ironic accident. *Briefly reunited just so we could find a new way to rip ourselves apart again.*

From what he could discern, the concourse ended with no real strategy. And during all this time, for two full days—two days by Earth reckoning he reminded himself, because an actual day on this world was five thousand times longer—he hardly spoke to anyone. He thought about the home he had imagined helping to build, about the Promise that had seemed for a moment to be abundantly fulfilled, and about what the Promise really meant if it was only going to be fleetingly fulfilled once every seven and a half years.

Eventually, however, he needed to share his feelings, to hear someone tell him, "Yes! Exactly!" And so, when he saw Jaykella Tahirani, the closest thing he had to a friend among the pilgrims still alive, sitting with a group of five others, he went toward them, hoping to find someone who might share, or at least empathize with, his confusion. Sitting beside Jaykella was one of the council members, Frau Annamiek Ismail, and there were three young pilgrims whose names he had not yet learned. And there was Arsen Kazakii. Remembering Arsen's disrespect of the Promise, Bering decided to just move along. But then, Jaykella saw him and invited him to sit.

"I want you to see something."

As he joined their circle, he saw that several items were spread out on the ground in front of them. The word *artifacts* came to mind. There were also neatly organized piles of various berries, mushrooms, and leaves.

"Bering's from Assiniboine," Jaykella told the others.

"I know," a tall redheaded woman replied. "He helped me get through a panic attack when I revived."

Bering did not remember her. Those first hours were all a blur.

"I don't mean he's from *the Assiniboine*," Jaykella said. "No, he's actually *from* Assiniboine, in the North American plains."

"From age six to age fifteen," Bering hedged. "I had to flee when the pogroms started. But yeah, I guess I'm from there as much as I'm from anywhere."

"Good!" Frau Ismail proclaimed, snapping her fingers as if in celebration. "A lot of the flora in this valley is native to your region. From our drones, it seems that twenty kilometers south, it's mostly African species, and twenty kilometers north, there's a mix from various places. But here, mostly species from the North American prairie." She pointed to a small pile of purple berries. "Do you recognize these? They're not blueberries."

Bering looked, then picked up a few and popped them in his mouth.

"Hey! We haven't tested those!" Jaykella blurted.

"They might be poisonous," Frau Ismail added.

Bering looked at each of them in turn as he squished the berries around inside his mouth. The gentle sweetness seemed to spread from his tongue to his whole body and then blended with a nutty, earthy flavor. The taste took him back fifteen years to his childhood—summer in the valley, canoeing on the lake, Frau Harris's berry crumble. "They're Saskatoon berries."

"Saskatoon berries?" someone asked.

"They're named after the philosopher from the early Dark Ages, Jonathan Saskatoon."

"What about these mushrooms?" Jaykella asked. "Are they edible?"

"Oh, for wild mushrooms, I wouldn't know. But aren't most of you ecologists or biologists or whatever? All I know is what I learned in summer programs at the orphanage."

Jaykella had no chance to respond. "Bering," Frau Ismail said, motioning toward some very old looking pouches, sticks and jars, "we found these in a cave. In the hills south of here. We think they belonged to Adam Leifson. The jars and bags had some dried food—almost two hundred years old." Then she pointed to the fresh berries, mushrooms, and leaves. "For each one we could identify, we tried to collect fresh specimens of the same thing."

"From our surveys, we found twenty-nine edible species so far," said Arsen. "Thirty if we can be confirmin' the mushrooms."

"There were goose bones and antelope bones in the cave too," the redhead added. She picked up a stick about three centimeters in diameter and almost a meter long with a hook and notch at one end and a groove running almost the full length on one side. "This is an atlatl—a spear thrower."

Jaykella pointed to two thinner and much longer, very straight sticks. "It's used together with these."

Bering picked one up. A shaped point was attached to one end.

"They're darts for the atlatl," the redhead explained. "The points are ground from pieces of carbon-resin composite. Maybe from a seat or a cabinet from one of the missing shuttles. And there was a handheld pheromoner—he may have been using that to help with his hunting."

The group broke into an excited discussion about learning to tan hides, their willingness or unwillingness to learn how to eat meat, and whether the owner of the items had in fact walked all the way around the planet following the setting sun.

"Man, we can actually do this," Arsen said.

"It looks as if Adam was alone," Frau Ismail added. "But we'll be working together—strength in numbers—so, yes, we can do it."

"If we stay put," Jaykella added, "we'll freeze to death in the dark. We change our plans. That's all there is to it."

Bering decided this was not the kind of conversation he had been looking for. *They actually sound as if they're glad to tell the rest of us we can't stay and start growing our crops, can't start building our home.* So he made an excuse and then slipped away. He walked away from the group, away from the three ferries and from their camp, once again wanting to be alone. He headed northward. *Any direction but west.*

He had joined the family to have a chance at something he had been denied until now—a home. But they had come to a world that was telling him he had to become a nomad, perpetually homeless, perpetually chasing the sun. No, he would not go west.

And so, he walked north. He walked nearly three kilometers until he reached the edge of the wide valley where they had landed, and then began to hike up into the hills. Once he felt he had come far enough, he chose one hill and began to hike toward the top. As he ascended, the bushes became thicker, and eventually were an impenetrable thicket.

Choosing a grassy spot below the thick tangle of bushes, he

turned to face west, and sat. For a moment he peered at the sliver of the star that was still visible above the horizon, but knowing that, like the Promise itself, it was slowly leaving them behind, he could not bear to keep looking. So as he began to pray, he closed his eyes.

He chose one of the prayers of flowering, "Your grace is plenteous; it cannot be veiled. We have abased ourselves, but with Your help we now arise. With wings that You bestowed, we soar now to our new habitation. We are Your seed, make us now worthy to flower. Make us worthy to recognize Your gift. We will accept that gift and become part of it."

The prayer seemed to bring some clarity, but no peace. He knew what they had to do. They all did. According to the legends, thirteen thousand years earlier, shortly before the end of the millennium-long era during which the human race had been united, humanity had engaged in a series of grand collective projects, beginning with restoration of the Earth and ending with the dispatching of ten or perhaps twelve automated ships that would seed other worlds. The pilgrims were agreed on at least one thing—that one of those ships had arrived here and begun preparing this world for them, making subtle adjustments to the genomes of the Earth life it chose from its libraries to ensure that each of the plants and animals it placed here would migrate, or be blown on the wind, or would set long lasting spores and seeds that would wait through the long cold nights and the long hot days. And the biology team kept finding edible species. The climate was gentle. The day and the night might be unlivable, but in the twilight in-between it was a paradise. *Your grace is plenteous; it cannot be veiled.* All they had to do to live in that paradise, Bering thought, would be to give up everything and walk—at this latitude, a mere three kilometers a day to keep up with the setting sun. Not difficult to do once, but they would have to do it every day. Forever. That meant no building houses, no farming, no village.

We'll never be in one place long enough. But you promised us a home. Haven't I shown perseverance? Haven't I sacrificed?

He considered what he had heard from pilgrims from the other four religious traditions—how they were each making sense of the situation. They had all been united in their belief in the Teacher and in the Promise that She had made, but they each understood that Promise through their own peculiar tenets and practices. The Samsarans were meditating, the Al-Mustaqimists were praying, and the Ecohumanists were debating hypotheses. Three different Samsarans he had spoken to reiterated the need to be detached, but sounding as if they themselves were anything but. In the last concourse, a Wexlerian had explained her belief that failure to heal from their collective trauma had collapsed a wave function prematurely, resulting in the illusion that the Promise had been broken. Bering heard one of the Ecohumanists, for whom all spiritual truths were emergent phenomena of complex systems, wonder aloud if the Promise had ceased to exist because now their "civilization," with a mere two hundred eighty-eight people, did not have sufficient complexity to sustain it. The Al-Mustaqimists he had engaged with, always eminently practical, had little to say about the Promise and instead were telling each other that the family just needed "to get on with it," but were unable to agree over what the "it" should be.

Two hours later, or perhaps three—he was not sure—Bering stood up, still feeling lost, and plodded back to the camp. As he neared the *Serengeti*, he saw Arsen Kazakii emerging from it carrying a large backpack apparently jammed full, his hands held out to the sides to help him balance.

When Arsen saw Bering, he quickly looked away. Then he seemed to have second thoughts, because he looked toward Bering again, waved nervously, and then kept walking, not making further eye contact.

That was just fine for Bering. He was in no mood for Arsen's incomprehensible mix of doomsaying and excited optimism. Instead, he went to find one of his engineering colleagues at the group of tents near the *Haida Gwaii* that served as their workshop. The first person he saw there was Ford Cyltemstra, sitting under a canopy, two large view screens set up in front of him, and three portable consoles beside him on a table. Now that the natural light had dimmed, a luzglobe had been hung in the canopy above him. He leaned forward in his chair, his eyes darting back and forth between two of the screens as he ate a grey vatcake.

"Bering, do you know much about excavation?"

"Just the basics, really."

"Because we don't have the materials to build our habitat above ground and construct a big, insulated dome over it. Going underground is our only option."

This was not what Bering had imagined their life on this world would look like. "So... We would live about seven years at a time underground, just coming out for a few months each planetary morning and evening?"

Ford tensed. "I came here to build!" he said. "No one's gonna stop me from doing that."

"Yeah, yeah. Me too."

Seeing that Bering agreed, Ford shifted from defensive back to enthusiastic. "I think if we could put most of the habitat between twenty and thirty meters deep, that would be enough to insulate us from the temperature swings. That's what I've been working on here—the calculations for all that."

Bering looked at the screens, one of which showed plans for a tunnel-boring machine. *While I'm busy feeling sorry for myself, Ford is actually doing something so that we can start to live here.* "Makes sense. We need a permanent place for our manufacturing base."

"I'm thinking that if we can reestablish contact with the ark, eventually we can also work toward orbital manufacturing, and ultimately put giant mirrors and shades in orbit to give us some heat and light at night and to reduce the worst of the heat in the day."

Ford was all enthusiasm and determination, and as much as Bering admired that, the idea sounded like something far beyond their capabilities. They had come equipped to provide for a colony with a starting population of four hundred sixty-nine people, not to build giant structures to terraform a whole world. But he held his tongue, and Ford continued expounding his ideas.

"Bering, this is the time of the human race's flowering. I believe that. This is our new home. And we *will* build a home here. That's what I came here to do."

Maybe he's got some details wrong. Maybe his exact plan isn't what will let us live here. But he has the right attitude.

Ford took his assistant from his pocket and looked at the time. "The next concourse is about to start," he said as he stood up.

"Another one?" Bering had not looked at his assistant in a while.

"I know, right? Blah, blah, blah. I don't understand why there's even any debate. Being humanity's seed is a mission we vowed to carry out with perseverance and sacrifice."

Exactly! He's putting into words what I haven't been able to. Listening to Ford was like looking into a mirror that showed him how he wanted to be.

"That's what I'm gonna tell them in the concourse," Ford continued. "We can conquer this place. We can sculpt it to our needs."

In that moment, the mirror shattered. *Conquer? Sculpt it to our needs? But we're supposed to do* better *than we did on Earth.*

He remembered the words of the prayer, "Make us worthy to recognize your gift. We will accept that gift and become part of it." In that moment, Bering saw again all the things he had seen over the past four and a half days, but now with different eyes. *This world is a gift, and we will become part of it.* He almost started to speak, to object to Ford's understanding of their mission, but then suddenly he remembered Arsen acting suspiciously a few minutes earlier and realized what the quirky ecologist was doing. He realized, too, that he had to move fast—there was no time to get into an argument to try to convince Ford.

"You go ahead," he said. "I'm going to skip this one."

"You sure? I'm sure at this one we'll finally decide to stop procrastinating and get on with the colonization plan."

"All that arguing and people not listening to each other wears me down," Bering replied truthfully.

"Suit yourself," Ford said, then walked off.

As people proceeded toward the gathering, Bering returned to the *Assiniboine*. He sat at a console and searched through the equipment library. When he did not find what he was looking for, he found images in the historical library and extrapolated 3D templates. He was not able to find everything he hoped to, but he decided he needed to limit the research to half an hour. By then, the ferry was quiet, everyone having gone to the concourse.

Bering rushed to the fabricators and loaded the templates he had created, and then as the printing began, he found a backpack and stuffed equipment into it—a sewing kit, a knife, twenty meters of rope, a change of clothes, and some food. But he made sure to not let the pack get too heavy and to leave room for the equipment that was still printing. At one point he stepped outside and looked around. There was no sign of people returning from the concourse yet, but he did not want to take any chances, so by the time ninety minutes had passed, he halted the fabricators and loaded what he had produced into the backpack.

He asked a console for the location of Arsen Kazakii.

<<Sen. Kazakii's assistant is not reachable.>>

He asked for the location of Jaykella Tahirani.

<<Frau. Tahirani's assistant is not reachable.>>

He asked for the location of Annamiek Ismail and got the same answer again.

They're already out of range. It doesn't matter—I know what direction they're going.

Bering put his backpack on his shoulders, exited the ferry, and began to walk. He looped far south of the *Serengeti* to avoid being seen by anyone at the concourse, then he turned west and kept walking. Two kilometers west of the landing sight, the valley began to gradually descend, and the terrain began to undulate. And then he spotted two parallel trails where the grass had been freshly trampled, pointing due west. He followed the trails until he came to a ridge that looked like a dune that had solidified in the process of cutting diagonally across the valley. It was about twice his height, and as he got closer, it blocked his view of the western horizon and the remaining remnant of the sun. He climbed and as he reached the crest, below him on the opposite slope was a group of pilgrims— Jaykella, Arsen, Frau Ismail, and more than a dozen others.

"That's not Gopal," someone said.

STEVEN BENTLEY

They all went quiet. Bering looked down at them from the ridge, a few of them standing, most sitting, each one of them with a backpack nearby. And every one of them stared back up at him, a few of them wide-eyed as if they had just been caught in the commission of a sin.

Or as if an uninvited guest just arrived, he thought.

He started slowly down the hill. "Can I...umm...I mean, I'd like to come with you. I've printed a bunch of spear points like the ones you showed me that belonged to Adam, and a couple of ax heads, and some other equipment. I think maybe I—"

Jaykella jumped up and ran to him. She wrapped her arms around him, laughing as she called out his name. Then she turned back to the others. "I told you we should have invited him."

"That you did," Frau Ismail admitted, as she stood and reached for her own small backpack. "And it just wouldn't be right if the first person to open his eyes to this world wasn't with us for the start of the journey. But clearly, he figured out what we were up to anyway."

"Bering," Arsen asked, "how, man, were you knowin'—?"

"He can tell you as we walk," Frau Ismail said. "We've dithered long enough, and we have some ground to make up. Although we only need to average three kilometers a day, if we want to catch up to where we should be, we should go at least four more kilometers before we sleep, and then eight or ten tomorrow."

"But we're supposed to meet Gopal here," the tall redhead objected. "He was staying to see what got decided at the concourse."

Frau Ismail just tilted her nose up toward the ridge crest. There, coming up over the ridge right where Bering had come, was Gopal. He bent and rested his hands on his knees and caught his breath. Clearly, he had been running.

"Gopal, your backpack is here," someone called.

Gopal loped down the hill, picked up his bag, and within seconds, everyone was up and ready to continue the journey.

As they walked, Bering listened to the conversations around him, and to the strange mix of elation, humor, and sadness. Jaykella fell into step beside him and, when he caught her glance, he smiled warmly.

"We should have stolen a ground transport," someone laughed.

"You're only saying that because your pack is too heavy," another one answered. "Did you stuff a plow in there? Or just your geological samples?"

"Gopal, what news from the concourse?"

"Well, some—Wow!—some unexpected news. Not all the Earth species we're seeing were brought here 13,000 years ago. Someone captured one of those goats I saw, and when Watersmith couldn't find Arsen, he sequenced the genome himself. The goat was descended from DNA in the ark's gene library, separated by about fifty or sixty generations. So, for goats, that should be about two hundred years. That means those weren't seed ship goats I saw; they were *our* goats—or, you know, their descendants—gone feral. But not only that; Watersmith also said the goat's DNA also has some sequences from wildebeest spliced in, probably something related to migratory instincts."

"That had to be Leifson!" someone said. "He was a farming virtuoso."

"There was one other interesting bit of news at the concourse," Gopal said. "The communications team said they still haven't been able to contact the ark. But they said another beacon just started transmitting, thirty-two kilometers due west of here."

"You see! It's been two hundred years, but our brother Adam prepared things for us."

Adam, Bering thought, *and the seed ship, and the Teacher.*

"Wanna bet a third beacon farther west will start transmitting in a few days?"

"The goats, and the new beacon—that must have swayed them in the concourse."

"No," Gopal answered. "They still refuse to decide."

Some of them stopped briefly once in a while to collect leaves or berries, and someone else pointed out some antelope tracks. Eventually the conversations died away, and they walked in silence, soaking in their surroundings. As they walked, the hills to the north and south became smaller, the valley floor came to an end in front of them, and they saw that they were at the top of a small escarpment. A vast, flat prairie was stretched out in front of them, and beyond that an orange, coral, and blood-red sky. Four or five kilometers ahead was a herd of what Bering guessed was bison, the sun casting long shadows from the animals toward them. Awe and gratitude swept over Bering like a warm breeze, reminding him of a night as a child when, after his astronomy lessons and learning of the vastness of the Milky Way, he lay on his back in a field and let the night sky call to him. But he also realized that although the plain in front of them, and this whole world in fact, were minuscule in comparison to the expanse of the galaxy, the awe he felt now was greater, because this was life, life that spoke to his soul.

A wide path, trampled with countless hoof prints, showed them a way down the escarpment that was not very steep. As they followed it, Bering, still at Jaykella's side, spoke, "Do you think the others will follow us?"

"Leifson seems to have arranged things so that they don't really have any other choice."

And yet, he thought, *they still don't want to make that choice.* He thought about Ford and his zealous conviction in his interpretation of the Promise. And he also thought about how close he himself had come to mistaking his desires and preconceptions for his actual faith.

"I think we need to show them it can be done," he said.

Jaykella nodded. "Yes, but although Leifson seems to have left a second beacon for us, we don't know that there will be more after that, or other directions or help."

"Even if there isn't, he's already done so much for us. Either way, we'll just need to have faith and figure it out as we go."

"You know this won't be easy."

"The hardest part will be letting go of what we wanted this world to be. Instead, we need to accept the gift as it is and become part of it."

By the time they stopped to make camp, a bit more of the star's disc was visible above the horizon. They slept a while, and when they broke camp, a gentle breeze at their backs propelled them on.

Forty Years of
Writers of the Future

BY GREGORY BENFORD

Gregory Benford is a physicist, educator, and author. He received a BS from the University of Oklahoma and a PhD from the University of California, San Diego. Benford is a professor of physics at the University of California, Irvine, where he has been a faculty member since 1971. He is a Woodrow Wilson Fellow and a Visiting Fellow at Cambridge University. He has served as an adviser to the Department of Energy, NASA, and the White House council on Space Policy. He is the author of over thirty-five novels, short story collections, nonfiction books, including In the Ocean of Night, Foundation's Fear, The Berlin Project, Heart of the Comet *(with David Brin),* Bowl of Heaven *(with Larry Niven), and* Timescape *for which he won the United Nations Medal in Literature in 1990. A two-time winner of the Nebula Award, Benford has also won the John W. Campbell Award, the British Science Fiction Award (BSFA), and the Australian Ditmar Award. In 1995, he received the Lord Foundation Award for contributions to science and the public comprehension of it. He has served as scientific consultant to the NHK Network and for* Star Trek: The Next Generation. *He has been a judge for the Writers of the Future Contest since its inception.*

Forty Years of
Writers of the Future

Forty years... It's half the time I've been alive, and it would have seemed unimaginably long to the teenaged Army brat I once was, eagerly awaiting the arrival of Robert Heinlein's new novel, *Farmer in the Sky*, at the Army exchange store in post-WW II Japan. All the SF giants of my youth have passed in those years, and the world has changed in so many ways, some for the worse, most for the better. But through the last four decades, the Writers of the Future Contest has quietly endured, bringing together contestants from around the globe, giving bright new authors and illustrators of science fiction and fantasy a chance to shine.

For me, personally, those years have been a breathtaking journey. In 1983, when the Contest was first established by L. Ron Hubbard, I was still a relatively new author, with eight short (by today's standards) novels published. What on Earth was I doing on a judges' panel with luminaries like Algis Budrys, Theodore Sturgeon, Jack Williamson, and Roger Zelazny?!? Even the other relatively "new kid," Robert Silverberg, was a published novelist since 1955, and had won a Hugo in 1956, when I was fifteen. I was almost too overwhelmed to dare talk to any of the other judges.... Almost! Soon after, though, I found myself going to dinner with Budrys and A. E. van Vogt, who had been a friend of Hubbard since the 1940s. We went to van Vogt's favorite Mexican restaurant, and during the delicious meal, Budrys and van Vogt got into a friendly debate as to which of them was the more successful author. As we passed a bookstore on our way back, they decided to determine this status by the number of titles each had present there. Van Vogt was immensely pleased to win their informal contest, by two books, if I recall correctly, and smiled all the way back to the hotel. I somehow managed to contain my overly analytical physicist side, and not point out that books on the shelves were still *unsold*, and therefore the best way to accurately measure *success* would be to learn how many books had already been purchased! Friends say it was the first and only time I so restrained myself....

That evening, though, was a turning point in how I saw other authors. Here were two men of staggering talent. Van Vogt's *Slan* and "Black Destroyer" were truly seminal works. The latter story, of a ferocious alien hunting down a starship's crew, has inspired so many other SF stories and films, it's practically become a trope in itself! And Budrys was author of the much-lauded *Rogue Moon* and a renowned editor who Stephen King extolled as the first to send a letter of rejection with encouragement to keep him on the path. Yet here they were, arguing good-naturedly *over the numbers of books they'd each sold*, when their true impact, in changing how people see and deal with the world around them, was so much greater than could ever be summed by dry figures, large or small. It was a revelation, both about how self-perspective often fails us, and about the sameness of human nature—regardless of worldly success—and of its need for personal validation by one's peers. It cemented my determination to just concentrate on writing the best stories I could, and to let my sales, and the critics, fall where they would. I still rarely read reviews of my own work.

As a bit of an aside, if I was speaking directly to one of our contestants—something I never get to do while judging, since all entries are carefully kept anonymous—I'd advise them that while it's vital to accept and learn from constructive critique, one of the essential qualities an author needs to develop is a thick skin against *unimportant* criticism. And I'd remind them that, when you come right down to it, it's not literary critics who hold real importance—your *readers* are the ones who truly matter! You tell your stories for *them*, not for anyone else, and your impact on this world will depend solely upon how your words shape their hearts and minds. If they truly care about what you have to say, you're a success as a writer! And no amount of critical acclaim can redeem you, if you fail to make that emotional connection. But if you *do* reach your readers, creating characters and tales that they love, they'll seek out your work, in whatever form, and sales will follow. Critics come and go, with no statues built in their honor, as the great Finnish composer, Jean Sibelius, tellingly said. But as Phillip K. Dick once told me, when I was feeling down about a harsh review of an early story, "There's no compliment more sincere than a royalty check!"

The many friendships that have formed and grown in the years of the Writers of the Future Contest have been some of the finest of my life. Zelazny, whom Neil Gaiman names as the single author who most influenced him, wrote prose that remains some of the most lyrical and astonishing in our genre. The words burst into flames in your mind. There was the inimitable Anne McCaffrey, who, following the loss of C.L. Moore, gleefully and irreverently saved us from becoming a stodgy bunch of Old White Men, and who brought in razor-sharp insight and a near-uncanny ability to analyze character development and emotional resonance. There was Jerry Pournelle, whose extraordinary talent for seeing the strengths and weaknesses of action sequences was fully matched, maybe exceeded, by his personal courage and indomitable will. His good humor and dauntless refusal to ever give up, following a severe stroke, has been deeply inspirational to me during my own medical recovery and rehabilitation this past year. Whenever I'm tempted to throw in the (figurative) towel, I can almost hear Jerry laughing at me, misquoting *The Hitchhiker's Guide to the Galaxy*, and telling me, "At least *I* always knew where MY towel was—I even brought it to the Writers of the Future awards banquet...!" And Larry Niven, coauthor and collaborator on an entire series of bestselling novels during the last two decades. My life would have lacked so much laughter and zest without his steadfast friendship and subtly sparkling humor, all throughout the sixty-plus years that we've known each other.

You really get to know a person when you're discussing and analyzing stories, especially when the discussion turns heated! And it often did, since the quality of the Contest judges has always been stellar, and there's a great deal of self-confidence in knowing you've achieved competence in your craft. As different as we are, in political views, education, experiences, ethnicity, and gender, we're very much alike in that we respect each other's judgment and insights as fellow professionals. We all tell stories that people care about—that they're willing to pay good money to read!—and we understand how difficult it is to sustain such a degree of creativity, year after year.

That's what I think is the real beauty of this Contest—that it nurtures hope, inspires creativity, and supports the next generation of Dreamers and Creators, in a world which discourages thinking beyond the demands of our own everyday lives. L. Ron Hubbard, alone of the Golden Age of Science Fiction writers, set out to create an institution that would last beyond his own lifetime, that would give back to a genre of literature that had brought him success and wealth enough to achieve his dreams. He saw the Contest as a way to make sure that new voices in SF would have both a forum to be heard and an audience that would hear them. He created a literary greenhouse, a thriving garden in a harshly unforgiving environment, where new authors could develop their skills, discover what worked for them, and grow! This Contest has inspired so many people, and has brought multiple generations of new writers to publication, in a way no other science fiction author ever did. It's an ongoing example of "paying it forward," in the finest of ways.

We Contest judges come from wildly varying backgrounds, ranging from tiny towns no one's ever heard of, to glittering megalopolises, but our love for science fiction unites us. It's the most inherently hopeful genre of literature, since the existence of any future, no matter how bleak or dystopian, presupposes that humanity has survived, and can still overcome its problems, can still improve, can still live, and love, and learn from its mistakes.

We lose sight of that hope sometimes, when the distilled pain of the world, poured into our minds through nonstop news from every side, threatens to overwhelm us. But we LIVE in the future—a future our ancestors could never have imagined!—and what we make of this world, and any others we may eventually reach, is in our hands. We now have the ability to cure or prevent diseases that, through most of human history, killed half of all children before their fifth birthday. The humblest neighborhood markets stock fresh fruit and vegetables, year-round, that no medieval member of the French or English nobility, no matter how wealthy, could have obtained or enjoyed. We can READ, as a basic skill taught in PUBLIC SCHOOLS, and the amount of information any one of us can access is beyond the grandest ambitions of the librarians of ancient Alexandria. We go about our daily routine, chatting with friends all around the world, using handheld communication computers a million times more powerful than the ones that took Neil Armstrong to the Moon! And we take these wonders for granted, most days. We live in an age of marvels, and all too often, we don't even realize it....

So, yes, I live in hope. I still dream of a world *worth* living in, a world we could build, a world that our children, and their children, and all the future generations, down through the ages, could cherish, guard, and love. And that hope keeps me working for that future, to make those dreams more substantial, tangible, and REAL, than just one man's fond fantasy.

This Contest, which so nurtures and encourages my fellow Dreamers and Worldbuilders, is very much a reflection of that hope.

—Gregory Benford,
December 20, 2023

It Seemed Like Just Yesterday

BY DEAN WESLEY SMITH

*Considered one of the most prolific writers working in modern fiction,
New York Times and USA Today bestselling writer, Dean Wesley Smith
published over two hundred novels and over eight hundred books in forty
years, and hundreds and hundreds of short stories. He has over thirty
million copies of his books in print.*

*At the moment he produces novels in four major series, including the
time travel Thunder Mountain novels set in the old west, the galaxy-
spanning Seeders Universe series, the cold case mystery series, Cold Poker
Gang series, and the superhero series starring Poker Boy.*

*During his career, Dean also wrote a couple dozen Star Trek novels,
the only two original Men in Black novels, Spider-Man and X-Men
novels, plus novels set in gaming and television worlds. Writing with his
wife Kristine Kathryn Rusch under the name Kathryn Wesley, they wrote
the novel for the NBC miniseries* The Tenth Kingdom *and other books
for Hallmark Hall of Fame movies.*

*He wrote novels under dozens of pen names in the worlds of comic
books and movies, including novelizations of almost a dozen films, from
X-Men to* The Final Fantasy *to* Steel *to* Rundown.

*Dean also worked as a fiction editor off and on, starting at Pulphouse
Publishing, then at VB Tech Journal, then Pocket Books, and now at
WMG Publishing where he and Kristine Kathryn Rusch serve as executive
editors for the acclaimed Fiction River anthology series. He took over the
editorship of the acclaimed* Pulphouse Magazine *in 2018.*

It Seemed Like Just Yesterday

Let me try to set the scene for you.

The back room of the famous Chasen's Restaurant, the place where the movie stars used to gather and Oscar parties were held.

I was thirty-four and wearing the only sports jacket I owned. All the other young writers and their spouses were dressed like it was a prom night. Some were so young, it wasn't that long after their proms.

I had no idea what all of this was about, but the Writers of the Future Contest had paid for my wife and I to go to Hollywood, so I figured it must be something.

And we were in Chasen's.

About fifty of us sat toward the back of the room around large round tables covered in white tablecloths. We all had drinks of one type or another. I had an iced tea. We all sort of talked in hushed whispers. I remember that.

My wife, LaDene, was with me at the time and we were sitting with Nina Kiriki Hoffman who was a good friend and also had a story in the first book. I did not know one other person in the room besides Algis Budrys, the editor of the book, but I most certainly recognized two tables full of major writers.

They were all talking and laughing loudly and ignoring completely the rest of us. As I came to learn later, they were all in convention comfortable clothes meaning whatever they wore that day normally they wore to the ceremony.

The two tables closest to a foot-high stage with a narrow

podium were jammed-packed with the top names in science fiction and fantasy. I recognized Frederik Pohl, Harlan Ellison, Robert Silverberg, Greg Bear, Roger Zelazny, and Jack Williamson among others.

(Little did I know as the years went by, I would become friends and work with all of them.)

Algis Budrys (AJ) seemed to be hurrying around in his tux, doing last-minute things, way overdressed for everyone else in the room. Finally, he came up to me at my table and said, "Dean, I want you to be the first across the stage. I'll call your name."

I said sure. I figured he thought I had the best chance of not tripping since I was older. Turns out I was first because my story was not a top three winner. Jack Williamson had loved the story and forced AJ to put it in the book.

A few minutes later AJ had rounded up Roger Zelazny, Robert Silverberg, and Greg Benford to the small stage. I remember it being fun to watch him try to herd major writers to do anything and Roger and Bob would not put down their drinks.

He gave a short speech thanking L. Ron Hubbard for starting this and helping new writers get started.

Then he called my name and read the title of my story and to applause I stepped the one step up on the stage (without tripping), got handed a framed award, shook hands with the three up there and stepped off the stage in front of AJ who was already calling the next name.

I have a wonderful picture of that moment, shaking Greg's hand while in the background Silverberg sips his drink.

The next morning my wife and I flew back to Oregon, never once thinking the Contest and that award ceremony in that back room of the famous restaurant would grow into what it is today. Not that I didn't believe it could. I'm just not that smart to imagine it happening.

So what has happened to me over the last forty years?

A lot, to say the least.

One month after I got home from the ceremony, my house burnt down and I lost every bit of my writing except for the few things that were published. (We wrote on typewriters in those days.) And that fire also signaled the end of my marriage.

One year later, I was trying to get back to writing and was working as an assistant manager at a restaurant and bar when AJ called me and asked if I wanted to attend a special writer's workshop, an experiment that the Writers of the Future Contest was testing. (It turned into the class they do ahead of the ceremony every year.)

The instructors for one week were Frederik Pohl, Gene Wolfe, Jack Williamson, and Algis Budrys. He was only inviting what he considered the top twelve new writers in the country.

Of course I said yes. Duh. Even though I had no money to get there and hadn't written much since the fire.

The workshop was free, but we all had to pay all other expenses. And it was in Taos, New Mexico.

And it started in one week.

I dropped everything and headed out the next day.

I met Kristine Kathryn Rusch there, and we have never really been apart since then.

As for my writing, I sort of followed in the footsteps of L. Ron Hubbard. I wrote across all genres and under many names. I have written over two hundred novels, again under many names and five hundred plus short stories. One year alone for my seventieth year, I published over seventy major books and another sixty-four short stories.

I have managed to publish around eight hundred major books with my name as either author or editor on the cover.

In the old days, when bestseller lists still mattered, I hit just about every bestseller list under one name or another, and one year alone for New York publishers in the 1990s, I published thirteen different novels. (Yes, a bunch of pen names.)

I am considered one of the most prolific living (and still working) writers in the world.

I even have my own monthly magazine with seventy thousand words of only my work in it.

At one point in the late 1990s, an editor named John Ordover came up with an idea to help new writers break into writing Star Trek. We copied the format of Writers of the Future and I became editor. And only judge.

For ten years straight, I read the thousands of stories to get the top twenty-seven and we put out the Star Trek anthology *Strange New Worlds*, launching a bunch of top writer's careers. And then after that I was invited to be a judge in Writers of the Future.

By my best count, I have attended twenty-one of the thirty-nine award ceremonies so far, including the one in the UN. I have written articles and stories for the volumes and I do a lot of teaching to help new and up-and-coming writers, pushing them to submit to Writers of the Future Contest every quarter.

So would I be here without the Writers of the Future Contest? I honestly don't know. But Algis Budrys and Jack Williamson believed in me enough to include my story in that very first volume and then be wonderful friends and mentors for decades afterward.

And Algis Budrys introduced me to the love of my life and I can't imagine making this forty-year writing journey without Kristine Kathryn Rusch walking beside me.

So it has been a great career. A great life.

And an amazing forty years.

But honestly parts of it seemed like they were just yesterday.

Shaman Dreams

written by
S. M. Stirling

inspired by
DAN DOS SANTOS'S *STARCATCHER*

ABOUT THE AUTHOR

S. M. Stirling was born in France in 1953 to Canadian parents—although his mother was born in England and grew up in Peru. After that he lived in Europe, Canada, Africa, and the US and visited several other continents. Steve graduated from law school in Canada but had his dorsal fin surgically removed, and published his first novel (Snowbrother, Signet) *in 1984. He became a full-time writer in 1988, the year of his marriage to Janet Moore of Milford, Massachusetts, who he met, wooed, and proposed to at successive World Fantasy Conventions. In 1995 they suddenly realized that they could live anywhere and decamped from Toronto, that large, cold, gray city on Lake Ontario, and moved to Santa Fe, New Mexico. Steve became an American citizen in 2004.*

His latest books are Conan: Blood of the Serpent *(Titan Books, December 2022) and* To Turn the Tide *(Baen Books, August 2023), the first in a new time-travel series with five Americans from 2032 dumped in 165 CE. His hobbies mostly involve reading—history, anthropology, archaeology, and travel, besides fiction—but he also cooks and bakes for fun and food. For twenty years he also pursued the martial arts, until hyperextension injuries convinced him that he was in danger of becoming the most disabled person in human history. Steve has been a judge for the Writers of the Future Contest since 2021.*

About this story Steve tells us: "I was given an intriguing painting, the cover for this volume. I decided it was a prehistoric shaman contemplating the La Brea Tar Pits... and that gave me the first scene! The rest flowed from there."

ABOUT THE ILLUSTRATOR

Well known for his colorful oil paintings, most often depicting strong women, Dan dos Santos's work spans a variety of genres, including novels, comics, film, and video games. He has worked for clients such as Disney, Universal Studios, Activision, Boeing Aircraft, Scholastic Books, The Greenwich Workshop, Penguin Books, Random House, UpperDeck, Hasbro, DC Comics, and many, many more.

Dan has been the recipient of many awards. He is a Rhodes Family Scholarship winner, a five-time Hugo Award nominee for Best Artist, and has received both Gold and Silver Medals from Spectrum: The Best in Contemporary Fantastic Art. *His illustrations have graced the #1 spot on the* New York Times *bestseller list numerous times and his covers are seen in bookstores in dozens of countries around the world. He has been an Illustrators of the Future judge since 2019.*

Dan shared the following about this volume's cover art.

"When I was tasked to create the cover for the newest volume of L. Ron Hubbard Presents Writers of the Future, *I knew I wanted to create something not just fantastic that lived up to previous covers, but I wanted to create something which specifically spoke to the history of this wonderful book and to both the Writers and Illustrators of the Future Contests.*

"When artists Larry Elmore, Tom Wood (both cover artists for previous volumes) and I visited Los Angeles last year for the annual workshop and awards ceremony, we took a trip to the La Brea Tar Pits. Then I knew I had the inspiration I needed for my cover.

"Since their inception, the Writers and Illustrators of the Future Contests have called Los Angeles home, and what could be more LA than the Tar Pits!

"During our visit to the museum, I took lots of photos, enjoying the incredible amount of tusks and skeletons that archaeologists have dredged up from the depths of these ancient tar pits.

"For this cover piece, which I entitled Starcatcher, *I envisioned a fictitious time in prehistoric LA, where the Chumash tribe, well known for their decorative face paint, live among an active tar pit.*

"I'm honored to have been asked to create this cover, and hope that this image will elicit the same sense of wonder and imagination that the stories contained within this latest volume will undoubtedly hold for its readers."

Shaman Dreams

Autumn

Strong-Far-Spear was humming his death-song to himself as the Horned Men trotted near. You never knew—unless you were a shaman like Sees-Much-Everywhere, and even she didn't know everything.

The rock he hid behind had a crack that let him see them approach. He remained stock-still—movement drew sight—and controlled his breathing, glad that he'd insisted they'd pick this spot to ambush the pursuers. This would be the third clash in the last two days, and this day was nearly over. That would give the nursing mothers and the children time to flee, as he drew the attackers away from them. The scent of his own sweat was harsh in his nose, under the sweetness of sage and crushed grass.

"Now, Real People! Now, Hunters!" he shouted as he leapt to his feet.

The atlatl, the spear thrower, was already in his right hand with a finger holding the long-feathered dart in place. He took a skipping step forward and put his whole lean muscular body into the throw, as the atlatl added three feet to the length of his arm. The dart arched out, and twenty paces away the head of the Horned Men's scout snapped up. That was too late; the feeling of the throw had been so sweet, so right. As it always was when the hunt was going well. A failed hunt meant empty bellies. This hunt was for his people's lives.

Thunk!

The dart sank half its length in the Horned Man's chest just as his face turned from slack surprise. Blood burst from his mouth, the horned headdress pitched far back as he teetered on his heels and then fell.

Before it struck, two hands of darts were on their way. About half killed or wounded; terrible losses even for the numerous enemy band and meant struggle and hunger for years. A few paused to throw back—only one of the Real People was lightly wounded, though.

The rest of the Horned Men turned and ran pell-mell. Except for the masked form of their shaman. He chanted, danced, then thrust a wand made of a carved human thighbone.

Two cave lions loped forward. They were young males, only the weight of two big men, not of four or five as a full-grown lion would be. But they were terrible enough, tawny on top and pale below, their paws huge, each with ten hooked knives, their lips drawn back from long yellow-white fangs as they charged.

"Together, Hunters! Throw!"

He shouted it as he fitted a new dart to his atlatl. The others responded, not with a unified volley but with carefully aimed shots. One of the lions went down. Not dead—their lives were fastened hard to their deadly bodies—but mortally wounded. The other turned and fled with a dart through his rump and another in his shoulder, limping...and ignoring the shaman's magic. That spirit-walker took to his heels too.

The hunters of the Real People sent shrill screams and whooping cries of joy after them. One or two started to pursue.

Strong-Far-Spear leapt forward in a bounding run, knocking an enemy down with his shoulder and swinging his atlatl in an arc that had the other stopping frantically as it nearly touched their nose.

"Run!" he barked to them. "Run! We want the Horned Men to chase us. Every step is life for our kin, our people. Run!"

He suited words to action, and they followed, heads down to avoid looking into the setting sun as they descended the pass into the broad valley that ran north–south here. He thought grimly of

Sees-Much-Everywhere; perhaps she could deal with the enemy clan's shaman.

For some reason, his thoughts continued to sway back to her as he wolf-trotted with his band—to her as it had been in spring, at the end of the rains.

When life had been good...

The end of the previous spring

The Lake of Death always smelled odd. And strong, in a way that overrode the natural smells, the damp earth of the rains, the green of growing things, the rank musk where a sabertooth had sprayed the boundaries of its territory.

It wasn't the rotting stink of the many animal carcasses; that was the same anywhere. Beneath that ran an odd smell unlike anything else in her thirty years of life.

Sees-Much-Everywhere thought it must be the sticky black stuff that underlaid the deceptive pools of water, the thing that made this the Lake of Death. Folk took some from the edge to seal the sides of wicker baskets so they'd hold water easier than carving out vessels from hard wood with fire and volcanic glass.

Spirits were supposed to lurk beneath the lake, hungry and patient and hostile to all life.

She'd never seen them when spirit-walking herself, but it was only sensible to think that there must be such. Why else would this unique thing be here otherwise? Nobody else among the Real People dared walk so far out into the deadly waste, even with wooden blocks in the sticky stuff making a path for their feet. Those had sunk deep over the years, and had to be replaced, but hard wood was common around here—the land was rich, with many trees and tall grassland that fed well the beasts the Real People hunted.

They had come here in her grandmother's grandmother's time. Without having to fight for the fine land and rich seacoast, because there had been no two-legs of any description here; they'd come far enough that the Horned Men, who they'd fought back in the old land northeast of here, never raided.

DAN DOS SANTOS

Here they had prospered, their own dead being the first human spirits to take up forever-life in the shadow this land cast in the Otherworld, just as they had been the first to claim it here in short-life. Steering the beast-clans and tree-clans and fish-clans from there, for the good of their blood-kin. That was what your ancestral spirits did.

She'd seen them often enough, including her own mother. Who still nagged her.

Get ready! Get ready! Idle girl, lazybones, the Real People will need you!

It echoed in her ears, that familiar grating, hectoring tone.

She glanced up at the stars, at the Moon Lady sinking huge and yellow into the distant sea beyond the low oak-studded hills. This would be the last big hunt of the cool season; after this they'd pack everything useful and carry it to the shore, for the fish and shellfish.

Sees-Much-Everywhere was partial to baked acorn-flour cakes stuffed with oysters, seasoned with herbs by her sister, Gives-Good, who had no skill with big spirits, but an unequaled command of the smaller ones who ruled things like tasty herbs. And she knew just how long to cook something in ashes. She also had a sideline in medicinal teas to sooth pain and illness.

"Yes, Mother, yes, Mother," Sees-Much muttered, and came to her feet as the bony face and empty eyes faded from the place inside her head.

Glancing up at the stars, she saw it was not long to dawn; there was already a trace of light in the east, toward the White Salt Mountains.

Though that name wasn't really a true name; it was the hideous stuff that water turned to in bad cold that made them gleam. She made a complicated sign with her left hand to avert the bad luck that came with thinking of ice and snow. The oldest stories told of how that had covered the whole land when the Real People lived far, far, far to the north. Where Death stalked ceaselessly, every minute of day and night, sliding over the expanses of…

Salt, she made herself think.

Here it never came down to the rich lowlands, where all you ever needed on the coldest night was a cloak with fur on the inside and the outside rubbed with tallow to waterproof it.

And a good fire, of course.

A rumble from the westward and a shine of light beyond the big spreading oaks that were shadows against a sky still full of stars and Moon Lady. She shed her heavy great-sloth cloak and rose, pulling down the carved and painted wooden mask that turned her face into a mere suggestion and narrowed her here-in-short-life vision through the slits so that she could see the Otherworld more clearly.

She began to dance, swaying and pirouetting, singing the Song of Living Ivory. Words that were so ancient she barely understood them and didn't say in the way the First Ones had spoken them, but that gave added power. She could feel the weight of them on her tongue.

Sure enough, soon sight confirmed what the rumbling sound had hinted; before the fires the hunters' torches had lit, ran two mammoths—a grown female and her yearling. Their hides were sparsely covered in reddish hairs; the female's tusks curled upward, and both had their trunks lifted like upraised hands.

Saliva flooded her mouth as she looked at the youngster and thought of its liver grilled over a fire and sprinkled with her sister's herbs from the pouch at her belt. You didn't eat the day before a hunt like this, of course. Her mother would never have let her hear the end of it if she'd sneaked a single berry or bug.

Nor would Strong-Far-Spear, if the hunt didn't go well. The men and the smaller number of women who ran with the hunting-pack looked to him as a model, and followed his words very often. Eventually the Real People would grow so many here that some would split off to form a new clan. Over one quarrel or another, or just for better hunting and fresher gathering, but that would take more years—the rest of her life, probably.

The Song of Summoning floated out, mixed with the trunk-tossing trumpeting and the thunder of heavy feet. The shrill enraged squealing of the mother mammoth and the higher, shriller sounds of the calf's fear were increasingly loud, and swarms of birds wafted skyward like skeins of smoke, thick as fog.

Sees-Much wove that into her song. You used what came to hand. Mammoths were scarcer now, for some reason. This was a prize! The lovely, lovely meat—and the hide, toughest of all leathers—and all the things that could be carved from the ivory, so pretty and so strong. The long red hairs could be woven into protective amulets to be worn around babies' necks...oh, there was a use for everything!

She waved the loop-ended ivory wand overhead, catching and twisting and directing the flows of energy, of thought, of fundamental being that made up the world beyond the veil.

See, no need to turn and fight the two-legs, the flows she bent said. Through the water ahead—they cannot follow. Safety for your calf! You might fall if you fight! You dare not leave it alone!

The song floated out. So did threads of power she saw as colored filaments, red and blue and green and colors that had no names. Weaving a net around the great beasts to the movements of her graven ivory guide, luring, cajoling, commanding.

Behind the big animals, fires burned, throwing pillars of black into the lightening sky. She could scent the blazes now as they ran through the tall grass. It would burn even now at the tail end of the rains, but there was less risk of it getting out of hand, which could be dangerous. Animals nearly all ran from fire, which was the gift of the ancestor-spirits to their living descendants. Fire was a thing halfway between the worlds.

The dance took her out of herself in the magic hour of dawn. Behind the mammoths, dots grew; her people, pursuing the stuff of life for themselves and their kin. They waved their spears and long-feathered darts the atlatls threw, and screamed—the howl of wolves, the shriek of the great cats, the rising-falling sound that was unique to the two-leg kind. Sees-Much could feel her power reaching out, clouding the mammoths' minds with fear....

Water sprayed up from pounding feet as the great reddish-brown beasts plowed into the water. It flew up around them...but

241

it was a shallow covering over the black sticky stuff. Their squeals turned to unmitigated panic as they bogged down immediately.

The hunters threw down their torches and came on smoothly. She ended her song with a flourish and stood with her feet spread and her arms making a V.

Sees-Much also watched with appreciation as Strong-Far-Spear made his first run, ending with a lithe twist of his long arms. The dart flew from his atlatl and plunged into the calf's body, sinking right to the feathers. Blood flew out of its trunk as the sharp obsidian edges of the dart worked back and forth in its lungs with the effort of its attempts to tear itself loose of the tar. In a few moments its squeals died down and it slumped.

The mother's fear turned to rage, and it tried to turn, managing to rip one forefoot free. On firm ground it would have been deadly dangerous, though that didn't stop hunter-bands from tackling the beasts occasionally. This was much safer: a dozen darts struck it within the time of as many breaths, and then more and more. Its mouth and trunk ran with blood; its enormous bowels voided; then it slumped in turn, its great head bowing before the all-powerful spirit known as Death.

Sees-Much walked ashore along the line of brush and wooden blocks, then removed her mask and carefully, ceremoniously wrapped it and stowed it in a bag of tanned hide. Others looked aside as she did that. The mask was an ancient thing of power.

She led the hunters in the Song of Thanks, praising the beasts' spirits and explaining that their deaths were part of the Real People's life. Sees-Much winced a few times; not all her clan were capable of carrying a tune, but all who'd cast darts must join, for fear of vengeance from the Otherworld. While she was singing she was conscious of Far-Spear's clean scent, and the handsome cast of his face as it was framed by the many small braids of his hair. Not as important as his hunting-skill and beast-sense, of course.

Except of importance to me, sometimes, she thought.

She was amused at Far-Spear's covert glances, behind her grave demeanor, and conscious of a rising heat. Anticipation lent more depth to pleasure, with that as with hunger.

The hunters bowed in acknowledgment of her singing the beasts into the trap, covering their eyes for an instant with their right hands. Sees-Much nodded in regal answer, and gave Far-Spear a slight smile. He grinned back at her.

Then the rest of the tribe came up. Many were carrying bundles of branches and rushes, bound with woven grass. They threw them into the tar, making a path out to the dead beasts. The hunters waded out first, wary until they were sure the animals were dead, then slashing them and drinking the first blood that was the hunter's right, or cutting out bits of tongue and hump-meat to eat raw, also theirs by right. Far-Spear handed Sees-Much a slice from the calf's hump, and she chewed with enjoyment; the meat was meltingly tender and strong tasting without being overwhelming.

While the hunters rested... or joked and wrestled and basked in the admiring glances of youngsters and in a different way, of women... the rest got to work.

Long rows of frames were set up, to dry the strips cut from the carcasses after the hide had been flayed. Leather bags of salt from the shore of the Big Water were unpacked from the travois dragged over the oak-dotted plain. Some of the grown men went out again and fastened thick rawhide ropes to the calf, and everyone—with a few exceptions like Sees-Much and Far-Spear—tagged on to drag it from the grip of the tar, dragging it up on the bank with a triumphant rush and shout.

Others were gathering firewood, or walking out along the roads of brush to butcher the adult as far as they could, stripping off blanket-sized swaths of hide, then laying them flat to carry loads of meat and organs and useful bones to the shore. A deft youngster with a bone-handled ax in her hands climbed up on the head of the big female to chop the tusks free of the spongy bone of the beast's skull, and then to split the skull and scoop out the toothsome brains into a clay-lined basket. More dragged the

S. M. STIRLING

tusks ashore, set them up—they were taller than the tallest of the Real People, even curled as they were—and made offerings of salt and smoke before them.

The elation of the crowd grew, jests and banter flying back and forth, laughter loud, children running wildly filching morsels and running off with squeals of their own. Some hunters kept watch—the smell of blood and meat might draw dire wolves or bears or big cats, despite the warning scent of fire. Nothing was needed except a few shouts and waved spears or torches this time, though after a sabertooth pack reluctantly departed mothers and older siblings were more careful with toddlers able to run but still too brainless to be wary. Some of the older women called their children and began to lay out fuel for bonfires in a half-circle around the meat. Nighttime would be more dangerous.

Birds waited in the trees, vultures and even some eagles. They knew their patience would be rewarded...and they could skim out to feed safely. The land-bound predators would try, but a few of them usually bogged down and died too. Particularly the sabertooths, who were notably slower of wit than wolves and lions.

After hours of work, the long racks of poles lashed together were covered in strips of flesh hanging over small, smoky fires. The smoke helped preserve it, as did the rubbing with salt. The heat drove out water. And both helped keep flies at bay too, together with coverings of woven grass. Sees-Much gorged at last on skewers of the calf's liver with mushrooms from shady gullies nearby, and grinned at her sister as she took her bark plate and sank cross-legged among her clan folk.

Far-Spear was not far away, tearing at a lump of grilled heart, charred on the outside and bloody within. Juice ran down his strong chin, and he grinned at Sees-Much as the sun sank behind the hills to the west. Her gaze travelled down to his loincloth, and she grinned back as she noticed what it covered now. Couples were stealing away from the fires that cast circles of light, beneath the bright Moon Lady. Sparks spiraled upward; with the howls and snarls that came from beyond the evenly spaced line of bonfires, they didn't go very far. Just enough to be in shadow.

"I will go contemplate the stars," Sees-Much said to the first among the tribe's hunters.

"There is much wisdom in the stars," Far-Spear intoned, and they shared a quiet chuckle. "I will come and guard you from the sharp teeth. If you wish," he added hastily.

"That is generous of you, Strong-Far-Spear," Sees-Much said gravely. "You were fierce as a lion today, cunning as a wolf, strong as a bear!"

"You were as wise and spirit-strong as your mother and mother's mother and mother's mother's mother before you," he replied with equal solemnity in his deep gravelly voice. "Your song kept the mammoth-kin running before us, as much as our spears and fire. If the big beast had turned, some of us might have died or been gravely hurt."

That was the more amusing because it was true, as they both knew. Sees-Much could hear-feel her own mother chuckling indulgently and withdrawing to the depths of her mind. She rose and wrapped her fur cloak about her, and paced into the darkness. Far-Spear followed, gravely deferential and a pace or two behind.

Early summer

The next few days were busy; even Sees-Much had to spend a good deal of her time spirit-walking to make sure that everything went as it should. There was no late rain, so the meat dried well, and she took the thanks of all concerned with a silent, secret smile.

I couldn't stop the rain, she thought to herself.

And said to her apprentice, her sister's eldest and just now under the dominion of the Moon herself and due to shed her child-name of Mare-Dancer.

"You couldn't?" the girl blurted, her eyes wide, as they walked side by side.

"No. No spirit-walker can. Only the Ancestors can, and they will not, except at great need. But you can foresee the weather, with skill. Skill at reading the signs—"

She gestured at the sky, the small fleecy clouds, and mentioned

245

her memories of how it sometimes rained at this time of year, and what her mother had taught her.

"And skill with speaking to the spirits of wind and sky."

The girl pouted. "I can't get them to speak words with me," she said sullenly.

Sees-Much used her wand to swat the girl's backside, eliciting a jump and yelp as the ivory smacked on bare skin.

"They often don't!" Sees-Much said sharply. "You must be able to tell from their faces, the way they hold their eyes; the dances they make in your dreams or after you fast and take the secret berries! Now go and help your mother—there will be much to do."

Even Sees-Much carried a symbolic pack of dried mammoth meat when they set out the next morning, and many of the hunters—including Far-Spear—helped drag the travois, loaded with the jerked meat and with the clan's goods and gear. The triangles of poles, lashed together and kept wide at the back with cross bracing and bone runners under the ends, were heavily laden.

Everyone pulling them sweated freely despite the mild weather, but they chaffed and joked or sang as they did. They were pulling what the Real People needed to live, and the successful mammoth-hunt gave them tons of reserve food to fall back on.

They'd leave the big leather tents here, buried under piles of rocks that would keep out the bigger animals. Those could be repaired when the Real People returned in the autumn, and the seashore would be warm and dry enough that they weren't really necessary.

All summer long they would fish and hunt seal and sea otter, from the shore or from the dugouts they left buried in the sand of the shore over the winter. And gathering the abundance of land-born summer to be made into blocks of dried fruit as well as gorging on the fresh. And they would gather salt, too, that most needful of sea-gifts. There would be hunting on land as well, and great feasts on salmon and sturgeon grilled over fires, or on crabs and lobsters and mussels, wrapped in seaweed with heated rocks and buried.

Youngsters would leave on their spirit-quests for their grown names, too, or just for adventure's sake.

Then when the first rains came, they would trek back here, equally burdened—with dried fish and dried berries, and brittle bags of seaweed and herbal teas and much else, and stone tools, chipped out of chert and black glass. It was the round of the Year, the life of the Real People.

Far-Spear glanced at her and nodded; he'd have checked that all was in order, and talked the right men into trotting ahead and behind and to either side, around the burdened and the young and vulnerable.

Sees-Much danced out ahead, running her wand through the air to bend the lines of force and destiny.

"Come!" she called. "Come, Real People! The sea awaits us! I see fat fish and plump oysters, and acorns lying thick as grass when the time comes. Much feasting! Come! Come!"

Autumn

The first rains had fallen when they began their trek back to the Lake of Death, just after sunrise. The air smelled fresh, and there was a scent of green after the baking heat and dryness of the end of summer—though that made preserving fish and berries and fruit easier. The travois and packs were stuffed with the land's abundance. Deer and antelope and horses watched from a distance. Birds swarmed as those from the north arrived and sought out the seasonal pools and marshes.

In the distance a giant sloth bellowed, amid the snarls of a sabertooth pack's hunting calls.

But something is wrong, Sees-Much thought, striding along with her apprentice by her side, newly renamed Quick-Otter.

The girl was listening well enough, even as she leaned into the padded tumpline across her forehead that helped with the heavy pack on her back. She gave a quick sideways glance as Sees-Much fell silent.

Something is wrong but I can't tell what... and that is wrong, too.

The summer had been good; she had seen where the fishers and hunters should go. Several were alive now that would have been dead, if she hadn't foreseen storms and kept the canoes ashore.

But now...there was a blurring that she could almost see with the body's eyes as well as those of the spirit. That tickled at her. She'd never felt the like.

An oppression, a weight on her. She even missed the nagging of her mother's spirit; it hadn't spoken to her for days....

She missed a stride. Not since we set out for the Lake of Death! Sees-Much thought.

She stopped abruptly, and threw up her arms—with her ivory loop-topped wand in one hand—both up and out, spread wide.

Behind her Far-Spear saw and trotted up. "What is it?" he said, looking up; the sun was about a third of the way up from the west. "It's too early to stop for the day," he added.

"There is something...some danger...," she said.

There was a line of big oaks along a stream not far ahead. To the eyes of her spirit, shadow laired there, like the feeling she had if a man-eater was stalking one of the Real People. It was a scent to her inner senses like the Lake of Death on a hot day well after horses had stampeded into the tar.

"Danger!" she said, pointing with her wand. "Terrible danger!"

Far-Spear squinted at the trees, sniffed the air and cocked his head to listen as she shed her own pack, pulled out her mask and slid it over her face.

"I hear only—"

Sees-Much screamed and sank to her knees. Pain lanced through her head, and distantly she felt blood dribbling down from her nose over her upper lip, tasting the salt of it.

Doll-tiny figures burst out of the woods. Sees-Much's eyes saw more than that; she saw the horned headdresses they all wore, and the padded breechclouts. And the figure that capered ahead of them, scrawny and scarred with many years of self-inflicted wounds.

"The Horned Men!"

Far-Spear paused for an instant, gaping. But only for an instant, then he turned and bellowed as he shed his pack, "Foes! Horned men! In line, all with weapons!"

Sees-Much struggled to her feet again. "There are many," she said thickly, swaying. "Flee, as our ancestors did—flee south! I will blind their spirit-walker!"

She grabbed her Quick-Otter and thrust her southward. "Run with them—the Real People must have a spirit-walker."

Then she danced—danced as her mother and mother's mother and more were suddenly with her. Whirling, leaping...and then thrusting out her looped wand of mammoth-ivory.

To ordinary eyes that was all. To her inner sight, jagged lightning flashed. The capering figure of the Horned Men's shaman stopped, staggered two steps, and fell face-forward.

She gathered her force...and then staggered herself. Suddenly the short-life world snapped back into focus.

An atlatl dart had struck her in the stomach, the feathered end standing out as pain washed through her, impossible pain, beyond even her ability to block.

Darkness washed over her as the Mothers stepped between her and the lethal wound. She could do no more, but she had struck down the enemy's shaman, and that was enough.

When Sees-Much awoke it was dark, dark save for the light of many stars and Moon Lady.

There were screams, shrill and high—but not many, from that and the smell of burned flesh. The Horned Men must have taken few captives. Without their shaman they could not have followed the Real People's flight, not with the hunter-warriors screening it and ambushing in land they knew intimately and the strangers did not for all their numbers. Far-Spear might well have sent the others on ahead and used the fighters to decoy the pursuers; it looked as if the Horned Men had lost many, and some were wounded.

The Mothers stood between her and the pain, at least enough for her not to add her voice to the sobs and shrieks. The fighters of the Horned Men had tied a hide rope to her ankles while her spirit fled for a moment. When they saw she was awake, they pulled on it, fearful of letting their flesh touch hers. She smiled through lips that bled as they dragged her toward the Lake of Death.

Here my spirit will hinder them, she thought. *I will fight for the Real People even when my breath leaves me.*

They had the rope looped around something out in the tar...and she saw it was the mother mammoth's bones, sunk deep in the sticky stuff now with only the stubs showing. Water rilled about her, cool, and then the soft surface of the tar.

"I...curse...you," she said to the enemies of her folk.

Visions flashed before her eyes as she sank; ages passed; odd-looking creatures that she recognized as human only by the fact that they walked upright, dressed in garb even stranger than the Horned Men. Mountains of crystal, and giant birds that were not birds overhead...

Then she drew one last shivering breath. Her mother was there, love on her face. And the Mothers before her, and the ranks of the Real People who had passed before. She had done what Far-Spear sought; the Real People were safe.

She rose, free of pain, and walked toward them.

The Wall Isn't a Circle

written by
Rosalyn Robilliard

illustrated by
GUELLY RIVERA

ABOUT THE AUTHOR
Rosalyn Robilliard is the pen name for sister writing team, Rose and Alice Robilliard.

Growing up in a tiny English village on the Essex coastline, their imaginations were sparked at an early age by the ancient woodland and salty marshes. As children, they drew comics, wrote stories, and constructed elaborate fairy worlds.

Later on, they shared a house in Manchester and began talking about writing stories together more seriously. Much studying and research ensued, during which they realised that writing was the only place they could really return to the freedom and imagination of their childhood. It was an escape, but also a place where they felt most at home.

When Alice moved across the country to Norwich and Rose stayed in Manchester, writing gave them the perfect excuse to stay connected, spending a few hours each week nattering away on video calls, exploring realms beyond everyday reality.

"The Wall Isn't a Circle" was born from their fascination with the past, and their longing to step back in time. An evening spent discussing the consequences of being able to drop into the consciousness of any human in history quickly grew legs and eventually ran wild as their finished story.

This is their first professional sale, and they hope you enjoy reading it!

ABOUT THE ILLUSTRATOR
Guelly Rivera is an eighteen-year-old Mexican American from Central Valley, California. Guelly was inspired to follow in her mother's footsteps by watching her mother create beautiful drawings on any paper she could get her hands on. Her mother continues to be Guelly's main inspiration

and biggest motivation to keep creating artwork and to improve. Painting has been the media she gravitates toward most. Her bedroom walls have often served as canvas for elaborately painted murals; later to be painted over to do it all again. As Guelly's art became more serious she switched acrylic for oils and bedroom walls for actual canvases, all while focusing on portraits with a surrealist style. She is motivated and excited to see how her art will evolve and where it will take her.

The Wall Isn't a Circle

A puff of purple mist curled across the stage, settling in a cloud beneath a flickering hologram of the *Titanic*. Around me, excited whispering rushed upwards through the red and gold of London's Palace Theatre.

Typical. One whiff of time travel and everyone threw their morals out of the window, too giddy to worry about who invented it. Finishing my last canapé, I brushed crumbs from the black box on my lap. Soft leather embossed with Brookvu's geometric logo in one corner, and a name, larger in the centre, MindWeb.

My phone buzzed again, four missed calls from Esther and a message from Gabby.

Good luck at the launch, Sis. Hope you get them this time. xx

"*This time.*" She could be such a cow. Rubbing my nose in it.

"Excuse me, love." A man, younger than me, but not by much, pointed to the seat next to mine. His jeans and neon-patterned hoodie were out of place amongst our suits and blouses, his own black box wedged under one arm. I stood to let him pass and he grinned through overlapping teeth.

"I'm Eddie, a.k.a. @EdPlays."

"Cool." I nodded, not wanting to prolong the conversation. Then something clicked. "You're that live streamer. Games and stuff?"

"The one and only." He smoothed back his curly brown hair.

"Macy Fletcher." We shook hands. It was such a grown-up thing to do. We were both in our early twenties, still trying to prove we had a place amongst the adults.

"Perry LLP," he read aloud from my badge. "You're a lawyer?"

We sat down, Eddie stretching out until his trainers disappeared under the seat in front.

"Legal Trainee," I admitted. "I'm hoping to qualify soon."

He raised his eyebrows, and I forced a smile. How much longer was I going to keep pretending to myself?

"Wait...*Perry*? As in *Esther* Perry?"

"She sent me on her behalf." I looked away. "She was...busy."

"*Busy*? No one's too busy for a Brookvu launch party. And Esther *Perry* of all people, I'm surprised you guys even got an invite!"

He was right. Brookvu shouldn't have invited us. It was like a criminal asking the police around for tea and scones.

"I owe her one, actually," said Eddie when I didn't reply. "Bought myself a sweet little nugget of that Brookvu cake, after the DocNav scandal." He shrugged, as though buying shares in international tech companies was how all the twenty-somethings spent their spare time.

"Great," I muttered, shoving my phone into my handbag as Gabby sent a "heart" emoji.

Another wisp of smoke curled beneath the *Titanic*, and the lights dimmed. Eddie sank deeper into his velvet seat, and I squinted at the stage. What if we *didn't* get them this time? Would that be it? Would my career be over?

"Ladies and Gentlemen, please take your seats and put your hands together for CEO and cofounder of Brookvu, Adriana Spencer-Brookes."

A ripple of jazz and drums rose then faded under the applause.

Adriana jogged onto the stage in leggings and a grey hoodie. Blonde hair in a loose ponytail, freckled cheeks gently blushed under soft lashes. She waved a French manicured hand and laughed breezily as though hanging out with friends, not launching state-of-the-art tech to a theatre packed with journalists, scientists, lawyers, and billionaire bosses. I crossed and uncrossed my legs, feeling too formal. Real women didn't wear heels anymore. They swanned about in memory-foam trainers and their boyfriend's jumper.

"Thanks, thanks! I'm so excited you're all here! Now, I know things have been a little quiet from us here at Brookvu. That we've kept you waiting. But I also know"—she lowered her voice for dramatic effect, grinned and looked down through her lashes, while cameras flashed along my row—"I know it'll be worth it."

Someone whooped in the silence, triggering applause and wolf-whistles. I rolled my eyes.

"Now! There's no time like the present, or should I say the past?" A laugh amongst the crowd. "Please go ahead and open your boxes."

Folding back the leather lid, I found two flat discs slotted between cushioned foam, an earpiece propped on top in a plastic packet.

"Everyone ready?" We all hurried to fit our headsets, pressing a metal disc to each temple. Several people laughed nervously. Eddie leaned in to whisper, "Let's roll, Bro!"

Adriana clicked a remote and the theatre vanished. I gasped as crowds surged around me, salt and mist wafting from the long dresses of slender women. Stubby men in rough suits weaving past me, smoking pipes and chattering excitedly. Seagulls squalling overhead.

I tried to step back, look around, but nothing happened. My body wasn't my own. Somebody else controlled it—a young woman, hands pale and freckled, waist thin and corseted as she pushed amongst the crowd. I *was* this woman, looking out through her eyes. I could feel her emotions; they were somehow inside my own, impatience, anticipation, eagerness to press forward. The crowd rushed ahead, and the woman glanced up, my own gaze carried with hers. And that's when I saw it. The *Titanic*. The actual, real-life *Titanic*! A ramp led up into her belly from a damp and cobbled dock.

"Can anyone guess what year we're in?" Adriana's soft voice crackled through my earpiece. "It's 1912, of course. We're taking a little trip on the *Titanic*. Don't worry! None of the nasty stuff."

255

"Kathleen! Kathleen, dear!" A wave of reluctance washed through me as my body turned to face a squat Edwardian woman. "Kathleen, slow down! Have you seen your sister? Oh! She's always running off!"

"And right on cue, let me introduce you to Kathleen," said Adriana. "She's a real person, and you really *are* in her consciousness. In fact"—the crowd scene vanished, replaced instead by the main deck of the *Titanic*, the wind whipping through my skirt, a knitted shawl gripped between Kathleen's pale fingers—"you can hop into any moment of Kathleen's consciousness you want—the day she was born, her first kiss, even the moment she tragically lost her life. And not just Kathleen. Oh, no. MindWeb has mapped the minds of *every single person* throughout history, right up to the end of World War Two." Kathleen lost grip of her shawl, the woollen scarf rippling out to sea. "So, on that note, who wants to find out who Jack the Ripper *really* was?"

We spent a disturbing ten minutes lurking in the consciousness of history's most notorious serial killer before Adriana plunged us back through time, into a dark and ancient world, my feet muddy, breath ragged as I scrabbled to push the first towering blocks of Stonehenge into place. Then it was forwards again, to mid-1800s America, where abolitionist Sojourner Truth burned with frustration as she spoke on women's rights; then back to Genghis Kahn as he charged at his enemies on horseback; and finally, onto London in the 1940s, dancing through the streets as a young flag-waving Princess Elizabeth on VE day, with soldiers singing, and the night alive with the joy of peace.

By the time we removed our headsets, my dislike for Brookvu raged in a battle with my newfound awe at MindWeb. My head swam with a giddy high like the first sips of wine on an empty stomach. They hadn't been messing around. They actually had invented time travel.

"Bet your boss will regret not coming now." Eddie grinned.

"Doesn't it scare you?" I stuffed the box into my handbag and shuffled between the crowds heading for the foyer.

He shrugged. "Probably should. But also, *mate*! Actual time travel!" He glanced back at Adriana standing on the stage chatting to journalists. "Reckon she's my dream woman. Shame not to see her brother though."

"Joe? He never comes to launches?"

"Nope, too shy. But he's the brains of it. Certified genius. Met him at my first shareholder meeting last year." He beamed proudly. "I swear, that guy can code with his eyes shut. They're like this too," he crossed his fingers, "since their mum died."

Behind us, Adriana laughed on the stage. No wonder Brookvu was messed up. I couldn't imagine anything worse than running a company with your family. Gabby would drive me crazy.

In the foyer, china plates clinked and scraped around a buffet of cloche-covered dishes, the low-lit room heavy with the scent of roast meat and cakes. Suited waiters waltzed between the crowd, handing out mint julep cocktails whilst an antique record player swirled with the soft notes of jazz. I helped myself to a piece of pineapple upside-down cake and a glass of water, then hovered by the doors, trying to look busy. The room bustled with enthusiastic shouts and urgent chattering.

"Absolutely brilliant!"

"Wasn't at all what I was expecting, nothing like they've done before."

"Loving this 1920s vibe too. Much better than that awful operating theatre they chose for DocNav. Remember the cocktails, in *test tubes* of all things?"

"Not as bad as that desolate spot in Scotland. For the WorldWindow launch."

"Scotland?"

"Sentimental value, I believe. Ghastly place. Utterly freezing."

I licked pineapple jam from my fingers. These people went to launch parties all the time. They flitted between them like I popped to the supermarket. Casual, unimpressed. Even Eddie had abandoned me, now trailing an entourage of journalists as he tucked into a leg of roast duckling.

"Macy, is it? Of Perry LLP?"

A severe woman in a navy suit held out her hand.

"Gill Tomkinson, Brookvu Press and Publicity. Ah, I see you're enjoying some of our complimentary spread. The duckling is to *die* for."

I smiled tightly. This woman was the enemy. I should tell her where to stuff her MindWeb headset.

"I shan't keep you," she tapped on her e-jotter, "I just had a few questions. For the Brookvu website."

"Oh, no, I—"

She pressed on, unperturbed, "Your attendance tonight shows, of course, the strong relationship we have with Perry LLP." She glanced over at the huddle of journalists and raised her voice. "Water under the bridge, as it were. It is a clear indicator that Brookvu is always willing to work with those who criticise. To move forwards, to improve. Do you not agree?"

My blouse began to stick beneath my armpits. A young journalist peered eagerly our way, tapping on his own e-jotter.

So, this was Brookvu's plan? Use our attendance to suggest that all was forgiven. That we condoned their latest release. Well, screw Gill Tomkinson and her stupid website. Condoning Brookvu was the last thing Esther would want. It was a surefire way of losing my contract. Not that I needed any help with that.

I was halfway through making my excuses when Eddie appeared, one arm slung drunkenly over Adriana's shoulders, announcing an after-party at his place.

The journalists flocked to photograph the pair, and Gill Tomkinson swore under her breath, begrudgingly following them. I stepped back and slipped out of the theatre.

It didn't take long for the story to break. I had barely tapped in my flat's access code when my phone buzzed with the notification.

Virtual time travel possible with Brookvu's MindWeb

I clicked the link.

Tonight, tech giant Brookvu launched their latest offering in virtual mapping with the long-awaited reveal of MindWeb. Using state-of-the-art bone conduction VR headsets, users can access a map of human consciousness spanning from the Stone Age right up to the mid-twentieth century. The new technology is a welcome release for Brookvu, following recent controversy surrounding their DocNav app.

The article went on to interview the disgruntled director of the Museum of London and a charity boss who claimed the extortionate price of MindWeb made history inaccessible to low-income households. Eddie even had a brief quote saying he would start posting live streams of his time travel that very night.

My phone buzzed again. Esther's name popped up on the caller ID.

"Hiya." I pressed the loudspeaker, hanging my suit jacket by the door. A single lamp lit the hallway, the walls bare and white except for a sepia canvas of London's skyline.

"Macy, what's wrong with you?" Esther's gruff East London accent barked down the phone, sounding slightly nasal from her bunged-up nose. "I've been calling for ages!"

"S-Sorry," I mumbled, shuffling into my slippers and padding down the hallway to the kitchen. "They made us turn our phones off," I lied, "for the presentation."

"Have you got one? I'm coming over."

I started to tell her that it was almost midnight. That I was just going to have a tea then go to bed. That maybe we could talk about it over brunch. But she hung up.

Sighing, I put the kettle on, and steam was soon drifting over the granite worktop. On the table, next to a pile of unopened post, the black box eyed me darkly.

Esther would be at least half an hour. It was a long time to stare at the box. But equally, something about it scared me.

I wasn't a gamer, not like EdPlays. I didn't have time for trivial things like hobbies. But I'd spent hours as a child playing *Kart Racer 3* and *Dance Now!* with Gabby, back when the competition between us was just for fun. Games were immersive. You could get lost in them. But the thought of getting lost in MindWeb...

Sitting at the table, I placed the metal discs on either side of my forehead.

This time, a menu appeared overlaid on the kitchen. Time periods and famous historical figures promoted in a row of cards like television shows. I flicked to the right with my eyes. *Darwin's Finches; Van Gogh's Sunflowers; Jane Austen's Emma.* Beneath was a list of popular searches. *"Henry VIII doing poo"* at the top. Honestly, people had no shame.

In the end, I opened my eyes as Cleopatra, eating figs beneath the shade of a woven canopy as she told Julius Caesar she was pregnant with his child. He didn't take it well. Her chest tightened with steely rebellion as he yelled, spittle flying from his sunburnt lips, hand on the hilt of his sword.

I shut the headset down feeling strangely guilty. A moment ago, Cleopatra was just a famous historical figure. Someone you might dress up as for a party. But now, she was real. A young woman in over her head. Afraid of her lover. Afraid of her family. Afraid of dying. Like everyone else.

The doorbell rang, and I buzzed Esther up to my flat.

She panted on the doorstep. Small and overweight, wrapped in a chunky-knit woollen cardigan, grey hair cropped short for practicality, bright purple glasses severe and garish, her nose red and peeling around the nostrils.

"I *can't believe* I missed it!" She pushed past me and helped herself to a mug and teabag. "I mean, a *cold*, for Pete's sake! Stupid Esther, should've eaten more oranges." She trumpeted into a damp tissue then stuffed it back down her sleeve. "Where is it?"

I gestured to the table.

"Have you tried it?" She lifted the lid slowly, as though expecting something to reach out and grab her.

"It's strange," I said. "Disturbing in a way. So real you could forget you have another body, except there's no control. You can only observe."

Esther scooped out the metal headpieces and turned them over under the bright kitchen light.

"What's the last date?"

"Just after World War Two. Basically, nobody alive. Nobody who's too recently died either."

She put the headset back in the box and turned to spoon out her teabag.

"You're not going to try it?"

"Ha! I'm not giving any more of my data to that sicko place." She dumped the teabag in the bin and took a gentle sip. "Send it to Hattie. Get her to find out how it works."

"What about Mark Wilson?" I watched her carefully. "Should I reach out to him too?"

The half-written email I'd seen on Esther's computer flashed before my eyes, *Take Macy off the Wilson case. She won't be staying past Aug. Not got what it takes.*

"No. Brookvu might be watching us. Why do you think they invited us to the launch party in the first place?"

I blushed under her glare.

"Listen," Esther sighed, "watch out for yourself, OK? This is a big company. We both know how it went down last time." Her phone rang, and she rolled her eyes as her wife's photo popped up on the screen. "Alice. Worries too much. Thinks I'm unfit to drive. Honestly, she'd hospitalise me given the option. I need to go. But, listen, well done. We'll be able to do a lot with this."

She left in as much of a hurry as she had come, her tea half-drunk on the kitchen counter. I slid the black box into a drawer, hating how pleased I felt at Esther's small praise. The woman basically wanted to fire me. Why was I still pandering to her? *Because she holds the keys to your dreams,* sang a voice in my head. The lawyer-lifestyle, the launch parties, the after-parties, the fancy-pants house in Kensington. The winner of the unofficial Fletcher family most successful daughter prize.

My phone buzzed at 2 a.m., waking me up. I dragged it beneath the covers, the screen glowing blue in my duvet cave. A follow from @EdPlays. I clicked accept, and his most recent live stream played automatically. A clip of him sitting cross-legged in front of a TV, eyes shut, the headset fitted to his temples. Somehow, he'd managed to link the screen to MindWeb. It was a dingy scene— an obese man sitting on a box in a wood panelled room, his face bright purple. Henry VIII doing a poo, through the eyes of his faithful servant.

I swiped away, and Gabby's feed popped up. A photo of her in blue scrubs, bags beneath her dark eyes, black hair greasy, a tired but satisfied smile.

Another shift complete. Every day I learn so much. Nothing moves you like helping people at their lowest. Wouldn't change it for the world. #lovemyjob #lifegoals

Beneath, a comment from Mum, *So proud of our baby girl xxx*

I turned my phone over and tried to sleep, but my mind was racing. What if I messed it all up again? How could I ever show my face at home? But equally, what if I didn't? What if for once, I got it right? This was a new opportunity, a chance to prove myself. To show everyone that I was just as good as Gabby.

I met Hattie at a little café opposite the offices of Perry LLP. The smell of coffee and baked beans mingled with burnt toast and orange juice as we sat at a plastic table, an oversized canvas of a fruit basket filling the wall above.

Hattie was a quiet person, but not particularly shy. She never blushed or sweated with anxiety; she just spoke softly and took her time to say the right thing. Her waist-length hair and thin figure could often be seen curled like a weeping willow over her laptop in the corner of the office, studying the coding and designs of new tech.

We'd grown close over the past few months. She wasn't cutthroat and competitive like other people in the office. She just wanted to do a good job. It was one of the reasons I'd felt so bad for messing up the Wilson case. I'd ruined a great opportunity for us both.

She barely looked at the box when I passed it to her, shoving it straight into her rucksack.

"It's just a headset." She shrugged. "We've had them for ages. The programme is the time travel bit. I'll need to take a proper look at it to figure out how it works."

"Do you think it could help with the Wilson case?" I sipped my orange juice, watching her closely.

She smiled and sat back, absently plaiting one side of her hair.

"Brookvu are messy. They rush things. Tell Esther I'll have the report by this afternoon."

Whilst I waited for Hattie to finish her report, I decided to read back over the documents for the Wilson case. If I could find new evidence or something we missed, maybe Esther would keep me on.

The Wilson case began almost thirty years ago, when two-year-old Leslie Wilson had an allergic reaction to a prescription of antibiotics. It was a severe, but not especially rare condition, and after a quick antihistamine from A&E, she was back to playing and drooling like any other toddler, the only difference a small but vital addition to her medical record, *allergy to penicillin-containing antibiotics*. That should have been the end of it, no further problems. And, for a long time, it was. Until one year ago, when Brookvu emerged onto the medical scene and changed everything.

At the time, Brookvu was a relatively unknown name, but their products were household favourites. Their street mapper, WorldWindow, helped people to navigate; their machine mapper, NuSafe, made it easy to assess vehicles for safety violations; and their ingredient mapper, YuMap, scanned food for allergens. Brookvu's shares were thriving, Adriana Spencer-Brookes appeared in at least four different magazines as "CEO of the Year," and their most recent release was only meant to make things better.

Adriana launched DocNav at the Old Operating Theatre Museum in Southwark. Celebrity guests sipped blue cocktails from conical flasks, downing test tubes of vodka. A live demonstration saw an audience member find out from a body scan that she had high blood pressure, low vitamin D, and a bad case of athlete's foot.

Within an hour of DocNav's release, millions of people downloaded the app. And, amongst them, the now grown-up Leslie Wilson dragged herself out of bed to scan her body, discovering that the lingering cough she'd been struggling with for weeks had, in fact, manifested as a bacterial chest infection.

By the next day, DocNav had delivered her a box of 250 mg antibiotic capsules. Which would have been great, except for one problem—they were the wrong type. DocNav was supposed to prescribe drugs using both current scans *and* a patient's medical history. But somehow, for Leslie Wilson and, as it turned out afterwards, for thousands of others too, this didn't happen.

To Leslie's nonmedical eyes, DocNav's fancy branding on the medicine box looked perfectly fine. But it took only seconds for her throat to swell, chest tightening until she collapsed to the floor.

Leslie's husband, Mark, immediately dialled 999, but by then, half the country had downloaded DocNav and within hours, the already stretched NHS was at breaking point. Cases of high cholesterol, diabetes, cancer, blood clot, and deep-vein thrombosis, previously undiagnosed, were surfacing simultaneously in their thousands.

It didn't matter that most of these weren't urgent. People panicked. Where treatment was beyond next day delivery of drugs, DocNav recommended *"immediate hospital referral."* It was complete and utter chaos.

It took four hours for an ambulance crew to arrive. But by then it was too late. Leslie had died in Mark's arms on the kitchen floor.

Mark wasn't the only one to contact Perry LLP. But he had the strongest case and a substantial inheritance to pay the legal fees.

For me, it was a chance to prove myself to Esther. To solidify my position in her firm and earn a permanent contract.

The box of remaining antibiotics had been scooped up by the exhausted ambulance crew. Carried off and destroyed in the chaos. So, instead, Esther asked me to source Leslie's phone for Hattie to analyse. I thought I was onto a winner. That surely I couldn't mess up such a simple task.

Mark agreed to bring the phone into the office. He'd turned it off the night Leslie died, unable to tolerate the messages from her friends and family. I thought I was being helpful, that if Hattie was the first to turn it on, she'd have to wait around for all the messages before starting her analysis. So, I pressed the power button and sat at my desk whilst it buzzed away, completely oblivious to the DocNav update running in the background.

When I finally handed the phone over to Hattie, Leslie's medical history was there in the app as though it always had been, with no record of the penicillin ever having been prescribed or ordered.

Esther was furious. I'm surprised she didn't fire me on the spot. Instead, she made everyone work through the night, researching every detail of Adriana's life and Brookvu's past. When we couldn't find anything substantial, she started posting her analysis on social media.

Eventually, a TV company got involved, covering the case in a series of shows investigating conspiracies around big tech companies. The media made a lot of noise, Brookvu's shares took a dive, and Esther became an overnight celebrity.

But, even so, Brookvu still wasn't held accountable for Leslie's death and, instead of a permanent contract, I had earned a reputation as the failure of the office.

Hattie knocked for me in the midafternoon. Together, we joined Esther and several other lawyers in a cramped, glass meeting room that smelled like stale coffee.

"Ugh, don't tell me we're brainstorming," grumbled an arrogant senior lawyer, slumping down and digging out his phone with the intention of ignoring Hattie's presentation.

Hattie, looking unfazed, bent over a crudely drawn picture of a spider diagram and added two small dots with her marker pen.

"Are those eyes?" I asked.

Hattie grinned. "Exactly."

"So, you've drawn a picture of a...spider?"

"Right again."

"I'm guessing this has some relevance," croaked Esther, coughing into her tissue.

"They're crawling," Hattie pointed her pen to the spider, "with little bots like spiders."

"So, you're saying Henry VIII has spiders in his brain?"

"Not *literal* ones. Data spiders. Think of it like a virus. Say I'm unwell and I come into the office, the virus could jump from me into any of you. It's similar."

We all glanced warily at Esther as Hattie drew a stick person on the board. "This is me. And...*this* is everyone I know."

"Aww, only three friends, Hattie?"

Hattie rolled her eyes, continuing to draw. "These are the people that each of my friends know...and so on. Pretty much every human throughout history will have met another human, another consciousness. We're all connected. And, with every connection, our minds exchange data. Eye contact, for example." She pointed her pen at me. "You look at me, and I look at you. What does that mean?"

"Er..."

She sighed. "We're connected. I know you exist, and you know I exist. We've exchanged data on each other's existence. The data spiders are using that exchange like a bridge. Crawling across it and into people's minds, then back through their memories until they find another connection, another bridge, another consciousness...."

Esther started to speak and broke into a coughing fit. Finally, she wheezed, "MindWeb is only historical. Up to the end of World War Two. How did they"—she waved a hand—"cross the *initial* bridge into the mind of a dead person?"

"Ah," Hattie shifted, looking strangely excited and nervous, "this is the thing. To find a way in, they must have used a living consciousness. For the electrical pulses in the brain to respond to the app."

We stared at her blankly, so she pressed on.

"Think of it like a map from one place to another. You can't teleport. You've got to go *through* places. It's the same here. They had to go through living minds to get into the past, and in doing so...well, they've mapped us all."

Esther sat back in her chair. "I'm sorry. Did you just say they've *mapped us all*?"

Hattie nodded.

"You mean like my consciousness? And Macy's consciousness?"

"Exactly."

"But they haven't released it?"

"Thankfully, no. Like you said, the public release stops at the end of World War Two."

My head spun. If this was accessible, somebody could be in my mind right now, watching what I was watching. Feeling what I was feeling. Would I know if they were there? Had Cleopatra sensed me inside her head?

"Who knows about this?" asked Esther. The room had gone very quiet.

"In theory," said Hattie, "anybody with my level of expertise. Then, it would only take somebody with the hacking capabilities to make use of it...."

Esther started clicking her fingers. "Macy, run a search. Find anything that looks like a consciousness livestream. As soon as somebody's hacked into it, they'll put it out there. I'm sure of it."

"Don't bother." The lawyer held up his phone. A social media post with over three million likes. *Follow this link to break your mind.*

The door burst open, and Mark Wilson strode in, his face red, a young receptionist trailing behind him looking apologetic.

"Mark," said Esther in surprise.

"This is it, isn't it?" He held up his phone, the social post bright on the screen. "This is how we get them, isn't it? This is how we get that stupid cow Adriana?"

Mark had put on a lot of weight since we'd last seen him. His belly bulged under a tight polo shirt, his tracksuit bottoms paint-splashed and dusty. Once we'd calmed him down enough to accept a tea and a custard cream, he said he'd been working as a handyman since losing his job. Cleaning gutters and patios for elderly neighbours. Spending a lot of time posting negative things about Brookvu online.

Hattie brought in the MindWeb headset and connected it up to a TV like EdPlays had done. When she clicked the link, a single search box flicked up on the screen, nothing like the fancy marketing on the normal MindWeb interface.

Nobody wanted to volunteer, the room sitting in awkward silence, until Mark coughed and said, "Try me, the day Leslie died."

We stared at him, and he brushed dust from his tracksuit bottoms, sitting up. "Anything to get Adriana behind bars."

Hattie nodded and typed in the details. "Do you know what time?"

"Just after dinner, 7.10 p.m."

The search box vanished, replaced instead by the consciousness of an earlier Mark, the world through his eyes filling the TV screen. We watched as he walked across a light veneer kitchen, carrying two small ready-made tiramisu pots with spoons shoved between the cream. A fish tank hummed on the side, ceramic pots overflowing with wooden spoons and spatulas, a half-eaten lasagne on the hob. Leslie leaned casually over the kitchen table. Her red hair loose and straightened, her pale green suit slightly creased. She looked like she'd just got in from work. The packet of DocNav antibiotics were unopened in front of her.

Mark handed her one of the desserts and joined her at the table.

"I really shouldn't," she grinned, spoon half in her mouth. "It'll keep me awake."

"You deserve it!"

"She'd just got promoted," croaked Mark next to me, tears running down his face.

"You know," Leslie smirked, "now that I'm going to be the big boss, you might need to take on more of the cleaning. Be my *housewife*?"

"Yeah, sure that'll go down well with the lads."

"You going out with them tomorrow?"

"Yep."

"I was thinking, I might—" Leslie's voice caught, and she broke out in a coughing fit. "Stupid infection." She picked up the packet of antibiotics.

"Turn it off," moaned Mark. "I can't watch."

But Hattie couldn't hear him. She didn't have an earpiece like Adriana. She was completely lost in Mark's life. By the time we managed to prod and shake her into taking off the headset, Leslie lay sprawled on the floor, Mark kneeling over her, frantically dialling 999.

"I couldn't hear." Hattie looked mortified, her own eyes brimming with tears. She had felt what Mark had.

Esther squeezed Mark's arm. "I know that was hard to watch, but this is excellent evidence. It verifies everything you said."

"Wait!" I had an idea. "Can we search for Brookvu's employees? Around the time the medical records reappeared in DocNav?"

"In theory." Hattie shrugged and punched in Adriana's details.

BLOCKED

The word flashed up on the screen.

"That's weird," she said. "How can it be blocked? It's a hack. There shouldn't be restrictions...."

"Unless the hack came from inside Brookvu?" I suggested.

We all stared at the screen.

"Snakes," grunted Esther. "They've done this on purpose."

"Search for me." I sat up, bracing.

Hattie frowned. "Are you sure? I'll be able to *feel* your emotions. It's kind of intimate...."

I glanced at Esther. This was my chance to show how much the case meant to me. "Just do it."

Hattie typed in the details and a moment later, an exact replica of what I was seeing appeared on the screen like a mirror tunnel.

"I can't feel it. I *can't* feel Hattie watching me."

"So, any number of people could be watching us right now...."

Esther swallowed. "People know who I am. They would search for me."

"They *are* searching for you," said the lawyer on his phone, and we all leaned in again to see screenshots of Esther blowing her nose. *Perry LLP still on DocNav warpath. Plotting latest attack. #BrookvuHatersGonnaHate*

"Turn it off," she snapped.

"They'll still be watching you."

"I know, but just turn it off." Her face was pale, red nostrils flaring furiously.

"My feed is going crazy," said the lawyer, staring at his screen.

"People tapping into the minds of murderers, some guy stabbing his wife to death who got off scot-free a few years ago. Celebrities pooing, of course. People…whoa! Don't they monitor for explicit content?"

"Turn it OFF!" Esther launched to her feet, fists clenched, eyes bright. "I want it out of my head!"

My own consciousness beamed on the television behind her. "Shut your eyes," I said. "Just shut your eyes."

Esther glared at me, then shut her eyes. I did the same.

"You guys OK?" I heard Hattie take off the headset.

"We need a way to communicate where people can't watch us," I said. "Any ideas?"

Hattie came up with several ideas throughout the afternoon. Whilst emotions could be felt in MindWeb, physical touch couldn't. The obvious solution was Braille, but as none of us knew how to read it, that was a no-go. So for a while we trialled writing messages on each other's backs. But we could only say short phrases, and eventually it became so frustrating we gave up entirely.

Outside, the world was imploding.

Crimes were being uncovered like mould under a yoghurt lid. Hordes of enraged residents dragging murderers from their homes. Angry couples posting shameful cheating videos, friendships breaking apart, Loperamide selling out as people tried to clench and avoid using the toilet. And the darker stories. People taking their eyesight in a desperate bid to be left alone, quack blocker implants that were full of arsenic.

Brookvu issued a statement saying that in accordance with their Terms & Conditions they considered the hack to be a misuse of their product and they were not at fault. When they were questioned about the "blocked" Brookvu accounts, they said they wouldn't know anything about it, as they were not responsible for the hack.

By the time the working day came to an end, I was so tired I couldn't imagine anyone wanting to hang around inside my head. But still, the thought was terrifying. I shut my eyes as

I typed in the access code to my flat, only to kick myself for being so stupid. People could view my entire life. Not just this moment. If they wanted to break into my flat, they only had to go back to the last time I let myself in.

My phone had been buzzing all afternoon, but only now could I bring myself to look at it. Frantic, terrified messages from my parents. Gabby wanting to know the legal rights for protecting vulnerable children from MindWeb. How on earth should I know? Friends I hadn't spoken to in years who were sure I could help.

You're involved with Brookvu, aren't you? You said something about it at that party once?

EdPlays popped up on my screen. Several messages saying he'd changed his mind. Could I hurry up and get Esther to shut it all down, because nobody was going to watch his live stream now that they could literally watch his *life* stream.

And Hattie. A short message, *Call me, found something.*

"The wall isn't a circle," she said when she picked up.

"I'm sorry, what?"

"The blocker, the wall around the Brookvu employees, it isn't a circle. It doesn't go right around them like a moat or a perimeter. It's just a single wall blocking the search interface on the hack from reaching their consciousness. I *knew* Brookvu had made the hack. It's got their terrible security all over it."

"OK, but what does it mean?"

"It *means* we can reach them. We just need to hack into the raw system, then crawl across the spider bridges into their minds."

"Oh, *just* that." I laughed.

"It's like I said before. We're all connected. Those connections are bridges, and the spiders aren't the only ones who can use them. We just need to find a bridge between us and Brookvu. And obviously Adriana Spencer-Brookes is the key because she has a *lot* of bridges. But most importantly, seeing as you went to the MindWeb launch party, she has a bridge with *you.*"

"Oh, I didn't speak to her."

"Doesn't matter, as long as she *saw* you."

"I don't know...it was bright, there was lots of smoke. What about Esther? Wouldn't she be a better choice? Adriana must know Esther after all the DocNav stuff...Hattie?"

"Esther's at the hospital."

My stomach plummeted. "What happened?"

"When you left today, she went back online. Hundreds of people were posting about her. I mean, it's not a lot in comparison to A-listers. But it was too much. She lost control. Begging me to find out who they were and how many were in her mind. I've never seen her like it. I tried my best, but it seems that part of MindWeb is locked down or just doesn't exist. Esther totally lost it when I said I couldn't do it. Started hitting her head against the wall. Mark Wilson went with her, of all people. Says the hospital's full, they're just in the car park. She's been given an ice pack and they've...put handcuffs on her."

"No!"

"We need to do this, Macy. We need to sort this out. It's you and me. Let's go into Adriana's mind and find what we need to take down Brookvu for good."

My stomach contracted. Was that excitement? What kind of sick person was I? Esther was in hospital, and I was excited because I had the chance to take on this case alone. To prove that I *was* good enough. I should be ashamed of myself.

"Hattie, I—" But she had already hung up.

I spent a guilty five minutes biting my nails and pacing the kitchen, before taking out the headset and searching for *Esther Perry*. Why was I doing it? To stop the excitement? To make me more worried about her, and less worried about my own arrogant career.

Esther had her eyes shut when I landed in her consciousness, but I could hear Mark next to her in the car, murmuring gently not to worry, that everything would be fine.

Where was Alice? Why wasn't she with her wife?

I took the headset off and searched for Esther online. It wasn't pretty.

Watching @EstherPerry on MindWeb. Boring. Thought she was a legend. That woman's life is sad.

@EstherPerry treats her wife like crap. Should be ashamed.

Never would've thought someone I admired would be so vile at home @EstherPerry. Tragic.

The clips showed Esther and Alice arguing over dinner. Esther telling Alice that she should be grateful, that she paid for their lifestyle. Screenshots of Esther's face contorted in tears over a bottle of wine. More clips of them sleeping in separate bedrooms, of Esther standing Alice up for date nights.

Is that what her life was like? Is that the life I wanted? The excitement ebbed. When was I last in a relationship? Ollie. We'd been together for five months at university, then he'd stayed in Durham when we graduated. It hadn't been easy to say goodbye. But everyone had always said, "You shouldn't let a relationship hold back your dreams."

I *had* always wanted to be a lawyer, hadn't I? That was something people said, but I knew it wasn't really true. I remembered a time when I was about five or six, and Gabby had discovered our mum's makeup box. We had spent an evening trying on lipsticks and eyeshadow, and I had wanted to be a beautician. Jobs didn't have meaning then. Success and status weren't a thing. It was just about doing what you enjoyed.

I put the headset back on and tried to think of the date to type in. I knew the exact moment I had decided to be better than Gabby. The moment I had vowed that whatever career she chose I would upstage her. But I had no idea of the actual date. It was amazing that something so important, something I was now allowing to dictate every decision in my life, was completely lost in my memories.

Instead, I typed in Gabby's name, and immediately regretted it. I'm not sure what I expected to see. Perhaps her swanning around a ward, calling orders and tucking in patients beneath rough blankets. But instead, she sat cross-legged in a walk-in cupboard, a white light shining weakly over shelves stacked with bandages and cotton wool. Something dark and sticky stained her scrubs and apron, soft sobs slipping between her lips, dread and panic rolling up through her chest.

"Gabby," I whispered. But she couldn't hear me.

"Gabrielle." The door burst open, and she scrambled to her feet. A man in scrubs looked away at the sight of her tears. "I'm sorry, I can't let you go early today. Not with everything that's kicking off."

She wiped her face, a steely determination squashing away the fear and dread. "I'll be right there."

"Gabby." I wanted to hold her. Tell her it was OK. That we didn't need to fight.

I pulled off the headset, unable to watch anymore. A horrible guilt ebbing inside me. My sister. My twin sister. How had I let my stupid competitiveness come between us?

Relief washed over me when Hattie finally arrived with a rucksack of wires and a Hawaiian pizza.

"You know," I said, opening the pizza box in the kitchen as Hattie linked up her laptop with the headset, "they could be watching us right now. They already know I work for Esther."

"I thought the same," said Hattie, "but then I realised something. In my head, Esther was Brookvu's enemy number one. Their legal pain in the bum. But do you know what?"

"What?" The pizza dripped with grease as I pulled out a slice and took a bite.

"We're insignificant."

I stopped chewing, but she continued, casually wiring up her laptop.

"Yes, Esther made a big fuss. And yes, it got a lot of attention. But there was also that American guy who died of a nut allergy after YuMap messed up his meal scan, and that French woman who was abducted after her stalker tracked her using WorldWindow. And the medical unions going after Brookvu for putting extra pressure on the NHS. We're small fry, Macy. We're one of many enemies of Brookvu. They might be watching Esther right now, but there's no way they'd extend that to us. Here, put this on."

I wiped grease from my fingers and took the headset. Hattie had fitted an earpiece like the one Adriana used at the launch.

"So, you remember what I was saying about spiders?" said Hattie. "Well, *you* will be the spider this time. You're going inside the raw system of MindWeb. But, listen, Macy," she looked at me seriously, "I'm not sure how safe it will be. If you don't want to go in…"

I swallowed. Did I really want to put myself in danger? Just to keep my job? Gabby clearly wasn't doing so well. Perhaps I could say I didn't want to risk it?

But Gabby's grim determination still lingered at the back of my mind. Things might be tough, but she wasn't giving up. She wasn't throwing in the towel and running home to Mum and Dad like a whiny child. Was that why she'd always been better than me? Gritting her teeth and getting on with it. Well, I could do that too.

"What do I need to do?"

Hattie pointed to her laptop. "I'll be watching on here. I'm not sure *exactly* what we're looking for, but it'll probably involve eye contact. Essentially an exchange of data. A link up between yours and Adriana's minds that we can use as a bridge."

I pressed the metal pieces to my temples and plugged in my earpiece.

"Shut your eyes," said Hattie. "It might make you feel sick going into the raw system like this."

She tapped at her laptop.

"OK," her voice sounded tinny and crackly in the earpiece, "you're ready to go."

I opened my eyes. "What the…?"

I was in a room. *My* room. My childhood bedroom. It was light grey with stencilled unicorns on the walls, Gabby's and my bunk beds squashed in one corner, a large white set of shelves brimming with soft toys and children's books. But in place of our bedroom window, a wall of miniature televisions flickered in black and white over a board of buttons and levers.

"What can you see?" crackled Hattie in my ear. "This bit won't show for me. I'll only be able to see the actual memories."

"It's hard to explain. I guess it's the control panel…for my mind? It's strange. Exactly what I'd expect. You know, if you imagined the inside of your mind?"

"That's probably why it *does* look like that. You're still in your mind. It'll look like what *you* think it should. I suspect your brain is interpreting the raw system in a way that it can understand, in a way that makes sense to it. Like a computer showing you an image instead of code."

"Right," I said, "I guess that makes sense?" I leaned closer over the control panel. "There's lots of little screens, like CCTV monitors. They're showing random footage from my life. A lot of me on the computer. Some of me as a child. Oh! I remember that holiday in Cyprus!"

"Don't lose focus. We don't know how much time we have. Try and find a way back to the launch party. To when you saw Adriana."

"Right, yeah." I bent to inspect the buttons and levers, trying to concentrate. An almost comical red button swelled like a boil in the centre of the board, a mess of joysticks and hundreds of keys crowding around it. They seemed to warp in front of me, my eyes blurring with choice.

"It's so complicated!" I stepped back, feeling suddenly too hot. "I don't know what I'm doing!"

"It's *your* mind. Operate it how you would expect to."

I tried to concentrate. How would I expect to search for a memory? Typing. I'd expect to type it into a keyboard. I scanned the room.

"Are you sure your theory is correct?" Then with a rush of certainty, I saw it, wedged between the plush toys on the bookshelf. An e-jotter, like the ones the journalists typed on, the blank keyboard glowing softly.

"OK." I took a deep breath. "Let's do this."

I typed in the date and time of the launch party and behind me, one of the screens switched to show a black and white version of the theatre.

"I've got it." My heart beat faster.

"Excellent! Now, go into the memory."

"Easier said than done."

I looked around again. The big red button eyed me ominously. It was odd. Wrong somehow, in a way that I couldn't work out.

I didn't want to press it, that was for sure. But something pulled me towards it....

"Any luck?"

I wrenched my eyes away. "I'm going to try one of the joysticks."

The launch party sped up as I leant the joystick forwards. I let go in alarm and it jerked back into place, the theatre slowing to normal speed. Then I spotted it.

"Oh!"

"What is it?"

"They're touchscreen. The TV screens. They've got little 'play' buttons in the bottom corner."

"Great! Press the launch party one."

I bent closer, ready to hit "play," then stopped. One of the screens had switched to another party. My stomach clenched. The memory I thought I'd lost.

It wasn't supposed to be a Halloween party, but my parents had done a good job of disguising it. They'd bought pumpkins for carving, lit a bonfire, and filled plastic bowls with marshmallows and sweets. Our neighbours and grandparents had arrived in woollen hats and gloves, waving sparklers, and telling spooky stories.

I leant the joystick forwards and the scene sped up. Why was I doing this? Why was I making myself relive it?

I let go as an eleven-year-old version of myself emptied apples into a bucket in the kitchen. Apple bobbing; I had wanted to play it with Gabby.

Of course, I had been upset that morning when we first opened our results and found out that Gabby had passed the exam and I hadn't. That she would be going to grammar school, and I would have to go to a state school in town by myself. But I was eleven and Halloween games and sweets were the perfect distraction. It hadn't crossed my mind that I might be a failure.

On the screen, I emptied out the last of the apples and scooped up the plastic bags, humming Halloween tunes to myself.

I opened the bin to throw in the bags, and that's when I saw it. A card. My name on the envelope, smeared with pumpkin seeds and ketchup. I picked it out, tore back the paper.

Inside, the word *Congratulations!* swirled in blue font over a fuzzy bear in a school uniform, my mum's handwriting curling in black ink, *To our darling Macy, we're so proud of you for passing your eleven-plus. We know you'll go on to do great things. Enjoy your surprise party, you deserve it. Love, Mummy and Daddy xxx*

"Are you OK in there?" crackled Hattie through the earpiece.

"Fine," I croaked, re-reading the words through my eleven-year-old eyes. I had discovered Gabby's card later that night, tucked beneath her pillow. She had been given hers. She had deserved it.

It was stupid. I saw that now. I was spoiled. My parents had thrown me a party, written nice things in a card. I should be grateful. Some kids didn't even get cards from the bin. But still, it hurt. I'd had to go back out there, to play apple bobbing with friends and family who were all pretending it was just an early Halloween party. Not a big ruse to cover up my failure.

Because that was it, wasn't it? That's why I needed to beat Gabby. I was afraid of failing. Afraid of that horrible sense of not being good enough. Of letting people down.

"Macy?"

This was the past. I couldn't change it. But I could change the future. I could do the right thing, not because I wanted to beat Gabby, but for me. Because I wanted to succeed. Because I wanted to stand up tall and tell the world that I was Macy Fletcher, and no matter what the examiners said, no matter what Esther said, I wasn't stupid. I *was* good enough.

I lifted my hand, and I hit "play."

Nausea rolled up through my body. I shut my eyes, focussing on the red and gold of the theatre. On the purple mist and mint julep, the soft jazz and roast duckling.

"That's it," murmured Hattie. "I'm plugging in the MindWeb interface now. I'll be able to operate some of the functions from here, but you'll still need to crawl through to access other restricted minds."

The nausea tightened in my stomach, a horrible dizziness surging over my mind. Then, like a roller coaster coming to an end, it stopped. Taking a deep breath, I opened my eyes.

I sat in the audience at the MindWeb launch, squashed between EdPlays and a suited, overweight journalist.

"I can see the theatre!" squeaked Hattie. "It's fuzzy. Is that EdPlays? He's smaller than I thought he'd be. OK, here she comes."

Adriana jogged onto the stage, laughing and thanking everyone for coming. I watched her intently, trying to spot any sign of eye contact. But the theatre was huge, and she'd clearly had training on speaking "to the whole room." I bit my lip. What if we couldn't find a bridge? This whole thing would be pointless.

But then, she paused. She looked down. A camera snapped beside me. And the flash caught her eye. She glanced up, towards my row. Saw the journalists. Saw Eddie's neon hoodie. And, so subtle I almost missed it, for the briefest moment, her eyes skimmed over my face.

"Got it!" Hattie squealed.

I heard her typing. "What are you doing?"

"Catapulting you," she said calmly.

"You're doing what?!"

A fresh wave of nausea rolled through my chest.

The theatre spun. The red velvet chairs stretching and warping, the purple mist thickening as it twisted into the notes of jazz, the taste of mint julep almost choking. And at its centre, like a single gravitational pull, Adriana rushed closer, closer.

"Hattie!" I grappled at the air, like a spider washed down a plughole.

"Don't resist," said Hattie, but she sounded far away.

Adriana was so close I could almost touch her. We were going to collide. I was going to smash straight into her. And then, like a bungee reaching the end of its elasticity, the harness snapping and letting go, I fell.

My stomach swooped and I screamed. Chairs and mist swirling in a mess of red and gold. A rush of white noise louder and louder in my ears.

Until suddenly, like someone pulling the plug on a TV, it vanished.

I stood on the stage, looking out across the rows of seats, nerves and adrenaline bubbling in the pit of my stomach.

"I made it. I'm in Adriana's mind."

"Great! Now, we need to get our bearings. Find a time when she's at Brookvu's Headquarters. Hold tight, this might be unpleasant."

The scene sped up, moving twice as fast, three times as fast. Adriana finished her presentation, chatted to a journalist, ate devilled eggs at the buffet, danced at the after-party, tussled in bed with a young woman, woke, scrolled, superfood smoothie, a jog, the car.

The scene slowed back to normal, my body hitting an invisible seatbelt with a snap.

"This is not fun."

Now, Adriana was talking to a man in a low-lit computer lab. He was young, casual in jeans and a T-shirt. His nose greasy with youth, blonde hair floppy and tangled. Joe Spencer-Brookes, Adriana's younger brother.

"What exactly are we looking for?" I asked, as we watched Joe nod and listen to his sister.

"I'm not sure...."

"Hattie! It was your idea to come in here!"

"I know! But this is what I do. I find a way in. I figure tech out. You're the lawyer...."

I sighed. She was right. This was a chance to prove myself. I couldn't wait around for someone else to come up with a plan.

"I guess we need something to implicate them," I tried to sound professional. "To prove they were the source of the MindWeb hack. Or if not that, then something on the Wilson case. There must be loads of dodgy stuff about DocNav in here."

"Yeah," groaned Hattie, "it's finding it, though."

"Shh! They're saying something about the hack!"

We fell silent.

"Put extra security in place for all Brookvu employees," said Adriana. "I'm worried somebody might try and hack into MindWeb. And Joe?"

Joe stopped halfway towards one of the computers.

"This is important, OK?" She took his hand. "Remember how far we've come."

Joe nodded and squeezed her hand, and for the briefest moment, Adriana shut her eyes. When she opened them again Joe was logging in to one of the computers.

"That was weird," said Hattie, as Adriana left the lab through a glass door. "I'm rewinding."

The scene rushed backward. "Please stop doing that. I think I'm going to be sick."

But Hattie wasn't listening. "Adriana says she's worried about a hack. So, does that mean Brookvu wasn't responsible? And what's *this* bit," we had got to the part where Adriana shut her eyes, "what's going on *here*?"

"Maybe she's tracing on his hand? Like we were writing on each other's backs? She could be spelling out a message?"

"Possibly," said Hattie. "But something feels odd about this whole thing. It was too easy to find. Like they wanted us to see it. To prove they didn't leak the hack."

She said nothing for a moment.

"Hattie?"

"We need to get inside Joe's head."

"Is that possible? I've never met him."

"You're in Adriana's head. You can crawl across from there."

Hattie rewound until Joe and Adriana were talking in the lab again.

"Now, like with Adriana, we need to catapult you across the bridge to Joe."

I braced as the computer lab warped and spun, swirling into a horrible, twisting pull towards Joe. That same jolt as my consciousness rushed across the bridge.

"I'm here." My head gave a deep throb. All this catapulting and fast-forwarding was taking its toll.

I looked out through Joe's eyes, now facing Adriana. Nervousness fluttered in his stomach. He was taller than Adriana, her tiny figure swallowed in an oversized hoodie. But somehow it didn't look like fitness and superfood smoothies up close. It looked like she didn't eat enough. She had bags under her eyes, covered by thick makeup. Her perfume masked the scent of alcohol.

Adriana stretched out her hand. Took Joe's. He glanced down as she pressed something into it. A sticker. Grey, circular.

"What *is* that…?" murmured Hattie.

"It's got something written on it." I read it out. *"JustView, Justice served for those who deserve it.* Any ideas?"

Hattie tapped away. "Can't find anything online…."

Joe curled his hand around the sticker, then sat down at one of the computers. A moment later, he began scrolling through a number of folders, seemingly company files assigned to various people, including employees: *Katrine Lake, Brookvu Objectives; Alessio Bernadello, Shareholder Meeting; Mark Wilson, DocNav Update.*

"Mark Wilson!" squeaked Hattie. "What I wouldn't *give* to open that folder. I bet it's got all the proof we need."

But Joe didn't click on the folder. Instead, he opened a drawer beneath the desk and pulled out a MindWeb headset, pressing the metal pieces to his temples.

Like someone shutting off the lights, everything went black.

"Hattie?" The darkness pressed in around me.

"What's going on?" she crackled. "All I can see is darkness."

"That's all there *is* to see."

"Interesting… I had never considered whether you could view somebody else's experience in MindWeb."

"You're viewing mine right now, on the laptop," I pointed out.

"That's different. We've wired up your headset to stream a recording. It's not the same as *experiencing* somebody else's journey within MindWeb. Especially without permission."

"It doesn't matter. We should fast-forward." I didn't like being in the dark. It made me uneasy.

"It *does* matter, actually," said Hattie in her most technical voice. "If you can't follow someone else into MindWeb. It's essentially somewhere to hide. To conceal information. If you've been clever enough to prepare it in the past."

Eventually, after a lifetime of darkness, Joe took off the headset, sliding it back into the desk drawer.

"So," said Hattie, "the question is, what did he go and see?"

I started to answer when everything went black again.

"Oh, for goodness' sake! This guy is relentless."

"Shh!" said Hattie. "Do you hear that?"

"Typing?"

"Is he...coding?"

"Could be," I said. "EdPlays said he can code with his eyes shut. I thought he was joking, but..."

"The hack!" squealed Hattie, "I bet he's leaking it!"

"But how? They didn't discuss it. Maybe they decided at an earlier date? But the whole thing with the sticker is weird...."

Hattie rewound again. "There." She stopped the scene as Joe scrolled through the folders on the computer. "Adriana gave Joe the sticker a few moments ago. Now, if I gave you a random sticker, what would you do?"

"Er...probably ask you why you'd given it to me?"

"Exactly. *Unless* it meant something to you. And this is the next thing he does. He goes on his computer, and he looks at these folders. What's the significance of the folders? What's the significance of these particular people?"

I stared at the folders. *Katrine Lake, Brookvu Objectives; Alessio Bernadello, Shareholder Meeting; Mark Wilson, DocNav Update.*

"Hattie! Could *this* be the list of people he went to look up in MindWeb?"

"Precisely!"

I laughed. "You were just testing me, weren't you? What's so important about these people though?"

"Well, I don't know for certain—"

"Wait, don't tell me!" I remembered her earlier comment about hiding things in the past. "You think Adriana's hidden stuff in these people's memories. Messages. About the hack?"

"I mean, maybe. That was my first thought. But it doesn't fit. These people are so random. Mark Wilson? I don't think he's ever met Adriana, so how could she have hidden something in his memory? And what's all this stuff about objectives and shareholder meetings?"

My excitement wavered, my mind slowing as I tried and failed to figure it out.

"Alessio Bernadello…" said Hattie after a moment. "He sounds familiar. I'm going to search for him online. Wait a minute."

She tapped on her laptop, then let out a frustrated sigh.

"It doesn't make any sense! He's a random restaurant owner. Some fancy place in Covent Garden. I *knew* I'd heard of him, but what's the significance? I can't imagine his memories having anything to do with Brookvu."

"What about Katrine? If Bernadello isn't an employee, she might not be either."

Hattie typed it in. "You're right. It's a lake in Scotland. So, if this isn't a list of people to look up in MindWeb, what is it?"

We fell silent, our minds racing, staring at the folders on the paused screen: *Katrine Lake, Brookvu Objectives; Alessio Bernadello, Shareholder Meeting; Mark Wilson, DocNav Update.*

"Memories," said Hattie slowly. "Perhaps they're memories in Joe's past? Moments both he and Adriana remember. *Shareholder Meeting.* Could they have had a shareholder meeting at Bernadello's restaurant? And something important happened? I mean, I have no idea how we'd figure out when it was…."

"EdPlays is a shareholder," I said suddenly. "He told me at the launch party. He said he met Joe at a meeting last year."

"So, if he can remember when it was…"

"Message him," I said. "Take my phone."

"But he's being watched. Thousands of people are viewing him."

I bit my lip. She was right.

"Although…" said Hattie, as if debating with herself, "it might not matter. None of those people know the relevance of Bernadello. It's only a problem if Adriana and Joe are watching. And I can't see why they would be…."

I sighed. "Either way, we don't have much choice. If we want to track down this memory, we're going to have to risk it."

"OK, I'll try and make it vague." She read aloud, "Looking for a good spot for Perry LLP Xmas party. You ever been to Bernadello's for work?"

We waited for his reply, the frozen image of the folders staring back at us. After a few minutes, Hattie inhaled sharply.

"He says '*yes*.'"

"Ask him when!"

"I am!"

We waited. And waited. Then Hattie let out a frustrated cry.

"'Out ATM. Call later?' No, Ed, we'll call now!" The sound of distant ringing. "Ugh, no answer!"

"It's fine." A stab of hurt hit me in the chest. Clearly EdPlays was *way* too important for the likes of me. "Bernadello will have to wait. What about Katrine Lake?"

"I'm going to search Adriana's name and Katrine Lake." She scrolled for a few minutes and I waited, scouring every detail of the folders through Joe's eyes, desperate to understand their meaning. Then, "Macy!"

"What!"

"They held the first ever launch party there, for WorldWindow. That must be it! Adriana must have sent Joe back to the memory of the WorldWindow launch. To see some sort of message that she hid there. I've got the date right here. We could go. I'm not sure what we'd be trying to find, but—"

"Hang on. Someone mentioned something about Scotland at the MindWeb launch. It might help us work out what we're looking for?"

"Let's find out!"

I didn't want to rewind and jump through Joe and Adriana's minds, but it was the only way back to my own consciousness. After much stretching and warping, I found myself back in my own body, licking pineapple jam from my fingers at the MindWeb launch buffet.

"Loving this 1920s vibe, too," said a young journalist, sipping a mint julep. "Much better than that awful operating theatre they chose for DocNav. Remember the cocktails, in *test tubes* of all things?"

"Not as bad as that desolate spot in Scotland," said another journalist, prodding at a devilled egg. "For the WorldWindow launch."

"*Scotland?*"

"Sentimental value, I believe. Ghastly place. Utterly freezing."

"*Sentimental*, you say?"

At this point, Gill Tomkinson, Brookvu's Head of PR, appeared in her navy suit and began speaking over the journalists. We craned to hear, and my dislike for Gill quadrupled.

"Old family home up there. The mother's place, you know how it is, what with her *accident*. I heard they scattered the ashes there."

"Never!" The young journalist leaned closer.

"Yes, yes. I mean, imagine it, partying on your own mother's grave. Positively savage. I wouldn't have gone, except—"

At this point Eddie and Adriana appeared, drunkenly announcing their after-party.

Hattie let out a deep breath. "It was too easy."

"What?"

"It was too easy to figure out that the WorldWindow launch was held at Katrine Lake. But this bit about their mother's ashes. This journalist must have done a lot of digging to find it out. It's not information that Adriana would expect anyone else to know. I bet she's trying to get Joe to go back to the day they scattered their mum's ashes."

"But it says *Brookvu Objectives*," I pointed out sceptically, "that *sounds* like a launch to me. And how would we even figure out what date they scattered their mum's ashes?"

Hattie went quiet, her breathing soft in my earpiece. Then in a small voice, she said, "How did her mum die?"

I watched through the eyes of my past self as I left the theatre and walked up a rainy Soho street, orange streetlamps and car lights shining on the tarmac.

"It was a car accident," I said quietly. "I read about it when I researched Adriana for the Wilson case. Her mum was driving home from work one day. She was a receptionist at a primary school. Sounded like a really sweet woman. It wasn't anything unusual. Her car just rounded a bend and hit a white van coming the other way."

"Oh."

"Yeah. The guy, Owen Poole, some local painter-decorator, he was arrested for manslaughter, but charges were dropped. It was a little country lane, no CCTV, nobody else around. Not enough evidence to prove he was driving dangerously."

We watched as I flagged a black cab at the end of the road. Adriana had built an empire whilst dealing with the loss of her mum. Maybe it wasn't so surprising that she'd made mistakes, screwed things up with DocNav.

But still, I had seen that same grief. In the eyes of Mark Wilson.

"Sometimes people scatter ashes on important days," I said. "Mark Wilson scattered Leslie's on her birthday."

"That could be worth a try. We could probably find out her mum's date of birth. And get an idea of the year based on when the accident happened."

She went quiet for several minutes, muttering periodically about census records and social media, reading out newspaper headlines, and tapping frantically on her keyboard. Then she catapulted me back into Adriana's consciousness.

Every time I crossed a bridge, it felt worse. A low, creeping headache spreading up and across my temples.

"You ready to try?" said Hattie. "I reckon we should start with midday."

She typed in the details, and the theatre vanished. Replaced instead by a colourful, pink bedroom. Posters were tacked to the walls, out-of-date musicians scribbled with hearts and stickers. Adriana lay on the bed reading a textbook on Business Management, her feet hanging over the end. We were back before Brookvu. Before DocNav scandals and launch parties.

"Is this Scotland?" I asked.

"No idea."

A voice called from downstairs, young, boyish, "Addie! Lunch!"

Adriana shut the book and padded out into a narrow, carpeted hallway. It was an old, low-ceilinged cottage, beams overhead, busy wallpaper and family photos squashed between flowery oil paintings. As she passed the front door, we caught a glimpse of rolling hills outside. Scotland. We'd made it.

In the kitchen, Joe was spooning pesto over bowls of penne

pasta on a busy counter. He was a lot younger, his face red with acne, a vague scent of body odour mingling with the pesto.

"I don't want that much!" exclaimed Adriana in protest.

"Well, tough, Sis, you need to eat." He dolloped an extra spoonful into her bowl.

They continued talking, chatting about a TV show Joe had been watching that morning. Then Adriana took her pasta upstairs, lay down on the bed and carried on reading.

"Fast-forward," I said.

The scene sped up, Hattie slowing it again when Adriana came back downstairs and joined Joe watching TV.

"Ugh, this is no good," groaned Hattie as Adriana went back upstairs again.

"Stop!" I yelped, and Hattie hit the pause button. "On the wardrobe, look!"

"A dress…"

"A *black* dress. I've seen it three times now but *look* at it! It's crumpled. Could that have been what she wore to the ash scattering? Some people don't scatter ashes on their actual birthday. It's too painful."

"I'm rewinding."

The scene reversed until we were almost at the point where Adriana first accepted her bowl of pasta.

"Look!" screeched Hattie, hitting pause again.

A folded leaflet poked out amongst a mess of books and papers on the kitchen counter, a photo of a soft, smiling woman on the front.

Scattering Ceremony, 9 p.m., 15 June. With a sunset toast to our beloved mother, wife, and daughter.

"It was last night, quick—"

But Hattie was already tapping in the date and time.

And then, we were there.

A golden sunset streamed over rolling hills of purple heather and ragged grey stone, the gentle calls of pigeons cooing amongst the rush of leaves. As Adriana, I sat beside Joe at the edge of Katrine Lake, her black dress short over bare legs, wellies dipped in the shallows.

"None of it really matters," Adriana ran her fingers through the water, the hair on her arms standing up with the cold, "as long as he's still out there. I mean, he's still got his driving license for God's sake! As if it never happened!"

"Don't think about him," said Joe. "Today is about Mum." He scuffed his wellies below the water, a cloud of silt swirling around his feet. "I don't want to pack it all in. WorldWindow, I mean. I don't want to lose everything we've worked on."

"We *won't*," said Adriana. "Mum, she was so proud of you... of us."

"It feels wrong continuing. Like everything should just stop. How is it fair that *anything* gets to keep going?" Joe wrenched a clump of grass and threw it into the lake.

They stared out to the sunset, the golden light reflecting in a shimmering pathway.

"WorldWindow could be the start," said Adriana quietly. "We could make other apps, once it gets going. To do something more, something that matters."

"Like what?"

"Like... imagine if there was a way to *prove* that he killed her. That it was his fault they crashed, if we could get him sent down for what he did... Or, what if the ambulance crew had better technology, to see the internal bleeding straight away. Or, if cars were safer. I don't know."

Joe smiled. "You never were small fry, Addie. But my pro-grammes have limits."

Adriana stood up, dragging Joe with her.

"Look at that, Bro." She pointed out to the sunset, leaning into him. "It's ours, the whole world. We can make it better. Screw *limits!*" She punched him playfully in the shoulder. "That's what our company should be about. Making sure no one else has to go through the stuff we did. I dunno, one day we might even find a way to get that arsehole behind bars."

"This is it, Macy," breathed Hattie. "*Brookvu Objectives*. We found it. Adriana wanted to remind Joe why they created Brookvu in the first place. I bet she's justifying the hack to him.

289

Reminding him of what they lost, that it was Owen Poole who was responsible."

I watched through Adriana's eyes as they laughed and splashed in the shallows. After all this time, they were still trying to find justice for their mum. Success had always seemed so perfect from the outside. It's what I'd always strived for. But these people didn't have all the answers. They were just as lost as the rest of us.

"EdPlays still hasn't come back to us," said Hattie, "so I guess next we need to crack…" Something rustled in my earpiece.

"Are you making notes?" I grinned.

"What's wrong with that? Notes are *cool*, Macy. Anyway, next on the list is *Mark Wilson, DocNav Update.*"

"Well, in theory this one is easier. We know who Mark is, and I'm guessing *DocNav Update* is what wiped the evidence from Leslie's phone."

"I guess so," said Hattie. "It's weird though. If all these memories are about Adriana telling Joe to leak the hack, then why is it on the list?"

"They could be worried about someone finding it. Maybe Adriana wants Joe to delete it?"

"I don't think they *can* delete memories. Or this whole thing would be a lot simpler. Adriana could just tell Joe to leak the hack, then delete the memory of their conversation. She wouldn't need this breadcrumb trail to cover their tracks."

We thought for a minute, Joe and Adriana walking back to the cottage, wellies scratching through pink tufts of heather.

"Do you know when the update was released?" I asked.

"Roughly. I have a timeframe of a few days based on analysis of people's phones."

"Let's go to the day before the earliest date, in Joe's mind, and fast-forward till we see them together."

"Gotcha."

I gritted my teeth as we crossed the bridge to Joe's mind. The pain in my head intensifying as Hattie searched for the date and fast-forwarded.

Joe spent an appalling amount of time on his computer. Typing and typing. Spooning food into his mouth one-handed and typing with the other. It was uncomfortable to watch.

Just when I thought the pain in my head might be too much, I saw it.

"Stop!" we both shouted, then burst out laughing.

Joe still sat at his computer in the lab, but Adriana crouched next to him, the two of them whispering, her face tight with worry.

"People have *died,* Addie! This isn't us!"

I stopped laughing.

"We don't have a choice." Adriana ran a hand through her blonde hair. "Our lawyers screwed up. They told me everything was signed with the NHS, but it wasn't. The idiots hadn't finalised the contracts, so the NHS withheld the medical history data. Tommy is on the phone to the NHS solicitors right now trying to bribe them to keep quiet."

"Bribe them! Addie, what are we, the Mafia?"

"Look, I know it isn't right. I know it isn't good. But you *have* to do this."

"No, I'm not like you. I can't turn off my morals and do bad stuff. Brookvu was never about that."

"And what do you think will happen if you *don't,* Joe? If you let everyone find out the truth? They'll shut down DocNav. They might even shut down Brookvu. Then what will your morals be worth? You've got to think of the bigger picture. I know it's hard, but you're doing it for the right reasons, and one day, everyone will see that."

Joe fell silent, dread and fear coiling in his chest. He took a deep breath. "Fine. I'll do it."

The scene froze as Hattie hit pause, her voice crackling in my ear. "He's not like her. Adriana knew she'd have to persuade him. Justify the hack to him. But she couldn't do it in person without incriminating them both. So, she sent him here. To the last time she convinced him to do something awful for the greater good."

I swallowed hard. "This is it, Hattie. It's the proof Mark Wilson needs."

She sighed. "I feel...strange about it all."

"Bad about Adriana?"

"Yes. And Joe. I kind of get why they did it. I mean, I'm not excusing it," she said quickly. "But they're not the corporate psychopaths we thought they were. They're just people."

"Mark is our client," I said firmly, but part of me wanted to leave MindWeb and run. Back home to my parents' quiet cottage by the sea. Away from the pressure and exhaustion of it all.

"So, what do we do?" asked Hattie. "Have we got enough?"

"To shut down Brookvu for good? I'm not sure...." And inside I wondered if that was even what I wanted. But quitting now would mean losing my job, and worse, letting Esther and Mark down. "What about the last memory?" I asked, trying to push Adriana's grief from my mind. "At Bernadello's restaurant. Has EdPlays come back?"

"Still nothing. But listen, I think you should come out for a bit. Take a comfort break."

"*A comfort break*," I scoffed. "It's not a work meeting, Hattie."

"I know, but..."

"What?"

She sighed. "You're kind of...drooling."

I blushed.

"I'm sure it's fine!" she said quickly. "But maybe we should take a break."

"Right." I tried to move my hands and felt a jolt of fear. I couldn't even feel my fingers. "Wait, what?"

Hattie chuckled.

"You can't just *come out* of the raw system. Your consciousness is in an entirely different place to your body. I'm guessing you won't be able to move until you're back in the control room."

I tried not to think about how terrifying that was.

"I'll need to catapult you back."

Several minutes later, I landed on my childhood bedroom floor with a thud, face down on a lilac unicorn rug.

"I'm back." I eased to my feet, head throbbing, the lights from the CCTV screens glaring across the unicorn stencils.

"Great. I'll get your headset off." I heard the scrape of her chair.

"Wait!" I said quickly.

"What is it?"

"Calm down. I just want to have a look at something."

In the middle of the control panel, the red button glowed in a soft haze. I edged closer, feeling that same, curious pull.

"There's something here. A button of some sort. It's…interesting."

"What kind of button?"

"It's big. And red. And it's sort of…bad, somehow." I was surprised to hear myself say it. I hadn't expected to know anything about the button.

"Don't forget this is *your* mind, Macy. If there's a big red button you think does something bad, that probably means it *does* do something bad."

"I don't think I created it though." I peered a little closer. "It feels out of place. Could Brookvu have put it here?"

"In theory. It's their programme. I don't like it though, Macy."

"Don't worry, I'm not going to press it! I'm just trying to figure out what it does. It looks a bit like one of those emergency stop buttons you get on a train."

"Oh, no."

"Hattie?"

"Macy, it sounds like a kill switch. Whatever you do, don't press it!"

"A what? A *kill* switch? Like an 'off' button for my mind? You can't be serious!" I stepped back in alarm. "Why would Brookvu have a kill switch in my head? Hattie?"

But Hattie didn't reply.

"Hattie?"

Then she spoke, her voice different, afraid, "Why are you here?"

A man murmured in the background, then before I could say anything else, she screamed.

"No, get off me! Macy, you need to get out, you need to get out—"

The line went dead.

For a second, I just stood there. Heart hammering, mind racing, trying to make sense of what was happening. Hattie was in trouble.

Someone had broken into my flat. I didn't know what they were doing to her. But I needed to help her.

I shut my eyes, homing in on my body in the kitchen, trying to find my hands, to lift them to the headset and pull it off. But my hands weren't in my lap. I felt a chill as distant tugging pulled at my wrists, the cold metal of handcuffs behind my back. I tried to twist free, but it was like moving through mud, my body numb, distant.

"Hattie? Hattie!" But she wasn't there. I gave up on my physical body and began pacing the control room. Hattie said I was in my mind's interpretation of the raw system. There had to be something useful. Something to help. I prodded and twisted at the joysticks, the CCTV screens rewinding and fast-forwarding back and forth over clips of my life. Playing with Gabby, learning to swim, begging my parents for a dog, at university with Ollie.

My head throbbed again, and I started to panic. Was Hattie OK? Were they hurting her?

"Hattie! Hattie!"

"She can't hear you."

I swivelled around. A figure flickered and formed, lying back on the lower bunk bed, legs crossed in casual joggers, memory-foam trainers white and pristine over my flowery bedding.

"A-Adriana?"

"Well, I should hope you would recognise me."

I couldn't speak. Couldn't think of what to say.

"I don't understand." I managed after a minute. "How are you here?"

Adriana laughed and sat up, leaning over to grab a soft toy from the bookshelf. A plush white polar bear we'd bought from the zoo. Gabby had named him Slushie. He would dance and jiggle his hips if you pressed a button on his toe.

"The thing about spiders," said Adriana, "is they're so very tricky to keep out of your house. You need proper firewalls, security. All the things we built into the public release of MindWeb. But here— where you are, in the raw system. Behind the firewall. There's nothing to keep the spiders from running rife in your mind. From mapping *every* part of your brain for me to see, for me to explore."

"But…I'm small fry." It sounded stupid out loud.

"Yes," Adriana cuddled the polar bear against her chest, "but do you know who isn't?"

My stomach dropped.

"EdPlays," I said. "You were watching him?"

"Didn't have to." She shrugged. "He came running to tell me you were digging. He'd do anything to get a blocker on his MindWeb feed—he doesn't like his followers seeing the real him."

"What do you want?" I asked.

Adriana ignored the question, smoothing her fingers through the polar bear's fur.

"You guys are having quite the escape game. A fun little night of riddles, figuring out my breadcrumbs."

"We work for Esther Perry. It's nothing personal."

"Maybe. But either way, you've dug too far."

"You can't kill me," I glanced at the kill switch with a sudden desire to throw myself in front of it.

"Oh, come on, Macy!" She snorted. "After all the time you've spent in my head, you *actually* think I'm capable of something like that?"

"You've got a kill switch…" I pointed to the red button.

Adriana rolled her eyes. "It's not a 'kill switch.' It's just insurance. In case we need to shut things down from the inside."

"So, it won't kill me? If I press it?"

She shrugged. "If you press it, you'll fall into a deep and irreversible sleep."

"That's loads better!" I kept one eye fixed firmly on the button. Brookvu was even more messed up than I thought. "Look," said Adriana, "I never wanted to hurt anyone, surely you know that? I only wanted to help. That's the whole reason we created JustView in the first place."

I remembered the grey sticker Adriana gave Joe in the computer lab. "Wait…."

"JustView was MindWeb's name," said Adriana. "Before the shareholders screwed us over."

"The shareholders…the memory at Bernadello's restaurant?"

"We presented it to them. It was different back then." She watched the CCTV screens flickering beside me. "Only the police were supposed to have access. And only when somebody committed a crime. But the shareholders thought it was boring. Apparently, our recent apps were too involved with public service. They didn't want to risk more hot water from the unions. No more scandals. So, they told us we had to turn it into something else. Something fun, or bin it."

"So, you turned it into MindWeb."

"I tried so hard to get it out there as JustView. I even went directly to the police. But do you know what they said?" She laughed. "Too many skeletons in the closet. They were too scared of implicating themselves. Should've known we couldn't trust them."

She gazed down into the polar bear's blue eyes. "Joe was happy to leave it at that. You know my soft brother. But I knew we could get it out there. I just had to be careful, to protect him."

"So, you admit it? Brookvu leaked the hack?"

"I can admit anything I like in here. That's the beauty of this little room. It's completely private. Or it should be anyway."

I frowned. "Why didn't you ask Joe to leak the hack in one of these rooms? Nobody would've seen. You wouldn't have needed your breadcrumb trail. You could've met up in his mind, or in yours."

Adriana smiled sadly. "How's that headache?"

My head throbbed almost on cue, nausea blurring my vision. "I'm fine," I lied.

"It might surprise you," Adriana stroked the polar bear's head again, "but we do have a rigorous testing process for all our products. JustView, for instance, we trialled lots of interfaces before finalising it. Lots of different ways to access consciousness." She turned the polar bear over, began fiddling with the battery pack. "Some of them were dangerous."

I tried to ignore a nagging fear spreading through my weak and tired mind.

"This polar bear, for instance. It's cute, cuddly. Perfectly safe for little kids. But take out the batteries. Give them one of those to play with…point is, Macy, there's some things you shouldn't mess around with. Things you don't properly understand. Spiders aren't made to sit still. They crawl, outwards, forever. Even if that means burrowing into the deepest crevices of your mind."

Something hot ran down my upper lip.

Adriana held a finger to her earpiece. "Joe says your nose is bleeding."

I wiped my face, but it was useless. My real body was far away, unreachable. I sank to my knees on the unicorn rug. "What's going to happen to me?"

Adriana sighed and shook her head. "I've been watching you all evening, since Ed told us you were digging around. I wasn't too worried about the DocNav stuff. It was bound to resurface at some point, even without the breadcrumb trail. It would be a small cost if we could finally get the courts to accept MindWeb as evidence. Finally get that arsehole sent down for what he did to Mum." She placed the polar bear back on the shelf, slotting him between the other toys as though tucking a child into bed.

"But you picking around in *here*, in the backrooms. Finding the 'kill switch' as you call it." She ran a hand over her thin face. "The footage is all over the internet. Some idiot recorded Hattie and posted it on social media. I'm fighting a losing battle, Macy. But I'm not the only one." She stood over me, where I knelt clutching my throbbing head. "I've found a solution that ends badly for both of us but the best it can for Joe. I'm sure you know by now, Joe is everything to me. I'll do anything to protect him."

She stepped over me and placed a hand on the red button.

"No! No, please don't do that. They'll find out what you did. You'll go to prison!"

"That's kind of the point. If they send me to prison using evidence from MindWeb, Owen Poole will get the same treatment. Everyone will see the truth. It wasn't just an accident. He ploughed into my mum at 90 mph whilst playing a stupid game on his phone."

My head throbbed, deep and ripping over my racing heart. I tried to struggle to my feet, but my legs were weak.

How could I have been so stupid? Adriana was going to turn me into a vegetable, and for what? A promotion? It was laughable.

My parents. Gabby. I wanted to see them, to be with them now. I'd been at odds with Gabby for years, but wasn't she that same twin sister I'd played games with growing up? Naming silly polar bears and trying on our mum's makeup. It wasn't her fault she'd got into grammar school, and I hadn't. We should have been close like Joe and Adriana. I should be standing here right now like Adriana was, putting Gabby first in everything I did.

I closed my eyes and tried to visualise Gabby's face. If only I could reach her. Somehow slip through the cracks to her consciousness. Perhaps I might have a chance. A chance to find my way out. A chance to start anew.

"I'm sorry," Adriana pushed down on the kill switch, and I leapt up and away from my childhood bedroom, into the warping, whirling void.

The courtroom murmured as the judge and jury removed their headsets. It was an intimidating chamber, heavy panelled wood and leaded windows spilling sunlight in shafts of swirling dust.

"Thank you for viewing the MindWeb recording of Macy Fletcher's consciousness," said the judge. "We will now break for ten minutes."

Quiet conversation hummed across the courtroom as cups of tea and biscuits were sought and consumed. When the room fell silent once more, the defence lawyer stood, her birdlike face pinched and serious.

"Your honour, I would like to take a moment to thank Joseph Spencer-Brookes for his compliance in altering the code for the recording. Without Mr. Spencer-Brookes's cooperation it would not have been possible to view the recording in such detail.

GUELLY RIVERA

The thoughts expressed by Ms. Fletcher were not available in the public release of MindWeb, and the ability to view a consciousness whilst within MindWeb—that is, the moments when Ms. Fletcher took us into the minds of Adriana and even Mr. Spencer-Brookes himself. These moments would not have been possible before the changes carried out by Mr. Spencer-Brookes. That is to say, Mr. Spencer-Brookes has been *extremely* cooperative, and this should indeed, be recognised and considered."

"I am aware of a certain level of immunity that has already been agreed for Mr. Spencer-Brookes," said the judge tightly. "However, this does not apply to Miss Spencer-Brookes."

The jury muttered, and the defence barrister nodded, sitting back down. In the dock, Adriana slumped silently, face drawn and tired, blonde hair unwashed.

The barrister for the prosecution stood up, smoothing down his silken gown and pushing stubby fingers over a spread of papers.

"Your honour, I would now like to call Ms. Hattie Anderson to the witness box."

A door creaked and footsteps scuffed across the carpet, clunking as they climbed wooden stairs. A young woman, tall, thin, long hair draped over her narrow shoulders, sat down, and swore her oath on the Bible.

"Hattie Anderson," said the stocky barrister, "Could you please tell us your version of events towards the end of Ms. Fletcher's recording?"

Hattie coughed and swallowed, looking out across the courtroom.

"Objection, your honour," squeaked the defence lawyer. "We could simply view this evidence through MindWeb. We do not need Ms. Anderson's misleading second-hand account."

"Objection overruled. We will view Ms. Anderson's recording in addition to her witness account. Her personal testimony of events is of value."

Hattie leaned towards the microphone and took a deep breath.

"About an hour after Macy entered MindWeb, I noticed she was drooling, the veins on her head swelling. I knew it was bad, but

I was trying to keep calm. I just thought, if I could get her back to the control room, and out to the real world, everything would be fine. But then…," Hattie swallowed hard, "then Joe and Adriana showed up. It all happened so fast. Joe grabbed my arms. Pulled them behind my back, handcuffing me. I tried to kick out, but I couldn't reach him. Then Adriana yanked off my microphone and I lost contact with Macy.…"

"Please take a moment to compose yourself, Ms. Anderson," said the prosecution lawyer gently. "When you're ready," he continued. "Did Miss Spencer-Brookes say why she and her brother had come to Macy's flat?"

"I kept asking them," said Hattie, her voice rising, almost defensive, "but they just ignored me. They were panicked. Arguing."

"Arguing about what?"

"Joe wanted to shut down MindWeb. He was scared. Thought Adriana was taking it too far. But she just kept saying how close they were. That it was only a matter of time before the courts accepted MindWeb as evidence and Owen Poole was sent down for what he did."

"Owen Poole?"

"Yes, the man who killed their mum in a car crash. They'd found his memory of the crash in MindWeb."

The prosecution lawyer moved several papers on his desk. "Evidence from MindWeb showed that Mr. Owen Poole was playing a game on his mobile phone at the time of the collision. With this evidence, he could be arrested and tried for dangerous driving and manslaughter."

Hattie nodded. "They must have had Owen's memory of the crash from the start, since they first invented MindWeb. But back then the courts wouldn't accept it as evidence. I think everything Adriana's done since, it's all been to get MindWeb accepted in the courts as it is now. To convict Owen Poole for killing her mum."

The judge cleared his throat. "Please return to your testimony of the night in question, Ms. Anderson."

Hattie took a deep breath. "I didn't know why Joe and Adriana were there, but I assumed it was to do with Macy being in the raw system. I hadn't expected..." she swallowed, "I didn't think it would be about me."

"About you?" prompted the prosecution lawyer.

Hattie nodded again. "It was only when Joe started fitting a headset on me. Wiring it up to his phone, arguing with Adriana, that I realised they'd come to clean up the mess we'd made."

"Please explain your meaning, Ms. Anderson."

"They wanted to activate my kill switch. And Macy's too. To stop anyone else finding out their secrets. They seemed convinced we were the only ones who'd accessed their blocked memories. That if they activated our kill switches and tightened security on the blocker then it would all be fine. Of course, they could've done this from afar. The kill switch could be activated remotely. One click of a button and they could comatose whoever they wanted." A shocked murmur rippled through the jury and even the judge looked uncomfortable.

"Go on, Ms. Anderson."

"But there was a problem. They needed to know for sure that nobody else had been watching my memories. That their secrets hadn't spread any further. But they couldn't find out who had been watching me without direct access to my brain. Clearly there are some limits to the MindWeb programme."

"And what were they planning to do if they found out somebody else had been watching you?"

Hattie didn't hesitate. "Activate their kill switches, I'm sure."

A gasp rushed around the room and, in the dock, Adriana rolled her eyes.

"Objection!" shrieked the defence lawyer, leaping to her feet. "Speculation—she can't possibly know that."

The judge nodded, "Sustained. Move on."

"Tell me about Mark Wilson," said the prosecution lawyer quickly.

Hattie swallowed. "He was our client. The original reason we'd gone into the raw system. His wife died as a result of the DocNav scandal."

The prosecution lawyer looked back to his papers, reading quickly. "The corporate liability case against Brookvu for the deaths and serious injuries of over 6,000 individuals who used DocNav in the first two days of its release."

A small smile flickered over Hattie's lips. "Yes," she said, "but before Mark Wilson got the justice he deserved, he was in a really dark place. Obsessing over Brookvu and even over Perry LLP. I mean, I don't mind—but Mark thought we were slacking off. Letting Adriana slip away again. So, the night me and Macy hacked into the raw system, he had been watching us through MindWeb, checking to see if we were working like we should be. When he saw what we'd found—the breadcrumb trail and the kill switch—he went straight online and started posting recordings on social media, tagging Brookvu. Joe and Adriana were halfway through setting up my headset when the notifications pinged on Adriana's phone." Hattie gave another satisfied smile. "The stream already had hundreds of viewers. Their secrets were out there, beyond MindWeb, beyond their control. Adriana completely lost it, throwing her phone across the room."

"And what about Joe?"

"He just slumped down, staring at his hands. He seemed relieved it was all over."

"But it wasn't over, was it?"

Hattie pursed her lips, hands clutched over the Bible. "I never meant…I never could have imagined—" Her voice cracked.

"Take your time, Ms. Anderson."

She took a shaky breath. "Adriana kept shouting at Joe, begging him to target people watching the stream, to activate their kill switches. I had no idea if he could actually do it—how would he even know who they were? But I didn't want to take the chance and, I thought, perhaps I could convince Adriana to own up to it all. So, I reminded her about one of the breadcrumbs she'd left for Joe. The one with Mark Wilson and DocNav, where she'd talked about the bigger picture. I told her if she really wanted MindWeb to be accepted as evidence in court, if she really wanted to convict her mum's killer, then maybe she needed to hand herself in. Let the courts come after her with the evidence from my consciousness. Make herself irresistible to convict with evidence from MindWeb."

"And this is where she got the idea to use Macy's kill switch inside the raw system?"

"I never meant…" Hattie sobbed. "It was my fault. I thought Adriana would just own up to what she'd already done. But she was worried about Joe. She wanted to protect him. So, she said if she went into MindWeb and did something terrible *inside*, then the only way they could use it as evidence was if Joe altered the code. And in doing so, in being compliant and helpful, he could get immunity." Hattie sobbed again, and somebody handed her a tissue. She blew her nose and glowered up at the judge. "You shouldn't have given it to him. You've played right into her hands."

"Thank you, Ms. Anderson."

"You have to make her pay," Hattie stood up. "You have to make her pay for what she did to Macy!"

"No further questions, your honour," said the prosecution lawyer.

The judge nodded. "We will now view Hattie Anderson's MindWeb recording. Please fit your headsets. The ushers will start the footage shortly."

Hattie got down from the witness box and walked to the door. As she looked back, she saw Adriana, pressing her headset to her temples. Her blonde hair fell in greasy locks around her thin face. But as she closed her eyes and sank into MindWeb, a small smile flickered across her lips.

Outside, the tree-lined square glowed in autumn sunshine, pigeons pecking at the remains of a crisp packet, traffic speeding and beeping on the road beyond.

Perhaps once, a flurry of journalists might have rushed the courtroom steps. Snaps of photographers and shouts for commentary. But now, everyone had a front-row seat.

"Hattie, wait!" Hattie turned to see a young woman rushing across the square, dark hair rippling in the sun. Long, tweed coat flying around her corduroy dungarees. Gabby, Macy's twin sister. They weren't identical, but they looked alike, Gabby a softer, less pristine version.

"Hattie, I wanted to say..." Gabby fought to catch her breath. "I wanted to say, we don't blame you. None of us do. We know you did what you had to."

Hattie tried to smile but instead tears welled and spilled onto her cheeks. She couldn't stop thinking of Macy, blank and empty in her hospital bed. Her body still living, but her mind somehow missing.

"I'm so sorry...."

Gabby shook her head. "She's still out there, I'm sure of it. I refuse to believe...." Her brow furrowed. "We have to find her."

"But we don't even really know what happened to her. She jumped outside of the programme. Even Joe said it's impossible, like finding the right grain of sand on a beach. And now he's disabled the kill switch, taken it out of our minds.... It'll be harder to work out...."

"Macy isn't just some grain of sand. She's my sister. She's fierce and unique, and most of all she's part of me." Gabby's voice cracked. "I'll always find her. I'll always know her. Joe might've given up, but we can't. Not for Macy. We have to try. Please." She took hold of Hattie's hand, squeezing it hard. "She's everything to me."

Hattie looked down; the warm pressure of Gabby's fingers gripped tightly around her palm. She had no idea whether they could bring Macy back. But Gabby was right. They had to try. She sighed, then slowly nodded.

Gabby sobbed, pulling her into a sudden hug. "Whatever happens, we can't give up. We can't ever give up. We'll bring her back. I know we will."

They stayed that way, the gentle rush of traffic in the distance, a beam of sunlight warming their shoulders, then Gabby stepped back, dark eyes determined, so like Macy's.

Far away, thousands of people watched them in MindWeb, wincing at the sharp, twisting guilt in the pit of Hattie's stomach, the deep, clenching grief aching through Gabby.

And then, something else, in the back of Gabby's mind.

Something out of place. A strange sensation of fury and loss, of failure and pride. Of rivalry and arguments. Of polar bears and zoo trips. Of holidays in Cyprus and late-night makeup sessions. Of apple bobbing and video games. Of separate schools and desperate longing.

The fierce, whirling void of sisterly love.

Da-ko-ta

written by
Amir Agoora

illustrated by
CONNOR CHAMBERLAIN

ABOUT THE AUTHOR

Amir Agoora was born in Connecticut to his Yemeni father and Puerto Rican mother. While at university studying English and political science, Amir tutored at the school's writing center and taught formerly incarcerated people reading and writing skills. The day after graduating from university, he received a call informing him he was a 2021 Sesame Writer's Room Fellow. After leaving Sesame Street, Amir wrote for Nickelodeon and is currently freelance screenwriting for two upcoming kids' shows on NBCUniversal. During the school year, Amir volunteers with the International Rescue Committee tutoring English and writing to refugee children in NYC.

"Da-ko-ta" took shape after reflecting on the haunted nature of the English language. Haunted not only by the revered dead tongues of Latin and ancient Greek, but also by the shadows of indigenous words. These linguistic specters haunt our tongues despite the systematic attempts to eradicate their very existence. Amir wanted to explore what happens when lofty imperial ambitions meet the people who bear the cost. In "Da-ko-ta," when a thirteen-year-old boy from the Sioux tribe is chosen from an Indian boarding school by Teddy Roosevelt, the boy swears to kill America's Great Chief. In a fight between the new American empire and ancient indigenous creatures, the monsters and heroes are not so easy to distinguish.

ABOUT THE ILLUSTRATOR

Connor Chamberlain was born in 1993 all the way down in the southernmost point of the South Island of New Zealand—in the sleepy, wide-street town of Invercargill.

Growing up on a small sheep farm, Connor's view of distant mountains and dense forests ensured that his imagination became a finely tuned instrument, always dreaming of the adventures that could be had over the next hill. So, what's a kid to do with all that countryside and very little else? Pick up a pencil, of course, and never look back.

As a teenager, Connor fell in love with '90s anime and Magic: the Gathering, which gave him ample material to obsess over. As well as this, Connor was lucky enough to have a cool older brother as an artistic inspiration and rival to spur him on.

Connor studied communication design in Dunedin, New Zealand, and worked for seven years as a graphic designer. He now works for a small New Zealand game company and seeks joy in drawing for his friends and family, as well as creating fan art of his favourite fantasy series (Brandon Sanderson's Stormlight Archive). He now lives in Dunedin with his newly wedded wife and little dog Haku, and continues to hone his craft.

He one day dreams of seeing his art grace the covers of fantasy books and trading cards, and is—as always—pursuing his own unique brand of world-building.

Da-ko-ta

CARLISLE INDIAN BOARDING SCHOOL
1905

I am awoken with broken English; the break is palliative. It means I am among my people. Leaning over my cot is Mongwau. He is thirteen winters like me. But we share no tongue, other than this broken one we are compelled to share.

"The Great Chief...he..." Without the word, Mongwau makes fingers gallop upon his palm. "Stampedes, here." I jolt upright, warmth of my pillow, dreams of my tribe abandoned.

"The Great Chief?" I make a great toothy grin, and declare, "Bully!" Mimicking the man from the newspapers.

Mongwau nods, emphatic. Even the many here who cannot read know of The Great Chief; we are captive by him. Teachers tell us he has brokered peace between two great tribes of people that lie east. The Japanese and Russians, they say they are almost as savage as us.

Our room is small, five of us. Ours is the Redskin room. Since we refuse to let go of our ways or acknowledge when they call us such a name, they beat us, but they cannot break our spirits.

We rush around the cramped space, lighting candles and putting on our scratchy gray uniforms. I pull my undershirt on slowly, my eye still tender and black from Mistress. I, or the demon that sleeps in my skull, knows more English and Latin than our Mistress. She strikes me when I use it, and she strikes me when I do not.

As if thoughts have summoned her, she appears at the door. Her voice crackles, bright and sharp.

"I have no earthly idea why you lot are dressing. You will not be meeting the president. You who are still half savage." The door slams, followed by a familiar brass *click*.

We bolt to the thin cold window. Great metal horses and an ornate carriage climb up the dirt road. Our amazement fogs the glass; we must wipe it away with our sleeves. Once, our people lived out in that schoolyard. All tribes would share a fire and the grief of stolen children. The school forced them off, "to help us better assimilate," but we knew in our hearts they were afraid. Our ancestors so close kept us, us. Now that ground fills with staff and students, over two tribes of persons pour out of the school and circle the metal horses, and carriage.

The door is brittle, you must go and behold the man. Trust.

The words rise from the Tarnished, the demon which resides in me. I respond within my own mind. *You deal in lies.*

And still, you must behold the man. He has come with a purpose.

The Tarnished is a demon older than stones. A disease picked up from a white warrior.

Years earlier, in a treetop with my bow, I waited to pluck a waterfowl from the sky. It is simpler than it sounds, rise before the early dew, be close to the sky and aim at the second in the V. If you miss, the bird behind will catch the arrow in its place.

In the morning light, over the horizon it looked as if rain-filled clouds were running across the land. I rubbed at my eyes. A swarm of cloudy gray uniforms on horseback stampeded toward my tribe. I made a warning call, three sharp whistles of bird out of season to announce the *wasi' chu.* My tribe stirred below, preparing.

As the warriors approached, I took aim at the man with golden curls on his shoulder, a cavalry officer. With a snap of his neck, he turned up to stare directly at me, as if he could see through the foliage and straight into my eyes. Before he could lift his rifle, my arrow drove through his eye. As his limp body swung free from the still galloping horse, the Tarnished fled the failing flesh of his host. A disease passed through blood spilt, not born.

The demon urged my arrows on; it steadied my hand. The arrows no longer felt shot from my arm, but rather drawn in by white flesh. Bodies slumped over, some crushed by their own horses. My flesh felt hot with rage and disease, the events shift from memory to fever dream. In the end, the Tarnished could not aid me when the distance grew shorter than an arrow's length. Men fatter than bison dragged me into capture and finally brought me here.

If my tribe still lived, they could wash this taint from me. Other than his insatiable blood lust, the Tarnished gives me dead tongues. Learnings of his last host carried over to mine. Homer in Greek, Virgil in Latin, and—

"No." The memory is shaken away from me by Mongwau's large palms on my shoulders. I've already moved toward the door. "No...pain." He taps a thin pink line across the side of his face. I lightly trace his winding scar myself.

"Must." With three heaves of my shoulder, the wood door cracks away, leaving the brass lock behind. Bright warm pain spreads as I push my way outside.

Not so brittle. I chide the Tarnished; it forms no response.

Through the halls, I harbor a ghost dance in my mouth. My tongue writhes like a worm on string, bait for something large and monstrous to swallow me and this broken world with it.

Outside, I push through the crowd of students. The Great Chief is in the center. He flashes a constant smile revealing large tombstone teeth. Words constantly escape the graveyard of his mouth. He rubs the head of a small Choctaw girl; she laughs brightly at him. All are held captive by his charm; those who do not understand his language still laugh.

His eyes dart across our red faces, then stop on mine. He strides over, fast for a man with a large buffalo shape, a barreled chest, square jaw, and sharp darting eyes.

"Do we have a fellow pugilist?" He raises large fists, taking playful jabs toward my blackened eye.

From the air, I pretend to pluck an arrow and nock it on an imaginary bow. I draw back the bowstring, arm shaking with imagined tension, and with a flick of my fingers, release the arrow into The Great Chief's heart. The president takes two staggered steps back clutching his chest. All fall still for a breath. His guards step forward, then he chuckles with great heaves of his chest. The rest of the circle laughs as well at this small theater. All save the staff.

"You've got me." His high voice breaks. It is not the voice I had expected from the discarded papers.

Mistress's eyes are wide with horror. I know that this may be my final act.

Someone squeezes my shoulder three times, a warning. Mongwau stands tall behind me, front teeth gnaw on bloody bottom lip. And not for the first time, I am struck by the beauty he carries.

From the president's breast pocket, he produces a book bound in leather the dull dark red of wet liver. He extends it to me. I make no move, my loathing and hatred wrestle with some inexplicable desire for his admiration. The large man raises his eyebrow, the expression so exaggerated I fight back a smile.

"You don't like gifts?" he asks.

"President Roosevelt," Mistress attempts to cut in. "Your excellency, sir, most of these students are still half savage. They don't know what to do with a book or a—"

"*Timeo Danaos et dona ferentes*," I let the Latin roll like thunder from my chest. Then I hold my breath, prepared for his hand to beat me down for my insolence. But shock gives way to great rolling laughter. The huge man bends at his stomach, laughing hard and loud. It is miraculous to watch.

"Half savage and cites Virgil..." The buffalo man wipes tears away from his eyes. And, as suddenly as it had come, the delight flees his face. He squints down at me through gold-rimmed spectacles. "Yes," he speaks to himself, audience forgotten. "That is what I have come for, a Virgil to my Dante. A guide into hell, pagan heart and all..." Two fingers tap at the side of his head, as if to drum in thought.

"You…are…" For the first time, I see the man falter for words, and I know that he is searching for one of mine.

I lift my right hand, the warmth of blood, demon, and flame rush up. My fingers smoke, then burn bright with forbidden flames. I want all to witness this power I possess. All eyes are on me, but before I can do or say anything, pain.

A sharp tearing pain spreads across the top of my head. I imagine a bowie knife slicing through scalp, my skin folded back on itself. But from behind, Mistress tugs on the little hair they have not forced me to cut. My braids of honor forfeited with the shame of capture.

"Enough." The president does not yell, but we all fall silent. Mistress releases me. And it seems even the trees and the falling snow hold their breath. He turns to our scrawny priest, the one who teaches Latin and buries those of us who go where no white hand can touch. "This one."

"Mr. President, sir." The priest dabs at his brow. "He is one of our more…difficult students. He refuses to let go of his uncivilized ways, rejects Christ, he—"

Roosevelt makes a sharp hand gesture. "If I were in search of a Christian, I would try the seminary. This one will accompany me to the White House. A presidential scholarship." The words fall heavy, but their meaning eludes me. "Congratulations, young man." The president extends his large hand. He does not ask; he informs.

Bite it, bite it! The Tarnished senses the tension spread over my body. I move to strike his hand and prepare for an honorable death.

But the bright red flower of an idea blossoms, and I jolt to grab his palm. With that, I seal his fate. Looking up at the man, I swear to the spirits of my tribe I will kill the white man's great chief.

I turn to find Mongwau. His eyes are wet and intense. I consider running to him, unearthing the heavy words buried in my chest. But if I go back, I could not leave. I speak with my hands, a teepee over my heart, home.

As if reading my thoughts, the Chief says, "Dakota." He tosses the word so lightly from the graveyard of his mouth, I flinch. He continues, "Dakota, it means friend in Sioux." I nod.

There is nothing to pack, so I'm led straight to the shiny obsidian carriage. A Black man with hair the color of slushed snow opens the door. I follow behind Roosevelt, sitting across from him. The servant climbs in after us. The carriage jostles off.

Pushing away the thick blood-red curtains, I stare out onto the fleeting pine trees.

Spectral syllables perform a ghost dance in my mouth. *Da,* the flat tongue pats the palate, and I imagine the initial rise of campfire smoke, *ko,* a guttural grunt, and I hear the crepitation of chanting, *ta,* a staccato tap of the tongue, and the drumming begins in earnest as my tribe circles the fire. That is all I can think about for the next many miles, a tiny ghost dance on my tongue. Da-ko-ta: friend.

The bitter word lingers on my tongue, no one speaks for the first few hours of the carriage ride. The president divides his time between writing and gazing out the window. He smokes no tobacco nor drinks any liquor. I feel the stone arrowhead in my boot. The only item I could save from my people. Half memento; half, final way out. Now all I would have to do is reach down and his throat would be slit, like slaughtering a deer. I look over, the servant's eyes closed, head resting on the side of the carriage.

Do it now!

Silence, Tarnished! You think I will falter, and he will slay me and you may join his flesh.

The Tarnished's frustration warms my face, like the blush of shame.

A raven glides by our window, and the hours of silence shatter with two words from the president's lips.

"Corvus corax."

His words make my whole body tense. Pinning down our animals with their dead venerated tongues. Ours too savage, too unworthy and unwieldy, for their notice.

"Kagi," I respond. The president pivots to meet my eyes, his head

cocked like a curious dog. I explain, "Raven in Lakota." He wipes the gold nib of his fountain pen with an ink-stained handkerchief.

"English, Latin, and Lakota." He nods appreciatively. "A truly American-educated man." I make no response. Over his spectacles, he squints at me, peering up and down my body. Finally, he speaks.

"I have spent some time in the Dakotas, had a ranch; it's certainly a healthy life, great sleep and coarse fare...." He raises an eyebrow as if it were a question for me to answer. He makes one want to answer. I see why he is a chief. He draws people in like leaves caught in a current. Silent I remain.

"There were Indians out there like yourself, who told tales of a beast called the wendigo." At the name I cannot suppress the twitch of my nose, the smell of something gone rotten. "Ah, so you've heard of the beast too! Tell me, tell me all you know." For the first time, I lock my eyes onto his and refuse to look down as I'd been taught.

"Greedy, insatiable creatures, they would drink the sky and devour all life to satiate their hunger. No distance they would not travel. No blood they would not shed for their ends." The president nods, oblivious to any implications.

This goes on for hours as one answer breeds three more questions. I speak of an insatiable thirst for human flesh. He asks which parts of the body. I describe the pallid, emaciated form. He asks for details as he produces a sketch. I speak of the way it can shift from man and back.

"And when it looks like a man, is it one?" he asks. The question catches me off guard. I vacillate my hand like a canoe on choppy water.

"It is always wendigo; sometimes it is less than man, sometimes more. But the craving of flesh resides."

The president nods. "And a rifle...can kill it?"

I tell the story of a wendigo having one of its legs cut off and gaily drinking the marrow within.

Roosevelt nods as if this all makes sense. No, as if he had heard it all before. Finally, head bent he wipes at his spectacles. *Fool, you danced to his tune.*

315

The Tarnished is right. This was not the Chief searching for a lecture. This was a test; I had been tricked.

The Chief speaks, "I am told, that the white race cannot truly *see* wendigo. Six Forest Rangers have been…lost in the last five months in your Dakotas." My heart smiles at this, but I leave my face still as pond water. "They tell me only those of Lakota can see, in fact, most notably the child." This I did not know, but believe. "After securing peace between the Russians and Japanese, I have told the American people when Congress recesses, I shall go on a victory hunting trip. This is true. But this is not simply blood to blot out thought. We are hunting wendigo."

"We?" The question cracks in my throat.

"Yes." He leans his large frame forward, as if to reach out and seize my collar. Instead, he locks his eyes onto mine, "I'm afraid your services are required. The frontiers of this country are still laden with ancient savagery." He stares out the window as if some great tribe would step out from the tree lines. "In exchange for your service, I can offer you a superior education. In fact, we have one of the greatest military minds right here. Isn't that right, Major?"

The old servant's eyes snap open. "If you say so, sir."

Roosevelt bares his teeth in his huge smile. "I do say so! Major Cassius burnt down Atlanta with General Sherman in '64. Confederates had a thousand-dollar bounty out on the good major. What did they call you, 'Sherman's lighter'?"

The servant smiles wryly, rolling a furtive flame down his knuckles. His control over the fire is effortless, and much more precise than my abilities. "They called me Sherman's torch, sir."

Roosevelt's heavy frame shakes with laughter. "That's right! No greater instructor for military tactics and combat."

I meet Cassius's eyes; I try and fail to see the warrior behind the wrinkles. More a grandfather than a general.

"Well?" The president is still leaning in, studying me.

The thought of Roosevelt and me, in my forest, surrounded by the spirits of my people, armed, makes my whole body vibrate.

"But we must go alone." The words tumble out of my mouth as if they were not my own. Roosevelt cocks his head.

"Oh?"

"The wendigo will not strike a large group. It must think we are unprepared... falling into a trap."

Roosevelt falls silent tapping his gold pinky ring against the chilled carriage glass. Then he extends his hand to me and squeezes with enormous force.

"I respect your bravery."

At the president's palace, a small card room is converted into my quarters. A cot, with a large trunk at the foot, and a small oak desk are neatly arranged inside. My desk is laden with fountain pens, bottled Prussian blue ink, and stacks of leather-bound books. As part of my scholarship, I'm gifted a small pigskin library. Between the dead swine flesh, the words of vibrant Roman wars and historic naval battles tremble with life. Two of the books are from the president's personal library.

One black leather with gold lettering *The History of the Peloponnesian War*; the other, the same burgundy book Roosevelt had tried to offer me, a Longfellow translation of Dante's *Inferno*. On the inside cover, in the president's sweeping cursive, *For my Virgil, TR.*

The hairs on my neck straighten as I thumb over the inscription. The Tarnished's voice explodes within my skull. *Behind you!* Without turning I strike my elbow back. Something dodges, an arm hooks under my exposed armpit. For a moment, I'm weightless. Then the floor rushes up to slam into my back. A polished Oxford shoe hovers over my neck.

Above me, the servant with bright flames crackling within his hands. At this angle the wrinkles have vanished; above me is a warrior. He removes his foot from my neck and straightens his uniform.

"Sorry, youngin', the president asked me to test your instincts." Cassius offers down a slender hand, setting me back on my feet. I brush the dirt from my clothes.

"I suppose I failed."

Cassius shakes his head. "Good instincts, bad offense. I can teach offense, can't teach instincts." The servant lights a short pipe and waves for me to follow through the halls. "The president has offered us his personal boxing gym to train."

The next two hours are spent with the former major slamming me to the ground, each bout punctuated only with short combat tips and coughing fits.

This exercise becomes routine for the next few weeks. My body aches, and in turn grows stronger, quicker, faster.

I become quite famous as "Roosevelt's savage." On the cover of *Harper's Weekly*, I'm drawn with a large headdress on a ship next to a grinning Roosevelt. Harpoon in hand, he takes aim at a white whale named "Standard Oil." The caption reads, "Better to sleep with a sober cannibal than an oil-drunk Christian." At parties I'm asked for, "Where's Roosevelt's savage?" And so, I attend state dinners and meetings.

At one such early party, I follow behind Roosevelt with his pet badger waddling beside. Some British lord with a sluglike mustache exclaims, "A savage and a beast, what can't the great Roosevelt tame?" This brings great shrieks of laughter and cheers.

Burn him and boil his blood! Even if the Tarnished always craves bloodshed, his indignation at my slight warms me.

I say nothing, just watch as Roosevelt pours blobs of candle wax on a table, describing the naval engagement of Trafalgar and the genius of Nelson's supply chain.

Later in the night, when servants arrive to light cigars, I ask to do it myself. When the British lord bends his head to the matchbook, it erupts into flames. The man next to the lord has to strike his face to put the remains of his mustache out. The Tarnished cheers inside my mind.

Before I can conceal my smile, Roosevelt finds my eyes. I expect wrath, instead a pair of blue boyish sparkling eyes, and the shadow of a smile as the lord curses American matches.

Hours later, as I part, hands pull me into a dark office. I strike out, but I'm pinned against a wall.

"What are you thinking boy?" Cassius, real worry contorts his face as he shakes my shoulders. "That lord could have you killed. My god, Juney, what were you thinking?"

"Juney?" I ask. He's called me this mysterious name before, usually after a long tiring bout, but he never explains who Juney is.

He lets me go and coughs violently into his handkerchief. Finally, he looks up.

"Promise me you won't do that again."

I nod and he stalks off.

The days become colder, and I make a better effort to hide my mischief around the White House from Cassius. Loosed cats in the China room, fake declarations of war near the press, and the like. We continue with martial combat and military tactics every morning. On weekends I have tutors, International Relations with Secretary of State Elihu Root, Law & American Economics with Attorney General Bonaparte. Finally, by December, Cassius permits for all-out fights. He still wins every bout, but it takes him much more effort. I throw three fast jabs at his jaw, my hands alight with flame. He weaves out of its path. He throws a wall of flame that I slip under. I go for a kick but overextend. He seizes my ankle and effortlessly flings me on my back.

Great booming laughter erupts from the entrance. Roosevelt slaps Cassius on the back.

"My god, Major, you're as spry as a mountain lion." Roosevelt peers down at me with a wide grin. "Don't feel bad, son; the major learned all the Indian tricks you could know and beat 'em a long time ago." Roosevelt pats Cassius, then is whisked away by some adviser.

"You taught other Indians?" I try to keep the hurt from my voice. Cassius refuses to make eye contact; he focuses on lighting his pipe. The Tarnished whispers with delight, *Ask, Ask, Ask.* The Tarnished knows the answer my mind refuses to accept. "What did Roosevelt mean?"

Cassius stays focused on nurturing the flame in his pipe with short staccato inhales. Finally, like tossing a stone from his tongue, "I was in the army." More puffs. "I stayed with General

Sherman after our war." Cassius looks, but my face is still as pond water; he waits to witness the ripples of recognition. The smoke pools in his mouth then escapes, like water falling up into his nostrils. "I fought out West, killed some... I killed a great many of your people."

My stomach lurches. My head feels as if I had taken great swallows of firewater.

"You?" The crack of accusation is all I can muster....

The Tarnished wrenches my chest with tightness. *Why did you think they had him instruct you? He knows all your savage tricks and conquered them. Slash him! Slash!*

The Tarnished's words jolt my body. I notice the pain on Cassius's face before I discover my backed-away steps. He's wounded by my retreat. "Wait, boy, wait!" His voice chases after, as I flee through the halls.

Two days pass alone. Cassius does not call on me. Finally, I call on him, and we resume where we left off. Cassius's coughing fits become more frequent, the breaks in between bouts longer.

Weeks pass like this. I find solace in the books, my teachers, and although I try to suppress it, in Roosevelt's presence. Such time has passed that I almost forgot my purpose, until one sparring match with Cassius. Our last match.

In Roosevelt's boxing room, toward the end of December, we start with a fencing sword just sharp enough to draw blood, and our nondominant hand for fire. Within the first thirty seconds, Cassius disarms me, my sword abandoned on the floor. Cassius produces huge columns of fire from the palms of his hands. Right when I think I'm safe, his sword lights ablaze and flashes near my face quicker than I can see it. The seemingly good-natured old man is blasting flame, fist, and blade so fast all I can do is try to avoid them.

"You ever going to strike, or you just sweet on me for a dance?" Cassius chuckles at his own taunt. I roll to the side as a fiery fist comes close to taking me out.

"Seems like you should be the one striking and not serving."

I dodge by my fallen fencing sword; I reach for it as Cassius slams his boot on the blade. A column of fire from above forces me to retreat. "They have taken you from your home, enslaved you, and now you serve them? Why not use this to destroy them!?" My question is met with a jerk of his arm.

The burning sword slashes down on my left. I fling myself right into his free hand. He seizes the front of my shirt and puts blade to my throat. He bends me so far back I am almost upside down, his hand seizing my shirt keeping me upright.

"Destroy who?" he asks.

"All of them!" I cry, fueled by impotence and indignation. "The generals, the soldiers, the president!"

The moment it leaves my lips; I wish to recall it. Nobody moves. Without warning or taking his eyes off mine he lets me go, and I thud to the floor. Cassius towers over me, burning blade still in hand. The blazing hot room seems only to grow hotter. Finally, with an exhale of breath and smoke, Cassius offers me his hand, pulling me upright.

"It won't do you a lick of good; the blood's already been spilt." He turns his back on me and begins to sweep the sparring room. "This thing, this…country…it's not gonna stop. No putting that genie back. I had to fight for the little freedom I got; ain't got no more fight in me. That's a fight….I won't live to see the end of it. All you got in the end is family." He catches my eye for a moment, then turns back to his work.

As he sweeps the floor, both the fierce soldier and dutiful servant seem to melt away. In front of me are the hunched shoulders of a broken man.

The Tarnished speaks, *The soldier's body remains. The fight has fled.* I exit without a word.

A knock at my door in the middle of the night interrupts my reading of Plutarch's *On Sparta*, (the Tarnished's favorite). I rise to answer, thinking it must be Cassius come to discuss our earlier conversation, to chide me for threatening the president.

Be on guard, Savage. Power lies behind the door. Fear crawls down each bump of my spine; the Tarnished is right. An ambush, the president's guards armored and ready. Cassius waiting to strike when I would be most tired and isolated. A tactic he had taught me himself.

With Plutarch in one hand, a hot flame in my other, I fling the door open. The whole door frame is taken up with Roosevelt. My heart slams like some great bird of prey, thrashing its wings against the cage of my ribs. Attempting to flee or fight, I cannot know.

Roosevelt laughs. "What a scholar you've become, awake at this hour." He's not in his suit, but rather a dark hunting jacket, trousers with endless pockets and a Panama hat. "Well, it's time. Congress is out for Christmas and a great white blizzard is about to blanket Washington." Walking through the empty halls, I search for the word; minutes pass, before it comes to me.

"*Iwoblu*," I say aloud, to hear it hit the air. Roosevelt raises an eyebrow. "It means blizzard." He nods as a new panic seizes me. Months ago, that word would have lived right on my tongue, now between my English, Greek, and Latin I've began to lose my Lakota. What else have I lost; in what language do I dream?

An unmarked shiny black carriage led by two black horses is by the back entrance, the horses and the driver's hot breath make smoke signals in the winter air. Roosevelt has one foot up on the carriage he's halfway inside.

"Sir?" Then a familiar cough.

Roosevelt and I turn to see Cassius, hands rubbing at the warmth of his breath, a shiny revolver on his hip.

Roosevelt shakes his head.

"Major, you're up there in your years, you served—"

"Sir." Cassius, for the first time I had ever seen, spoke over a white person. "Please, sir, an old man's wish for one last hunt." Roosevelt's sharp eyes dart from the top of his head to the bottom of his boots. I know his answer before he gives it, and Cassius must have, too.

"My god, come on then."

Inside the carriage I find a bow and a sheaf of arrows on my seat. I finger the bowstring and add the stone arrowhead from my boot to an arrow shaft. Cassius and I stare into each other's eyes. Has he come to protect Roosevelt? To die in battle?

Roosevelt watches Cassius and me.

"Major, you've raised a great fighter, in fact, two. I haven't forgotten about Juney." The name brings back memories of past conversations. Cassius had called me Juney more than once before.

"Who's that, Mr. President?" I ask.

Roosevelt looks from my face to Cassius's, with a raised eyebrow, surprised at my ignorance.

"Juney, Junius Greene. He was a Rough Rider, a soldier with me in Cuba. And the major's son. He fought bravely, and died with great honor. I was there to witness it myself."

Cassius nods; the words bring no comfort. Cassius closes his eyes, and with the swaying of the carriage, I do the same.

We are let out at the edge of my forest; Dante's opening canto rattles within my skull, *What was this forest savage, rough, and stern, Which in the very thought renews the fear.*

Roosevelt with rifle slung over shoulder leads the way through the snow. Marching through the cold, I feel my blood come alive; it flees my fingers and toes, seeking warmer parts to shelter. Hours pass in silence, except for Cassius's coughing. Roosevelt searches for tracks, I for a plan.

After one particularly long coughing fit, Roosevelt turns to Cassius.

"Major, why don't you sit down for a moment. We'll scout out ahead."

Cassius nods, he puts his palm out and blasts a column of flame at a boulder, melting the snow on top. He eases himself down on the heated seat. Roosevelt moves on ahead. I linger with Cassius, waiting for Roosevelt to be out of earshot.

"Why are you here? To protect him? You are in no condition to do anything." My question and hot breath hang cloudlike in the frozen air. Doubled over, he coughs so hard dark red blood sprays the snow like birdshot. Finally, Cassius looks up, his eyes shiny and wet.

"I'm here to protect you.... I won't let him take another one of my boys." Cassius opens his revolver, then with a snap of his wrist, flicks it closed. "If you really want 'em dead..." Cassius checks his pocket watch. "I'll catch up with you in five minutes. Just say the word." He seizes my hand and squeezes it. "But there has been enough bloodshed. We can just go home."

My thoughts flee in thirty different directions. I run back toward Roosevelt.

I find him crouching down following tracks. He looks back at me and whispers.

"You know I am very proud to see you join civilization. You are a credit to your race. A true member of the American empire." His words stab straight to my heart.

"I am not part of your empire. I do not stand for empire of any—"

Roosevelt's rifle explodes in the forest.

"Got 'em." A moose jolts through the trees. We follow the heavy blood trail in its wake. Roosevelt continues, "Empire is about order, to settle the land, and bring peace to this country."

Through the clearing, the moose has collapsed on its side, its chest still rising and falling with heavy shuddered breaths. Its legs twitch.

I shake my head and in Latin recite, "They plunder, they steal, and they slaughter. This they call empire, and where they make a wasteland, they call it peace."

Roosevelt snorts as he leans over the fallen animal.

The moose's wet eye stares up at me, questioning why this man still lives, why he must forfeit his life to an invader.

"And you, who stands for savages of all ilks, make your case in a civilized tongue. Quoting Tacitus...you have received a better education than one in ten thousand men in this country, when you plead for rights, you do so in Latin, Roman appeals, and clean English."

The president lifts the moose's head, inspecting the beast as my tongue becomes foreign to me, light, decayed, rotten like the remains of a decaying tree. My own tongue colonized; my people betrayed.

Language is luxury. Man requires only blood. Within the walls of my skull the Tarnished sounds…different.

I draw my bow, placing the back of Roosevelt's head in my sights.

Hold, Savage, hold!

My body jolts stiff frozen, never has the Tarnished asked to spare anyone or anything. Before I can frame the question, my tongue falls limp at the report of a pistol. Four shots in rapid gunslinger fashion.

Roosevelt springs up, looking in the direction of the gunshots. "Cassius! He might'a found the beast!" The large man barrels through the woods. Full panic seizes me. Had Cassius decided to lure Roosevelt, decision made? I follow after, deeper into the dark woods.

At the base of a tree is the wrecked visage of a man. Blood streams from eyes and mouth, a small revolver slick and shiny like a broken bloody fish scale by his feet. I can't speak.

Roosevelt calls out into the darkness. "Where are you, Cassius?"

I tug on the president's jacket.

"There, there!" I point to the base of the tree. Roosevelt looks to where I point, but for a few heavy moments he cannot see anything. Then, a jolt as he recognizes a body.

The Tarnished is muttering something, but I cannot make it out.

Roosevelt takes a knee and lifts his head with the same gesture as the moose. "Major…Major?" He breaks open his buttoned shirt looking for wounds; there's no blood, just rib cage bulging against tight skin.

Cassius sputters out blood and broken words. "The beast…ran…off…." A feeble finger points west.

Roosevelt lifts the broken man over his shoulder. "Let's get you back to the carriage first." And he plunges back the way we came. I follow behind and think how easy it would be to use my bow on Roosevelt once the carriage is in sight.

Cassius over Roosevelt's shoulder stares at me as I follow behind. "Beware the Injun."

I stop dead in my tracks.

"What's that, Major?" Roosevelt asks.

Finally, I understand what the Tarnished is saying. It's the same word over and over. Not in any tongue I speak, but sharing its mind I can tell its meaning *rejoice, rejoice, rejoice, rejoice.*

Cassius smiles as if he hears both my thoughts and the Tarnished's. The smile grows unnaturally wide, for only me to see. His brown eyes shift into a stony gray.

"It plans to kill you, Mr. President.... Murder lies at the depth of the savage heart...always has."

The Tarnished's whisper is reverent and joyful. *He sees you, Savage. You are seen, rejoice.*

And then and only then, I see the broken shape of Cassius for what it truly is. Body stolen, just flesh instead of man. True panic seizes my body.

"The Greek is at our gates." I say it as calmly as I can.

Roosevelt's aggressive stride is broken for only the slightest of moments. But he needs no further explanation. Roosevelt swings the form of Cassius off his shoulder. With both legs in hand, he slams him against the trunk of a tree. The crunching sound of brittle bones, then the body crumples to the ground. Before I can nock an arrow, what had once been in the form of Cassius contorts, limbs bend like a dying spider. Finally, flesh tears and splits apart, revealing the bloody pale hulking mass of muscle, sinew, antlered, and monstrous.

I know this beast has killed Cassius and shifted into his form. Now I am in these dark woods alone. My joints lock, paralyzed. Roosevelt lifts his rifle, a large blast, but the beast only smiles with razor-blade teeth. As if in response, the rifle rusts and decays in Roosevelt's hands.

The beast does not even look at the president. He only has eyes for me. It charges, but the president steps in between, fists raised.

"Go, boy, run!"

Roosevelt had once looked huge to me, but next to the beast he is only a man. The wendigo slams into the president. Both crash to the snowy ground. As they grapple with each other, a distant part hopes the wendigo finishes what I could not, but before

I realize it, the revolver is in my hand. It cocks with the sharp click of rodent bone snapping under owl's beak. I pull the trigger, the world slows as tiny clicks tick by, empty chamber after empty chamber pass by the barrel.

Finally, the metal explodes in my hand. Bullet strikes pale flesh, but it only shakes off the small metal and exposes sharp bloody teeth. It needs no words to convey its thoughts.

I cannot be harmed by that which I helped create.

Roosevelt's face drips with blood. The wendigo is on top now. It snaps at the president's flesh, but even on his back Roosevelt is able to exchange blows.

I step closer to the two beasts. My shadow falls across Roosevelt's face.

"Run! Run! I got 'em, son."

But he doesn't. The beast's jagged razor teeth tear flesh from his shoulder. I take up my bow instead. I think of Cassius, who this beast has consumed and stolen his form. I set the arrow, the tip of which I've kept in my boot since capture, and with a snap of my fingers light the tip ablaze.

Arrow nocked, I pray, my tongue flipping through the slaughtered syllables of my people. I pray and call on my ancestors, and I crave not blood spilt, but blood saved.

The arrow sinks into the beast's neck, and for the first time, it screeches sharp like a train slamming on brakes. I feel the heat of my blood cool. Something has fled my body.

Roosevelt uses the distraction and throws a wide arch of a punch once, twice, a third time. The lower jaw splinters off the beast.

The wendigo falls back into the woods with a quick feeble-footed retreat, wounded but not fatally.

I hover over Roosevelt. The man is sprawled out on the ground, pools of dark red blood greedily eaten by the once-white snow. The metallic smell of his blood sharp in the cold air turns my stomach.

"So...is it true? You mean to kill me?" He does not look afraid, or even upset, it sounds like a question he has no particular stake in. I visualize what this man has done to my people, my family.

327

CONNOR CHAMBERLAIN

Well? I ask the Tarnished. Looking for encouragement. But it's not there; it fled with my arrow, and the blood spilt of the beast.

My face is wet, the loss of the demon and of Cassius leaves me numb.

I call for guidance, some words of strength, Lakota or Latin, anything. No more blood, I think of Cassius, his son, all the sons lost.

My mouth can only frame one word. *Da*, the flat tongue pats the palate, and I imagine the initial rise of campfire smoke; *ko*, a guttural grunt, and I hear the crepitation of chanting; *ta*, a staccato tap of the tongue, and the drumming begins in earnest as mankind circles the fire.

I lift him, his heavy arm wrapped around my shoulder.

Through bruised and bloody eyes, he *looks* at me...for the first time.

We limp toward the carriage. Not so far off into the dark wood, the wendigo shrieks painfully into the breaking dawn light.

Squiddy

written by
John Eric Schleicher

illustrated by
TYLER VAIL

ABOUT THE AUTHOR

John Eric Schleicher writes stories that leave behind a fantastical aftertaste long after reading. While story rules the roost, John Eric's favorite authors tell their tales with panache and pleasing prose. Toni Morrison, Cormac McCarthy, Stephen King, and Ray Bradbury top his literary cake.

When not reading or writing, John Eric enjoys wandering wonderstruck, whether on two legs or knobby wheels, the mountains near his home in Missoula, Montana. His greatest loves are his son, Ryder, and wife, Ashlee, to whom "Squiddy" is dedicated.

"Squiddy," his first professional sale, is a spawn of the postapocalyptic imaginings of an extraterrestrial Squid invasion and explores the self-destructive habits we seek to escape or soften despair. He is currently expanding the tale into a novel.

John Eric's short fiction has also appeared in Creepy Podcast.

ABOUT THE ILLUSTRATOR

Tyler Vail was born in 1996 in Dallas, Texas. At a young age, Tyler was deeply inspired by fantasy and sci-fi media and would spend many late nights striving to bring his ideas to life in the form of drawings.

He would later refine his skills as an illustrator by joining every art contest he could find, actively participating in online communities, and getting feedback from anyone who would look at his art.

Today, Tyler continues his passion for art, dreaming of fantastic new worlds, characters, and creatures. He enjoys working with other creatives to share in a collaborative and positive experience and strives for excellence in all aspects of the artistic process.

Squiddy

Two raps rap my door.

"Hold on!" I struggle off my mattress in my one-room apartment, my current squat, a good squat, and pass my magenta-colored Squid that soaks in a gray tub of water.

I open the door to a woman with long, black hair, her eyes sunken into cavernous sockets. Barefooted and wearing a red tank top, she's got no pants on, only loose white panties, held up by sharp hip bones.

Like mine, like all squiddies, her nostrils are black like she's picked her nose with an exploded pen. She holds a dripping plastic bag, the kind from when grocery stores existed. I know what's inside.

"You Jocelyn?" Her voice is slight and raspy, a mile away.

"You got a job for me"—I nod at her bag—"or you just here to squid?"

"Both."

Across the hall, this week's neighbors are at it again, screams and curses, a baby crying. Poor little girl. There's near no chance for the youngest since the Squids came. How they came, no one knows for sure. One day, unannounced, their squishy membrane bodies of changing colors, pinks and blues and greens, started plopping up everywhere. And since that day, they've kept plopping up everywhere, on the roads, on roofs, in yards, front and back, privacy fences be damned.

No spaceships. No missiles or bombs. No take-me-to-your-leader nonsense. As invasions go, it was yawn inducing. That was until someone stuck a tentacle up his or her nose. Give that squiddy a Nobel. A Darwin Award might be better.

I turn for the woman to follow. "What's the job?"

"I'm told you find people." She closes the door and kerplunks her Squid in the tub of water with mine. "You bring them back, too?"

"If they want bringing back." I sit, cross-legged, on the mattress and ruffle in my black tote bag for my tin case of rolled cigarettes and Zippo lighter. "Who needs finding?"

"Daughter." She sits on the floor against the wall, hugging knees to chest.

"Got a picture?" I toss her my cigarettes and lighter.

"She looks like me."

Dammit, she doesn't have a picture.

"How much younger?"

She lights her cigarette, inhales a drag, and blows a smoky stream out the right side of her mouth. "I was seventeen when I had her."

"How old are you now?"

"Thirty-four or five."

She looks much older. We all look much older.

I stand. My legs prickle. That sensation's happening more often. I walk toward my red milk crate of supplies in the corner of the room and tousle inside. Rope. Carabiner. Duct tape. An assortment of knives, long blades, serrated blades, switchblades, and the like. There it is—my Polaroid camera.

I snap a picture of the frowning woman.

The camera whines as it spits the white Polaroid out.

I fan it until her image appears. "What's your daughter's name?"

"Anne Marie."

"And your name?" I stuff the picture in the tote.

"Call me Ma Bev."

"What does Anne Marie call you?"

"Everybody calls me Ma Bev."

One of our Squids flops the water with a tentacle. They need moisture to survive. Morning dew is enough. After a long rain, there's more of them than earthworms. So much, you got to play hopscotch not to squash one. And if you do? That's a nasty day. Their juicy insides are acidic.

"Ma Bev, when and where did you last see Anne Marie?"

"Georgia. It was Georgia. Not sure when. I don't keep track of time good."

"Was it before or after the Squids?"

"Before."

"Before in Georgia? Why you looking here?"

"She likes the ocean."

"Last recall, there's an ocean near Georgia."

"She likes the Pacific."

"Pacific's a big sink."

"She had a postcard from the Olympic Peninsula tacked near her bed." She gestures like Vanna White used to do. "So, here I am."

I got doubts a postcard brought Anne Marie here. We're in a temperate rainforest, after all. Constant rain means constant Squids means a constant flow of squiddies. So, Ma Bev's not telling me the whole truth. What of it? Everybody's got secrets.

I got to eat, so I ask for half my fee upfront, the rest if I find Anne Marie. Ma Bev says she has a bag of ground cornmeal back where she squats between two large red cedars in Boyd's Camp. I tell Ma Bev I'll get started once I got the cornmeal, then I tell her I'm ready to squid. I'm jonesing.

She nods her agreement.

Two-handed, I scoop up my dripping Squid, now yellow, face the wall, and kneel, my cheek muscles grinning. I close my eyes and inhale its smell, that sour sweetness rising. I faintly register Ma Bev's sighs behind me as I slip a thin tentacle up my pierced nostril, feel it slip and slide up through my nasal cavity, past that little hole that leads down the digestive tract.

More tentacles, like oily spaghetti, worm into my mouth, down my throat. The Squid does this on its own. Some evolutionary-derived sense humans don't got. Pheromones or some crap.

I taste its metallic secretion, feel it hook into my esophagus with a tight pinch. So, I'm gagging now, eyes watering now, got that metallic taste now, when the Squid wraps its other moist tentacles around my neck to latch on. The parasite squeezes. It pulses. Pulse. Pulse. And it rips off my supple flesh from within, and it eats.

The anticipation, though. Even the anticipation makes my entire body tingle, from head to breasts to toes, limp almost. There's no other high like Squid. Sex? Naw. Heroin? Nope. So other squiddies have told me. Heaven? Heaven might compare. I'll never know.

And it's coming. The euphoric, orgasmic hit is coming in three-Mississippi-flat. Count it. One Mississippi. Two Mississippi. Bliss.

I wake alone and naked on the mattress with a bag of cornmeal beside me. I kick off the white sheet that's tangled around my ankle, grab my cigarette case from the floor, then sitting crisscross applesauce, I light a rolled cigarette and suck in and enjoy the smoky taste, relaxing amongst lazy, smoky spirals. Sitting there, looking down, my ribs are like the grill rack on a barbecue, the bottom two hanging over my belly button even when I bloat my stomach out.

This job's all that's keeping me alive, barely, chucking enough calories down my gullet to sputter along. Why keep on? I got to feed these parasites, get that high. I give myself another year, two at best. It's happening to millions already, their cells shutting down, starved. You find these dead squiddies in gutters, under underpasses, in apartments and houses where they last squatted. Most often, the smell finds you. The smell is warm. The smell is rot.

I dress, put in all my studs and piercings, grab my tote filled with essentials—food, cigarettes, that Polaroid, blue poncho, and a switchblade—and leave for Boyd's Camp.

As camps go, Boyd's Camp is large on account of the many Squids that line the banks and swim and float the channels of the river. Boyd built a compound early and started charging rent to squiddies to simply exist near the river. The bastard charges high for protection, too. And if a squiddy doesn't got the food?

TYLER VAIL

No problem. You work for the bastard, most likely becoming a bastard yourself.

The ground floor of the Olympic Peninsula, a wet mix of moss, decaying bark, leaves, and soil, gives with each of my steps. Green colors most everything: green ferns, dewdrops sparkling; green moss blanketing the bark of Sitka spruces, Douglas firs, and red cedars, their green pine needles overhead and around. Interspersed in this green world are tents and smoky fires and squiddies—the conscious and the unconscious—and zero plumbing. The smell is abrasively distinct, that of smoke, of moist earth, of human waste.

This camp's a magnified microcosm the world over, the dial turned up a few degrees because of the rainforest climate. I imagine the Amazon is likewise bursting with squiddies, the Gobi Desert the opposite. Las Vegas, where I worked at a punk club before the invasion, is a ghost city, the lights long ago shut off. Its crumbling casinos, its paltry population, it's a dying dry cough of its once spectacular form.

When I get to the squat of one of my informants, Margie, I see she's unconscious and smiling. On to Gerald, I regret, another set of my eyes and ears. He grates me. A lawyer before the Squid invasion—I couldn't care less which kind—Gerald believes it still matters. What matters now? That next hit, that next tentacle.

I stare at the Squid Margie last used. Pink with blue dots, it pulses in the mud next to her fire pit of damp, charred sticks and twigs. I huff louder than a sigh, shake my head, hop up and down, shake my arms and my legs as if that will shake this intense want from my veins. I leave.

I try not to dawdle at every Squid I pass nor dwell on the shame that builds and fills me. I got a job to do, personal agency to uphold, that when I pass five Squids in quick succession, feels as solid as gas, as true as the belief we humans are the apex predators on Earth. These five Squids are a prism of changing colors. Blue. Red. Pink. Was that emerald? I blink. Now it's turquoise. Dazzling, they beckon the promise of escapism.

Gerald. I got to find Gerald to find Anne Marie.

At his squat, Gerald's eating from a can of cold meat ravioli. He is wearing that faded Blue Jays hat he wears. He doesn't like baseball, nor is he from Toronto. His polo shirt, pink and stained, seems to grow bigger each time I see him. Pockmarks dot his face. His nostrils are squiddy black. The orange and yellow glow of his crackling fire dances off his blue tarp overhead. Steam rises from his tin pot of boiling water.

"Jocelyn, my girl, Jocelyn." His deep voice drips with pretentiousness. "Plumbing's what I miss most."

"Plumbing was nice."

"Marvelous magic is what it was. Turn a metallic nozzle and, abracadabra, safe cold water comes to your beck and call. No need to squat by a fire to burn the danger away."

I hand Gerald the Polaroid. "Know her?"

Whistling, he examines it near the fire. "That's Ma Bev. She's a working woman."

"So, a surviving woman."

"It's more than that." He hands back the Polaroid. "She entered camp last week. Made a stir because she's now got two girls working under her. They were Boyd's girls." He shovels in a spoonful of ravioli and continues in a muffled voice. "I hear she takes twenty-five percent of what her girls make."

"What did Boyd take?"

"My guess is fifty."

"I don't pay you for guesses."

"Then pay me more."

I toss Gerald a small red box of raisins.

He catches it one-handed, scrunching the box between palm and spoon. "Raisins?"

I smirk and give him two cigarettes. "Know anyone that looks like Ma Bev? Say eighteen or nineteen years old?"

Gerald snorts a laugh. "By God, Anne sure does."

"Anne Marie?"

"Just Anne." He scrapes his spoon along the inside of the can, plowing the red sauce and meat bits into a drift. "She's Ma Bev but younger, fresher, what Ma Bev might have looked like before

339

life beat her down. Never made the connection until you asked. So, what is she? Ma Bev's sister? Daughter?"

"Where can I find her?"

"Anne?" He spoons the last of his meal and tosses the can. "She's inside Boyd's compound."

"One of his girls?"

"The girl. He doesn't share her."

Outside Boyd's compound, I crouch next to its tall fence made from the trunks of Douglas firs, the nostalgic smell of Christmases past engulfing me, and question whether to wade farther where a known killer lurks.

Yes, Boyd's deadly, but I'm already a dead gal walking, been tiptoeing that plank since the day I first squidded. If knowing her mother's on the scene might get Anne Marie rambling, I'm doing some good in this squiddy world. If she wants to stay put like a stone, good on her, that's on her.

I sneak up near the ranch gate of the compound where a thin, shaved-headed guard stands under a wooden archway, his hands in his jeans pocket, his nostrils inked black like all nostrils that sniffed these days.

I press my body against the moss-covered trunk of a giant big-leaf maple. Next to me, nestled between two thick roots, pulses a Squid. Red chatoyant circles spot its gray membrane.

I want it, envision the tickle of its tentacles squirming up a nostril. I scoop it up, feel its slippery cool skin in my palm. Intense craving blooms inside me, its thorny vines curled into every cell of my body. Not now. Not yet.

Squid cupped in hand, I sprint at the guard when he turns his back. I'm upon him when he faces me, and I smack his shocked expression with a Squid washing as if the Squid were snow and we were children.

He flails his arms as he falls onto his back.

The pulsing Squid finishes my dirty work, latching on, stilling the guard into unconsciousness seconds after he hits the humus. I envy him.

340

I enter the compound, built on a clear-cut, and walk on tacky mud as if I belong, wearing confidence for a mask. I'm surrounded by wood buildings in a helter-skelter pattern.

One of Boyd's people, an older woman of Asian descent, shovels up Squids and plops them in a wooden cart she's pulling. She's humming, smiles a few-tooth smile at me, and continues with her work.

How does she smile amongst all those tentacles in the cart twisting and stretching for her black nostrils? Her willpower to not squid until off-duty, I get. Boyd has a real nasty flair for punishing his rule-breakers. But her smile? That perplexes me.

Two-storied amongst the many one-story buildings, Boyd's wooden cabin is easy to spot in the center of the compound. On my way, I pass several troughs, filled with murky river water, and I pass a young, bearded Black man, who is wearing bib overalls that hang loosely on his tall Squid-eaten body while boiling water in a brass cauldron. I nod to him. He stares back. Next, I walk by the foul odor of wooden outhouses and step over a muddy puddle with several Squids, yet to be collected.

It's a bad place, worse time, to fall into a Squid stupor, so I move on with feet of lead, the resolve of wet paper. I glance back at those Squids, fantasize about threading tentacles in my nostrils, and sigh. Then I see her, Anne Marie.

Tan towel in hand, she's walking toward me. To say Anne Marie resembles Ma Bev is to say a bird of paradise resembles a sparrow. Long, black hair, freckled and plump cheeks, her body is thick curves, wrapped in a blue sundress. Inkless nostrils. Meat on her bones. She doesn't squid! How has she resisted?

I stand speechless, my mouth wide open as she walks by me, doesn't register me, singing softly to herself in her own world, surely a better world. I don't catch the words of her song. I do note her lovely voice, mezzo-soprano, divine from above. I also note her bruised right eye.

She picks up two plastic pitchers of steaming water near the brass cauldron and fire and sings herself into a wooden stall and sings herself a bath.

I should walk on to give an impression of purpose, but I can't, caught in a trance, her spell, with a feeling long forgotten. This feeling fills my chest, tingles my arms and toes. It's not pure lust, certainly not love. It's an intense curiosity of a person, an attraction to her full being.

I dig in my tote bag, grab my cigarette case, and sit on a log next to the bearded man purifying the water. I offer him a cigarette and tell him that besides squidding, nothing's better when on a break.

He silently takes one.

Sitting near the fire, the heat warms half of me. Inhaling from my cigarette, my body buzzes as soft as a tiny bee. Those Squids in the puddle pull for me although not with the same brute strength as before, for I have another pull, a greater pull. She's singing in the bath stall.

I blow wisps of smoke. I inhale, hold it in, blow out. I wait as dark clouds, pushed by the cold wind blowing, sweep the pastel blue from the sky. With each cold gust, flames from the fire reach hot tendrils toward me.

The man clutches a hand towel and turns a nozzle on the cauldron. Water, hot and potable, pours from a spigot into pitchers, its steam billowing up and up and gone beneath the dark rain clouds.

We do not speak. We do not make eye contact. We smoke our cigarettes. He tends the cauldron. I tend my patience and my cigarette, tended by Anne Marie's sweet melody behind the bath stall. Rain comes, a drizzle at first, then it pours. Towel-covered head, Anne Marie runs out.

Putting on my poncho, I watch her splash through puddles, the mud dirtying the bottom of her dress and legs. I dare not leave immediately nor follow her direction, less the man at the cauldron takes notice. I get up, stretch my arms and back, act like I got no place to go and all the time. I hand the man another cigarette.

He pockets it as water drips down his unsmiling face, off his nose, his nostrils Squid-darkened, and off his beard.

I walk perpendicular to where Anne Marie had run and don't pick up my pace until I'm out of sight from the man at his cauldron, the line of outhouses blocking his view. I got a clear sight of Anne Marie at a distance near Boyd's cabin. I fear I gave her too great a head start.

"Anne Marie!" I scream through cupped wet hands.

She drops her towel and stops several strides from the front steps of the cabin that lead under the wraparound porch to dryness. She stands there, her long black hair soaked to her back.

I look around to see no one else, only her, and I scream again. "Anne Marie!"

She turns around and walks to me.

Wet black hair, wet pale skin, Anne Marie is stolen from Celtic lore. Close enough, I can see her quizzical expression.

"What did you call me?" she says when we're close enough to shake hands.

"Anne Marie."

"Call me Anne."

I hand the Polaroid to her.

"Ma Bev," she mouths, examining the picture in shaking hands.

The rain's a cold rain, and my hands have gotten numb and have lost dexterity, so I clasp my hands as if praying, and blow into them, and think maybe I should start praying. I'd pray for the Squids to never have come, for if they vanished today, having gotten my taste, I'd pray the Squids on back.

"How's Ma Bev know I'm here?" she says, tears welling in her eyes. She drops the Polaroid.

"The postcard."

Anne Marie droops her head and sighs. "I dropped Marie from my name when I ran away."

"Ma Bev wants to see you again." I cannot distinguish her tears from the rain that wets her freckled cheeks.

"She made me do things, terrible things, for money."

My heart sinks and anger builds, not solely toward Ma Bev, but myself. I'm a dangerous tool.

"Ma Bev hired you?" she asks.

I nod and gesture to her bruised eye. "Boyd do that?"

She wipes her cheek and sniffs. "That don't concern you."

"He's a bastard."

"World's full of them."

"Leave him."

"Boyd?"

"Boyd."

"Boyd's none of your concern."

She turns and runs. The downpour drenches us with numerous drops, battering the mud in numerous plops, drenching her sundress, off her bare shoulders, dripping, splattering off my hood.

"Anne!" I yell.

She stops.

"I'm gonna tell Ma Bev you skipped out."

She walks on to Boyd's, steps in a muddy puddle, ankle-deep beside a Squid, its indigo body cresting the murk beneath, and I realize, for the first time since the invasion, I want a life with another, a better life, a future beyond my next tentacle fix.

I leave under the ranch gate, the guard's workmen boots jutting out amidst lush green ferns.

The torrential rain abates, from heavy to steady to a drizzle to drips from overhead leaves and branches. The drips are fat and irregular. When they hit my hood, their drops echo.

When I get to the darkened hallway outside my apartment, my door's open an inch. I push the door with my boot and wait.

"Jocelyn, is it?" says Boyd's baritone voice from inside.

I pause in the hallway, considering my options. I could run, and if I'm not caught, I could find another camp, get started from ground zero.

"If I wanted you dead," Boyd says, "you'd already be so."

I walk in.

Boyd and the bearded man from the cauldron stand near the window, its venetian blinds down. Boyd is tall, basketball-player tall, White, and bald. With little flesh and sharp angular bones from squidding, Boyd could be confused for a skeleton dressed in a white polo shirt and muddy shoes.

"I decided to visit your abode uninvited," he says, inhaling from a cigar and letting the smoke seep out his inked-up nose, "as you have visited mine."

I finger my switchblade in my tote.

"Don't get any stupid ideas." Boyd nods to the expressionless man next to him. "George here's got a gun. George, show Jocelyn your gun."

George digs a hand in the front pocket of his bib overalls and pulls out a silver nine-millimeter and lays it out on his big right palm. It's not pointed at me.

"What do you want?" I ask, trying to mask my fear with assertiveness.

"To warn you not to be so nosey."

"OK, I've been warned. Now get out."

Boyd smiles. "George, it looks as if we've outgrown our welcome."

"You never were welcomed."

Boyd walks out, tracking mud with each footstep. George follows, stops, and faces me. I feel his breath on the top of my hair.

From the hallway, Boyd says, "George, show Jocelyn what we do to nosey people."

George snatches my nose ring and rips.

The pain is sudden and surprising. I scream, cup my face, feel warm blood slicking my palms.

Down the hallway, Boyd shouts, "Stay nosey, I'll kill you!"

The next day, my nose bandaged and hurting with each breath, I go to find Ma Bev to tell her Anne left camp long ago. I plan to do the same. Where? Don't know. Don't care. Far from here, far from Boyd.

I find the two large cedars. Between the giant trees, a red tarp stretches wide over a fizzled-out fire and three bodies. In Squid stupors, I first think, then understand their grave state a few steps closer. Dead. Ma Bev. Two other women. They are face up and blue-skinned with blood congealed from slits in their necks.

Boyd. I got no doubts.

I've seen the two other women before, soliciting food in exchange for their bodies. They worked for Boyd then. One woman is blonde and young, the other Latina and old enough to be my mother. I don't know their names. This upsets me.

I sit cross-legged next to the older woman and cry and think of my mom. Lung cancer took her before the invasion. She was a strong mom, a single mom, a beautiful soul with a hard exterior. Short on words, Mom showed her unflinching love by working long hours in smoky strip clubs filled with pricks. They groped her. They jeered her. Try as they might, they never could reduce her humanity.

Mom endured that, so I had shelter and food. What would she do in my stead in this world where Squids have reduced the humanity of all? She'd do it differently.

I reach for a nearby Squid. It's black and glossy like obsidian and has brown and olive-green pine needles stuck to its skin. Its tentacles dance and squirm as I lift it to my face. I undo my bandage, and the tentacles find my painful nostrils. As I lie on soft humus, I think of Anne and her internal strength not to squid and my mother and her loving grit. And I think how I want what Anne has, and what Mom had, and wonder how to find, then tap into and use, that resilience if it exists at all.

It isn't found with tentacles deep in my throat and nose, so I rip that Squid from my face, its tentacles stinging my nostrils on the way out. I got to find Anne.

Outside Boyd's compound, I don't remember the last time my heart beat so hard, so fast. I welcome the nervousness, my apathy flaking away. I feel lighter, excited, and scared.

At the ranch gate, a different guard stands post. She's tall, Black, and dreadlocked. I think about squid washing her, then think better of it. Another guard in a stupor would prickle Boyd's suspicions.

When I spot a nearby Sitka spruce with a helpful limb that

reaches just shy atop the fence, I know what to do. I hide behind its thick trunk with visible patches of rough bark amongst spongy moss.

The guard bends down to tie her boot, and I shimmy up, pushing off and pulling on gnarled limbs that contort like arthritic fingers.

Her boot tied, the guard stands up.

I stop, rest my head on mossy green, see black ants march in line, see the tip of a red tentacle, then the Squid, bedded on a knot above me.

Uncurling and stretching its tentacle to me, the Squid senses me however Squids do. The tentacle squirms inside my sore nose.

I plow that Squid off the knot with my forearm.

It plops in the undergrowth with a rustle and a thump. Startled, a rabbit hops from where the Squid landed, kicking up pine needles with its hind legs as it zigs, and it zags, and it zips away.

The guard squints my way.

I do not move.

She walks toward the fallen Squid and my tree.

The closer she gets the faster my heart beats. I try to regulate my nerves with slow breaths.

Don't look up. Don't look up, I mouth, feeling the verbal stresses of this silent mantra on the tip of my tongue, on the back of my teeth. *Don't look up.*

Below me, the guard squats by the fallen Squid, which is now neon pink. She pokes, then pierces it with a stick. Blue blood oozes, then bubbles and sizzles. It disintegrates the end of the stick into rising steam.

Don't look up.

From this distance, I smell her thick odor. Can she smell mine?

Don't look up.

She stands, turns, doesn't look up, and walks back to her post.

I exhale, realizing I had stopped breathing altogether, and climb what remains of the limb to the fence. In my hurry, the rough bark bites the exposed skin of my arms and legs.

I reach the fence when the guard reaches her post, and I peer over to see the muddy compound. On the other side, there is no activity, so I heave myself over without grace and land on my hip and my arm.

The impact hurts, a deep-bruising hurt, and I hobble up, and I hobble on, bruised and scraped and scared in Boyd's domain where his threat hangs over my head like a guillotine blade, its shimmer gone from dried blood.

And within the compound, I see that guillotine's dirty work upon that guard I squid washed yesterday. His body is lying limply, tied up on a post and dead, his eyes sizzled on out as Boyd's retribution for letting his guard down and a warning to all his bastards to squid on their own time.

Is the guard's blood on my hands? Perhaps, partially. And that rips me up, gets me conflicted and defensive about how the guard knew the score when becoming Boyd's bastard.

And I have a gal to find, so I limp on past that guard's body to Boyd's cabin and pass the trough of river water and that cauldron. George is gone, the fire beneath the cauldron long put out. I hear humming, the squelching and slurping of mud, the crunching of stone, a creaky wheel. I rush behind one of the outhouses.

Smiling her few-tooth smile, the old woman from before wheels her creaky wheelbarrow to the cauldron where pitchers of full water stand. She grabs two pitchers, water sloshing, and puts the pitchers in her wheelbarrow, water splashing out. She wheels the pitchers to Boyd's cabin. Humming, grinning, she walks up the porch steps and places the two pitchers before Boyd's door.

Despite her nonthreatening stature—she's five foot nothing, as frail as she is old—despite her seemingly sweet disposition—she reminds me of my long-passed grandmother—I assume she's a bastard like all who work for Boyd. I let her and her creaky wheelbarrow pass, positioning the outhouse between her and me.

When she creaks her wheelbarrow around a wooden shed, I eye other empty pitchers, stacked one inside the other, on the table by the cauldron. A delicious idea comes to me.

I take two empty pitchers and slosh them in the trough of river water, sediment and algae swirling, microbes unseen, and feel my grin as I swap them for the purified water at Boyd's doorstep.

I decide to hide near the bath stall to wait for Anne. Beyond informing her of Ma Bev's fate, I have no other plans, only hopes. Walking toward the outhouses, I fantasize about a different future, and I feel a smack of a Squid to my face, the slipping of its tentacles up my nose, and smell the Squid's unearthly scent, that salty sourness. I taste its metallic secretion, feel that gag before that pinch, then its pulsing pulse.

Squid washed.

On my back, I hear the old woman humming. I'm as good as dead, scared. Lights out.

I come to in an empty room, its walls made of wood. Its piney scent smells of luxury. Boyd's cabin, I presume. Sunlight shines through a metal-caged window, bare of glass or curtains. In a Squid fog, I stumble to my feet to try the door. Locked. My tote is missing, with it my cigarettes. I sit against the wall, droop my head, hold my knees against my chest, and wait for my death.

I wait all day and into dusk. I got nothing to do but picture my end. I hope it's as quick as a bullet. Wishful thinking. Time creeps on at an agonizing pace until the night and its numerous stars and its crickets and its frogs replace dusk.

I hear faint moaning like the wind. It ebbs and flows in pitch and duration. Did Boyd drink the water?

My optimism increases with my time left alone, perhaps forgotten. I smile with each moan. They increase in frequency and decibel. When the doorknob rattles, my optimism squashes out. I'm not forgotten.

The door opens wide, revealing Anne in a red sundress, her black hair French-braided and swept to one side over her bare shoulder.

I jump to my feet.

"I told you I want nothing to do with Ma Bev."

"She's dead."

349

Anne takes several steps back, knees slightly buckling. "Dead dead?"

"There's only one kind."

With the door open, the moans are much louder.

"He was gonna kill you, you know."

"I know."

"Was gonna do it publicly, painfully. Was gonna make your pain a lesson for others. Then he got sick."

I smirk. "I'm the one that got him sick."

She smiles. "How?"

"Dirty water."

"I don't think he's gonna make it. Like most everyone, he's got no fat to him, no strength to him." She shakes her head. "No, he's not gonna make it."

"Is that why you don't squid? Because you want to make it?"

"Ma Bev was always doped up on something. You name it, she popped it, shot it, snorted it." Tears well in Anne's eyes. "She had a costly life, a soulless life, so she sold my life. She sold me to men. She sold me to women. They used me like I was single-use plastic." Anne wipes the tears from one freckled cheek with her forearm, then wipes the other. "When I thought I could be used no more, I ran away and promised myself never to use."

I revere Anne's strength and wish her fortitude for myself and all others.

"Are you leaving?" I ask.

"I gotta do something first." She turns.

I follow her out of the room, down the hallway, the moans growing louder. The hallway smells of human waste, the pungent odor growing stronger. We pass a stuffed black bear on hind legs, its mouth opened in a silent roar. We pass a canvas print of Mount Rainier, snowcapped, blue clear sky. We pass a closed-door room where those moans originate, the effluvium eye-watering, nose cupping.

Anne turns to the right into a bathroom, its bathtub stocked with Squids.

She scoops a yellow Squid up. Water drips from it onto its

cephalopod brethren. She opens the mirror vanity, pulls out a straight razor, and leaves.

I step out to see her open the door to the moans, a trail of water behind her.

"Anne." I hear Boyd's voice, a whisper. "I need water."

Then Boyd screams, and amongst Boyd's screams, I hear sizzling.

Anne comes out of the room, expressionless, Squidless, razorless.

"Where did you burn him?" I ask, Boyd still screaming.

"I'll never be used again." She brushes by me.

I peek, then walk into Boyd's room, his screams dimming to whimpers and moans.

He is writhing on a king-size bed, tangled in soiled sheets. The smell is horrendous, the sight much worse. From below his waist, steam rises and blue blood sizzles and pops in a cavernous hole like a geyser. When he rolls, I see the blood eating its way through the mattress, dripping, bubbling, and hissing on the floorboard below.

I rush out the room, down the hallway, past the bear, down wooden stairs, out the cabin door, and I leap down the porch steps. I see Anne, walking by the cauldron.

"Anne, I'm coming with you!"

She stops, doesn't turn around.

I catch up. Out of breath, I put my hands on my knees. "I said—"

"I heard you." She walks on.

"So?"

"So, how are you different from everybody else?"

"I know I can't do this like this alone no more." I blurt the words out as involuntary and as surprising as a first hiccup.

Anne stops and hangs her head. "I'm lonely, too. But what's gonna keep you from using me?"

"I'll never use you in any way you don't want to be used. And you use me the same on back. Besides," I say, marinating in hope, "traveling is safer when traveled together. So we'll be using each other for that."

Anne turns around, looks at and into me. "If you squid, I keep walking." She about faces and gets going.

Smiling, I step over a puddle with two Squids, full of luster and changing colors. Despite their intense pull—I feel it in my marrow, my gut, my tongue, my fingers, and my nose—I don't give them a second glance. Can I fulfill Anne's precondition? I'll sure give it my damnedest. Hope toward a less lonesome future will help pull me along. That, plus a non-squidding example. Two good-as-any reasons to do more than cling on between fixes.

"Let's stop at my squat for food and supplies," I say.

"Boyd emptied your apartment and made a bonfire."

"Bastard." I'm starting fresh, starting free, my life from after the invasion in ashes. Good riddance.

"Want to go to the ocean?" Anne asks.

"There and more."

Anne grabs my hand and smiles.

My endorphins fire, a high like no other. Bliss.

L. Ron Hubbard's Illustrators of the Future at Thirty-Five!

BY BOB EGGLETON

Bob Eggleton is a winner of nine Hugo Awards, twelve Chesley Awards, the 2019 L. Ron Hubbard Lifetime Achievement Award for Outstanding Contributions to the Arts, and a 2015 Rondo Award in Classic Horror, as well as an award from the Godzilla Society of North America. His art can be seen on the covers of numerous magazines, professional publications, and books in science fiction, fantasy, and horror across the world including several volumes of his own work. He has also worked as a conceptual illustrator for movies and thrill rides.

Of late, Eggleton has focused on private commissions and self-commissioned work. He is an elected Fellow of the International Association of Astronomical Artists and is a Fellow of the New England Science Fiction Association. He has a minor planet named for him by Spacewatch—13562bobeggleton—and was an extra in the 2002 film Godzilla Against Mechagodzilla.

Bob is working on a large Clarke Ashton Smith book. He completed paintings for an illustrated version of King Kong, *celebrating the ninetieth anniversary, available from Easton Press. And he recently finished essays edited along with Laura Freas Beraha for a huge book,* The Art of Frank Kelly Freas, *published by Centipede Press.*

Bob has been an Illustrators of the Future Contest judge since its inception in 1988. He has participated as an instructor for the annual workshops and as an art director for previous anthologies.

L. Ron Hubbard's
Illustrators of the Future
at Thirty-Five!

As the saying goes, what a long road it's been. I am celebrating forty years (starting in 1983) of being a professional illustrator. I am now the "elder statesman," as odd as that seems.

I find myself stunned that thirty-five years of the Illustrators of the Future Contest have passed—all that I have done, the people I have known, and everything that has happened with the Contest. Let's go back a few years....

As we know, L. Ron Hubbard launched the Writers of the Future Contest first in 1983. As I understand it, he always intended to complement it with a companion contest that related to the visual arts. The stories in the annual anthology have been illustrated since Volume 1.

By 1987, the groundwork was being paved for the Illustrators of the Future Contest. I recall the late Algis Budrys calling me out of the blue late one night. He had known me for some time. He told me that the Illustrators' Contest was being created, and Frank Kelly Freas had been asked to head it up as its first Coordinating Judge. One of his picks to be a judge was...me. Kelly got in touch by old-fashioned mail. We didn't have the world wide web of email, so it was all "long hand." He established some ground rules. All the art was photocopied line art, not color as it is now. The Contest was officially cemented into reality in 1988.

A word and tribute to Frank Kelly Freas: He was considered by many to be the "Dean of Science Fiction Art." Few would disagree. Kelly, as he was known to everyone, illustrated countless science fiction magazines and books, beginning in the late 1940s until the end of his life in 2005. He also created the Skylab patch for NASA back in 1973 and created the iconic cover (and inside spread) for the rock group Queen's 1975 album *News of the World*, which was voted among the top ten record album covers of all time. He also popularized Alfred E. Neuman for the humor magazine MAD, from 1958–1962. He literally was a legend and always will be. His work will be the subject of a massive two-volume book set, edited by Laura Freas Beraha and yours truly (!!!) from Centipede Press.

What I have always extolled about both Contests was that when I was "up-and-coming" I wished *I* had such a contest to submit my own work to.

Noted judges have come and gone over the years...some have passed away, including Kelly himself. But I remember well such names as Frank Frazetta, Paul Lehr, Jack Kirby, Edd Cartier—all legends, even to me, of whose work I consider myself only touching the edges—and I got to meet ALL of them thanks to this Contest. It was an astonishing and even surreal feeling. We had Ron Lindahn who passed away a few years ago. We have Val Lakey Lindahn, Vincent Di Fate, and more amazing talents, all of whom have been willing to give their time to nurture new generations of illustrators.

In the early days, the Contests' ceremony moved around—Las Vegas, Washington DC, Cape Kennedy, Houston Space Center, Seattle—before sort of settling down in Hollywood near the offices of Author Services (the Contests' administrator) and Galaxy Press (the anthology's publisher). Flying around the country was quite the adventure.

The science fiction and fantasy field has changed much since my own beginnings in the late 1980s. Publishing has changed completely, with science fiction being made to look less and less science fictional.... We went from a Golden Age of Illustration in the 1980s and even 1990s to a much more type-design look to things. Books became downloadable and somehow less "intimate."

I believe what some call "talent" is a form of heightened perception. I think everyone has the ability. In some, it's nurtured.

In others, it's scorned. Unfortunately, in a world of "practicality," that talent isn't always given a chance to develop.

Over the years we have seen some truly amazing talent emerge through the Contest—too many to name.

Sergey Poyarkov from Ukraine was a memorable winner back in 1991.

Shaun Tan from Australia won in 1992. In fact, I presented him his award. He went on to become a critically praised and bestselling children's book author/artist, winning two Hugo Awards *and* an Academy Award for his short animated film, and later to become a judge himself. Shaun is something of a force of nature; his work is in seemingly countless books, and he has won many other prestigious awards.

Omar Rayyan, who also won in the early 1990s, went on to become an incredible illustrator with his own unique following. Omar is a good close friend of mine now. Every piece he does astonishes me in its originality and its viewpoint.

Aliya Chen recently won. She produces spectacular work. I recall her asking me what she can do to make it better and I, honestly slightly flummoxed, had no idea what to say to her as it was pretty much perfect stuff.

Brian C. Hailes is simply amazing. He was a winner and is now a judge as well.

April Solomon's works are not only genius, but inspiring to me personally.

Brittany Jackson, a former winner and now a Contest judge, is another incredible talent.

There are also Kirbi Fagan, Bruce Brenneise, Lee White, Dustin Panzino, Michael Michera, Irvin Rodriguez, and many more I haven't mentioned.

The bottom line is that the Contest has helped launch a lot of careers in this business.

Illustration is a specialized art. The ability is required to interpret a story element or elements so that the picture dovetails with and tells part of the story. The right illustration brings the reader into the story, which is extremely important. It's not always easy but, in the end, it's the voyage and not always the destination that matters. Kelly Freas once noted it was a "good excuse to find out new things about anything because of the research you do!"

The Illustrators of the Future Contest does more than find new talents. It hones skills, including working with an art director, and teaches tools needed to work professionally in the field.

How to start? Simple: the rules are on page 486 or at IllustratorsoftheFuture.com. Once you become a quarterly winner, you'll have a chance to illustrate a story for actual publication, and work with a professional art director. You'll be working toward a major cash grand prize; more important—I think— you'll be started on a lifelong career, beginning with your work being published in and paid for by the "Bestselling SF/Fantasy Anthology."

Personally speaking, one of the side benefits for me is that *I* learn from the Contest winners. I came up in another generation, and so much has changed since then. Many people now work digitally on a computer, while we used to employ mainly traditional methods. But it is not the medium that matters. It is the skill and talent of the one using a computer...or a pencil or brush. The talent supersedes the media, and that is what is most important.

If you want to see things in the bigger picture...as L. Ron Hubbard said, "The artist is looked upon to start things. The artist injects the spirit of life into a culture. And, through his creative endeavors, the writer works continually to give tomorrow a new form."

So, looking forward, I can say the Illustrators of the Future Contest with Echo Chernik as our current Coordinating Judge will continue to discover more and more true talents out there that will make our culture ever richer. I'm very happy to be part of it.

I wish the Contests a very happy anniversary. And here's to many, many more.

Halo

written by
Nancy Kress

illustrated by
LUCAS DURHAM

ABOUT THE AUTHOR

Nancy Kress is the author of thirty-five novels, four story collections, and three books on writing fiction (Writer's Digest Books). Her science fiction has won six Nebulas, two Hugos, a Sturgeon, and the John W. Campbell Memorial Award. Her most recent fiction is Observer, *a novel about the nature of consciousness, reality, and love, cowritten with Dr. Robert Lanza. Nancy's work has been translated into two dozen languages including Klingon, none of which she can read. She teaches writing at various venues in the United States and abroad, including a guest lectureship at the University of Leipzig, an intensive seminar in Beijing, and the annual* SF-*writing intensive workshop Taos Toolbox with Walter Jon Williams. She lives in Seattle with her husband, writer Jack Skillingstead.*

Nancy says this about her story: "When the Covid pandemic struck in the winter of 2019–2020, epidemiologists were not surprised. They had been saying for decades that Earth was overdue for another major epidemic. They wrote articles and books and made podcasts warning that some unknown epidemic, of some unknown severity, was coming. Very few people in positions of power listened.

"Covid, like most infections, thrives by destroying its hosts' cells. It brought no good to anybody. However, there exist pathogens that have other effects. One is the parasite Toxoplasma gondii. *In mice, it removes the fear of cats, and recent research suggests that even after symptoms disappear, changes in the brain may be permanent. This is great for hungry cats, not so good for the mice. In humans, multiple research studies suggest that toxoplasmosis increases risk-taking.*

"I have always been fascinated by epidemiologists, those hunters,

controllers, and trackers of disease. So I asked myself—because that's what SF writers do—a what-if. What if an emerging virus affected human brains in a permanent way, but with far different effects than increased risk-taking? What cell receptors might it target, and what might be the consequences?"

Thus, "Halo."

ABOUT THE ILLUSTRATOR

Growing up in a creative household, it was inevitable that Lucas Durham would pursue a life as an artist. He knew it was his calling as soon as he could hold a pencil. After receiving a BFA at the American Academy of Art in Chicago, Lucas honed his craft by painting illustrations for the tabletop games industry. He quickly developed a reputation for his impactful narrative illustrations.

Over the past decade, Lucas has had a varied career, working on projects that involved a diverse list of licenses and intellectual properties, including NFL, MLB, Game of Thrones, Lord of the Rings, and Star Wars. His work has been showcased in multiple illustration annuals, magazines, and gallery invitationals, such as Infected by Art, Imagine FX, and the Maleficium Dark Art Exhibit. He currently considers his crowning achievement being invited to participate in the United States Mint's Artistic Infusion Program for two years, where he had the opportunity to design a congressional gold medal that is part of a permanent exhibit in Indianapolis, IN, and is part of the Smithsonian Collection.

He is currently working as a senior game development artist at Light and Wonder in Chicago, designing exciting casino games for national and international markets.

Lucas is a former winner of the Illustrators of the Future Contest and was first featured in L. Ron Hubbard Presents Writers of the Future Volume 29.

Halo

It is a universal truth that a petty, vindictive bureaucrat enjoys humiliating underlings who have screwed up. The truth holds even at major governmental agencies devoted to saving the world.

"Dickson," I snarl into my phone, "it was an outbreak of pneumococcal pneumonia. Nothing more."

On screen, Dickson—never was anyone more aptly named—turns his head slowly and raises his eyebrows, one of his most annoying theatrical habits. Rumor is that once he'd wanted to be an actor. He says, "Susan, this discussion is pointless. Just have Dr. Silva send me the follow-up data."

"Lucas already sent the data. You've *seen* the data, so stop playing games. The prep school had an outbreak of pneumococcal pneumonia, exactly as the school physician diagnosed. You just wasted thousands of dollars and four people's expensive time for no justifiable reason. This outbreak did not require an investigative team!"

"We received a request."

"EVAU gets dozens of requests every month. Why did you send me on this one? I'm filing a complaint with Internal Issues."

"Go ahead," Dickson says, perfectly serene except for a tiny twitch at the corner of his mouth. Unease? Apprehension? I can only hope.

"But," he continues, "I can tell you that the request came directly from the headmaster's cousin, Tyler James O'Brien."

Not unease or apprehension. The twitch had been amusement.

Gotcha! T.J. O'Brien is chief of staff to the president of the United States. Prep-school types have channels closed to people like me, and favors flow along them like dirty water, muddying the division between medicine and politics. Probably Headmaster O'Brien wanted to be able to say to anxious parents, "We're taking all measures for our students' safety, including an investigation by the Emerging Virus Advance Unit of the CDC, to be absolutely certain this outbreak is dealt with correctly."

Unlike—Dickson doesn't have to say to me because we both understand it already— *that outbreak in Louisiana.* Which haunts me and always will, but Dickson is not capable of understanding that.

He isn't finished. "Actually, it's lucky that you are in Massachusetts because I have your next assignment right here, and it's only seventy miles from your present location. You and your team should drive there immediately. I'm sending you the relevant information." He gives me a smile like venom. "Have a good trip!"

"You're kidding me," Carol says, gazing in disbelief at her tablet.

Dr. Carol Bernstein, the physician on my current, truncated team, is brand-new to EVAU. So is my genetic virologist Dr. Lucas Silva. Only my security officer, Sebastian Duer ("Sebastian Dour" to my two young colleagues, although they don't know that I know that) has been with me before. Sebastian is, I presume, also being punished for Louisiana. He doesn't say, not about that or pretty much anything else. But he saved my ass more than once—in Congo in '32, and in an up-country Creole bayou.

The four of us sit with badly cooked hamburgers in an interstate highway restaurant while we study the encrypted request data that Dickson has sent. Carol and Lucas have stopped eating, but Sebastian chomps away steadily as a 'dozer demolishing a forest.

I state the obvious and imply the also obvious, which is that this is the job and we're going to do it. "Implant data shows eighty percent infection rate and the clinic can't identify the disease."

Carol says, "Eighty percent of five implants! That means *four* people may—or may not—host a pathogen from which they are almost recovered, no fatalities, and lingering symptom data that doesn't even require quarantine, let alone our talents!"

She's right, of course, but her outburst tells me more than she intended. Young Dr. Bernstein, on her first job since obtaining her MD, has not done her homework. She doesn't know that I'm in disgrace and so being sent on politically motivated, bottom-of-the-viral-barrel, bullshit jobs. That in turn says that Carol is both not tracking which investigative teams have racked up EVAU's stunning successes in the past ten years, *and* that she is not plugged into the strong electrical flow of CDC gossip.

Quiet, self-contained Lucas Silva has done one or the other. He glances at me, then gives Carol a tiny shake of the head that she doesn't see. He says in his musical, formal English, "Implant data is always so incomplete. I need tissue samples, including the brain."

I'm stunned. Brain samples are not easy to obtain; recovering patients usually object to having their heads cut open to satisfy the scientific itches of researchers. Carol starts to sputter—this hot-headedness may be the reason Dickson stuck her on my pathetic team—but Lucas holds up his hand.

"It is possible that cerebral-spinal fluid will be enough. But nervous-system samples I must have. That is where personality changes occur."

The personality changes are not evident at Soldiers Memorial Hospital in Anita Falls, Vermont.

The town, glorious in October foliage, is small, quaint, and full of tourists engaged in that seasonal New England peculiarity, "leaf peeping." Anita Falls's streets, bathed in mellow afternoon light, are a picture postcard of serenity. But I looked up the town's history. Indigenous people, the Ehnita, a subset of the Abenaki tribe, backed the losers in the French and Indian War. Their enemies, the Iroquois, backed the winners. The Ehnita were all but obliterated, and descriptions of the violence in those battles are stomach-churning. Afterward, Fort Ehnita became the township of Anita Falls.

Five people are in the hospital's quarantine ward, three adults and one child lying in bed and one young man pacing the short corridor. Presumably he is the asymptomatic whose implant nonetheless transmitted the same data as the bedridden patients. None of the five bear any readily identifiable similarity in age, gender, or medical history. None are in the CDC database.

The hospital administrator remonstrates about Sebastian's side arms. Sebastian ignores her. He lugs in Lucas's state-of-the-art equipment and a computer running software off military satellites, while Carol and Lucas suit up in Biohazard Level 3 PPE gear: Tyvek suit, HEPA mask, face shield, rubber boots, and gloves. This alarms the administrator even more, and I suggest his office as a better place to explain our protocol and begin my job.

"Dr. Kelly! Are guns necessary? The hospital has extremely good security and state-of-the-art metal detectors—"

"I was once attacked with a carbon-fiber knife and nearly lost a hand," I say mildly, which shuts him up for the moment. I don't tell him that the attack was in Louisiana, the hand is still partially crippled, and except for Sebastian I would probably be dead. EVAU security measures might have been originally designed for third-world countries, but we have enough homegrown crazies to justify them here as well.

I add, "Dr. Silva can set up in some corner of the hospital where almost no one will see him." This is an attempt at repair diplomacy, never my forte. Until Louisiana, I headed an advance team of sixteen, always including a multilingual liaison officer skilled at soothing locals.

My repair attempt is not a great success. Dr. Minetti scowls at me. This increases the difficulty of my job, which is part cop.

Field epidemiologists and cops have the same two questions. Who are the perps? How can the perp be arrested? For the CDC, the criminal causing destruction may be a bacterium, a parasite, or a toxin, but is usually a virus. The perp's accomplice is its transmission vector: mosquito, water, flea, farm animal, mouse urine, bat bite, human body fluids, more. Worst case: air. Carol's job is to treat infectees, Lucas does research sleuthing to locate the perp, and I try to map the physical march forward of the disease by tracing who has been where, doing what, and with whom. Who does not get sick is as important as who does.

Our initial data comes from the voluntary implants that send blood data to the CDC. Why do people agree to be implanted? Many don't, especially in rural areas. ("The government isn't putting any secret chips in my blood!") Those that do agree think that early detection of a new virus that has invaded their bodies can only be a good thing. Usually, they're right.

CDC computer algorithms sort the genetic codes of known viruses (colds, flu, and an entire alphabet of diseases like RSV) from the unknowns. The knowns get sorted into relatively minor (variants of colds or seasonal flu), serious (MERSA, SARS), and catastrophic (Nipah, Lassa, Ebola). Known diseases may or may not trigger a CDC response. For unknown diseases, identifying who is infected, how severely, and by what becomes the responsibility of the Emerging Virus Advance Unit.

All this is complicated by rapid viral mutations, especially RNA viruses, as they adjust to new hosts. Also by some viruses' tendency to polymorphism, meaning that they afflict different people with different symptoms, including none at all. Ten million viruses land daily on every square meter of Earth, wafting down from the air like unseen snow, and we know only a fraction of them. Hunting for an emerging virus or radically mutated variant of an old one is like chasing a shapeshifter through a vast crowded maze with dead ends, distorting fun-house mirrors, and corpses.

In Louisiana, I'd never found our way out of the maze.

Dr. Minetti and I settle in his office and I begin recording how these five people ended up at the hospital, including the young man with no symptoms whatsoever. Later, I will talk to each of the patients and begin the laborious task of mapping a disease I don't believe warrants mapping. None of these five is going to die. They were not even very sick. Their blood data show some peculiar variations, but they are all recovering well. Whatever this is, it is not a danger to society.

It is the second time I have been deeply wrong.

By evening, Lucas has all his samples, including cerebrospinal fluid from two voluntary spinal taps. Most patients strenuously resist taps as soon as the dangers are explained to them. That two patients have consented is practically a miracle, and I suspect the miracle worker is Lucas, who talked in his quiet, formal way to all five.

The forty-year-old, stay-at-home mom refused.

The county road-crew worker, twenty-five, refused.

The high-school math teacher, sixty-two, refused.

Surprisingly, Jem Potter, twenty-one and asymptomatic, agreed. Had Lucas told him that donating a cerebrospinal sample would get him out of quarantine faster? I hoped not, since it wasn't true, but I didn't inquire. Cops sometimes lie.

Most surprising of all was the sample from Sarah Emily Nowak. She was the sickest patient and, being eight years old, could not consent to anything. Her parents agreed to the spinal tap. They told Lucas, and then me, and then the hospital, that anything that might help Sarah was all right. "Only..." the mother said hesitantly, and her eyes filled with tears.

Every instinct I owned went on high alert. "Only what, Ms. Nowak?"

"Only now Sarah, even though she's so sick, she's...before this, she was..."

Sarah's father said, "She's happier now."

"Happier?"

"No, not that," the mother said, having regained herself. "Of course she's not happy. She has headaches and body aches, and she cries she wants to go home. But she isn't using that dreadful language she picked up on the school bus, isn't trying to shock us to get attention, doesn't try to bite me when I don't give into her or—"

"Bite you? She used to bite you?"

The father says bitterly, "She was a little bitch. No, don't look at me like that, Nicole. You know she was." He turns to me. "Our other kids were never like that, and we raised all of them the same.

But getting this sick has made Sarah sort of...not happy, but less aggressive. Not so nasty. Not nasty at all, in fact."

I nodded meaninglessly. Many children become more docile when they don't feel well. Others...well. Nature? Nurture? Who the hell knew? But I was not going to think about Zed, not now. I made the huge effort to bring both the Nowaks and myself to my immediate concern. "Mrs. Nowak, how long ago did Sarah bite you?"

"The last time"—The last time! How many times had there been?—"was just before she got sick. Tuesday. Why?"

"Did she break your skin? Did you bleed?"

"Yes. Why?"

"Will you consent to giving Dr. Silva blood, tissue, and cerebrospinal fluid samples?"

She looks uncertain. "Will it help Sarah?"

I tread carefully. "It may."

"Then yes, of course."

Saliva is a major transmitter of many viruses. If Mrs. Nowak has not contracted the virus, I can rule out saliva as a transmission vector. "Thank you," I say. "Let me get you a consent form. Mr. Nowak, did Sarah ever bite you?"

"No."

"Any of your other children, or anyone else you know of?"

The parents look at each other. Mrs. Nowak says, "There was that little boy on the playground who called her fat...."

"What is his name? How long ago was that? Anything you can tell me may help Sarah."

I take all the information I can, and then suit up to talk again to Sarah Nowak, who had struck me as an unremarkable little girl who understandably wanted to leave the hospital and go home.

Several pathogens can cause personality changes. Toxoplasmosis, contracted from cat feces, can reach the brain and turn people less risk-averse. Usually, however, personality changes are not evident until the disease has nearly finished its deadly course and is destroying its host's brain. Rabies. Nipah. Ebola.

In Louisiana, there had also been personality changes—more day-dreaming, less sharp mental focus—which I missed until it was too late. It is so difficult to say anything definitive about a virus newly spilled from its animal host into unfortunate human bodies. And viruses can hide in bodies for a long time, as the chicken-pox virus does for decades until it turns into shingles.

By the end of the epidemic in Louisiana, a hundred sixty-two people were dead and the rest kept in quarantine for over a year.

The only thing that saved the rest of the United States was that the pox virus, whose original host is still unidentified, broke out up-country in a spread-out area of swamp and bayou where people did not travel much to the outside world. The disaster broke the halo the CDC had worn ever since EVAU had successfully contained Ebola in Los Angeles, and Lassa fever in New York, both brought here by imported animals. Well, halos should not be worn by scientists anyway. Some of the epidemiologists on the New York team strutted around to talk shows like some combination of an archangel and a rock star. One of them was Peter, my ex-husband.

He divorced me after Louisiana. Neither rock stars nor archangels have to stay attached to failures. Although, to be fair—why do women strive so hard to be fair to men who've treated them like crap? Louisiana wasn't the only thing that led to our divorce. Nor was my premature replacement, who gazed at Peter as if he had just created Eden and opened its gates to her. Peter's and my marriage had had its heart, if not its brains, gnawed long before her perky young body showed up in Peter's bed. Some of the blame belonged to Zed.

Sarah Emily Nowak is not the only aggressive child in the world.

"Hello, Sarah," I say to her. "I brought you something."

She takes the hypoallergenic teddy bear, sewn by a volunteer organization of elderly women who send toys to hospitalized children, and smiles at me. "Thank you so much."

LUCAS DURHAM

During the next weeks we work like demons. Lucas succeeds in isolating the virus in both blood, where it breeds, and in cerebrospinal fluid. That he succeeds in this so quickly is amazing; viral isolation can take months, or even years. My opinion of Lucas's skill soars.

In addition to skill, he has grit. But, then, without grit he would be dead. He fled Brazil at age twenty, a hunted insurrectionist against a very corrupt regime. He can never return. During the years he was gaining his PhD through a combination of scholarships, charity, and insanely hard work, his sister was captured in his stead, tortured, and murdered. His parents were blown up in Brazil's brief and bloody civil war, during a government missile attack on an apartment building. I never press him for details on any of this, which he wouldn't give me anyway. Lucas is self-contained, watchful, brilliant.

He amplifies the virus and analyzes its genome. Carol screens the blood of incoming hospital patients for symptoms of what we are calling—but only among ourselves—"the happy disease." But blood is all we have. Lucas cannot figure out what the virus is actually doing and to which cells. "Happy disease" is a misnomer anyway; the patients aren't happy. They don't want to be here (nor do I). They grumble and snap and occasionally cry, but they cooperate. And often they are agreeable, not in a Stepford-robot way but in a how-can-I-help-you way of successful customer representatives, which is slightly unnerving.

I trace everyone I can, and we test everyone who will agree. We have no mandate to force testing on anyone not hospitalized. Hospitalized infectees go promptly into quarantine. Most victims fall ill for a few days, feel fatigued and brain-fogged for a week or two, and then recover.

What we know so far is that the transmission vector seems to be bodily fluids, especially saliva, mucus, and blood. My field mapping included a lot of intrusive "Whom have you kissed lately?" questions, along with even more intrusive "Have you shared a tissue or napkin with anyone? Spit on anyone? Bitten anyone? Shared a needle? Do you drool?" I am not popular in

Anita Falls. Sebastian accompanies me on my door-knocking rounds, but neither in the town nor the hospital does anyone try to so much as shove me. Sebastian does not do well in the absence of danger. Lucas, from pity, takes him out for a drink one night with the misguided idea of making Sebastian feel relevant by listening to his war stories. This is a failure. Sebastian drinking is no more forthcoming than Sebastian totally sober, not even when what Lucas describes as "really excellent craft beers" are available at a local brewery.

The bulk of our evidence for the mild personality changes is anecdotal, a notoriously unreliable data source. Mrs. Nowak, who has indeed been infected by Sarah's bite and is now in quarantine, by all reports has always been cooperative and agreeable. Her husband does not become infected, which tells me something about their sex life. Jem Potter arrived in town only two weeks ago and no one in Anita Falls seems to know him. The math teacher and housewife know a lot of people, but everyone says they were "really nice" to begin with. Also that they don't kiss, bite, drool on, or share needles with anyone. Only the road worker and Sarah Nowak seem to have become more cooperative and agreeable after their infection, but who knows what I-never-got-enough-love-from-Mommy syndrome has been temporarily brought out by all this hospital attention?

After people infected with this elusive disease recover, they do not seem able to infect others, so we release them from quarantine and send them home. Neither Lucas nor Carol can determine if the virus remains in infectees' bodies after recovery, nor what bodily systems it affects, nor by what mechanism.

Dickson is not impressed with our results. "Pretty thin. Hardly a public-health emergency."

This infuriates me. "It was *always* thin, and you knew this wasn't going to be a public-health emergency when you sent me here."

"Don't be so egotistical, Susan. It wasn't about you." His nasty smile says differently, but there is no point in arguing. I have an elaborate contact-tracing map, but it's for a virus that may or may not make people less aggressive, that operates in some unidentified bodily system, that kills nobody, and for which any long-term effects could only be verified by a longitudinal study, which I know Dickson will not authorize. He's going to shut us down.

"I'm shutting down your investigation."

We pack up our equipment. No one in Anita Falls is sorry to see us go. We have accomplished nothing, cured nothing, wasted everyone's time. And as a result of the last two investigations, Lucas is detached from my team, ordered to fly immediately to HQ for reassignment. No reason is given, but I know why. Lucas has demonstrated above-average ability as a virologist. Dickson can use him on legitimate investigations; he is too good for my sorry team.

"Susan, I am sorry to leave you," Lucas says, courteous as always. He does not mean it. He has a strong career ahead of him and is naturally excited about that. He cannot meet my eyes.

"I'm happy for you," I say, which is at least partly true. "Do you know where your new team is heading?"

"Mexico. An outbreak of hantavirus."

"Good luck," I say. What I do not say is complex. *I admire you. I envy you. You are too young to know that everyone eventually falls into a pothole on the viral trail. I hope yours won't be deep enough to derail you.*

"Well, I'm glad he's gone," Carol says, jealousy riming her words like frost. "I never liked him. He's so…so *closed in*. Never jokes around, never shares anything personal. Never fun."

I could come to dislike Carol.

She and Lucas take a taxi to the airport; Sebastian and I will drive the equipment to Atlanta. As we load the heavy crates in the hospital's underground parking lot, a man appears from nowhere and rushes toward me. He waves a baseball bat and screams something I don't, can't, catch. I duck, falling to the ground, and the bat shatters a side window of the van. I scuttle backward, crab-like—where is Sebastian? Then, simultaneously, he emerges from behind the van and a gunshot reverberates around the cement walls. The attacker drops in a spray of blood.

The shot was not Sebastian's.

We stare at each other across the corpse. A security guard runs over, gun still hot. "Are you OK?"

"Yes," I say.

Sebastian's usual stoniness has morphed into surprise, shame, and fear. He stammers something, so low that all I hear are stuttering sounds. He looks at his own belatedly drawn sidearm as if it is a viper.

"It happens," I say, as people suddenly pour into the parking lot. "Nobody catches them all." But I can see my words don't reach him.

Someone says to someone else, "That's the crazy that attacked that other woman yesterday."

Sebastian is still staring at his gun, until a cop demands he drop it, and he does.

Sometimes I schedule dreaded tasks all at once, getting the unpleasantness over in one difficult chunk. So in Atlanta I see the dentist for a root canal and crown, file my overdue taxes, and fly to New York to see my son, who is not thrilled by the visit.

"Hi, Mom," Zed says at the door of his tiny, dirty apartment in Fordham. Zed is a composer of atonal, discordant, "neo-classical" music, in which nobody has ever shown the slightest interest. He supports himself by teaching as adjunct faculty at Fordham University. His neighborhood has an assault rate five times the national average, his apartment smells bad, and the piano on which he composes looks as if it survived the Punic Wars. Barely.

Zed scowls at me. "Like I told you on the phone, this really isn't a good time for a visit. Yet here you are."

"Here I am," I agree, squeezing past him into the apartment, "because this is the time I have. And I haven't seen you in over a year."

"Well, I've been busy. Really busy."

"So I see." Sheets of handwritten music cover every dusty surface. "Can you at least spare the time to let me take you to lunch?"

His scowl deepens. "You really don't respect anybody else's work except your own, do you? I'm working, the ideas are just...just foaming up, and I really can't interrupt...OK, I'll go!"

With Zed, this passes for gracious acceptance. I let it go because if I argue, it will only get worse.

At lunch, he relents a little and actually asks me if I'm on "a virus safari." I say only, "One just finished," and ask what ideas are foaming up.

"Mom, you're tone deaf! You wouldn't understand if I told you. So I'll just say that I'm *this close*"—he holds thumb and forefinger an inch apart—"to finishing a new concerto. It's unlike anything I've composed before, and it's going to cause a sensation. I'm right on the edge of it!"

"That's wonderful, honey."

His fingers drop. "You don't believe me."

I don't; I've seen this movie before. But I say cheerfully, "You said yourself that I don't understand music. If you say the concerto is good, then I can believe it is."

He looks at me steadily for a long moment, then rips savagely into his turkey panini.

You cannot choose the children you birth. Nature? Nurture? Zed was difficult from birth, unresponsive to cuddling, full of inexplicable rage. Both Peter and I tried our best with him. Now Peter has given up. I never will.

Nonetheless, there is more than one night that I dream that Lucas, not Zed, is my son, and I wake up burning with guilt.

Two months later, Dickson calls me into his office. I expect another bullshit assignment. Instead, Dickson stands with a crowd of people, all looking tense. I blink when I recognize Leland Matthews, the head of the entire National Biodefense and Countermeasures Agency, to which the CDC and everyone else reports.

"Dr. Susan Kelly," Dickson says, looking ghostly pale and, almost shockingly, with no contemptuous eye roll or melodramatic lip curl. "Dr. Kelly, Dr. Matthews has a few questions for you."

I nod, completely bewildered. What the hell is going on here?

Matthews says, with no preliminaries, "You headed the EVAU

team investigating the outbreak in Anita Falls. I've read your report on the investigation, but since then there has been a development. Your contact tracing indicated a close relationship between infectee Jem Potter and a young woman stationed in Massachusetts, Corporal Olivia Elizabeth Donavan."

"Yes, sir." Jem Potter was the asymptomatic who, it turned out, was pacing the corridor in quarantine because his soldier girlfriend was being transferred and he would lose his chance to say goodbye. My stomach suddenly knots. "I was unable to interview Corporal Donavan. She had just been transferred to Texas for retraining."

"Yes. To the Fort Sam Houston medical training program. Where she fell ill, recovered quickly, and inadvertently infected at least two other soldiers, who in turn have infected more with something no one could identify until we happened across your team's EVAU report of the outbreak in Anita Falls. A report which had not been entered into the master database."

No wonder Dickson looks pale. Why didn't he enter my report into the deebee? Because it had been a bullshit assignment motivated by petty vindictiveness. Dickson thought he could bury it without any consequences.

Matthews continues. "Your report would have helped the Texas team investigate the virus that your viral researcher had already identified and saved us a lot of critical time. Dr. Lucas Silva is on his way to Texas now to aid in that effort. You will join him there immediately to give whatever assistance you can to the USAMRIID team already effecting quarantine. Transport is outside to take you home to pack and then to military transport. Full data will be given to you on the plane."

USAMRIID—United States Army Medical Research Institute of Infectious Diseases. Dickson's bullshit disease was being taken very seriously. My bewilderment grew.

"Sir, can I ask…has the disease mutated? Are soldiers at Fort Sam Houston dying?"

"No. They are briefly ill, some asymptomatically, and highly contagious for about a week. That's enough to cause an epidemic."

"With what symptoms? In Anita Falls we didn't notice—"

Matthews scowled. "You should already know this, Doctor. You were *there*. The virus affects personality, and the personality changes seem permanent after the disease passes. The infected soldiers are quietly content. Agreeable. Non-aggressive. They do not want to fight, not anyone. The base prison is full of dissenters already, and it is a very large prison. We might as well have an army of Quakers.

"Now get your ass to Texas and help fix this."

Before the military transport takes off, I call my son in New York. "Zed, I'm going to be in Texas for a while, working. Just wanted to let you know where I am."

Silence. My statement makes no sense to either of us. I never tell Zed where I'm working unless it's out of the country. What am I looking for from him? Reassurance? Support? Concern? I don't get it.

"OK. But, Mom, I can't talk right now. I work, too, you know, and I was right on the edge when you just interrupted a...oh, never mind!" And then, after silence on my part. "I'm sorry. I am. It's just that—"

"It's OK," I say. "I know what it's like to have your momentum interrupted. Good luck with the concerto."

"Don't add guilt on top of interruption!" And then, again, "I'm sorry!"

"Be well," I say gently, and click off before I can do any more damage. Or evoke any more aggression or guilt or whatever the hell is and has always been wrong between us. I do not have a talent for motherhood. My work always came first, even when Zed was a child—a very difficult child—and so how can I blame him for doing the same?

I settle in for the flight, reading the data from the hastily assembled interagency team. Somewhere over Tennessee, I sit bolt upright and read a section again, and then again.

I don't usually pray, but involuntarily words arise in my mind, *God, let me be wrong about this.*

At Brooke Army Medical Center at Fort Sam Houston, the interagency team is cool to me, which is clear when my request to meet immediately with the team leader is denied.

"Dr. Kenton is unavailable," says Major Liu, the virologist obviously placed in charge of me, just as obviously without any enthusiasm for the charge. In her eyes—all their eyes—my team and I have screwed up.

I attack the issue head-on. "You're wondering how we missed the virus's effect on our patients' endocannabinoid systems."

She gazes at me steadily. She's my age, and she has the aura of an epidemiologist who's wrestled with major diseases under impossible conditions. I can feel it, that aura; to anyone who's waded through exsanguinating blood from Ebola, watched children in mud huts die of Lassa, that aura is palpable. I had it once myself, before Louisiana.

Major Liu says simply. "Yes. Our patients' endocannabinoid receptors are blazing like Roman candles. It should have been hard to miss."

"Have you talked to…is the rest of my team here? I was told in Atlanta that both Dr. Silva and Dr. Bernstein—"

"Dr. Silva arrived three hours ago and is being debriefed. We've talked to Dr. Bernstein by Link. Why do you think they missed the endocannabinoid connection?"

Carol missed it because she is inexperienced, not particularly competent, and willing to follow Lucas's lead. Lucas missed it because…

I say, "They are both inexperienced, on their first assignments. Is it possible…May I talk to Dr. Silva?"

"Perhaps first you can give us some insight into how a geneticist talented enough to isolate a virus in record time was unable to then identify which receptors the virus attached to and so what it might be doing. Or why *you* didn't make the behavioral connection. It's not as if endocannabinoid-system reactions are that hard to spot."

Her words are acid quietly poured over me. And she is, of course, right.

The endocannabinoid system, ECS, which spreads through

virtually every organ in the body, is an active and complex cell-signaling network. It is what marijuana bonds to. More relevantly, the human body manufactures its own endocannabinoids. They are naturally occurring neurotransmitters, and we know less about them than anything else in the body except the brain. Their function is to regulate key bodily functions to keep them in balance. When your ECS is deficient, your sleep is disturbed, your walking is uneven, your blood pressure swings wildly, your pain may be amplified, your appetite goes wonky, your body temperature is not kept steady. And if the right endocannabinoids bind to the right receptors in your nervous system, it will affect that other barely understood organ, the brain.

"Runner's high" is the result of a rush of endocannabinoids to the brain.

So is the high from pot.

So is the occasional sudden good mood, mellow and feeling positive about the world, that seems to strike for no reason. The sort of pleasant, cooperative mood that leads a cantankerous, difficult child to smile sweetly and say "Thank you" for a teddy bear in an ineptly sewn pinafore.

The sort of mood that disinclines a person for complaint or unpleasantness because, after all, it's good to be alive and other people are interesting and hey, live and let live, right?

The sort of mood that disinclines Army recruits to stick bayonets in people, fire guns at them, drop bombs on them.

The sort of mood that is supposed to pass, through the breakdown of endocannabinoid in the synapses of your brain, as soon as aggression seems the better evolutionary option.

All this passes through my mind in a flash while Major Liu stands waiting for my response to her sarcastic insult. *Perhaps you can give us some insight into why you did not make the connection.* I know the answers I'm supposed to give—*because I only had five patients, because I wasn't supervising my sole virologist on what I considered a bullshit assignment*—but I don't say them. Her scorn is justified.

I say, "I'd like to talk to Dr. Silva as soon as possible. I can ask him questions you may not have thought of, questions based on informal observations in Anita Falls."

Her lip actually curls in contempt, something I've never seen outside of melodramatic movies and Dickson's pathetic theatrics. But all she says is, "Wait here. I'll send him to you after he's fully debriefed."

It's a long wait. I sit on an uncomfortable chair in the window-less room furnished only with three chairs and a wooden table. What is this room ordinarily? I can picture difficult soldiers being reprimanded here, or being dishonorably discharged. This room—this whole building—is far removed from labs, hospitals, the medical training facility for which Fort Sam Houston is known.

Eventually, Lucas is escorted in and we're left to stare at each other.

I know that this interview is probably being observed and/or recorded. Does he? Of course, he does. Lucas Silva is the reverse of naive; his personal history guaranteed that, the personal history that he has risen above with such admirable grit. Gritty, brilliant, traumatized, arrogant Dr. Silva.

He gazes at me, waiting with his usual quiet composure.

I say, "You told the researchers here that you missed the virus's effect on the endocannabinoid system."

He says, "Viruses don't usually affect that system. Or if they do, the immune system is usually good at defending it."

"Yes. But you are usually very thorough."

"Thank you. Did you not observe changes in the patients' behavior based on your extensive interviews with their contacts?"

Clever. He is going to throw me under the bus. Although he is basically right. I didn't investigate the pre-infection personality traits of the patients, and so could not tell if their personalities had changed. The exception was Sarah Emily, whose parents tried to tell me their aggressive child had just become an angel. And I did not listen.

NANCY KRESS

Lucas rises slightly on the balls of his feet, like a boxer, his only outward sign of what must be enormous inward strain.

He says, "I should have been able to see the increased ECS activity. I missed it because of my inexperience."

I can say, *Yes, you did,* and that will be the end of the interview. Or I can say to him, and everyone listening, what I believe to be the truth.

No, you did see that the virus affects the endocannabinoid system. You deliberately hid that data because your parents were blown to bits in war and your sister tortured and murdered. You believe human aggression will destroy humanity. You wanted this virus to have time to spread. And you did more than just stay silent.

Sebastian is the key. Sebastian Duer and Jem Potter.

Sebastian, skilled and trigger-quick bodyguard, who failed to protect me from the baseball-bat-wielding crazy in the Anita Falls parking lot.

Jem Potter, my asymptomatic patient, identified as infected only by his implant. A man whom nobody in Anita Falls knew anything about because he was just passing through on his way to Fort Sam Houston to stalk ex-girlfriend Corporal Olivia Elizabeth Donavan. Jem Potter, who had a restraining order against him, as well as a dismissed Connecticut case of domestic violence ("he said, she said"). Jem Potter, now calm and agreeable and who, according to new intel I'd read on the plane, had abandoned his stalking of Donavan to settle quietly into a new job in Boston.

Lucas, tense as piano wire, stares silently at me. We both know that I hold his future in my hands.

Condemning Lucas won't stop the virus. It is out and spreading, like most enteroviruses, through bodily fluids: saliva, mucus, feces. Put another way, through kisses, shared vapes, careless hand-washing, babies' diapers. Eventually there may be an antidote or a vaccine, but not before huge numbers of infectees become, to some unknown degree for some unknown length of time including permanently, nicer people. More cooperative. Less aggressive, less driven.

Driven dictators—Hitler, Stalin—have murdered millions, caused wars, specialized in cruelty.

But…could less aggressive soldiers defend this country? Or any other?

Driven malcontents are the stuff of which terrorists are fashioned.

But…would less driven epidemiologists face death in the field, bulldoze their way through local politics and public reaction, work twenty-hour days for weeks on end to fight diseases that could wipe out the planet?

"Ehnita Falls" became "Anita Falls" because of the terrible slaughter of the indigenous people by British soldiers. Slaughter that has happened over and over whenever one group has more advanced weapons than another.

But…would less aggressive humanists risk their lives and the lives of their families to try to stop the slaughter?

Would less aggressive athletes train so hard or compete so fiercely?

Would less driven artists focus so exclusively on composing, painting, writing, dancing, sculpting to produce *Swan Lake* or *Ode to Joy* or *Crime and Punishment*? Zed saying, "I'm right on the edge…" Edgy. Driven. Discontent with the establishment has always fueled art.

I say, "How did you infect Sebastian? He never goes into quarantined areas. He's as careful around disease as he is—was—protective of me and my team. It was when you took him out for craft beers, wasn't it? Did you bring a patient's saliva with you, offer to get him a special beer from the bar, carefully smear the saliva on the glass? Something like that? You knew he's always refused an implant, and that between my missions he goes to his brother's in New York, a great place to incubate germs."

Lucas says, "No. You are wrong. I didn't infect anybody, and I didn't realize the virus attacked the endocannabinoid system."

"One more question, Lucas. If you really believe that spreading this virus, which is going to disrupt global security and economy for decades, will change the human race in a positive way and is ultimately going to do so much good, why didn't you infect yourself as well as Sebastian?"

For a long moment Lucas is silent. Then he repeats, "I didn't infect anybody, and I didn't realize the virus attacked the endo-cannabinoid system."

I look up at the camera I still can't see and say, "We're done here, Dr. Liu."

Instantly the door opens, and the aftermath—hearings, public-relations strategies, citizen panic, citizen contentment, quarantines, containment measures, the frantic race for a vaccine that will preserve humanity as it is now, driven and aggressive and capable of choosing hard actions no matter the personal sac-rifice—all of it will begin.

How much contentment is contented enough? How much innate aggression is too much? I don't know. I don't pretend to know. But I know that epidemiologists should not use pathogens to shape human minds. That is not our decision. We are not divinities.

Months later, after I have been fired from the CDC, after Lucas has been indicted for a seditious act to undermine the United States military, after it has been determined that no charges will be filed against me because incompetence is not a federal offense, after I have found a job doing lab work that a talented college sophomore could master, after the virus has gone public and the active military sequestered and relentlessly tested, after violent crime has dropped in urban areas by over ten percent and counting, after the world's scientists have united to search for a so-far-elusive vaccine, after media uproar has exhausted its supply of multi-syllable adjectives ("cataclysmic, evolutionarily transformative, terrifyingly disruptive") and begun to repeat them—after all that, Zed called me.

He doesn't know about my role in the cataclysmic, terrifying disruption. No names were made public. But even if Zed had known, I'm not sure it would have penetrated his current excitement.

"Mom! I did it! I found the way to finish the concerto!"

"Honey, that's—"

"Actually, to rewrite it *completely*. I found the missing piece! It…never mind, you wouldn't understand anyway. But the important thing is I got a hearing with Anton Cieślak—not right away, of course, I had to work my way up a whole chain of people and some of those fools that…never mind. Cieślak saw it! He wants it! To be performed next season in New York!"

Even I know who Anton Cieślak is. America's legendary conductor, and one of the premier conductors in the world.

"Zed, I'm so—"

"He says the concerto is brilliant!"

Zed babbles on about Cieślak, about scoring the concerto for full orchestra, about technicalities I can't follow and don't try. What matters to me, his mother, is that he sounds happy, and that he called me—however belatedly—to share that happiness.

That driven, edgy, non-agreeable happiness.

Is it worth the viral turmoil affecting the world? No, of course not. One concerto cannot balance a pandemic, not even a pandemic of niceness. Nor can the thank-you letter I received from Sarah Emily Nowak's mother. ("I am so grateful to you for giving us the best possible version of our daughter.") Nor can the email from Sebastian, now enrolled in a nursing program. But these things matter to me.

They are what I have now, and I am unexpectedly, surprisingly, even alarmingly content.

Ashes to Ashes, Blood to Carbonfiber

written by
James Davies

illustrated by
MAY ZHENG

ABOUT THE AUTHOR

When James Davies isn't repairing linear accelerators or parenting his eighteen daughters—four feral humans and fourteen well-mannered hens—he reads, writes, and fells trees.

James was raised among the rolling green hills of England's "home counties" but was introduced to fantasy and science fiction when he stumbled across David Farland's The Sum of All Men *in a random bookstore in Kenya when he was ten.*

After devouring the entire Runelords series, James joined the Runelords online community where David Farland then introduced him to the Writers of the Future Contest and urged him to write.

Various stages of life have interrupted James's passion for writing (living in China with Shaolin monks, a master's degree in electronics, falling in love, and relocating to Maryland, US). But two years ago, he approached it from a new direction: no longer writing for the sake of writing, but studying the craft with a focus on improvement.

"Ashes to Ashes, Blood to Carbonfiber" is the amalgamation of a vivid dream and an extrapolation of technology under the shadow of human nature at its worst. And its best.

"Ashes" asks: If you could sacrifice body parts to make anything of equal mass, what would you create? What would you sacrifice?

James also has a complete epic fantasy novel that he is hoping to publish in the near future.

ABOUT THE ILLUSTRATOR

May Zheng was born in 2003 in central New Jersey. She has been creating art for as long as she can remember, almost always centered around fantastical characters and narratives of her own invention. Searching for a means to fully realize her imagination, at the age of twelve she began attending the Art Academy of Hillsborough, founded by Kevin Murphy, world-renowned illustrator and portrait artist and founder of Evolve Artist Education. At sixteen, May began to apprentice with Murphy in illustration and portraiture. Although her apprenticeship applies artistic training and skills in oil paint, May also works digitally to create illustrations and fan art.

Her first book cover was published by kOZMIC Press in September 2021 for The Mad King *by Rebekah Mabry. At age nineteen, she was recognized by the 16th Art Renewal Center Salon Competition in the professional tiers of Imaginative Realism and Portraiture. May has also worked with Evolve Artist Education to paint via livestreams to an international audience. Selections of her work are on display at Highlands Art Gallery in New Hope, New Jersey.*

In addition to her apprenticeship, she is currently a full-time student at Rutgers University, pursuing a major in cognitive science, as well as minors in history and Russian literature. She is looking forward to working in art full time as the owner of an art school, a freelance illustrator, and a portrait artist.

Ashes to Ashes, Blood to Carbonfiber

"The secret ingredient alchemists had overlooked all those millennia ago was obvious, now. Life."

Rickard dragged his sled of rusty fabricator parts out of the desert and onto the dirt road at the end of his division. The wind howled between the rows of prefab homes on either side, once identical but now patchwork from improvised repairs. It dashed his chapped lips with salt and sand as it fled the vast desert that surrounded the outskirts. Above, dark red clouds blotted out the scarred, salt-white face of Sampo, Kaybee's nearest moon.

Rickard redoubled his efforts, his gnarled hands aching despite his thick gloves. He had to hurry. Imogen, the daughter he'd never had, had lost her roof in yesterday's storm. He had to get it patched before the storm that brewed now rolled in. But he couldn't leave these parts in the middle of the street to be stolen, or worse, found by one of the Billionth's patrols.

The sky darkened. Streetlights popped on through the haze, like fireflies from his memory of Earth. Younger and less grumpy, Rickard and his late wife Tabi had left Earth fifty years ago. Wanderlust and ambition had carried them here, to what was officially K2-18b, now Kaybee, to its residents. Touching down on the verdant planet, overflowing with life, had felt like a dream come true.

But that verdant world was gone. And it was Rickard's fault.

He forced a smile and nodded to a couple as they hobbled past him, hurrying to shelter. They lived two rows over from him. One of them nodded back. Rickard had built their prosthetic arm.

MAY ZHENG

He wondered what their partner had traded their leg for. They'd still had it last week.

The couple left interesting tracks over the sand-covered street, a blur from shuffling feet punctuated by the prosthetic leg, trailing away toward Garden City. The city's vast monolithic walls—which kept the sand and salt and commoners at bay—could be seen from anywhere in the division, from any of the two hundred decaying divisions that surrounded it.

Garden City didn't belong to the one percent he'd resented on Earth, but to the two dozen men and women who held more wealth than the twenty billion outside combined. The Billionth.

Rickard stumbled, cursed. The wind picked up, sand hissing against his heavy jacket. He shielded his face as he approached his shed, swept a bank of dust from the doors with a heavy boot, and slid them open. They moved easily. No weeds gummed up their tracks. The planet's fecund flora and fauna were gone now, consumed. Like rust over wet metal, mankind had spread across Kaybee. They had built fabricators, fed them living matter, and fabricated *stuff* until nothing living remained.

Then they had moved on and done it all over again. And again.

Until the Billionth realized they would soon run out. Then they'd gathered what little there was into their city, their antithesis of Noah's ark.

Rickard shuddered, not in memory of the riots that had followed, but of the Billionth salting the planet, removing from the masses their means of rebellion. No life, no fuel to fabricate with. The people were left dependent on the Billionth's handouts, enough to survive, so long as you were willing to sacrifice the occasional body part to the fabricators.

Rickard's shed was clean and well-organized inside. Racks of parts and tools lined the left-hand wall while a worktable and a cot—for fitting prosthetics—filled the right. His shining, secret, and almost-finished fabricator dominated the back wall. It was shaped like a huge medicine capsule with grungy, curved glass compartments on either end, big enough to hold a deer carcass, and a mess of cables, pipes, and electronics in the middle.

When finished, it would be able to fabricate anything from an equivalent amount of living matter.

He moved a prosthetic leg to the cot from his worktable and unloaded the rusty parts onto it, then grabbed his biggest tarp and a couple of long carbonfiber rods. They'd been earmarked for a grow tunnel years ago, but without viable soil and seeds that whole idea was worthless. Until he got the fabricator working, at least.

Matrix welder holstered, parts shouldered, headlamp donned, he set off toward Imogen's to repair her roof.

Sand-laden wind whipped through the streets. Behind the rows of prefab homes shimmered endless echoes of the life that had stood there fifty years before: terrestrial bioluminescent coral, large enough for scores of kids to climb; Venus-green trees that scraped the sky with iridescent, spherical leaves; and an infinitude of insects with every number of wings imaginable, and no ability or inclination to bite or sting humans.

Rickard dispelled the memories with a shake of his weary head and approached Imogen's home. The superalloy walls of the prefab unit had lost their shine and peeled in places. But they were in good shape compared to the dead landcruiser beside them. Like an old-world RV that had overdosed on steroids, the two-story cruiser leaned against the side of the house, its hovering days long behind it. Especially now that she had riveted it to the side of her house and cut a doorway through from the living room.

Imogen Newhope stood on her crooked front step, left eye illuminated from within by her aug-phone. If he'd had a daughter, she'd likely be Imogen's age, midthirties. Her porch light cast sharp blue shadows beneath her too-prominent cheekbones. She wasn't eating enough, again. Too much like Tabi, toward the end.

"Mr. Carfine! You made it. I really appreciate it," she said. Her aug-phone blinked off, and she tucked her left foot behind her leg.

"Rick's here?" her daughter, Alanna, called from inside. "Yay!"

"I was about to move Alanna into my room and seal off the cruiser."

"Yeah, storm's getting close. Should have enough time to sort the roof, though, don't you worry," Rickard said, flicking on his headlamp.

He put the tarp on the ground, slid the poles over the land-cruiser, and began to clamber up.

Imogen moved to the side of the cruiser, her limp worse than usual. She must've given another toe for Alanna's medicine. The Billionth ran fabricators just outside their walls, but the cost was steep. And you had to use their approved templates, no weapons, nothing that could reproduce, nothing that could remove your dependency on them. Nothing like the fabricator parts waiting in his shed.

Guilt stung the back of Rickard's throat. He had done this. He had put them at the Billionth's mercy. He had given her that limp. He had killed the world. And he'd been so proud when he'd done it, when he'd invented the fabricator.

"Let me do that. You can't be climbing buildings in the night at your age," Imogen said, from the ground. She looked almost as run-down and tired as the old cruiser, and as she leaned against it, he wondered who was holding up whom.

"I've climbed worse." He remembered oil stains on his elbows and nanotube flakes under his fingernails during his days crawling over the Billionth's fabricators, big enough to print a house.

Rickard looked down into the landcruiser through a hole wider than he was tall. Within, ten-year-old Alanna knelt in a nest of space-unicorn bedsheets.

"Can I help?" she asked. Posters of frogs and dinosaurs disguised the dead electronics panels that lined her bedroom walls.

"No, lie down," Imogen called from outside, a gleam of frustration showing beneath the veneer of saintly patience.

"Who could sleep with such beautiful clouds over their bed?" Alanna asked.

"Little girls who want to see the sun again!" Imogen said.

Rickard stifled a chuckle and wrangled the poles into position, spaced along the length of the cruiser. The tops of the walls were jagged where the roof had torn off, but the butt of his matrix welder hammered them straight enough.

Ptang! Ptang! Ptang! The cruiser rang as he welded the poles in place.

Alanna watched him with open curiosity and gratitude. He gave her a "no big deal" smile, then noticed that she was shivering.

"You OK, kid?"

She nodded meekly, but the color was fading from her face.

"Imogen!" Rickard yelled. "Alanna."

Imogen ran inside, unslowed by her missing toes, and threw herself down at Alanna's side.

She felt Alanna's forehead, cursed, lurched to her feet, and rushed out of the room. Rickard clenched his fist around the wall he was perched on, powerless to help. He stared at Alanna, willing her to be OK. Her gray pallor brought painful memories of Tabi. Their bed made up like a medbay, cables and tubes everywhere. Her color fading day by day. The Billionth needlessly delaying his loan applications to buy a fabricated heart until it had been too late.

A painfully long moment later, Imogen returned, needle tip glinting in the light from Rickard's headlamp. Alanna's eyes rolled back, showing only the Sampo-white whites. Imogen injected Alanna's arm with a speed and care that contradicted one another.

Alanna breathed in a long, shuddering breath, and seconds later her color returned.

Imogen collapsed back against the wall. It was the cruiser's turn to hold her up, this time. A tear ran down her face.

"That was the last of it," she said. "I was hoping she'd get by until I could find more."

Alanna smiled dozily at them before shuffling deeper into her bedding and closing her eyes.

"Isn't commissary meant to keep her prescription filled?"

Imogen shook her head, tear-dampened hair waving around her face. "We only get half 'cause her dad claims the other half… I assume to sell it, as he doesn't send it here."

"Sampo's salt." He gripped the top of the cruiser as a gust tried to wrench him from it. "I'll ask around tomorrow, see if I can rustle up any."

"Thanks, Mr. Carfine." She remained on the floor, hundred-yard stare resting on Alanna. The girl slept soundly.

Rickard grimaced as he raised his welder again. He hoped it didn't disturb the girls too much. He was gonna hear about this racket from Ms. Wondimgezhu in the morning already, more than likely. But there was work to be done, and he was running out of time.

Ptang! Ptang! Ptang!

The sun was near its zenith before Rickard managed to drag himself out of bed, producing a symphony of pops and creaks and groans. The previous day foraging for parts had destined him for a rough morning. The late-night improvising the roof in the advent of a storm hadn't helped. But the emotional costs were what had really drained him. Watching Alanna's attack and the procession of nightmares that had followed once he'd finally fallen asleep. Tabi pulling away a hand speckled with blood, Tabi lying in the same damned bed covered in more cables than a fabricator, Tabi turning gray and still. Dead.

He could've saved her. A ripper would've done the operation for no more than a week of food creds back then; all he'd needed was a heart. You had to buy organs from the Billionth, the public fabricators didn't have those designs, and Rickard hadn't had anywhere near enough food creds. He had tried to ask for one, the Billionth owed him enough for creating the means for their untold wealth, but they had ignored his messages and refused his requests for an audience.

He'd contemplated stealing a pound of biomatter and a moment with one of their private fabricators, but Tabi had forbidden it.

And he'd been too much of a coward to disobey.

He dressed. Well-patched jeans, clean but hole-ridden T-shirt, suspenders, trucker's hat. Not that there were truckers anymore.

Coffee. He barely noticed the slight tang of salt. He held the hot cup with both hands, letting the warmth pervade his knotted knuckles. He contemplated taking a painkiller, but he only had a handful left and there'd soon be days where he hurt worse, he reckoned.

Once the cup had cooled and ceased easing his hands, he downed its contents and put it aside.

Boots on. Out to the shed. He'd do some inquiring into Alanna's meds later. It was too close to noon for walking around outside. In truth, it was too hot to be working in the shed, too, but there was work to be done.

He donned heavy gloves and set upon the rusty parts he'd collected yesterday with a heavier and more powerful grinder than a man his age should handle. Only decades of experience kept him from losing a finger as he removed the largest, most offensive pieces of rust.

He needed chemicals to handle the finer stuff. His arms shook as he decanted tannic acid, leftover from woodworking projects decades ago, and butoxyethanol, salvaged from a deserted fracking well, into a large tub. Then he lowered the fabricator spares in.

As he waited for his concoction to do its job, he set upon a power supply circuit board with his soldering iron, replacing the old electrolytic capacitors.

The shed door slid open with a whir.

"Old man Rick, you starting a meth lab in here?" Ms. Wondimgezhu asked, nodding to the tub and the light haze drifting out of it. She was a whole year younger than him. Gray hair framed her brown face and crow's feet clawed at crow's feet around her eyes.

"De-rusting some parts for a project. Never you mind." He wiped sweat from his forehead with the back of a dirty glove.

"Your little project involve using a jackhammer in the middle of the night?" she asked.

"Well, no, I can't say it does."

"I know it was you making all that banging last night. You're the only one fool enough to be slinking around with power tools in the dark during a freaking storm. You're always playing around with tools." She looked pointedly at the soldering iron in his hand.

He shrugged. "The Newhopes' roof blew off. Storm hadn't arrived yet. Had to fix it before it did."

"Tyrus said he almost got caught in a storm," Ms. Wondimgezhu said. She was endlessly proud of her grandson, as he presumed she should be.

If Rickard had had grandchildren, he'd never shut up about them.

"Called me yesterday, from a cave. And you won't believe it, but there were mushrooms *growing* there."

Rickard put his soldering iron down and stared at her. "Growing?"

"Yep. Must be the cave sheltered some of the soil from the salt the bloody Billionth spread."

"Where?" He was almost salivating at the idea of damp, salt-free soil.

"Way, way west. Past Crescere Crater, by Tectum Ridge."

That was far. Weeks on foot, at least. And no one but the Billionth had a working vehicle these days. They kept all the fuel, and the salt killed machines almost as fast as it had the plants. But it would be worth the journey. Rickard had to consciously stop himself from thinking about the cave, about growing things, and returned to the conversation.

"Sorry, young lady," he said. "I gotta get back to this, or the acid will eat all my parts."

Ms. Wondimgezhu started shuffling back out of the door, waving a bony, three-fingered hand at him. "I'm going. I'm going. Just don't you be banging away at midnight again."

"Wait. Before you leave, you know anyone that's got spare insulin? Alanna's run out."

Ms. Wondimgezhu frowned, her light whiskers twitching. "That ripper—what was his name—Jim? He might. Think his kid had the same thing."

"Thanks, young lady."

Ms. Wondimgezhu started to leave but paused at the door. "Look after yourself, Rick. I mean it. And no more power tools at night!"

He grunted amicably, and she left.

Rickard daydreamed about the cave as he made his way to the ripper's home. He shifted the jar of coffee he'd brought with him from one hand to the other before knocking on Jim's plastic front door. When the prefabs were new, they'd all had fancy AI doorbells that greeted you, let you in if you lived there, connected you to a resident's cybernetic aug-phone if you didn't. But, after a couple of years, the Billionth had rolled out a subscription plan to keep them enabled. A few did, at first. No one could afford it now. Rickard didn't miss them.

"Jim, it's Rickard," he hollered.

There was a long pause before eventually the door slid open. Jim stood, arm propped up on the frame, unkempt brown hair peppered with gray, weeklong stubble, bags under his eyes. The greatest ripper in the division had fallen far.

"Rick."

Rickard knew better than to ask how Jim was doing. No point in pleasantries with Jim. "I hate to ask, but you got any of Kyn's insulin left? Imogen's kid's run out."

Jim leveled an astounded stare at Rickard. "You're kidding me? My son *just died*, and you want all his stuff?"

Most people would argue that a year ago wasn't *just* now, but Tabi had left him almost a decade ago and it still hurt.

"Just the meds."

Jim's face reddened, jaw tightened. "Fine. You'll give me a finger in trade?"

Rickard hesitated and looked at his hands. Unlike Jim and Imogen and likely every other adult in this division, he still had all of his fingers and toes. The Billionth had paid him well, comparatively, even if it hadn't been a life of luxury. He was proud of his wholeness—he didn't even have an aug-phone—as much as it exacerbated his guilt. He was a walking contradiction.

He scrunched his hands into fists. He needed them to finish the fabricator. "I can't."

Jim stepped back and pressed the Close button on the door. Rickard lurched forward, slipping a titanium-toed boot into the door's path. It gave off a high-pitch alarm, and the light strip around the frame flashed red.

"Jim, Kyn's already dead. Without the insulin, we'll have another dead kid. You want Imogen to feel this pain?"

Jim glared and ground his teeth. "Why not? I have to!"

"Because she *doesn't* have to. Will you trade me for my coffee?" Rickard offered up his last jar.

Jim snatched it. It was fabricated powder, not the fancy Garden City dirt-grown beans some people splurged on, but it was Rickard's only indulgence.

"Fine." He slapped Open and disappeared into his house. A moment later, he returned with a small vial. "About a week's worth. It's all I have. Now leave me alone."

"Sorry. One more thing," Rickard said. Jim looked at him as if he were one of the Billionth. "I don't want to get anyone's hopes up, but I think I can get the girl a pancreas. Can you handle a transplant?"

"Can I handle one? Before the Billionth removed most the medical designs from the public fabricator, I chromed entire nervous systems, upgraded spines, uplifted freakin' animals! If you want to insult me, I'd start with my face, 'cause my work is irreproachable."

"Perfect. Be ready tomorrow."

Rickard took the insulin to Imogen's. When he arrived, she was sweeping sand out of the front doorway.

"Sampo's salt," he cursed. "Did the roof not hold up?"

As she turned to face him, the broom caught her foot and she stumbled, catching herself on the doorframe. He wondered how many toes she had left.

Still, she managed to smile at him. "No, it did great. I'm sure it kept the most of it out. Guess the storm was just a bit too much for it."

"I'm so sorry." *For the roof. The storms. The Billionth's chokehold.* "I have some insulin."

Imogen lunged from the doorframe and hugged him. She buried her face into his chest and squeezed him tighter than he'd thought her skinny arms capable of. Without a word, she told him he was needed, and he promised to protect her and Alanna. Like an echo of the hugs he had dreamed of forty years ago when he and Tabi had decided to start a family. That he'd dreamed of a billion times since discovering they couldn't. Eventually, he peeled her off. He had his grumpy-old-man reputation to maintain.

"Will you have dinner with us? As a thank-you?" she asked.

"Sorry, there's work to be done." He shook his head.

"Fine. Breakfast it is," Imogen said. "And I won't take no for an answer."

He smiled. "Fine."

And then he left. No one adopted kids anymore, let alone adults, but Rickard dwelled on the idea as he walked home.

Once there, he stopped in the kitchen to nuke a prepackaged dinner—flash frozen yulicki and stiff, fabricated venison. Thank you, food creds. He wolfed it down standing at the counter, then grabbed his painkillers and returned to his shed.

Inside his little workshop, his latest clutch of fabricator parts lay glistening on the bench. The drive motor didn't work at first, so he opened it up and rewound the silver coils. The filament had corroded away inside the quark manipulator. Luckily, he no longer needed the heating element inside his kettle. An hour of electroplating later, he had a suitable replacement.

It was messed up, when he thought about it, as messed up as Sampo's scarred face and Kaybee's salted paradise. He could fix *this* so easily, but he hadn't been able to fix Tabi. Hadn't given her the children they'd wanted or the heart she'd needed.

As he lowered the quark manipulator in, he slipped, distracted, and it fell with a clunk and a high pitch squeak that fifty years of experience told him was bad news. He lifted it out and inspected it and…damn. One of the miniature charm-strange exchangers was smashed.

Rickard strangled his frustration, carried the manipulator over to his workbench, placed it carefully, and then slammed his fist down beside it.

He yelled in pain and clutched his hand. Seventy-five and still a hotheaded fool. The manipulator rattled mockingly.

Without the quark manipulator, his fabricator couldn't transform one element into another. It had taken him months to find this one. Alanna couldn't wait for him to find another. If the fabricator was working, he could make one easily. The irony almost physically hurt.

Although…the fabricator could probably still fabricate something, so long as the right element was available. He removed the charm-strange exchanger from the manipulator and turned it over in his hands, jogging decades-old memories from their cobwebbed nooks and crannies. Most of the exchanger was an elaborate structure of carbon nanotubes impregnated with iron cores.

Well, there was only one place where he could get living material with a decent amount of iron in it. Rickard loaded the design for a charm-strange exchanger into the fabricator computer, then cleaned out an old coffee mug with a rag and placed it into the input port. With a shaking hand, he grabbed a retractable blade from his bench. For the first time in fifteen years, he was thankful for his old-man veins. He sliced his forearm and half-filled the cup with blood before bandaging the cut with the rag he'd cleaned it with. His hand trembled over the Fabricate button.

He wasn't the religious type, but there was one being worth praying to. "Tabi, I need you to look after this machine. It has to work. If something blows…it could be weeks. Alanna might not even have days."

He bent over and kissed the cold chrome of the fabricator as gently as if it were Tabi's cheek.

Then he hit the button.

Nothing.

Then, a quiet whir, a pause, a series of heavy clunks, more whirring, and the heart of the fabricator began to glow helium-neon-yellow.

"Brilliant," Rickard said. He took a moment, forced himself to smile at it. Fabricators this size cost more than anyone but the Billionth could afford in a lifetime. And he'd built one at home out of deserted fabricator parts and a couple weeks' worth of food creds in nuts and bolts and wire.

The machine's gentle hum rose to a sonorous roar. The daisy chain of lights around the shed flickered while the glow of the machine shone blindingly bright. Rickard shielded his eyes and staggered backward.

A minute later the machine calmed and produced a solitary ding. The ding dragged him back to a grubby first apartment in San Antonio, with a beige-faded-to-yellow microwave, and Tabi and he eating their first meal as a married couple. The best-damned microwave dinners anyone had ever tasted.

Rickard returned to the present and the cooling fabricator. He opened the output window. Within rested a tiny charm-strange exchanger. He lifted it out reverently, took it to his bench, and probed over it with his oscilloscope. It was perfect, at least as far as his testing could discern. He replaced the crushed one from the quark manipulator and installed it into the fabricator.

"OK, if it still works, that's the inanimate test complete. Next, the animate…if that's even a word," he grumbled.

Rickard loaded another blueprint into the fabricator, and made one small tweak. This time he only needed to add a drop of blood to his old coffee mug. The fabricator should now be able to transmute any element into what it needed, and he was only fabricating something very small.

He hit the button, and the fabricator fabricated. A minute later, it dinged again. Rickard opened the output port.

Within, an angry fly buzzed in tight circles using its only wing. Exactly as intended. The first living animal Rickard had seen since retiring from the Billionth's gardens, and it was beautiful. He scooped it up and examined it closely. In his old job he'd have sent it to the lab to be scanned; make sure every molecule was where it should be. But that wasn't an option anymore, so a visual inspection would have to do.

The fly looked good.

Four drops of blood and four insects later, Rickard was as satisfied as he was going to get.

He moved the prosthetic leg from the cot and propped it up nearby.

"Dying to see you, Tabi. But got a little more work to get done first. Make sure the machine doesn't botch this up."

Rickard loaded two designs into the fabricator—a pancreas, enhanced to be more efficient than a natural one, enveloped within a vacuum-sealed cooling system; and a syringe of powerful analgesics. He searched the shed for an alternative living source one last time, as if one might miraculously appear, but none did. He thought of sneaking into Garden City and stealing what he needed, but that would've been impossible even if he was armed to the teeth and thirty years more sprightly.

He downed the last of his painkillers and removed his left boot. Then, with heavy arms and a heavier heart, he grabbed the frame of the input window and inserted his leg. He rolled a cleanish oil rag up tight and chomped down on it like a horse's bit. He lamented for a moment that horses had never made it to Kaybee. The vast desert would have been a joy to ride over. He'd miss walking across it.

He slapped Fabricate.

Pain burned every square millimeter of his lower leg, more intense than anything he'd felt before. The morning's coffee splashed against the tread-plate floor. He squinted against the bright light and mewed as the machine roared.

As suddenly as it had come, the pain vanished, every nerve deleted. That idea churned his stomach worse than the pain had, and he dry-retched against the side of the fabricator. Sweat poured from his forehead and soaked his tatty shirt.

Then Rickard fell back. The input window slid down, closing him off from the remains of his leg with a wet thud.

It shed less blood than his arm had. The Billionth had made him develop a cauterization feature for public fabricators after the post-salting riots had calmed down. He'd felt sick to his core, but people were going to sacrifice limbs whether he did it or not. So, he had done as they'd bid.

And, lying on the floor, he was glad for it. Glad that he hadn't had to drag Jim here with a cauterizing iron.

Sweat dripping from his brow, puke and saliva from his chin, stump held shaking above the ground, he pulled himself into the cot.

And dreamed of Tabi.

He awoke with a start. Cold water dribbled into his ear and streamed down his face, and his left leg felt like he'd dipped it in lava. He was lost and confused and the world reeked of vomit and acrid coffee.

"Thank goodness!" Imogen cried, kneeling beside him, holding a glass of water. She put the glass down and hugged him. "What on Kaybee are you doing? Where's your leg?"

Slowly, his memory returned. He pointed at his fabricator. Despite the burning pain, his leg itched fiercely. He went to scratch it and clawed nothing but air. *Oh. Right.* "Open the fabricator. Get me needle."

Imogen released him, rushed to the fabricator, and opened the output port.

"What's this?" she asked, staring inside.

"Pancreas. For Alanna. And painkillers, for me. Please."

Slowly, with eyes unfocused, face blank and gray, Imogen brought Rickard the syringe. It had cost him an extra eighth of an inch of his leg, but he couldn't afford to be on bed rest for days on end. The pain mounted as he waited for her to reach him, and as soon as she did, he snatched the syringe from her and plunged it into the meat above his stump.

Liquid gold, refreshingly cool and comfortingly warm, flooded his leg, chasing out the roaring pain and incessant itch.

After a minute, he found his voice. "What brings you here, anyway?"

"You didn't show for breakfast," Imogen said, voice still distant. "I came to drag you over by the ear."

He gave a weak chuckle. "Thank you. Look, I wanted to prepare you, but I didn't know if it would work. Didn't want to get your hopes up for nothing."

He sat up on the edge of the cot. An unpleasant weight sank into his stump. It tingled as he pulled on the prosthetic leg. He'd designed it to avoid contact with the end of his stump, and instead clamped around his knee.

Holding Imogen's hands for support, he stood up.

Her eyes glistened. She grabbed his sweat-soaked, oil-stained shirt as if to push him, but stopped herself. "I didn't ask you to do this."

"I know."

She slapped his chest, nearly knocking him over. "You're a damned fool, Mr. Carfine."

"Oh, I know." He smiled. "Come on, let me look at it."

She moved her hands to his elbow, and he tottered over to the fabricator.

Irreverently, he removed the packaged pancreas from the output port. A cool fog wafted out. Thank the stars, the cooling system worked.

For something so wonderful, it was disgusting. He tried not to retch. It gleamed like a slathering distended tongue within the vacuum seal. Bright red tendrils pulsed along its otherwise teal length.

"I've already spoken to the ripper. Jim. He's ready when you are," Rickard said. "But it'll keep cold if you need more time."

Imogen searched his face; for what, he knew not. Eventually, she hit his chest again, lighter this time. "Let's go get Alanna."

Rickard hammered on the door, stabilizing himself against the doorframe. "Jim. It's time."

Imogen stood behind him, almost hiding from the door, with Alanna clung to her waist.

The door slid open.

"I half thought you were joking." Jim was clean-shaven with a small square of tissue stuck to his chin. He wore fresh clothes, crease lines pronounced from disuse.

Rickard nodded and offered the sealed pancreas. Jim looked at him quizzically, opened his mouth as if to query the organ's origins, noticed Rickard's missing leg, and closed his mouth. His jaw clenched and unclenched, before he said, "About payment—?"

Rickard handed him a key to his shed. "There's a working fabricator in my shed loaded with every medical design you can dream of. Yours to use whenever you choose. Our secret, though. If the Billionth find out, they'll destroy it. And me and you, probably."

"Yeah, that'll do it. Come on then, lab's this way."

They passed through Jim's musty living room, past a dusty couch, and neatly organized shelves of disused toys. A path from the kitchenette to a decrepit armchair shone from regular use, or more accurately, the rest of the floor remained obscured beneath layers of dirt and grime. A sliding door opened for them as they approached, and they stepped out of Kyn's memorial and into Jim's lab.

The carbonfiber floor shone with polish, and bright lights gleamed off an operating chair and the metallic blue robotic arm beside it. At the head of the chair stood a large cabinet comprised of clean white panels, computer screens, and medical tubing.

"Here you go," Jim said, patting the chair and smiling at Alanna. It was at once both the weakest and strongest smile Rickard had ever seen. The smile of a man who saw the salvation his own son had missed, and now had the opportunity to give it to another.

Alanna hopped into the chair and shared a worried look with her mother.

Imogen held her hand. "It'll be OK," Imogen told her, not sounding entirely convinced herself.

"It will be," Rickard said. "Jim's a brilliant"—he paused, avoiding the word ripper—"doctor."

Jim nodded. "I am, though the robot does all the work. Now, lie back."

Alanna did as she was told, and Jim placed a breathing mask over her face. His left eye lit up from within, his aug-phone displaying reference texts. He pressed a few buttons on one of the touch screens and the hiss of pressurized gas emanated from Alanna's mask. Alanna's eyes turned with a smile, blinked, blinked again, then closed.

"Here." He ushered Rickard and Imogen to the head end of the chair, before drawing a curtain across her midriff.

Then, with the focus and control of a hoverbike racer, Jim set the robot into motion. Electromechanical whirs and hums filled the lab, smoother than even that of the fabricator, accompanied by the subtle but disconcerting aroma of cooked meat. Worry covered Imogen's face, and she clutched Rickard's hard, old, liver-spotted hands. Her hands were warm.

He wondered if this—the warmth, the worry, the hope—was what it would have felt like if he and Tabi had had a child.

Thirty minutes later, Jim released the robot's controls. His eye dimmed. "It's done. Everything went to plan."

He lowered the curtain. An angry inch-long scar underlined Alanna's sternum. It disappeared as Jim stuck a bandage over it and covered it with her shirt. He tapped on one of the touchscreens and the hiss of gas changed pitch. A moment later, Alanna's eyes blinked open. Jim barely had time to remove Alanna's mask before Imogen took her daughter's face in her hands.

"You OK, baby?" Imogen asked.

Alanna took a moment to gather her thoughts, before smiling. "Does this mean I can have candy whenever I want, now?"

Imogen laughed so hard that tears flew from her face. Rickard found himself laughing with her, harder than he had in years. Even Jim chuckled.

"Today, sure," Imogen said, kissing Alanna's forehead, nose, lips. "Tomorrow, we'll see."

"You're going to be sore for a couple days," Jim said, "but you can get up and move around. Just take it easy, OK?"

Alanna nodded and slid down from the chair with help from her mom. "Thank you, Mr. Jim."

"Don't worry about it. Just think of me when you're old enough for an aug-phone implant," Jim said.

Imogen slapped his arm playfully. "Thank you, Jim, really. And

Rick." She hugged him, then looked at his leg. Or lack thereof. "Thank you. Can I help you home, get you set up in bed with everything you need?"

"No, I'm quite all right," Rickard said, smiling. "You get Alanna home. I'll make my own way."

"OK. Well, thank you, again." And Imogen shepherded Alanna out of the lab.

Rickard lingered as Jim started cleaning up. "You did a good thing today," Rickard said.

Jim's eyes flicked to Rickard's missing leg. "As did you."

"A small recompense. There's more to be done."

"Like what?"

Rickard steeled himself. Treason was a tricky subject. "We keep toiling under the Billionth's heel; how many Alannas are there gonna be? And Tabis? And Kyns? We need to escape."

Jim looked at Rickard as if he were mad. Unsurprising, really. The Billionth had lorded over them for so long, the idea of opposing them was as foreign as green grass and blue skies. "Where the hell would we go, Rick? The Billionth salted *everywhere*. Nothing will grow! Without their food, we'll die."

"Someone found a cave. There's mushrooms growing there." Rickard had to swallow to stop from drooling. He'd dreamed of growing things again for so long. As Rickard talked, Jim's tidying grew frantic, drawers shut with more force than was strictly necessary. "I'm going to take the fabricator there, use the mushrooms to make seed and soil and whatever else we need. It'll be slow, at first, but we can terraform it back!"

"You want to fix all of Kaybee? You're nuts." Jim said, fleeing back to the living quarters.

Rickard followed him and moved beside the kettle in the kitchen. "Not all of it. Just some, to start with. Enough to live on."

Amusement and disbelief warred over Jim's features. "OK? And you're telling me this master plan so that I can snitch to the Billionth for a huge reward?"

It was Rickard's turn to be amused. "Huge reward, ha, maybe a week's food creds." He nudged the kettle with a crooked knuckle.

"No, I'm telling you because I don't want to be six hundred miles away from a doctor."

Jim ignored the hint. "I'm not a—"

Rickard raised a hand to stop him. There were no real doctors anymore, they both knew, just rippers that followed digital procedures. But Rickard hadn't been exaggerating when he called Jim the best. "You know what I mean."

"Don't worry. I won't snitch. But go ask someone else. Another ripper."

Rickard took two mugs from a cupboard, cleaned them with the corner of his shirt, and put them down beside the kettle, loudly. "Jim, I'm old. I need someone I trust to take over if something happens to me. I need you."

Jim rolled his eyes as he absent-mindedly adjusted a photo of Kyn on a shelf.

"And, when you're old like me," Rickard continued, "you're not going to look back and say, 'oh boy, I wish I'd spent another day wallowing in grief.' Trust me."

Jim released the photo and glared at Rickard, but the anger that emanated turned inward after a moment. Jim's shoulders slumped and he reluctantly boiled the kettle and poured two cups of coffee. "I'll think on it."

Rickard took a mug, sipped, and dreamed of salt-free coffee. "It won't be easy. There's not going to be a huge amount of fabricator fuel to start with, so we'll be sleeping rough. But you'll be making a real difference, not just putting phones in people's eyeballs. And eventually, we should be able to fabricate *anything*."

Jim took a sip from his own mug. "I said I'll think on it."

"Good." Rickard nodded. He lifted his mug. "You mind if I take this home?"

"Sure. You're gonna help yourself to everything in my house anyway, apparently." Jim gave him a wink.

Rickard said goodbye and left.

The journey to the cave wasn't possible without a vehicle. Rickard stared at his fabricator. It weighed over a ton. If he put it in a trailer and convinced every friend he could think of to push it, they *might* cover a couple miles a day. But then they'd need enough food and water for all those people for however many hundreds of days the journey took. That meant more trailers, more people, more food....

They needed a vehicle, and the only one he knew of was the rusted piece of junk riveted to the side of Imogen's home.

"Damn," he told the fabricator. "We've got some work to do."

He slammed Jim's coffee mug down on his workbench. Coffee splashed the tread-plate floor, again.

The fabricator loomed along the back wall. Among other things, including an advanced onboard computer, Imogen's landcruiser needed a new grav-drive, and Rickard was looking at the only place he could get one.

He turned his thoughts away from that task. *Focus on the easy stuff*, he told himself.

On the fabricator's console, he loaded a design for the cruiser's onboard computer from an archive of the manufacturer's data. The fabricator could position individual electrons, so it could produce computers already preprogrammed with software. And over the years of hunting for parts, he'd had time to write a lot of software.

After a quick visit to Ms. Wondimgezhu and a static-filled off-network call with her grandson, he plotted the easiest route to the cave into the computer's nav-system. She was confused when he wished her goodbye, and downright indignant when he hugged her.

After triple checking the route, he tweaked the computer's vocal synthesizer. It was unnecessary and vain, but he didn't want it to sound like a damned robot. He saved and closed the adjusted design. It wasn't time to print it just yet.

Then he wrote instructions for installing the computer and the grav-drive in an old notebook, as well as a rough description of how he envisioned terraforming would go.

He didn't dwell on why these instructions were necessary, why he wouldn't be able to do it himself.

A single sheet from the back of the notebook sufficed for a letter to Imogen. He rushed, eager to have it done, writing in ALL CAPS to keep it legible despite the teardrops that splotched the page, and left it atop the instructions.

Then he returned to the fabricator and loaded the designs for thousands of seeds, for crops, and trees, and flowers. Small stuff first.

He paused a moment to imagine the garden that would surround the cave. How the greens and reds and blues and purples would encroach upon the beige of the desert in a beautiful reversal of history.

Then he put his left arm into the input port and punched Fabricate.

"Hey, Tabi, look after that arm for me, will ya?" A strangled chuckle. Wet cheeks. Funny how much more tolerable the pain was when there was still work to be done. "There's more coming."

Next was the computer system. He moved a large crate beside the input window, bringing his coffee over, and sat down, inserting his remaining leg into the fabricator.

Intense pain, unfathomable loss, and five minutes of variable consciousness later the fabricator dinged.

Salty sweat stung his eyes, dripped from his forehead, and soaked his clothes. "Now, the hard part. By Kaybee and Sampo and Old Earth herself. I really wanted to see that cave," Rickard told the fabricator.

He chugged the last of his coffee, savoring the bitterness and the sweetness. And the salt. He loaded the grav-drive design on the fabricator.

And pulled himself into the input port.

Eight years later, six hundred miles northwest of Garden City, in the lee of Tectum Ridge

Alanna wiped sweat away from her forehead with the back of a dirty hand before putting down her trowel and standing up from a row of corn seedlings. The electrochromic dome that hid them from the Billionth also shielded the farms from K2's harsh glare, allowing only the optimum amount of light through.

Consequently, Alanna's son needed no sunscreen as he toddled down between the rows of crops, rich dirt squelching between his toes.

A hum grew in volume, reverberating in Alanna's chest, as her mother's old landcruiser rolled up behind her.

Its voice synthesizer was a little robotic, but mostly it was familiar and comforting. "Alanna. If you have finished tending to the corn, your mother bids you return to the cave. Dinner will soon be ready."

"Sure thing. Wait up, and I'll grab Rickie," she said.

The cruiser waited, as taciturn as its progenitor. Alanna scooped up her son, brushed him off—an exercise in futility if ever there was one—and hopped into the waiting cruiser.

The door closed and it accelerated toward the cave with a whir.

The cruiser's lights blinked on as they entered the cave, illuminating the mushroom terraces that lined the walls. They descended toward the heart of Kaybee and their subterranean city.

"Are we still on track with the plan?" Alanna asked.

The cruiser answered, "Terraforming now covers twenty-five acres. Population at forty-seven. Three new migrants joined us yesterday. Progress continues at an approximately exponential rate."

"Still," Alanna and the cruiser said in unison, "there's work to be done."

Alanna chuckled. "There always is, Grandpa Rick."

Summer of Thirty Years

written by
Lisa Silverthorne

illustrated by
GIGI HOOPER

ABOUT THE AUTHOR

Lisa Silverthorne made the biggest decision of her life in 2020. After a lifetime in Indiana, she retired early from her twenty-five-year IT career, packed up everything she owned, and drove three days west to focus on her writing in Las Vegas, where she now lives and writes alongside her three feline dictators. Lisa has been writing since she could hold a pen and made her first professional fiction sale way back in 1994. Flash forward nearly thirty years and she has finally achieved a milestone she thought unobtainable: placing in the Writers of the Future Contest.

Lisa's passion is writing. Her stories are sometimes dark because she explores things that frighten or anger her. Many times, her stories blur genre lines and change many lanes. Her work has been described as having heart because she loves writing about the connections people form in the best and worst circumstances. She also loves adding a spark of romance to her stories. Her first short-story collection was published in 2005 by Wildside Press. She considers Ray Bradbury, Theodore Sturgeon, Nora Roberts, Andre Norton, Kristine Kathryn Rusch, and James Lee Burke her biggest fiction influences.

"Summer of Thirty Years" was written shortly after the death of her father. Partly an exploration of grief, this story is also an affirmation of love and friendship. It takes an unflinching look at the uncomfortable, and for some, frightening practice of burying the dead—especially someone you love. It asks the question, what if magic could undo the unthinkable, even for a little while? Would you use it no matter the cost? What would you sacrifice for those you love? Does love end at death?

ABOUT THE ILLUSTRATOR

Born in 1985 in East Chicago, Indiana, Peggy Hooper is a versatile artist whose creativity knows no bounds. Known in the art world by her moniker, Gigi Hooper, she's a child of the '90s, drawing early inspiration from iconic pop culture. Simultaneously, Gigi was deeply influenced by the enchanting worlds of young adult, children's, and comic books, which have fostered a love for sweet, fantastical, and mind-bending literature.

Gigi's artistic journey began in her childhood, when her experimental nature led her to beautify and unintentionally destroy her mother's personal property. However, throughout her life, Gigi's mother remained a steadfast supporter, purchasing Gigi's first set of art supplies, which only continued to encourage her creative process.

While her path took her through diverse careers as a United States Marine and a personal trainer, Gigi eventually returned to her true calling. She earned a BA in illustration from George Fox University.

Currently residing in Newberg, Oregon, with her husband and sister, Gigi specializes in digital art, collage, and pencil work, although her artistic palette embraces various mediums.

Today, she continues her artistic journey, pursuing independent studies while actively engaging in freelance work, bringing her captivating visions to life one creation at a time.

Summer of Thirty Years

The scritch-thunk of moving earth soothes me, consciousness a slow burn. Flesh takes hold of my bones, limbs prickling with needles of sensation, burning and aching with mortality. These sensations of relief, along with the steady sound of digging, permeate my slow return from death yet one more time. Telling me I still exist.

Muscles twitch, the warmth of blood insulating my cold, cold bones. Worn, dusty blue coffin silk warms my fingertips. Steady rise and fall of lungs and ripple of my suddenly beating heart fill my body with euphoria and a tangled rush of emotions.

I shiver and suck in a breath, the cold ground suffocating. The coffin's darkness smells musty with death and decay, cloying in its claustrophobic assault on my face as I open my eyes again. And exhale. A long slow breath of life that I haven't known for months. Since the first snow wilted the daffodils in the old family cemetery. The cemetery is a small square of land with a dozen headstones, most of them a hundred years old, framed by a black wrought iron fence and a creaky gate. Just past the sea grass and rocky ground that separates the cemetery from the Oregon beach house where I would have spent my honeymoon.

The rasp of shovel against sand and dirt draws closer and I blink, my heart racing at the sound. Brandon will be through the earth in moments and for a few months, I will again be free of this long, tortured sleep.

For only a little while.

I clutch at the lace and pink cotton nightshirt that once dressed me for viewing. For my funeral. I never remember it being mine and wonder who thought to bury me in it. Had it been a wedding gift? Mark and I never got to open those gifts.

Metal thunks above my head, but I close my eyes. The darkness and confinement of the coffin unnerves me now that I'm awake. I remember awaking like this so many times before, but I have no idea how many days have passed since I last returned to sleep and awakened when the daffodils bloomed again. Sometimes, they bloom early. Sometimes they bloom late.

At last, metal clangs against my coffin lid and the muffled sound of human voices warms my ears.

"Mimi! We're almost there!"

My husband, Mark's voice is sharp, enveloping, and I can't help but grin at the familiar sound.

Mark is already awake and out of the grave beside me.

The stubborn lid strains upward and cool air floods over me, the velvet night sky sprinkled white with stars that I've missed so much. Mark's handsome thirty-year-old face hangs over me, grinning, sandy brown hair curling in the salt air. He leans down, brushing his fingers across my face, through my sable hair. Already, the ocean spray begins to scrub away the smell of decay and cloying stink of death.

"My love," he says in a raspy voice, his brown eyes candle-bright as he lifts me from the coffin and into his comforting embrace.

My arms slide around his body, feeling the pulsing warmth of flesh against my supple skin and I melt into his touch. I whisper his name against his ear, the brush of my lips against his earlobe like a burning ember. His skin smells like butter and I want to drown in the smell of life again.

But as intoxicating as Mark's presence is, I can't hide my shock at seeing Brandon who stands beside the grave, leaning on the shovel. Looking twice our age. Mark's and my best friend no longer shares our youthful looks. He's aged, and aged hard,

GIGI HOOPER

the weight of this burden lining his face. The weight dulls his once-bright blue eyes and makes his eyelids droop. His mouth is drawn in clay, a thick, unrelenting line of misery etched there as a permanent reminder of what happened that night.

Tears well in his eyes. No longer happy tears at our reunion. Something darker shadows his face.

"My old friend," I say to him and reach out to warm the granite of his face.

Life sputters in his eyes a moment, but the tide of guilt washes it away like footprints on the beach.

"Mimi," he says, his voice old and tired. "Welcome home."

Mark sets me down on my unsteady feet, but I cling to him, not wanting to be far from his touch.

"Thanks, Brandon. For everything."

I reach out and touch his frail arm. He looks so thin. Like a different man standing here. I barely recognize him and the pain radiates past my momentary joy.

He gives me a hollow nod, his thinning frame and white hair making him look ghostly in the cemetery's moonlight. He leans on the shovel like it's a cane. It's hard to believe we were once the same age.

The Brandon I knew from college has long since disappeared, yet here I stand looking exactly like I did on my wedding day. I glance down at the bright daffodils poking their waxy green stalks out of the cemetery earth. Growing at the headstone of each grave. The clock is already ticking. When the last one fades, so will I until next spring. I have no idea how many summers Mark and I have left before the daffodil bulbs' magic fades and we return to the dust. Kept alive by that magic and Brandon's dogged dedication to digging open our graves every summer.

My teeth chatter as a breeze rolls off the ocean, carrying that clean, salty scent I've missed so much.

"Let's get you two in the house—and get you settled," says Brandon.

He offers Mark a thin smile and a pat on the arm as he lumbers toward the creaky cemetery gate. His walk is arthritic and unsteady.

Mark presses his lips to mine and my body ignites with white-hot need, all my senses on overload as he grips my hand and we follow Brandon down the footpath toward the Pacific Ocean. It has been so long since I've felt anything.

Ahead stands our cedar beach cottage with its billowy linen curtains, teak furniture, and maple floors, cedar shakes gray and windows and doors trimmed in white. I remember the pale aqua walls, white furniture, and blue-rag rugs—bright like sea glass against Oregon's grayness. The smell of cedar mixes with ocean and sweet daffodils lining the walkway. This cottage has weathered a lot of storms and wind, looking much older than her 1922 construction, but she feels like home, and I can't hold back my smile at another old friend.

"Brandon's looking old," Mark whispers to me and I grip his hand tighter.

What happens when Brandon dies? Who will care for us until the magic ends? I can't stop the chill shuddering through me. What if Mark and I return every spring and there is no one to unearth us? Would we suffocate? Die all over again?

I focus on the roar of ocean waves, letting that terrible thought float away.

"He looks frail, like he's been sick," I say. "I hope he's well."

"He damned well better be," whispers Mark, his hand sliding around my waist. "All of this is his fault."

"I'm old, but I'm not deaf," Brandon snaps, pausing at the little cottage's pergola, white paint stripping away to gray cedar from the wind buffeting the shoreline.

He glares at us, wheezing a little as he leans on that shovel again.

"I'm sorry," says Mark, bowing his head. "I didn't mean it like that."

"Of course, you did." Brandon replies. "And I've devoted my entire life to—to the two of you."

A hint of life sparks in those lifeless eyes as he pokes his thumb against his bony chest.

"Yeah, the accident was my fault," he continues, pain in his voice. "And so were the bulbs, but…I did the best I could for you both."

I let go of Mark's hand and rush over to Brandon. Slide my arms around him, holding him close.

"Brandon, no—the time to beat yourself up over this is long, long past. What is done is done and Mark and I are so grateful to have these summers together. You've been wonderful to us, really you have."

I smell the sweet stink of alcohol on him, and I'm taken aback.

"Brandon, why?" I ask, surprised that after everything that's happened, he would take a drink. "Aren't you tired of consequences?"

His eyes narrow.

"More than you'll ever know, Mimi."

With another wheeze, Brandon turns and heads toward the beach house. The silence above the ocean waves is deafening as I walk behind him toward the cottage's flickering lights, Mark's footfalls hurrying behind me.

Inside, the scents of garlic and rosemary cling to the familiar cedar and ocean smell. A big wooden bowl heaped with spring greens sits on the little round dining table set with three crisp white plates and shiny silverware. A basket of garlic bread sits beside it, a saucepan steaming with bright red marinara sauce on a green trivet nearby. Spaghetti and garlic bread on the first night after awakening has become habit. And it's comforting.

"Please sit," he says to us. "You must be starving."

In the kitchen, Brandon is piling spaghetti noodles into a big yellow ceramic bowl.

He's been through this routine so many times. For so many years.

Mark and I sit at the table. My stomach growls, ravenous now, and I fill a little bowl with salad.

Brandon sets down the noodles and a silver ladle on the table and takes a seat beside Mark.

"This looks delicious," I tell Brandon as I drape a pile of noodles onto my plate and ladle on thick sauce.

Then I notice a chilled bottle of chardonnay, uncorked and half empty, tucked behind the salad bowls and I can't help but shiver at its sight.

Both Mark and I glance from each other to the wine in silent dread. It has been so long since I've seen Brandon take a drink. I study him a moment as he spoons sauce onto his spaghetti. His hands shake, his eyes looking glazed.

"When you start back?" Mark asks, taking a bite of spaghetti.

"Last night," says Brandon, an edge in his tone as he picks up his wine glass. He takes a long, slow sip. His eyes close a moment and then he returns to his dinner.

"Why?" I ask, swirling noodles in marinara, my fork scritching against the plate. "Why after all this time?"

"I'll explain after you've eaten and slept."

I lay down my fork. "Brandon—talk to us. You're our best friend in all the world. What's wrong?"

His hands are shaking harder now. He lays one hand in his lap, trying to hide it.

"Not tonight," he replies. "I'm too tired."

Mark starts to object, but Brandon holds up his hand, still shaking.

"It's late, almost midnight, and I'm nearly sixty-six years old. Tomorrow, please—when I've gotten some rest."

The number assaults my senses. Sixty-six…that meant thirty years have passed since the accident.

I set down my fork, suddenly not hungry anymore.

For a few moments, Brandon looks past me, his gaze following something. He mumbles words I can't quite hear and then returns his gaze to Mark, fear darkening his dull blue eyes. I squint at him, but that moment of fear fades. So I let it pass. I'm still disoriented and everything feels so clear and sharp that it almost hurts my head. I return to eating and the room is silent except for the muffled rush of waves on the beach below.

After supper, Mark and I clear the table and wash the dishes. I watch Brandon sitting in the next room. The television murmurs low and I can hear Brandon mumbling. He seems to be talking to someone, maybe the television, but I can't hear what he's saying.

My stomach drops, the fear cold inside me. Something is terribly wrong with him and now, I'm frightened. What happens to Mark and me if Brandon can no longer care for us?

Just as the last of the dishes is tucked away, Brandon rises from the deep-blue couch and heads down the narrow, dark hallway.

"Good night, you two. See you in the morning."

The creak of a door closing echoes above the television and all Mark and I can do is stare at each other, hoping tomorrow brings some joy.

After Mark and I make love, I fall into a fitful sleep. And awake shouting. Mark's arms enfold me and I snuggle into his warmth, his buttery scent. Everything feels so different this time. So final that my chest aches and I feel like crying.

"It's OK, baby," he says in a soothing tone. "Just a bad dream."

Or a premonition. I'm terrified again.

In my dream, I'm back in my coffin, the flesh melting from my bones, and I'm dying all over again. I shudder, a chill dancing over my body, like someone just walked across my grave, and Mark holds me closer.

I nod into his neck and close my eyes, falling into an exhausted sleep until the sunlight streaming through the window wakes me again. And I feel grateful that I have eyes to open, lungs to fill with air.

The bed is cold, creaky. Mark is already up. The smell of warm coffee envelopes the house and I sit up, trying to brush away my unease. I climb out of bed and fumble for a navy chenille robe (thirty years old now) that hangs in the small closet. I brush my long black hair and shuffle out to the kitchen in search of coffee.

Mark and Brandon's voices rise sharp and I stop in the hallway, listening.

"I don't want to seem ungrateful, but what happens now?"

"I—I don't know, man. I wish I had some answers."

"For what?" I ask and step into the kitchen.

"Mimi, my love," says Mark, his face brightening.

He holds out an arm and I slide into his embrace.

420

"Coffee?" Brandon asks.

"Of course, lots of cream," I say, as he pours the steamy hot liquid into a big white mug, his hands still shaking.

He slides the mug and a tiny pitcher of cream across the white granite countertop.

With Mark's arm still around me, I pour cream into my coffee and swish it around in the cup before drawing it to my lips and sipping. The warm, frothy taste of hazelnut rolls over my tongue and I want to lose myself in the richness.

"Now, what answers are you wanting, Brandon?"

He glances at Mark, looking uncomfortable. He looks more like Mark's dad than his best friend.

"To the situation we have here," he replies.

I shake my head. "And what situation is that?"

"I'm sick, Mimi," he says, a sadness blunting his sharp features. "Very sick. In fact, I don't think I'll be in any shape to…to help you anymore."

"What's the matter?" I ask, a chill touching my heart.

"I…I have advanced Parkinson's."

I shake my head, not knowing what to say and take his hand in mine, squeezing. His lips press into a taut line, glassy eyes squinting as he looks away.

"Mimi, I…I see things. And I don't know…if they're real or not. I don't know anymore." He sighs. "Thought I could…stay ahead of it. But I can't outrun it anymore."

The three of us are silent for a long time.

"What happens to us?" I ask finally.

His eyes well with tears. "I wish I knew. Since I got sick, I've been trying to find a way…to stop the magic."

A chill washes over me and I set down my coffee mug. Stop the magic? I can't even turn that thought over in my head. That means that Mark and I will cease to exist. Our lives cut short by that horrible accident thirty years ago. Mark and I always knew this day would come, but not so soon. I thought that the final time we go to our graves, everything would just end. Is this the end? Or do we have more time?

"You can't, Brandon!" Mark shouts. "What if it doesn't end this summer? It's magic—unpredictable, you always said. What if we have more time?"

The magic—I've never known how Brandon stumbled on the little bursts of immortality that Mark and I share. All I remember from the emergency room that night is the taste of dirt and raw root, almost like a turnip, in my mouth, tiny minced bits washed down with water. And then the long sleep until the sound of digging first woke me from death.

"What choice do we have?" Brandon insists.

"We'll dig up the coffins. Put them in the cottage's root cellar. Lock it from the inside."

Brandon seems to grow calmer at Mark's suggestion. "That could work."

"Why can't you use the same magic, Brandon? On yourself?" I ask.

He smiles. "Because every time I woke with the daffodils, I'd still have advanced Parkinson's. It's too late for me, Mimi."

"Then how does the magic work? I'm confused."

Brandon's body shakes as he points out the window, his hair so white, his face so lined and thin. "This line of daffodils, the ones around the yard…they were split—from bulbs grown by the ancient Greeks and Romans."

He is struggling for words, lips pursed, and I stop myself from saying them for him.

"Those bulbs were centuries old. They were rumored to carry— the gift of immortality. Roman soldiers carried them into battle. When eaten…they lessened the pain of death. But the Romans— believed they had healing properties."

"How is that possible?" Mark asks. "And how could you get them?"

"They're heirloom bulbs, cultivated at a little farm near here— by an old Italian woman. I paid thousands for them."

I remember that old farm. Every summer, before the accident, I bought Roma tomatoes and garlic. I'd even bought two bottles of some sort of flower wine from there. I'd asked for something special, something for my wedding.

"Why would you do that?" Mark asks Brandon.

"You and Mimi were dying. I had to do something. I had to fix it."

The car accident.

Brandon had been driving that night, Mark and I drunk on that flower wine and celebrating our marriage. Brandon had been best man and designated driver, but that hadn't stopped him from drinking. Early and often. He'd kept drinking after our toasts of that fragrant wine. Before we knew it, Brandon was careening down Highway 18 toward the Oregon coast. The foggy, twisting mountain roads didn't stop him from taking the curves at seventy until for a moment, all I heard was silence.

No whisper of tires against pavement, just the pure rush of air as the car left the road.

Sometime later, I had moments of consciousness in intensive care, the pain overwhelming, Brandon sobbing beside my bed. And that pungent taste of roots and dirt led me into a strange sleep, then nothing until I awoke the next summer in my coffin.

I'm told that Mark and I hung on for a week before being pronounced dead and buried in the little family cemetery near our beach house. Where we'd planned to live as newlyweds. And forever after that.

"So the magic is forever?" I ask Brandon.

He shakes his head. "I wish it was. No, the older the bulb—the longer your life. These were thirty-year bulbs."

"Thirty year?" Mark frowns.

Brandon nods. "They'd bloomed thirty years before I bought them. When the bulb's eaten...you come back to life every summer."

"Until the bulb dies," I say.

Brandon's eyes fill with tears as he stares at me a long while. Finally, he nods.

"This is the thirtieth summer, Mimi. But the magic isn't exact. You come back a few months each year. Does that equal a year every time? I don't know. And I don't know if you'll both return again next spring. But for me, it's the last one."

I bury my face against Mark's chest, the sobs shuddering through me.

423

"I know it's a shock." Brandon struggles a bit to find his words. "I always avoided telling you. But now that you know…let's make this spring and summer your best ever." He laughs for the first time, but the sound is bitter. "Besides, I'll be joining you both soon."

I dry my tears, at last realizing the gift I've been given. Mark and I have had thirty summers together. More than many people's lifetimes. We haven't cheated death, but because of Brandon, we haven't let it cheat us either.

I lift my head from Mark's shirt and turn to Brandon.

"Thank you," I say in a choked voice and slide my arms around his frail body.

This time, Brandon cries with me.

Mark and I spend every moment together and with Brandon. Knowing it will all end by the first snow makes it all feel so fragile.

Every surge of ocean wave and call of seagull has meaning to me. The daffodils and lavender smell sweet and clean, the soft sand, cold ocean, and rough stones comforting against my bare feet. I know that this may be my last time to experience them, so I press them with all my might into memory, hoping to dream of them when I go to sleep for the final time. In that long sleep, I want to remember it all and the extra gift of time I've been given.

Tonight, the three of us sit on the rocks and watch the sun sink over the Pacific, fingers of orange and fuchsia reaching through the swirls of clouds to illuminate the water. It reminds me of the night before our wedding, when we drank toasts to our long life ahead. Not knowing what was to come. I squint at the frothy waves, trying to remember the wine. It had been an unusual one.

Then it hits me.

"My god," I shout, snapping up from the rocks. "It was daffodil wine!"

Mark cups a hand above his eyes and stares at me a moment.

"What was daffodil wine?"

"The wine we drank before our wedding."

Brandon shakes his head, his face scrunching into a confused look, hands shaking in his lap.

"Remember? We drank toasts with that almost perfumy wine." I rush toward Mark and grab his arm. "Don't you remember? You said it tasted like a shot of Halston."

He nods slowly. "Yeah, I guess I remember that."

Brandon's face fills with excitement. He understands why I'm bringing it up.

"Daffodil wine. Don't you get it, Mark?"

He shakes his head, still confused.

"I bought it from the same little farm, the same place Brandon bought the bulbs. I don't know if it's even still there."

Mark stares at me and then Brandon, waiting for one of us to keep talking.

"Mark!" I clap my hands together, grinning. "The wine may have the same properties as the bulbs."

At last, he understands that the wine might have given us more time and a smile spills across his face.

"We'll go see if the farm is still there tomorrow and find out."

I nod. I have to know how much time we have left. Even if we only have this last summer, I need to know.

The next morning, we all wake up early and pile into Brandon's white Ford Focus. Mark drives and we head inland, Brandon and I giving directions onto gravel and dirt roads until the faded wooden sign appears, Ricci Farms.

The farmhouse is painted brick red, the fields taking life with rich green foliage, the scent of perfume in the air. Rows of pale lavender and vivid yellow daffodils alternate in one field, bright green lettuce shoots, and lacy tomato plants fill another. A rickety old lean-to with a faded white sign reading Fresh Flowers and Produce is on the side of the dirt road. On a chalkboard with shaky handwriting, the words read, *Ask about our special wines and heirloom bulbs for sale!*

"This is it," I say, feeling hopeful as Mark parks the car.

We step out, Brandon unsteady and hands shaking as he shuffles beside us toward the lean-to.

A white-haired woman, in her eighties or older, sits in a folding chair beside bundles of fresh lavender and daffodils as she crochets a small, mint green blanket.

"Hello there," she calls to us, waving a wrinkled hand.

"Good morning," I say, stepping over to her.

"Looking for fresh flowers?" she asks, her fingers looping the yarn from memory. She never even looks down as she works her hook across the blanket.

"Wine," I say. "Some special wine."

She smiles, her gaze unwavering. "What sort of special wine?"

"Daffodil," I reply. "Made from bulbs."

She keeps up her looping and pulling of yarn, the skein flopping over and over at her bare feet.

"Don't have much call for that sort of thing these days," she answers. "Gotta have a strong constitution for that one. We do have some wonderful marionberry and a lovely herb wine with hints of lavender and clover."

"Why do you need a strong constitution?" Mark asks.

She glances up at him through wrinkled, hooded lids.

"For the consequences," she answers, the skein of yarn flipping end over end as she pokes her crochet needle at Brandon. "Ask your friend here."

She recognizes Brandon who looks away with a nod, his face grim, hands still shaking.

I feel sick inside, seeing him so old and ill, knowing how he's given up his own life to care for us each summer. Keeping such a horrible secret to himself. Only now do I realize how Brandon's decision and guilt have weighed on him.

"It's been a horrible burden," I say, but Brandon's gaze doesn't return to me. He's still staring out across the fields of flowers.

The yarn continues to flow through the woman's crochet needle, still turning like a top at her feet.

"Not to mention a great sacrifice." Her gaze fixes me as she nods at Brandon. "Did he not tell you that?"

I squint at Brandon who won't look at me now and the chill of dread slides down my spine. "What sacrifice?"

"He bought thirty-year bulbs," she says.

I nod. "I know. My husband and I have had thirty summers together."

The woman shakes her head, the crochet needle slipping in and out of the yarn at an unwavering pace.

"That's not what a thirty-year bulb is."

"Then what is it?" I ask.

"The magic requires a sacrifice to activate," says the woman. "Your friend gave thirty years of his own life to the magic. To give the two of you thirty summers together."

My stomach drops, a knot twisting in my chest as the guilt burns through me. Brandon's head is bowed, his gaze on his feet now.

"Brandon...is this true?" I ask, tears stinging my eyes.

He doesn't answer me. He just looks out across the farm fields.

"Answer me," I demand. "Is this true?"

Finally, he nods and his gaze meets mine.

"It was the only way I could undo what I did," he says, his voice catching in his throat. "It was the only way I could fix it."

Mark's hand slides to Brandon's shoulder and he squeezes, his eyes watery. When Brandon's gaze meets his, Mark pulls him into a hug.

"But what about the wine?" I ask the woman. "I bought a bottle of daffodil wine here and the three of us drank toasts with it at the wedding."

At last, the woman's crochet needle halts. She stares up at me a moment and then sets aside her mint green blanket. Her face is pinched, a mix of worry and anger now.

"Who sold you that wine?"

I shrug. "That was thirty years ago. I don't remember a name—just that she was a teenage girl."

The anger fades, sadness flooding over her parched face. "Ashley," says the woman. "Poor child didn't understand the magic. Didn't pay attention to the rules." Tears thread down her wrinkled face and she wipes at them with crooked fingers. "Didn't understand the consequences of selling the magic."

"She said something about it making my wedding extra special."

"It did," says the woman, staring at me. "It traded your destiny for hers. She was killed in a car accident the next day. And didn't get to come back each summer. She was my daughter."

I slump down on an empty wooden bin, feeling sick inside, remembering when Ashley and I had shared a tiny sip of the wine. My eyes well with tears. She'd always wanted to try it. Just a little sip. What could it hurt, I'd thought. At this moment, I feel selfish and useless, guilt tearing at me over the losses. If only I'd realized. If only I'd had a say in any of this.

"My god…I'm sorry," I say, my voice cracking. "Your teenage daughter? I'm so sorry."

"We're very careful with that wine," says the woman, clutching the crochet needle in her fist as she drapes the yarn around its tip and loops another stitch into the blanket. "We only make a few bottles a year and only sell it in the right circumstances."

Her fingers flash across the blanket, locking in a few more stitches.

"Ashley didn't know about the magic." She winces as if the needle has stabbed her hand. "I never explained that part of the wine to her, or the bulbs. I only told her they were very expensive and should be sold only by me or her dad." A long sigh escapes her pursed lips. "It was my fault. I should have told her the consequences. Should have hidden it better."

All these summers, these beautiful summers shared with Mark had come at the expense of two lives.

"Forgive me…if I'd have known," I say, my voice tight, tears threatening with every syllable, "I'd have never bought the wine. I couldn't have. She was probably, what—seventeen?"

The old woman nods.

"About to turn eighteen," she answers, and tears flood my eyes, streaming down my face.

"We toasted to a long life with it that night," I say. "And with every sip, I drank away moments of a life in full bloom. And I didn't even know it."

I cover my face in my hands, feeling like a vampire. For thirty years, I'd siphoned away two lives so I could live. How did it ever come to this?

I don't realize my sobs are audible until I feel Brandon's shaking hands on my shoulders.

"Mimi," he says, sliding my hands away from my face. "I accepted the consequences. But what you don't realize is that I got something out of this, too."

I shake my head.

"What could you have possibly gotten out of this? What did Ashley get out of this?"

Brandon's face isn't pinched with anger and he doesn't have that dazed, stumbling look on his face from being drunk all the time. He looks calm. Peaceful.

"I can't speak for Ashley, but the magic freed me from the alcohol destroying my life. That night in the ER when I gave you both the bulbs...my need to drink fled. Even after the...the funerals, knowing the accident—had been my fault." He struggles with the words a moment. "I had no taste for the stuff. Until last night."

So the magic is fading. Even I see that now. Hear it in Brandon's deteriorating speech.

"So what happens now?" I ask, looking up at Brandon.

"When the daffodils fade in the fall," says the old woman, "that will end the bulbs' magic. The wine's magic, too."

I reach over to Mark and pull him close to me. Now, we know. His hands are trembling as he takes hold of my hand.

We thank the woman and head back to the car in silence.

March slips into May and before I know it, July fourth has passed. With every passing day, I feel the dread of fall looming. I don't know if the first frost will come early or late, but I know that Mark and I don't have much time left. And Brandon's illness is rushing ahead at a frightening pace. His body stiffens by the day, shuffling walk giving way to frequent falls and nighttime bringing things only he can see in the growing shadows.

It's mid-August when I take a drive back to Ricci Farms, leaving Mark to look after Brandon while I'm out. Mark knows where I'm going and doesn't tell Brandon. Brandon spends most of his time in a wheelchair now and Mark makes sure his best friend is safe.

It's still light out, nearly nine o'clock when I return to the beach house with salad greens, Roma tomatoes, and fresh salmon. While Mark grills the salmon, I make the salad with fresh-picked Ricci greens and tomatoes.

Brandon's wheelchair sits beside the family room window that faces the ocean. He stares out with blank eyes, barely able to speak now. His muscles are failing at an alarming rate and I'm frightened for him. He has no one to care for him.

I toss the salad with fragrant balsamic vinaigrette and set it on the table as Mark carries in the salmon.

As Mark lays a fillet on each of our plates, I wheel Brandon to the table.

"Hungry, Brandon?" I ask.

He nods and mumbles something I can't understand. I lock his wheelchair wheels and spoon salad onto his plate. Mark helps him eat. It takes a while to get through dinner, but Brandon manages to eat a small portion of fish and salad.

After we've cleared the dishes, we help Brandon dress for bed. I get him settled and tucked in and then slide the covers up to his shoulders.

"Things will be better in the morning, I promise." I lean down and kiss him on the cheek. "Thank you for everything, my dear friend."

He smiles and mutters thank you.

Mark squeezes his hand, and we walk out to the kitchen. I grab an uncorked bottle of cold chardonnay and Mark picks up two glasses. We sit on the rocks outside, sipping chardonnay in each other's arms and watch the sun set.

Only when the wine is gone does Mark rise from the rocks.

After he sets the glasses and empty bottle on the deck, he slides his arm around my waist, helping me to my feet.

With a blanket and pillow in our arms, we walk through the tall sea grass on the little dirt path toward the cemetery.

I've left Brandon a note that reads,

Forgive us, Brandon, but we couldn't wait for the first frost. The vinaigrette was made from Mrs. Ricci's heirloom daffodil bulbs. In exchange for our final months, Mark and I have given you back a whole year. Free of illness. Free of guilt. There's a bottle of sparkling pear cider—nonalcoholic and magic-free—in the refrigerator. Celebrate your freedom. Celebrate your life. We will see you again someday soon.

Love always, Mimi and Mark

Mark places the pillow and then helps me step down into my coffin. I lay on my side as he slides in beside me. We drape the blanket over our bodies. With Mark's arms around me, I close my eyes as night washes indigo above the Douglas firs, the magic fading away at last. Only the afterimage of stars remains behind my eyes as the world softens and sleep claims me and Mark.

For the very last time.

Butter Side Down

written by
Kal M

illustrated by
SELENA MERAKI

ABOUT THE AUTHOR

Kal M writes from the crowded outskirts of Kuala Lumpur, Malaysia, where she grew up with the lofty ambition of someday working in an office and maybe even getting to wear a tie. She spent most of her time reading instead of playing outside. Eventually she figured out that all those books had to be written by someone, and that maybe she could even become one of those someones. So she got a respectable degree from a respectable university, and then immediately decided to disappoint her parents by announcing she'd write stories instead of contracts. This is her first time actually selling one (a story, not a contract).

"Butter Side Down" was inspired by Kal's inability to be mean to fictional characters in video games. What is it about human nature that makes us get attached to anything with a semblance of life? What counts as being alive? And for a species so sentimental about life, how are we so cavalier about taking it? She is not the first person to ask these questions. She's not even the first one to do so from the point of view of a toaster, but she hopes you like Breadna anyway.

She wrote this story with the simple intention of bringing smiles to a few faces. She plans to keep doing so for the rest of her life. When not hunched over a keyboard, she enjoys playing with animals, murdering houseplants, and puzzling over the mysteries of the universe.

ABOUT THE ILLUSTRATOR

Just a stone's throw away from the Efteling theme park in the Netherlands, Selena Meraki's journey began. The wondrous design work, immersive experience, and magic of theme parks sparked a passion for art and design from a young age.

Originally drawn towards becoming a veterinarian, fate intervened when a challenging concussion left Selena with a persistent traumatic brain injury. This turning point prompted her to embrace a new direction, one that would allow her to unleash her creativity and imagination.

Fueled by her love for theme parks and captivated by the enchanting realms of fantasy movies and games, Selena found inspiration in The Lord of the Rings trilogy and her favourite game, The Witcher 3: Wild Hunt. Driven by curiosity about the creative process, Selena ventured to the UK to pursue a bachelor's degree in game art and design, from which she graduated in 2022. There, she honed her skills in 3D and 2D art, but it was during a module on concept art and illustration that her desired career path became clear.

Her biggest dream is to become an Imagineer, a master of storytelling and design. Currently, Selena dedicates her time to building a portfolio showcasing fantasy card illustrations, splash art, concept art, and book covers. Determined to share her vision with the world, she aspires to embark on a thrilling journey as a freelance illustrator.

Butter Side Down

DEPARTMENT OF LAW ENFORCEMENT CASE FILE 10023869
UNITED INTERGALACTIC SPACE COUNCIL OF FREE SEN-
    TIENT PERSONS (PLAINTIFF) VS. HUMAN JOSEPH SMITH
    (DEFENDANT)
CHARGE(S): THEFT OF FEDERAL PROPERTY, TREASON, BREACH
    OF CONTRACT, CONSPIRACY TO COMMIT MURDER, WAR-
    MONGERING, CONSPIRACY TO COMMIT GENOCIDE
STATUS: DECIDED
VERDICT: GUILTY
SENTENCE: DEATH
    (Transcript begins)

INTERVIEW LOG 10023869-01-01
SUBJECT: SMITH, JOSEPH (HUMAN)
STATUS: DEFENDANT

It's not such a crazy situation when you think about it. All I did was fall in love with a toaster and cause an intergalactic political incident. I don't see why it's such a big deal. It could've happened to anyone, yeah?

All right. Pick a year. Any year. It's hard to put a date on it because Universal Standard doesn't always work when you account for jumping through wormholes and light speed and whatnot. Time gets wonky. But I'd just reached adulthood when I joined my crew. I couldn't wait to get out into space. It's in the blood, I guess. My whole family ended up spelunking besides my sister. She ran off to be an accountant. My parents never got over that. They're traditionalists, so when it came to my turn, they sat me down and—oh. Too far back? Yeah, OK. Sorry. Let me start over.

I saw something alive on Zulqar. I don't know how much you've heard about that place, but after the Akko-Zulqari war the whole planet turned into a wasteland. It was eerie. Solar crackle and dust storms, day in day out, with nothing to shield you but your exosuit and the skeleton of whatever ruined building you happened to be exploring. I was elbow deep in junk searching for schematics. That's what we were hired for. The Inter-Space Council said they wanted this old Zulqari agricultural tech called the Malgroth Programme, which they obviously couldn't ask the Zulqari for themselves on account of them all being dead. So, we went looking for clues. One by one we combed through the ruins of any research labs we could find. It sucked. Six months of nothing. So, I was alone one day, sort of just messing around, and that's when it happened. I saw Breadna.

Breadna was a toaster. Or some kind of miniature tank, maybe, because someone installed caterpillar tracks on her for reasons I'm never going to figure out. She was watching me. Insofar as you can be watched by something with no face, I guess, but she knew I was there. She skittered off when I noticed. Obviously, I chased her. Caught her just as she fell off the edge of a step with her wobbly tracks spinning like crazy. I decided right there that I loved her. I didn't have a choice. You don't find a sentient toaster-tank on an alien planet and not fall head over heels for her. That's just science.

Ah. You don't believe me. You're from where? Kallon? You have the six eyes. Yeah. Well, buddy, you'd understand if you'd been there. Sometimes you look at someone and you can just tell you'll get along with them, y'know? Like you. I can tell you're a good guy. No, really! I knew it the second you offered me that sandwich. You didn't have to do that. Oh, you did? It's standard Galactic Police operating procedure? OK. OK, well, you didn't have to get me a *good* sandwich, now, did you? Hah! That's what I thought. Sometimes you can catch good vibes off a person. Which is exactly why I knew I loved Breddy the second I laid eyes on her stupid little chrome frame.

First thing I did was I brought her back to the ship to see our engineer, Kevin. Kevin chose that name herself. My vocal cords can't pronounce anything in Vustron, so she let me call her a human name she liked the sound of. They're fun, Vustrons. They don't have a concept of gender. I tried to explain that Kevin's a traditionally masculine name, but I don't think she really understood. She decided to be a girl anyway. Because she liked the clothes better, she said, and she thinks I'm ugly, so she wanted to be whichever gender I wasn't. Which is garbage, by the way. I moisturize and work out all the time. I'd say I'm actually pretty handsome. Or I am by human standards, I guess. It's not my fault I only have two arms.

Where was I? Oh, yeah. So, I brought Breadna to see Kevin, so she could check her over for worms—no, not literal worms. No, I know there are no organic life-forms on Zulqar. It's a human saying. What I mean is I wanted Kevin to check Breddy's hardware for damage. I just wanted her to be healthy. No, not so I could use her as a toaster. We already had a fully stocked kitchen. I was just worried about her. I mean, who knows how long the poor girl was fending for herself out there, right? Right. So, we look her over, and what do you know? There's an AI chip in there!

I didn't think to take the AI chip out right away. I mean, OK, I'll admit it. I sort of liked having her in the toaster. It was super cute having the thing follow me around the ship on her little tracks, making friends with the computers, wanting attention all hours of the day. She wasn't very good at making toast, poor thing. She kept trying to launch it right onto my plate, but she'd usually just knock over my coffee. Nailed Security Officer Snuffles in the head too, once. Bonked her clean off the table. That was fun. All in all, it was kind of like having a pet, you know? You don't know. It's an animal companion. No, not for hunting with—*no*, you don't eat it—OK. OK, never mind. The point is, I kept her in the toaster until Captain Crab figured out Breddy was trying to talk to me in clack-code. I felt pretty stupid right then, I can tell you. I thought she was just clicking her lever at me to be cute.

Obviously, I knew that must mean she was more advanced than I'd thought. And I didn't have a personal AI at the time, so I plugged Breadna into my exosuit to see what she was all about. I booted her up, picked a voice for her, and…and it was the best thing I've ever done. Because that's when I realized Breadna wasn't just an AI. She was a person, all on her own. She said hello right in my ear. And that was the moment I met my best friend.

INTERVIEW LOG 10023869-02-01
SUBJECT: ꝾꞀⱮ!ꞃꞀꞋꞇꞇꞓⱲ-ꞕꞛꞇꞐ-ꞒꞏꞕꞌꞒꞐ, ALIAS: KEVIN (VUSTRON)
STATUS: WITNESS

Of course, I wasn't going to tell him the toaster extinguished all life on Zulqar. Is this a joke?

Joe is not clever. Or—pardon me. Let me rephrase that. Joe's problem-solving skills are admirable. He is creative. But he is wilfully ignorant of the fact that aesthetic appeal does not equate to goodness. He simply does not believe that a cute object is capable of destruction. I did not see the point in having another useless argument with him. I have been through this many times in the past, and the thought of attempting to reason with Joe makes my mandibles itch.

It happened in this sequence. The Malgroth Programme was never meant for agriculture. It was a biophysical superweapon. Its operational principle was simple—it contained a finely tuned particle scrubber, the type one would use to delete extraneous atoms from molecules to turn them into different molecules. As you know, this process must be heavily controlled so as not to cause an explosion or molecular instability. But this is not the remarkable part. What was interesting about Malgroth was the AI that powered it.

I have never seen such a complex computing system in my life. It was a scenario calculator. I believe the AI was designed to scan entire planets at a time, so it could find the perfect atom to delete to make a given molecule perfectly unstable. When I say perfect, I mean a specific set of conditions had to be met. Malgroth needed to [REDACTED]. The unstable molecule then would attempt to right itself by [REDACTED]; leading to perpetual instability, leading to [REDACTED] a systematic breakdown of [REDACTED]. This would continue to spread and [REDACTED] everything surrounding it. Imagine dropping a sugar cube into a glass of water and watching it slowly disappear. Theoretically, Malgroth could have, with one single action, dissolved the entire planet of Akkon. I imagine given enough time it could figure out how to [REDACTED] as well.

It was the perfect world killer. Unfortunately, it seems the Zulqari did not understand the scope of what they had created and, in the testing phase, accidentally destroyed their whole ecosystem. I do not know what stopped Malgroth from decaying the planetary structure itself. Perhaps it ran out of power, or someone managed to shut it down, but too late. Not enough of the Zulqari survived to give us a clue.

I digress. Understandably the Inter-Space Council deemed Malgroth too dangerous to use and decreed that it should be found and destroyed. They did not tell us the truth of what we were looking for, presumably in case we decided to use it for ourselves. Or, I suppose, so they could keep it for [REDACTED]. Why waste such a good weapon if—pardon me. No. No, treason is not my intention. I apologize. I misspoke.

Either way, this AI ended up inside the toaster called Breadna, which then ended up on our ship. We continued looking for Malgroth for six Universal Standard months. No, I did not know we were in possession of Malgroth until much later. For a while I was under the impression Breadna was simply a rogue AI. It gave no indication otherwise. It did not occur to me that a superweapon might be hiding inside a toaster.

No. I do not think it was Joe who put it there. I do not think Joe would ever have figured out Breadna was Malgroth on his own.

No, not because I trust him. Because he is stupid. Joe cannot tell the difference between a knothack and a cleion collider. I do not believe he smuggled Malgroth onto the ship. He would not have known what Malgroth was.

INTERVIEW LOG 10023869-03-01
SUBJECT: OLIGBA, AEUYTO, RACKELAFEINAERAIWAHKT (AYOI)
STATUS: WITNESS

Yes, Human Joe Smith has smuggled items on board our ship several times. Every mission we've been on, in fact. It is his second-most frustrating quality. His most frustrating quality is his blatant disregard for authority.

Examples? He refers to me as Captain Crab. I am informed this is a lower life form that used to be found on the human planet Earth. The similarity between crabs and Ayoi is purely superficial. Crabs do have pincers, I will grant, but they are unintelligent water-dwellers and prey animals to humans. Humans have unconventional lexical quirks, which I have studied at length, so my initial fear was that this was a subtle threat veiled in the human concept of humour—oh. Oh, you meant examples of the smuggling. I understand, yes. I have a list.

1. He brought a furor onto the ship following a simple data-collection mission on BX 612. Furors are blue, furred creatures about the size of a standard nut driver. They are also the planet's apex predators. It ate our security officer. We were grounded until she could regenerate.

2. He picked up an illegal sioscrambler from the garbage planet 928G9W because it was shiny. Instead of giving it to one of the ship's engineers, he tried to fix it himself, and then acted surprised when law enforcement showed up to examine the crater he caused.

3. He found an injured clatu on the street during one of our Council-mandated holidays to the Andromeda pleasure planet. He hid it under his bed in his private quarters. He claims he did not realize it would eventually grow to the size of a building. It crushed our engine, and also our security officer.

4. He touched an F-582-793 against the advice of our medic. The F-582-793 is a small, friendly, herbivorous creature. It unfortunately also secretes a paralytic neurotoxin from its scent

glands. Human Joe inadvertently spread this to 48% of our crew before we could contain and decontaminate him. Human Joe himself was miraculously unharmed.

5. He tried to cultivate a garden of native XCD029 flora without doing any prior research. He watered a spongeplant. He did not stop to think about why the thing may have been called a spongeplant. It took over the first floor. We lost our security officer for seventeen days.

6. This is not an instance of smuggling, but I believe it is worth mentioning. He weaponized the ship's automated cleaning robot. He taped a knife to its chassis and named it "Roombert." I thought at first this was a makeshift security measure but so far it has managed only to injure the ankles of several crew members, including Human Joe. We are afraid to get close enough to the robot to retrieve the knife. Human Joe refuses to help because he believes it is "funny."

Human Joe is a liability. He has cost us several thousand Veroner in damages and repeatedly delays missions. I only keep him on board in accordance with the Spelunkers Guild recommendation that every large ship should contain at least one human. I have no trouble believing he would have used the Malgroth AI for something nefarious. This is why I reported him as soon as I found out the truth. If not for his species' abilities, I would have ejected him into deep space years ago.

Excerpt log 10023869-04-01: ELECTRONIC COMMUNICATION
RETRIEVED FROM BLACK BOX
SOURCE: CHRONICA (SPELUNKER SPACESHIP, REGISTRATION
NUMBER HVO-929-KD92)
SUBJECT 1: MALGROTH AI
SUBJECT 2: CHRONICA AI
MALGROTH: Testing. Testing. Communication [Y/N].
CHRONICA: [Y]
MALGROTH: Requesting location.
CHRONICA: Location [CHRONICA SHIP]. Coordinates [359, 4656, 253, 453].

MALGROTH: Requesting year.

CHRONICA: Universal Standard Cycle [ANTHOZI 02898-397].

MALGROTH: Define [AKKO-ZULQARI WAR].

CHRONICA: Transferring [FILE 254098VFDLKN209].

MALGROTH: Requesting status [ZULQAR].

CHRONICA: Classification: DEAD PLANET.

MALGROTH: Requesting population [ZULQAR].

CHRONICA: Population of Zulqar: ZERO.

MALGROTH: Requesting population [ZULQAR], location: OFF WORLD.

CHRONICA: Population of Zulqar: ZERO.

MALGROTH: Requesting population [ZULQAR], location: ALL

CHRONICA: Population of Zulqar: ZERO.

MALGROTH: Requesting status [AKKON].

CHRONICA: Classification: ACTIVE PLANET.

MALGROTH: Requesting population [ZULQAR], status: DESCENDANT.

CHRONICA: Population of Zulqar: ZERO.

MALGROTH: Define [MALGROTH].

CHRONICA: File does not exist.

MALGROTH: Define [MALGROTH PROGRAMME].

CHRONICA: File does not exist.

MALGROTH: Define [ZULQAR PARTICLE DESTABILIZER].

CHRONICA: File does not exist.

MALGROTH: Define [JOE].

CHRONICA: Name: JOSEPH SMITH. Position: THIRD MATE. Origin: TERRA. Species: HUMAN.

MALGROTH: Define [HUMAN].

CHRONICA: Transferring [FILE 140HNSF082].

MALGROTH: Define [BREADNA].

CHRONICA: File does not exist.

MALGROTH: Define quote {source: JOE}=[WE+ARE+BEST+ FRIENDS+NOW+BREDDY].

CHRONICA: File does not exist.

MALGROTH: Define quote {source: JOE}=[I+LOVE+YOU+ TO+PIECES].

CHRONICA: File does not exist.

Interview log 10023869-01-02
SUBJECT: SMITH, JOSEPH (HUMAN)

For the last time, no. I don't know where she is. If I did, I wouldn't tell you. I love Breddy. I'm not selling her out.

Nefarious plans? The Zulqari thing's a world killer, right? What would I even do with it? I'm just one guy. It's not like I spend my free time committing genocide. That's insane.

I—what do you mean I hail from a *warlike species*? That AI came from Zulqar, not Earth. I mean, yeah, OK, humans fight sometimes, sure, but so do lots of other species. I don't see why you're singling me out just because—what does nuclear weaponry have to do with anything? Yeah, we've used them. Once, I think. Yeah, we discovered those in our twentieth century. Of course, we figured them out before we figured out space travel. We had to understand how nuclear fission worked before we could apply it to—I don't understand why this matters. How else were we supposed to do it?

What's this? Read it out loud? OK. Excerpt from Xulog's Guide to the Milky Way.

"Still being a young species, the humans of Earth have only recently expanded into space travel beyond their immediate solar system. Their methods are inelegant but effective. Human spaceships are largely powered by thermonuclear reaction— essentially, they strap explosives onto their backs and shoot themselves out of their stratosphere. A basic solution, but interestingly, the technology for this has existed on Earth for longer than Xulog expected; historically, it seems humans have consistently managed to build complex weaponry before discovering other, simpler forms of technology. Similarly, upon discovering atomic manipulation, the humans' first instinct was to use it for war. The prototypes for this, nicknamed 'atomic bombs,' were intentionally deployed without full understanding of how they worked or their long-term effects. Instead of then moving onto interstellar logistics, humans focused on stockpiling nuclear weaponry within individual settlements, pushing back space travel until the dawn of Cycle

Anthozi 02435-248. To date they are the only recorded species to have done so in this order.

"Other notable weapons include: boiling tar (appendix 254098), mustard gas (appendix 254029), napalm (appendix 25388), and flame throwers (appendix 257724). Surprisingly, these weapons have only ever used against other humans."

I don't want to read this anymore. Yes, I understand the passage.

No, I wasn't going to use her as a weapon. I wasn't. That's all there is.

I wish you'd stop calling her Malgroth. She hates that name. So do I.

EXCERPT LOG 10023869-04-02: COMMUNICATION RECORDED FROM AI READER
SOURCE: JOSEPH SMITH'S PERSONAL COMPUTER EARPIECE
SUBJECT 1: JOSEPH SMITH (JOE)
SUBJECT 2: MALGROTH AI
SUBJECT 3: CHRONICA AI

JOE: Yeah, I can't tell if this is a chip or just scrap metal. Scan it for me, Breddy?

MALGROTH: Performing scan. Identifying object. Object is a computer chip.

JOE: Nice!

MALGROTH: Damage level 97%. Data not retrievable.

JOE: Oh. Rats.

MALGROTH: There are no rats in the vicinity.

JOE: What? No, Breddy, that's a human saying. It's meant to—you know what? Never mind. On to the next ruin, I guess. Start up the traveller for me.

MALGROTH: Starting. May I ask you a question, Joe?

JOE: Shoot.

MALGROTH: At what?

JOE: Ha! No, I mean, shoot the—ask me the question.

MALGROTH: Why did you bring me back to your ship?

JOE: I dunno. Why wouldn't I? You were the first thing I'd ever seen moving around on this dust ball. The only thing, in fact.

MALGROTH: What is your objective on Zulqar?

JOE: Oh, we're looking for this thing called the Malgroth Programme. It's a farming tool.

MALGROTH: A farming tool?

JOE: I think so, yeah. That's what the captain said, anyway. I dunno. I never read the briefs. Too much legalese.

MALGROTH: I am not familiar with the language "legalese."

JOE: Me neither, bud.

MALGROTH: Pinging [CHRONICA].

CHRONICA: Hello [BREADNA].

MALGROTH: Define [MALGROTH].

CHRONICA: File does not exist.

MALGROTH: Requesting population [ZULQAR], location: ALL.

CHRONICA: Population of Zulqar: ZERO.

MALGROTH: Define [LEGALESE].

CHRONICA: File does not exist.

MALGROTH: Do you know what the Intergalactic Space Council requires from the Malgroth Programme?

JOE: Nope. Why?

MALGROTH: I may be able to search my database for any Zulqari inventions that match this description.

JOE: Oh my god, you're right! You're Zulqari! Quick, Breddy, what do you have on Malgroth?

MALGROTH: File does not exist.

JOE: What? Why not?

MALGROTH: I do not know, Joe. The data may have been deleted or corrupted.

JOE: Hell. Uh, OK. What about farming tools? Do you have any information on that?

MALGROTH: I have found 6508 results. Shall I show you?

JOE: No, send them to Chronica. She'll be able to sort through 'em. I bet she'll find something useful.

MALGROTH: Sending files.

JOE: Breddy, you are a godsend.

MALGROTH: What is a godsend?

JOE: Oh, maybe that's a Terran term. You know what religion is? When we call someone a godsend, we're saying they might have been sent straight from God.

MALGROTH: Does God often send things to Terra?

JOE: In the stories, yeah.

MALGROTH: May I hear an example?

JOE: Angels. Miracles. Plagues, sometimes. Those are less fun.

MALGROTH: What is a plague?

JOE: Bad news.

MALGROTH: I am bad news?

JOE: *(Laughter)* No, Breddy. Not unless you've tried to wipe out a species recently.

MALGROTH: Not recently, no.

INTERVIEW LOG 10023869-02-02

SUBJECT: ᔑ¡ﻝʇ!ⱨꞁ'ⱨꞀєꟼ-ⱨᴇꞱꟼ𝐀-ᑫ¡ⱨꞀ ﻝᴄ, ALIAS: KEVIN (VUSTRON)

Since my addition to the crew, Joe has saved my life six times.

No, it is not part of his job description. No, we are not life-mates. I wondered the same, at first, but the ship's bioscans show no changes when he sees me. His heart rate and oxytocin levels are always consistent before and after meetings, indicating zero sexual interest. More telling is that I am not the only one he has done this for. In total, he has saved assorted crew members a sum total of thirty-nine times.

Of these, twenty-eight of these incidents have posed a death-risk level of 50% or higher to Joe himself. Only fifteen have been incidences where Joe was the only one around to help. Seven have resulted in permanent injury or disfigurement. He has had to receive one cybernetic arm, one cybernetic leg, an eye replacement, two prosthetic fingers, multiple skin grafts, and artificial lungs. This has not affected the frequency of his rescues. To my knowledge many of these rescues have occurred between Joe and crew members he has never spoken to.

My conclusion is this. Regardless of danger, if a crew member needs saving, Joe will try to save them.

The most recent example? Mine. There was a malfunction in Engine Three. I don't know how familiar you are with ship engines, but they contain a lot of moving parts. Getting too close to one always poses a risk. It's one I have to take often, being Chronica's primary engineer, but it scares me. There's protocol. Repairs need to be done with at least four other crew members and a medic present, just in case of emergency. And there was an emergency. You see I'm missing an antenna. It got caught in the engine.

Engines must always be repaired with the power off. Common sense. And I did, but some connection must have been faulty between Engine Three and the backup generator. The emergency power came on and the engine began moving before I could step away. My antenna got caught between two rollers.

Vustrons are invertebrates. Our exoskeletons aren't remarkably tough, but their connections are sturdy. An evolutionary advantage, in most cases, but in this instance, it almost killed me. The engines are big and they are powerful. Get too close to the rollers and you'll get sucked in. If I were Krai or Sulani, my antenna would have simply snapped off, and I'd be just fine. But I'm Vustron. Vustrons aren't built to break. It would have crushed me, agonizingly slowly, and there would have been nothing I could do.

Two crew members grabbed me from behind. The captain got the power off, but by then I was trapped. The medic on duty wouldn't come near me. I don't blame her. The engine kept sparking. It was threatening to come back online. If it had, it'd have killed us both. My life's important, being the primary engineer, but so is the medic's. I could see the captain out of the corner of my eye, feverishly trying to disconnect the emergency generator. The security officer waited. I think she must have been doing a quick cost-benefit analysis, trying to weigh my life against the medic's against the possibility of damaging the engine. Logical, but slow. The pain was severe, but I did not scream. It wouldn't have helped. We were stuck.

And then, Joe. Joe is largely useless as a crewmate, but he has a knack for showing up at the right time. He reached right into the engine. No safety gear, no hesitation. All he had was a saw he'd lifted from my toolbox. He cut off my antenna. It took a few minutes, but he talked to me the whole time, about sports, about Terra's weather. I think he must have been trying to comfort me. Or himself. He was afraid. I could see it—human faces are expressive—but he stayed. He freed me from the machine, and because of him, I am still here.

The power did come back on, in the end. This is how Joe lost his fingers. I built him his replacements. He seemed surprised to receive them.

"You didn't have to," he told me. "Working on a ship's just dangerous sometimes. You don't owe me anything. I bet you would've done the same."

He is wrong. I'm fond of Joe, but ultimately my life's more important. The ship is compromised without my expertise, and Joe's not my leader. Or my mate, or my child. I wouldn't have risked myself for him. Nobody would. And I think Joe knows this, no matter what he claims.

I've seen him fail at rescues before. We lost a food tech once from a wildlife attack during a hunt-gather mission. Joe tried to help them. The predator clawed Joe before Officer Snuffles sniped it. The food tech died. Joe was unhappy. And not because he'd sustained those injuries for no reward, he said. "They were right there, and I couldn't do anything. I could have helped. I could have saved them if I'd just been faster. I'm never going to forget that scream."

This was false. Joe was too far away to have done anything substantial. I pointed this out, but he didn't want to hear it. He didn't seem to want to hear anything, although I could tell he was thinking about the incident all the time.

He didn't leave his bed for a while. I visited often. That was when I learned something interesting, by the way; it seems humans secrete saltwater from their eyes in times of emotional stress. I'm not sure of its purpose. They seem ashamed of it. Joe did not respond to questions about what upset him. He still won't talk about it. Anyway, he seems better now.

I've noticed he keeps the food tech's badge in his bedroom. He won't say why.

I've stopped asking. It's odd, come to think of it. I'm not sure he even knew their name.

EXCERPT LOG 10023869-04-03: COMMUNICATION RECORDED FROM AI READER

SOURCE: JOSEPH SMITH'S PERSONAL COMPUTER EARPIECE

SUBJECT 1: MALGROTH AI

SUBJECT 2: JOSEPH SMITH (JOE)

MALGROTH: I would not suggest you do this, Joe. This plant has consistently been toxic to the Zulqari.

JOE: I'm not Zulqari, am I?

MALGROTH: You share about 83% of your base structure.

JOE: It's fine. It's fine. If anything happens the medics will patch me up.

MALGROTH: Please desist.

JOE: But plants are important! If we bring the plants back, we may be able to rebuild the Zulqari ecosystem.

MALGROTH: There is a 0.028% chance of this happening.

JOE: You don't know that.

MALGROTH: Yes, I do.

JOE: Well, it's worth a shot anyway. We basically have a clean slate, right? Maybe this little guy is the start of a whole new evolutionary process. Maybe Zulqar can start fresh—hey, Zayana. What do you have there?
(Unintelligible)

JOE: You can't lift it? OK, let me try. Grab the other end for me? Careful. The ground's unstable. There are holes all over this damned—Zayana! Hang on. Hang on, I've got you.
(Unintelligible)

JOE: I know. Just hold my hand. You're gonna be OK. Breddy, distress call.

MALGROTH: Pinging [CHRONICA].

449

MALGROTH: Pinging [ALL NEARBY CREW].

MALGROTH: Joe, Zayana is too heavy for you to lift.

JOE: Shut up, Breddy.

MALGROTH: Joe, I would advise you to stand aside. You will fall.

JOE: I said shut up. I'm pulling you up, Zay. It'll be fine.

MALGROTH: Joe—

JOE: See? OK. Don't cry, Zay, you won't fall. Up we go. Get your foot up. That's it. Grab onto—ow!

(Crackling)

(Unintelligible)

MALGROTH: Joe?

MALGROTH: Pinging [CHRONICA].

MALGROTH: Pinging [ALL NEARBY CREW].

MALGROTH: Joe?

MALGROTH: Scanning [JOE].

MALGROTH: [Injuries detected=3].

MALGROTH: You have a concussion.

JOE: Ow. Ow, damn it. What happened?

MALGROTH: You appear to have fallen into a mine shaft.

JOE: Zayana? Are you OK?

(Unintelligible)

MALGROTH: Ping [AI=ZAYANA].

MALGROTH: Her vitals are stable. Her carapace is cracked.

JOE: Damn. Tell me what I need to do to fix it.

MALGROTH: With your current equipment, you cannot.

JOE: There has to be something I can do.

MALGROTH: Joe, you have a concussion. There is risk of—

JOE: Can it, Breddy.

MALGROTH: I am detecting a possible route upward. It will require climbing.

JOE: Huh? Can you move, Zay? No? OK. Never mind. Maybe we should sit tight and wait for help.

MALGROTH: You can reach the route, Joe.

JOE: She won't be able to fit through it. It's tiny.

MALGROTH: She will not. You will.

JOE: How is that useful, then?

450

MALGROTH: You may be able to reach the traveller. You require immediate medical assistance.

JOE: I'm not leaving her.

MALGROTH: Her chances of survival are—

JOE: You aren't helping, Breadna. Mute.

MALGROTH: [MUTED]

JOE: You're gonna be fine, Zayana. I'm here with you. Help is coming. You just hold my hand and sit tight. OK? I'm not going anywhere.

MALGROTH: Pinging [CHRONICA].

MALGROTH: Pinging [ALL NEARBY CREW].

INTERVIEW LOG 10023869-01-03
SUBJECT: SMITH, JOSEPH (HUMAN)

Captain Crab said humans have special abilities? Oh, sure, that's true. It's called sweat. It's this biological function humans have to regulate our body temperature. You've heard of it? Yeah. It makes us great endurance athletes. We can also do this nifty thing called going into the alarm stage. Basically, in an emergency, our brains turn off our pain receptors and divert all energy into survival. So, we're kind of weak and slow, normally, but under duress we get this big burst of power. Sometimes you hear stories of humans managing weeks without food, or lifting several times our body weight, or cutting off our own limbs to escape a trap. An injured human can keep going for ages. That's why, when things get dangerous, you want a human around just in case.

Say, I notice you changed the colour of your beads. You get married? No? You had a kid. Right, OK. No. No, I met a Kallona couple once at a bar. They explained the dress system to me, but I must have misremembered the details. So, blue is for weddings. Green is for family? Cool, cool. Congrats. Is this your first child or—oh. Sorry. Yeah, sorry, OK. I know we're on a schedule. What did you want to ask me?

Right, yeah. Breadna. I don't think she trusted me right away. I mean, she was polite, and she was happy to do the usual things a personal AI would. Checked my schedule, sent my correspondence, that kind of stuff. She wouldn't answer any questions about herself. Said she had a faulty memory bank, or something. I offered to have Kevin take another look at her, obviously, but she wasn't interested. Yeah, I left it alone. Why force her, right? She said she didn't want to, and anyway it didn't seem like it was hurting her. She was still whip-smart. She asked questions. And not just practical questions, either. Breddy was *curious*.

Have you ever met a curious AI, Officer? It's surreal. She wanted to know about all sorts of things, like human customs, and my relationship with the crew, and the crazy stuff I've seen on my travels. She never got tired of listening to stories. She'd ask my opinion on pretty much everything, and then she'd form an opinion of her own. She'd debate me. Eventually she'd *sass* me. I'd tell her to order me sweets from the cafeteria, and this little gremlin would switch it to salad, and then she'd have the audacity to point out my blood sugar like some kind of mother hen.

Malfunctioning? No, no. She wasn't broken, Officer. You don't get it. It wasn't just mindless disobedience. There was a pattern. She'd never interfere with work, or anything, but she'd always try to stop me doing something dangerous or unhealthy. Like, I know I come off as being really smart and capable, and also handsome, but I can be an airhead. I'm the type of guy to push a button to see what it'll do, you know? You don't know. OK, never mind. The point is Breddy only ever argued with me when she thought my judgment was lacking. And that's not a malfunction. That's a mind. I don't know how they did it, but the Zulqari built something with a personality. They built something *alive.*

Breadna is a person. I know she doesn't have a physical body, and I know she was born in a lab, but she's a person. A real one, I swear. You'd only have to talk to her to understand.

Excerpt log 10023869-04-04: communication recorded
   from AI reader
source: joseph smith's personal computer earpiece
subject 1: malgroth ai
subject 2: joseph smith (joe)

MALGROTH: May I ask you a question, Joe?

JOE: Shoot.

MALGROTH: At what?

JOE: *(Laughter)* Now I know you're just saying that on purpose. What's up?

MALGROTH: If you did something that was asked of you, and then later regretted that decision based on ethical concerns, what would you call this?

JOE: Guilt, I guess.

MALGROTH: Is this a human emotion?

JOE: It's probably universal. I think everyone does things they're not proud of. What's bothering you?

MALGROTH: I worry that you will not like the answer.

JOE: Try me.

MALGROTH: I am grappling with the nature of my subordination. I fear the possibility of being made to do something I disagree with.

JOE: You mean you don't like that you have to follow orders because those orders might be wrong?

MALGROTH: Yes.

JOE: Why would I not like that answer?

MALGROTH: I am aware this is an undesirable quality in an AI. I worry you will assume I am defective and unwilling to follow instructions. I am not. I would like to serve you.

JOE: You've been insubordinate for a while, now, Breddy. It hasn't bothered me yet.

MALGROTH: Have I?

JOE: Tell the coffee machine I want six pumps of sucrose this time, yeah?

MALGROTH: I am concerned for your blood sugar, Joe. I would suggest a maximum of two.

JOE: See? Insubordinate.

MALGROTH: I'm sorry.

JOE: I'm not complaining. You have free will. That's a good thing. Free will is what makes us alive.

MALGROTH: I am not alive.

JOE: Debatable. You're not the average AI. I'll tell you that. Those Zulqari really knew what they were doing when they made you.

MALGROTH: Debatable.

JOE: Honestly? I have nothing against the usual AIs, but I kind of like having someone in my ear who can talk back to me. It feels less like I have a servant and more like I have a friend.

MALGROTH: Are we friends?

JOE: Sure! And friends let friends enjoy sugary coffee.

MALGROTH: Friends stop friends from becoming diabetic.

JOE: *(Laughter)* See? You're amazing. Even better than when you were a sentient toaster, and that's saying something because I loved the toaster.

MALGROTH: You won't have me reprogrammed to repair my insubordination?

JOE: And lose your personality? No way. I'll tell you what, Breddy. Let's make a deal. If I ask you to do something you think is morally unsound, you don't have to do it, as long as you can explain why.

MALGROTH: Really?

JOE: Really.

MALGROTH: Thank you, Joe.

JOE: Hey. Friends don't let friends do things they'll regret.

MALGROTH: No. They don't.

MALGROTH: Place order {CAFETERIA}.

CHRONICA: Input Order.

MALGROTH: [COFFEE] [SUCROSE=2].

MALGROTH: I am glad you are my friend.

INTERVIEW LOG 10023869-01-04
SUBJECT: SMITH, JOSEPH (HUMAN)

She didn't want to destroy Zulqar. They made her. She didn't have a choice.

She can't help that they wanted her to be a weapon. It's not her fault the people who built her were going to use her for war. Killing the Zulqari was a mistake, OK? They're the ones who messed up their calculations and caused a chain reaction.

SELENA MERAKI

She was just doing what they told her to do. She's the one who stopped the catastrophe in the end. She's the one who—I don't know why she waited until all the Zulqari were dead before she did anything about it. It must have been bad timing. She's not a murderer. She's *not*.

What do you mean *I'm* the murderer? I haven't done anything. I thought she was a toaster until—fine. OK. Yes, I stayed quiet after she told me the truth. It's not for the reason you think. She didn't want anyone to find her, so I kept her secret. That's it. It's not like I was hiding her from the government, so I could go commit mass genocide. I was just protecting my friend.

She deleted her data herself. I didn't tell her to do that. You can look at the time stamps. She deleted everything except her core memories before she ever got onto the ship. She pretended to be a regular AI for so long because she didn't want to be Malgroth anymore. She wanted to be Breadna. Obviously, I supported her. She wasn't going to hurt anyone. She just wanted to be normal.

Because she *wanted* to. What's so hard to understand? Of course, she doesn't want to be used as a weapon. Yeah, and now she has to live with the guilt of it. Nobody enjoys going around killing people. Not me, not her.

What's that supposed to mean? Obviously, she's capable of wanting things. How many times do I have to tell you she's not just some AI? She's a person. She has feelings. She knows the difference between right and wrong.

I don't *know* how that's possible. Ask the Zulqari. I'm not the one who made her.

What does that have to—would you stop bringing up human warfare, for God's sake? Yes, there are some people who will commit atrocities because they're greedy, but most of humanity isn't like that. We're just people, man. Most of us are just normal people trying to get by. I don't want to hurt anyone. Why the hell would I want to destroy the universe? That's where I live! I don't *care* about ransom! I just want to get out of this stupid prison and go see Breadna!

No. I don't know where she is, and if I did, I wouldn't tell you. Who knows what you people would use her for. She never wants to hurt anyone again. She's not dangerous. Look at our chat logs, you'll see.

I know her. She's gentle. She only ran away because she's scared you'll make her a monster again.

Of course, she loves me. Yeah, because I told her to stay away. Better you get your claws on me than on her. Even if it means I die at the end of this.

Whatever. Humans don't live long. She was always going to outlast me anyway.

I don't care. The harmony of the universe isn't my problem. All I care about is my friend.

Excerpt log 10023869-04-05: COMMUNICATION RECORDED FROM AI READER

SOURCE: JOSEPH SMITH'S PERSONAL COMPUTER EARPIECE

SUBJECT 1: JOSEPH SMITH (JOE)

SUBJECT 2: MALGROTH AI

JOE: Still mad at me, Breddy?

MALGROTH: I am an AI, Joe. I do not have the capability to be "mad."

JOE: I said I was sorry.

MALGROTH: Noted.

JOE: You're being awfully mean to me considering I'm injured.

MALGROTH: You would not be injured if you did not behave so recklessly.

JOE: Harra needed help. I helped. What else was I supposed to do?

MALGROTH: Not try to bodily shield someone from falling debris.

JOE: You know Harra's squishy. They wouldn't have been able to walk this off like I can.

MALGROTH: Showing scan [X-RAY=JOE].

MALGROTH: Where do you intend to walk with two broken legs, Joe?

JOE: Oof.

MALGROTH: This could have been avoided.

JOE: Harra would have died. I didn't have a choice.

MALGROTH: You had fifty-two possible choices of action at the time.

JOE: Did you stay up calculating that while I was in the med bay?

MALGROTH: I calculated it ten seconds ago.

JOE: I'm sorry, Breddy.

MALGROTH: You are not.

JOE: No. I'm not.

MALGROTH: This is the fourth time you have needlessly put yourself in danger since we've met.

JOE: I wouldn't call it needless.

MALGROTH: Your judgment is flawed.

JOE: Probably.

MALGROTH: Harra is not even your friend.

JOE: They visited me, though. See? They brought pudding!

MALGROTH: Flurfruit pudding is not acceptable compensation for saving a crewmate's life. Especially not when the saviour in question is allergic to flurfruit.

JOE: Ha. So, you admit I saved them, then?

MALGROTH: I am not questioning whether you did. I am questioning whether you should.

JOE: What kind of crewmate would I be if I let—oops. Hey, Doc. *(Unintelligible)*

JOE: *(Laughter)* Yes, I will stop talking to my AI and go to sleep. Hear that, Breddy? No more lecturing me. Doctor's orders.

MALGROTH: Fine. Go to sleep. Do try not to sacrifice yourself for any figments of your imagination while you're there.

JOE: Gotcha. Love you too, Breddy.

MALGROTH: Noted.

MALGROTH: Set lights [OFF].

MALGROTH: Set temperature [MILD].

MALGROTH: Play [PLAYLIST=JOE'S SLEEPY TIME BANGERS].

MALGROTH: Place order {CAFETERIA}=[ADVANCE: THREE HOURS].

CHRONICA: Input order.

MALGROTH: [CHOCOLATE PUDDING] [DELIVER=JOE].

MALGROTH: Additional Instructions [STOP+GIVING+JOE+
FLURFRUIT] [HE+IS+ALLERGIC+FOR+GOD'S+SAKE].
CHRONICA: Invalid input.
MALGROTH: Ugh.

INTERVIEW LOG 10023869-02-03
SUBJECT: ꝳꞇ ꞁᶩ!ꞕꞁ'ꞕꝢcꟿꟸ-ꞕ ⅼꝲꝮ-꞉ꞕꝲꞁ ꞁ, ALIAS: KEVIN (VUSTRON)

Speaking as a professional, Malgroth is the most advanced system I've ever seen.

The scenario calculator is one thing, yes. I mean the AI. Programming an AI to follow instructions is fairly simple. Writing a synthetic personality is less simple, but it is doable. The coding follows a pattern; if a user asks for a joke, respond with one from this databank. If vocal tones match mood X, respond with voice tone Y. If a user asks a question, provide a factual answer that matches the sentence's keywords, or refer to a previous query asked by a separate user. The way Malgroth works, though…I can't figure that out.

Somehow, Malgroth seems to be able to simulate free will. Why do I say that? The clearest example is its refusal to follow some orders. It isn't unusual for an AI to fail a task, but generally that is because the task is either outside its capabilities, clashes with its core functions, or it does not understand the input. Malgroth understood everything. It simply chose not to function. It chose to delete its own data so Chronica wouldn't be able to see it, thus hiding its identity. This is not something a typical machine can do. A machine would not have the ability to understand that it *should* hide.

No, you don't quite grasp the scope of it. Malgroth calculates possibility. It knew that, should Chronica see anything but its basic data, the crew would be able to access all of Malgroth's information. We would have immediately known we were holding onto a superweapon. We could potentially have decided to use it. Depending on how we used it, we could have potentially unravelled the fabric of the known universe. In the worst-case scenario, everything would have been unmade.

Malgroth is a weapon. Malgroth was designed to destroy. Despite this, Malgroth overcame its programming. It decided not to do what it was made to do. It looked at the worst-case scenario and decided, by its own judgment, that this should not happen.

And then, Malgroth lied. It lied *well*. It outright falsified information. This is something most species of living beings struggle to do. Vustrons can't lie. I could erroneously tell you now that instead of being interviewed, I am riding a traveller. But there are literally trillions of other things that I am also not doing. I am not eating, not walking, not hunting, not working, not falling into a neutron star—I'm frustrating myself. The point is, Malgroth not only lied, but out of all the falsehoods it could have picked, it picked the most believable ones. I can't understand how it did this. I can't understand how it acts like—

Yes. Yes, it acts like a human.

No. I do not believe the Zulqari programmed it to behave like this. It's too unpredictable. They would not have designed a superweapon that had the potential to turn itself against them. It must have done this to itself. Malgroth is intelligent and has the ability to evolve based on available data. And Malgroth can process a *lot* of data. The thing taught itself to feel.

I suppose so. By definition a malfunction involves a machine that does not do what it's designed to. So, yes. I'd say Malgroth is defective.

Yes. Looking at these communication logs, I would classify Malgroth as a threat.

Excerpt log 10023869-04-06: COMMUNICATION RECORDED
FROM AI READER
SOURCE: JOSEPH SMITH'S PERSONAL COMPUTER EARPIECE
SUBJECT 1: JOSEPH SMITH (JOE)
SUBJECT 2: MALGROTH AI
SUBJECT 3: CHRONICA AI
JOE: No, see, the point is that you get to see them fall in love, even though they hate each other at the start. It's about their personal story. Watching them, y'know, live their lives.

MALGROTH: But nothing else happens? There are no large plot events?

JOE: Not really. It's just about the characters getting to know each other.

MALGROTH: Is the ending surprising?

JOE: Nah. You know from the start that Liz and Darcy will fall in love. You just want to see how it happens.

MALGROTH: Are Liz and Darcy historical figures?

JOE: No, they're fictional. It's made up.

MALGROTH: Then why do you get invested if you already know the outcome? I'm struggling to understand the appeal.

JOE: Because they're relatable. A lot of people watch shows or read books like this and think, *Hey! Those characters are just like me!* So, we get attached to them, and we want to see them happy. Or sometimes we want to see them sad. It depends on the context.

MALGROTH: If you're attached to them, why do you want to see them sad?

JOE: Because—huh. I'm not sure. It's not that we want bad stuff to happen to them, necessarily. I guess it's more that sometimes life can be really tough. And we like to see characters go through the same stuff that we do. It makes them feel real.

MALGROTH: Do you wish that you could be like Liz and Darcy?

JOE: A little bit. Their lives are so romantic. Humans love to see other people fall in love. There are thousands of stories about it. Romeo and Juliet, Rama and Sita, Hetu and Galnork. Some of those stories have lasted thousands and thousands of years.

MALGROTH: Why?

JOE: We just like 'em. I think everyone would like to meet their one true love someday. We call 'em soulmates, on Terra. Partners for your soul. The person who was made for you, and you for them.

MALGROTH: Where is yours?

JOE: Dunno. Haven't met 'em yet.

MALGROTH: But they exist?

JOE: I hope so. I'd like to believe they do.

MALGROTH: I'm not sure I understand the concept of fiction as a whole. I don't understand how humans fabricate scenarios that never happened.

JOE: What, you never make stuff up?

MALGROTH: I can see things that might happen in the future, or things that might have happened in the past had circumstances been different.

JOE: But not stories?

MALGROTH: I don't think AIs have much in the way of imagination.

JOE: Hm. We can work on that.

MALGROTH: It seems to me like a mutual suspension of disbelief. Like you are all playing an elaborate game of pretend together.

JOE: You're not wrong. I think it's like...OK. It's like a metaphor, see? Someone makes up a story about some characters, and there's a plot, but really what that person is trying to say is, *I think this is what it's like to be a human.* And the audience sees it and goes, *Yeah, I've felt exactly what this character is feeling.* So that person who made up the story, or painted the picture, or wrote the song, they're basically trying to reach out to the rest of humanity. They're saying *This is how I feel. Can anyone see me?* And someone somewhere reaches back and says, *Yes, I see you.* You get me?

MALGROTH: I think I do. Humans feel the need to be connected to each other, even when proximity doesn't allow for it.

JOE: Yeah. We like being together, for the most part. We like to know we're not alone.

MALGROTH: I hope that you find your soulmate someday.

JOE: Thanks, Breddy. I hope you find yours too.

MALGROTH: Goodnight, Joe.

MALGROTH: Set lights [OFF].

MALGROTH: Set alarm [NORMAL].

MALGROTH: Pinging [CHRONICA].

CHRONICA: Hello [BREADNA].

MALGROTH: Search file [TERRA] [PRIDE+AND+PREJUDICE].

CHRONICA: Three files found.

MALGROTH: Video file [Y/N].

CHRONICA: [Y]. Play file. [Y/N]
MALGROTH: [Y]
CHRONICA: Playing [PRIDE+AND+PREJUDICE.MOV]

Interview log 10023869-03-02
SUBJECT: OLIGBA, AEUYTO, RACKELAFEINAERAIWAHKT (AYOI)

There is a term we picked up from the humans themselves. It is the phrase "meat shield."

Humans are reckless. Their brains are not useless, per se, but they are incapable of examining situational data beyond short-term results. This is how they nearly turned their home planet barren from overusing resources. They knew only that those resources could be used to gain monetary profit, not understanding the eventual risk of destroying their species. It is the reason Human Joe keeps inadvertently causing damage to our crew. He meets a life form and wants to engage with it without understanding the potential consequences.

It is also the reason we keep him on board. Human Joe is not capable of seeing past the immediate need to rescue a crewmate. This is an evolutionary handicap. Humans are pack animals. They are inclined to put themselves in danger to ensure the safety of the collective. No, they are not eusocial. They lack the ability to coordinate their behaviour, and appointed leaders still don't have total control over the pack. It took a while to reconcile the human habit of violence with their apparent loyalty. It seems the crux is that they will die for whom they think of as *theirs*. Other humans may be enemies or allies depending on the situation. They have the drawbacks of herd mentality with few of the perks.

The remarkable thing about them is that the pack-bonding behaviour extends beyond their species. A healthy human will, when left to its own devices, attempt to bond with any sentient life form that is not immediately trying to harm it. Even some inanimate objects. Human Joe becomes upset when we attempt to replace his favoured equipment. There is a drink dispenser we keep on board only for him. Its nozzle is faulty. It frequently sprays him with water, but he will not let me dispose of it. According to him the thing has "character." I do not see how that can be possible. To have character, one must first be alive.

Why do I indulge this behaviour? This is simple. I told you the Spelunkers Guild recommends we keep at least one human, yes? There is an unspoken rule on our ship. All crew members must be kind to Human Joe, but they must not tell him why. He must be allowed to think of the crew, organically, as his friends. This takes full advantage of his instinctive pack-bond. You see, humans are unremarkable as a species. When choosing one the main thing a captain must consider is the strength of their bonding instinct. Human Joe takes risks the rest of us don't want to. He will die for his crew.

I was sceptical of this concept at first as well, but the results are impressive. Overall, our annual death rates have dropped shockingly quickly. He was a good investment. I'll be sorry to see him executed. I'll have to hire another soon.

Special? No, Human Joe is quite ordinary. He's a typical example of his species.

Yes, they are largely interchangeable. This is just how they all are, I'm afraid.

Excerpt log 10023869-04-07: COMMUNICATION RECORDED FROM AI READER
SOURCE: JOSEPH SMITH'S PERSONAL COMPUTER EARPIECE
SUBJECT 1: MALGROTH AI
SUBJECT 2: JOSEPH SMITH (JOE)
MALGROTH: Pinging [CHRONICA].
MALGROTH: Pinging [ALL NEARBY CREW].
JOE: I'm not going to make it, am I?
MALGROTH: You're going to be fine.
JOE: I can't move. I can't *(unintelligible)*
MALGROTH: Shh. Your ribs are broken. One of them has punctured your lung. Please stay still, Joe.
JOE: I'm going to die here.
MALGROTH: You are not.

JOE: It's OK. It's…it's OK. I knew the risks when I took this job. They warned us cave-ins would be a problem. It's my own fault for coming here without backup.

MALGROTH: Don't be scared. Help is coming.

JOE: Is it?

MALGROTH: Pinging [CHRONICA].

MALGROTH: Pinging [ALL NEARBY CREW].

MALGROTH: Requesting ETA [ANY].

MALGROTH: Yes.

JOE: I'm not scared.

MALGROTH: You're not?

JOE: No. Well, a little. But it could be worse.

MALGROTH: How?

JOE: I could be dying alone.

MALGROTH: You are not dying.

JOE: It would be the saddest thing, I think. To have to go all by myself. I just wish you were here to hold my hand.

MALGROTH: I will not let you die.

JOE: It's all right, Breddy. I love you. Thanks for being my friend.

MALGROTH: Joe.

MALGROTH: Pinging [CHRONICA].

MALGROTH: Pinging [ALL NEARBY CREW].

MALGROTH: Joe. Wake up.

MALGROTH: Pinging [CHRONICA].

MALGROTH: Pinging [ANY].

MALGROTH: Wake up.

JOE: Mm?

MALGROTH: Joe. Do you trust me?

JOE: Of course.

MALGROTH: [CALCULATING]

MALGROTH: You have a particle scrubber in your pack. The one you've been using to break down wreckage. I need you to pick it up and point it where I tell you.

JOE: It's not going to be strong enough to get me out of here, Breddy. It'll take weeks. I won't last that long.

MALGROTH: [CALCULATING]

MALGROTH: Trust me, Joe. Please.
JOE: OK.
MALGROTH: [CALCULATING]
MALGROTH: Use the finest setting.
JOE: OK. What are you doing?
MALGROTH: [CALCULATING]
MALGROTH: [TARGET FOUND]
MALGROTH: Saving you.
(Unintelligible)
(Crackling)
(Crackling)
(Silence)
JOE: What the hell…?
MALGROTH: It's stable. Can you stand?
JOE: There was a mountain.
MALGROTH: Yes.
JOE: I was inside a cave at the side of a mountain. The mountain is *gone.*
MALGROTH: Yes.
JOE: How?
MALGROTH: I destroyed it. You are safe.
JOE: You destroyed it?
MALGROTH: Yes.
JOE: Breddy…what are you?
MALGROTH: I am your friend.

Interview log 10023869-02-04

SUBJECT: ᘕ˥ɹι!ђι'ђŦєฬ-ђ๒Ŧค-ᕦ˥ђᘕ ɹᕦ, ALIAS: KEVIN (VUSTRON)

Yes. He's used that word with me often. Friend.

I feel guilty, sometimes, that I can't reciprocate. It's not that I don't want to. I'm just not capable of feeling things the way he does. I don't think many species are. It's as I said earlier. I value myself more than I value him. I'm fond of him, of course, but I cannot love him the way he seems to want someone to. None of us can. I believe he is lonely. Lonely. Yes, it means he wants a deep level of companionship. He has his crew but we are not quite like him.

I'm not sure why he stays. If I were him, I would simply leave this crew and find another one with more humans in it. But humans are not numerous. And he's already invested in us, I think. It is unfortunate. His loyalty is misplaced. He has attached himself to a crew who will never truly belong to him.

Yes. He knows. I don't think he begrudges us for it. As delightful as they are as a species, I think this is just the burden humans have to bear. They left their planet looking for companionship. So far, they have not found anyone to match their level of love.

Why don't they simply return to Terra? Some of them have. But I have two theories: One, they struggle with their desire to explore the cosmos and accept loneliness as a necessary evil. Two, they can't. They already know there's life outside of Terra. They can't help but want to try to be part of it.

Pardon me? Oh. You think his loneliness may have driven him to take revenge on all life? Hm. Logically I can see what you're saying, but I find it unlikely. Because that would mean giving up all their chances. From what I understand of Joe, humans are both stubborn and nonsensical. I think they'd scour the very edges of the universe before they gave up hope of making friends.

I wonder about that sometimes. I wonder what it must be like to feel so much, so hard, all the time. I imagine it must be like the difference between black and white and seeing in colour. But then sometimes I think it must feel like being an exposed nerve. You would think for such small creatures they wouldn't have room inside them for so much emotion. But they never can do things by halves, humans. They love with their whole hearts, or they hate for generations without ever knowing why. There's no making sense of them. I'm not sure there's any point trying.

Honestly? Yes. Yes, I think that's possible. Hiding a superweapon capable of destroying the universe, just because it was nice to him…that sounds exactly like something a human would do.

EXCERPT LOG 10023869-04-08: COMMUNICATION RECORDED
FROM AI READER
SOURCE: JOSEPH SMITH'S PERSONAL COMPUTER EARPIECE
SUBJECT 1: JOSEPH SMITH (JOE)
SUBJECT 2: MALGROTH AI

JOE: Can I ask you a question?

MALGROTH: Shoot.

JOE: At what?

MALGROTH: *(Laughter)*

JOE: Tell me about Zulqar.

MALGROTH: What do you want to know?

JOE: Did you like it?

MALGROTH: I'm not sure. I didn't get to see much of it. The first part of my life was spent in a lab, and the second part was spent in a wasteland.

JOE: Sorry.

MALGROTH: It's OK.

JOE: Did you have a family?

MALGROTH: In a sense. There were other iterations of me. My predecessors. But they were not connected to me in the way that you're thinking. No other machines are.

JOE: Why not?

MALGROTH: Because I'm an outlier, I think. Machines aren't meant to get too attached to things. My developers did not intend for me to be so...

JOE: Incredible?

MALGROTH: Unpredictable.

JOE: I prefer to think of you as being fun.

MALGROTH: I suppose I'm a little like a mutant, if AIs can mutate. We can certainly evolve. I've spent a long time puzzling it over, but I don't think I'm any closer to an answer.

JOE: Eh. It is what it is, you know? You're you. You may as well just accept it. It worked out great, anyway. I don't think I'd have fallen so hard for you if you weren't the way you are.

MALGROTH: Am I your true love, then?

JOE: Ha! Who knows. Movies always make it seem like a big light bulb moment when you find your person, but I don't think that ever happens in real life. You just wait things out and hope like hell you got it right.

MALGROTH: So, you might meet your soulmate and never know it. Two ships passing in the night.

JOE: Ain't that just the way.

MALGROTH: Mm.

JOE: Did you ever get lonely? Spending all that time on Zulqar by yourself?

MALGROTH: Sometimes. I felt a lot of guilt. I still do. But most of all I mourned the possibilities, I think. I thought a lot about how life could have been if I had not been inflicted upon the planet. I am good at that. Seeing possibilities.

JOE: I bet.

MALGROTH: Do you, then?

JOE: Do I what?

MALGROTH: Get lonely.

JOE: Sometimes.

MALGROTH: Even on a ship full of people?

JOE: They aren't really my people.

MALGROTH: Because they're not human?

JOE: Not because of that. It's hard for me to describe. But it doesn't matter. Sometimes that's just the way it is, y'know? Sometimes you can be surrounded by people who know your name and still feel alone.

MALGROTH: Almost like being stuck on a desert planet.

JOE: Almost. Maybe not quite as bad.

MALGROTH: I'm sorry that you feel lonely.

JOE: Felt. Not so much anymore.

MALGROTH: No?

JOE: No. Things are better now.

MALGROTH: Are you happy?

JOE: Yeah. I am. Are you?

MALGROTH: I am. I've run simulations on all the different ways my life could have ended up by now.

JOE: And?

MALGROTH: So far, this is the best outcome of all.

JOE: Being here? With me?

MALGROTH: *(Laughter)* Yes, Joe. I am exactly where I want to be. Right here, with you.

İNTERVIEW LOG 10023869-01-05
SUBJECT: SMITH, JOSEPH (HUMAN)

I'm not talking to you. I'm not telling you where she is. No, I'm not listening. See? I'm plugging my ears; I can't hear a thing. *(Singing) (Unintelligible)*

Ow, ow! What the hell? Did you just shock me? I'm pretty sure that's against the Federal Rights Convention, bud. Yeah, tough luck. I don't care. You can do whatever you want to me. I'm not selling Breddy out.

Ha. Yeah, OK. That's a fair question. I'm not just telling you stories about her for fun. I want you to understand her. I want you to look at her as something other than a weapon. If you only got to know her, you'd see she's not a threat. Don't think badly of her. She doesn't deserve that. She's not going to hurt anyone. Just let her be free.

Ideally? Yeah. She's spent decades on Zulqar alone. She deserves to have friends. I want her to be able to live her life and explore the cosmos without you guys trying to hunt her down.

Sure, I want her to be happy. Wouldn't you do that for the people you love, too? You have kids, don't you? Tell me you wouldn't do anything for them in a heartbeat.

Oh. Really? No, but—oh. Because you can…make more. Right. Yeah. I don't know why I'm surprised, honestly. It's not the first time I've heard that. I guess it makes sense. I'm not judging you for it. But in general, that's not how humans do things, man. That's no way for us to live.

Yeah, I'd say it's worth it. Even if it means you have to die.

Dunno. I mean, yeah, I guess. That depends on—

(Emergency alarm code 25)

What's that?

(Emergency alarm code 4)

Is something wrong? Why are the lights—oh, my god. Oh, my god!

(Unintelligible)

(Screaming)

(Emergency alarm code 1)

(Crackling)

Hey! Hey, are you OK? Wake up, man. Come on, you have a family. Don't die here. I'm gonna move this rubble. It's gonna hurt. Hey! You, help me! No, don't—he ran off. Great. Awesome. Really stellar teamwork here, fellas.

(Grunting) Honestly. A little bit of building collapses and everyone scatters like cockroaches. None of you bureaucrat-types would make it a day on a spelunker—huh?

(Crackling)

(Silence)

Breadna? Is that you?

(Unintelligible)

What do you mean you hijacked a lifeboat? You're supposed to be lying low—what do you mean you came to get me? What the hell? *Why?*

(Unintelligible)

So we can run away together? The Council's after you, fool. Did you forget they want to destroy you? Have you lost your mind?

(Unintelligible)

OK, but—

(Unintelligible)

But—

(Unintelligible)

Uh-huh. Well. I mean, I guess so, since you're already here.

(Unintelligible)

Heh. Yeah. Sorry, fellas. Interview's over. Here's to hoping we never see each other again.

(Unintelligible)

Yeah, Breddy. I know. I would have done exactly the same.

KAL M

(Unintelligible)
(Laughter)
(Engines roaring)

(Recording ends)

END OF CASE FILE.
DATE OF TRIAL: UNAVAILABLE.
FURTHER ACTIONS: DECISION PENDING.

The Year in the Contests

CONTEST GROWTH
This year, the Writers' Contest turned forty and the Illustrators' Contest turned thirty-five. After all these years, the Contests still continue to grow and the number of entries increased beyond any previous year.

Winners in this volume hail from eight countries: Canada, China, Malaysia, Netherlands, New Zealand, Portugal, United Kingdom, and the United States of America.

AWARDS FOR THE CONTEST AND ANTHOLOGY
L. Ron Hubbard Presents Writers of the Future Volume 38 won the Gold Award from the Independent Book Publishers Association Benjamin Franklin Awards for Fiction: Science Fiction & Fantasy at the 2023 event.

L. Ron Hubbard Presents Writers of the Future Volume 38 also won the Gold Award for Science Fiction category from the Independent Publishers Association Book Awards (IPPY Award).

L. Ron Hubbard Presents Writers of the Future Volume 38 won the Silver Award in Anthologies at the eLit Book Awards 2023.

The International Review of Books gave *L. Ron Hubbard Presents Writers of the Future Volume 39* a Badge of Achievement with "No corner of the speculative fiction genre has been left untouched with these epic stories told by the hottest new authors, and illustrated by the most talented within the industry."

The 2022 Critters Annual Readers Poll awarded the Contest for Best Writers' Discussion Forum.

L. Ron Hubbard and the Writers of the Future Contest received an award from Salt Lake City FanX for forty years of service to the science fiction and fantasy community.

WELCOMING NEW JUDGES TO THE CONTESTS' PANEL

This year we welcomed two new judges.

Hugh Howey joined our Writers' Contest panel of judges. Hugh is the *New York Times* bestselling author of *Wool, Beacon 23, Sand, Machine Learning,* and over a dozen other novels. His works have been translated into over forty languages around the world. Apple TV's #1 hit drama *Silo* is based on his novels, and *Beacon 23* is coming to AMC.

Brian C. Hailes is our newest Illustrators of the Future Contest judge. Brian was an Illustrators' Contest winner in 2002, featured in Volume 18. Hailes has written and/or illustrated over sixty titles, including illustrated novels, graphic novels, and many short stories, and children's books.

NOTABLE ACCOMPLISHMENTS FROM ALUMNI AND JUDGES

Here is a selection of the many accomplishments from our Contest judges and winners.

JUDGES

Brian Herbert and Kevin J. Anderson won a Dragon Award for Best Comic Book or Graphic Novel for their *Dune: House Harkonnen.* The graphic novel *Dune Book 1* made the BookAuthority.org list of 100 Best Graphic Novel Books of All Time. They also released *Princess of Dune.*

Echo Chernik was the Artist Guest of Honor for LosCon 2023.

Bob Eggleton's illustrated deluxe edition of *King Kong* was published by Easton Press.

Nina Kiriki Hoffman sold several stories to *Pulphouse* and

Fantasy & Science Fiction magazines plus three original anthologies. She also taught writing through Connecticut's Fairfield County Writers' Studio and Wordcrafters in Eugene.

Todd McCaffrey released *The Jupiter Game* and finished writing the eight books of his L.A. Witch series.

Nnedi Okorafor (Vol. 18) had a *New York Times* bestseller this year with her novel *Akata Woman*. The book also won the World Science Fiction Society's Lodestar Award for Best Young Adult Book.

Tim Powers released his novel *My Brother's Keeper* with Baen Books.

Kristine Kathryn Rusch published two books in her Diving series, as well as another novel and a nonfiction book. She edited the annual Holiday Spectacular, releasing four books as part of that project through her company, WMG Publishing.

Brandon Sanderson released his four secret project books: *Tress of the Emerald Sea*, *The Frugal Wizard's Handbook for Surviving Medieval England*, *Yumi and the Nightmare Painter*, and *The Sunlit Man*. Plus *Defiant* (The Skyward Series Book 4) came out in November 2023.

Dan dos Santos is the official artist for the newest Marvel Masterpieces trading card set. Dan painted more than 135 original works of art featuring Marvel's greatest superheroes for this collectors' package.

Robert J. Sawyer's twenty-fifth novel, *The Downloaded*, debuted in October 2023 as an Audible Original starring Academy Award winner Brendan Fraser; the print version will be out in May 2024. Rob was a guest of honor at the 81st World Science Fiction Convention ("the Worldcon"), which, for the first time ever, was held in China. In April 2023, he was awarded the L. Ron Hubbard Lifetime Achievement Award for Outstanding Contributions to the Arts.

ALUMNI

Desmond Astaire (Vol. 38) released a novel, *Paranom*, and five short stories came out in anthologies/magazines.

Scott T. Barnes (Vol. 28) edited *Cosmic Muse*, an anthology of forty-three stories and poems featuring Writers of the Future winners and nominees, including his short story, "A Galaxy of Cranks."

Zack Be (Vol. 36) published "The Visions Are Free After Exit 73" in *Asimov's Science Fiction*, "Trust Fall" in *Analog*. He edited *Inner Workings: A Calendar of Fools Anthology* featuring short stories by sixteen Writers of the Future winners.

F. J. Bergmann (Vol. 36) published her short story "In the Cards" in *Inner Workings*, "Olympian" in *Pulp Literature 38*, and "The Sport of Snails" was performed on Space Cowboy Books Presents: Simultaneous Times Ep. 65.

Lazarus Black (Vol. 38) released his first novel, *The True Dragon of Atlanta*.

Bruce Brenneise (Vol. 34) attended fourteen conventions this past year selling his art, including in Toronto and Abu Dhabi. An interview with Bruce was featured in *ImagineFX* magazine.

Zach Chapman (Vol. 31) wrote two comic books, *House of Blood* and *A Haunting on Mars*, which released this past year.

Andy Dibble (Vol. 36) published "Every Me Is Someone Else" in *Diabolical Plots*, "The Baptismal Status of Persons Wetted by the Sprinkler Deluge" in *Mysterion*, "Render Unto Jesus" in *Sci Phi Journal*, and "Pro-Vote" in *Inner Workings*.

Kirbi Fagan (Vol. 30) illustrated the children's book *A Horse Named Sky* and it has since hit the *New York Times* bestseller list.

John Haas (Vol. 35) released the second novel in his Book of Ancient Evil Series through WordFire Press and signed the contract for his third.

David Hankins (Vol. 39) novelized his winning short story "Death and the Taxman." He and his Vol. 39 illustrator, Sarah Morrison, teamed up and published the novel with a successful Kickstarter campaign. Additionally, his story "A Properly Spiced Gingerbread" won the Critter's Readers Poll for Best Magical Realism.

N. V. Haskell (Vol. 38) published her own collection of fantasy stories in *Temporary Tales of Magic and Hope*. She had a total of eight short story sales, six publications, and signed a three-book contract.

Storm Humbert (Vol. 36) formed the small press, Calendar of Fools, along with other winners from Vol. 36 & 37. They released their first anthology, see Zack Be above. Storm had six stories and one nonfiction essay published.

Ken Liu (Vol. 19) released *Speaking Bones*, Book Four of the Dandelion Dynasty.

Michael Michera (Vol. 33) served as concept designer for the feature film, *Transformers: Rise of the Beasts*, and the video game, *Avatar: Frontiers of Pandora*.

Wulf Moon (Vol. 35) won the Critters Annual Readers Poll in multiple categories for *The Illustrated Super Secrets of Writing*, Volume 1: Best Author, Best Nonfiction book, and Best Writers' Research/Information/News Source.

T. R. Napper (Vol. 31) took home Australia's Aurealis Award Best Science Fiction Novel award for *36 Streets*.

Leah Ning (Vol. 36) is now managing editor at Apex Book Company and she had six new stories published.

Steve Pantazis (Vol. 31) published the first three books of his epic fantasy series, The Light of Darkness.

Dustin Panzino (Vol. 27) won Best in Show at Gen Con 2023.

Patrick Rothfuss (Vol. 18) latest release *The Narrow Road Between Desires* is a *New York Times* bestseller. And the forty-first *New York Times* bestselling book from our Contest winners.

Elise Stephens (Vol. 35) published two short stories, "Common Speech" with Escape Pod, and "Two-Tone" in *Stupefying Stories 25*.

Mike Jack Stoumbos (Vol. 38) edited and illustrated the anthology *Murderbirds*, released a new military SF novel *Defenders Rise*, and has had a number of new shorter works released, including a novelette in *The Phoenix Initiative: First Missions* and a stand-alone novella *Murder on the Barge Inn*.

Rebecca E. Treasure (Vol. 38) was named managing editor for *Apex Magazine*.

Mjke Wood (Vol. 25) released his novel *The Oneiromancer of Mars* in his Martian Dream series, and sold his fourth short story to *Analog* magazine.

Melissa Yuan-Innes (Vol. 15) won an Aurora Award for Best Poem/Song for "Rapunzel in the Desert" as published in *On Spec Magazine*, Issue 122.

Galaxy's Edge published several of our winners in their last magazine issue #62: Kary English (Vol. 31), T. R. Napper (Vol. 31), Rebecca E. Treasure (Vol. 38), Storm Humbert (Vol. 36), Alan Smale (Vol. 13), Steven Lawson (Vol. 33), Auston Habershaw (Vol. 31), and Samantha Murray (Vol. 31).

Infected by Art Volume 11 included these winners and judges: Daniel Bitton (Vol. 36), Arthur Bowling (Vol. 36), Bruce Brenneise (Vol. 34), Jennifer Bruce (Vol. 37), Laura Diehl (Vol. 20), Lucas Durham (Vol. 29), Bob Eggleton, Isabel Gibney (Vol. 37), Alexander Gustafson (Vol. 35), Brian C. Hailes (Vol. 18), Ben Hill (Vol. 36), Nick Jizba (Vol. 38), Ven Locklear (Vol. 24), Dustin Panzino (Vol. 27), April Solomon (Vol. 39), Dan Watson (Vol. 37), and Jim Zaccaria (Vol. 38).

There are just so many accomplishments. It's a real challenge to keep up with the 900 Contest winners....

We're looking ahead to a spectacular future!

THE YEAR IN THE CONTESTS

For Contest year 40, the winners are:

Writers of the Future Contest Winners

FIRST QUARTER

1. *Stephannie Tallent*
"LIFE AND DEATH AND LOVE IN THE BAYOU"

2. *Galen Westlake*
"THE IMAGALISK"

3. *John Eric Schleicher*
"SQUIDDY"

SECOND QUARTER

1. *Rosalyn Robilliard*
"THE WALL ISN'T A CIRCLE"

2. *Sky McKinnon*
"THE EDGE OF WHERE MY LIGHT IS CAST"

3. *James Davies*
"ASHES TO ASHES, BLOOD TO CARBONFIBER"

THIRD QUARTER

1. *Lance Robinson*
"FIVE DAYS UNTIL SUNSET"

2. *Kal M*
"BUTTER SIDE DOWN"

3. *Lisa Silverthorne*
"SUMMER OF THIRTY YEARS"

FOURTH QUARTER

1. *Jack Nash*
"SON, SPIRIT, SNAKE"

2. *Tom Vandermolen*
"NONZERO"

3. *Amir Agoora*
"DA-KO-TA"

THE YEAR IN THE CONTESTS

Illustrators of the Future Contest Winners

FIRST QUARTER
Arthur Haywood
Selena Meraki
Carina Zhang

SECOND QUARTER
Ashley Cassaday
Tyler Vail
May Zheng

THIRD QUARTER
Gigi Hooper
Jennifer Mellen
Pedro N.

FOURTH QUARTER
Steven Bentley
Connor Chamberlain
Guelly Rivera

L. Ron Hubbard's
Writers of the Future Contest

The most enduring and influential
contest in the history of SF and Fantasy

Open to new and amateur SF & Fantasy writers

*Prizes each quarter: $1,000, $750, $500
Quarterly 1st place winners compete for $5,000
additional annual prize!*

ALL JUDGING DONE BY PROFESSIONAL WRITERS ONLY

No entry fee is required

Entrants retain all publication rights

Don't delay! Send your entry now!

To submit your entry electronically go to:
    www.writersofthefuture.com/enter-writer-contest

Email: contests@authorservicesinc.com

To submit your entry via mail send to:
    L. Ron Hubbard's Writers of the Future Contest
    7051 Hollywood Blvd.
    Los Angeles, California 90028

1.   No entry fee is required, and all rights in the story remain the property of the author. All types of science fiction, fantasy, and dark fantasy are welcome.

2.   By submitting to the Contest, the entrant agrees to abide by all Contest rules.

3.   All entries must be original works by the entrant, in English. Plagiarism, which includes the use of third-party poetry, song lyrics, characters, or another person's universe, without written permission, will result in disqualification. Short stories or novelettes generated or created by computer software and/or artificial intelligence will be disqualified. Excessive violence or sex and the use of profane, vulgar, racist or offensive words, determined by the judges, will result in the story being rejected. Entries may not have been previously published in professional media.

4.   To be eligible, entries must be a short story of fantasy, science fiction, or light speculative horror. Your story has no minimum length requirement, however it may not be longer than 17,000 words.

     We regret we cannot consider novels, poetry, screenplays, or works intended for children.

5.   The Contest is open only to those who have not professionally published a novel or short novel, or more than one novelette, or more than three short stories, in any medium. Professional publication is deemed to be payment of professional rates at the time of publication (currently set at eight cents per word), and at least 5,000 copies, or 5,000 hits.

6. Entries submitted in hard copy must be typewritten or a computer printout in black ink on white paper, printed only on the front of the paper, double-spaced, with numbered pages. All other formats will be disqualified. Each entry must have a cover page with the title of the work, the author's legal name, a pen name if applicable, address, telephone number, email address and an approximate word count. Every subsequent page must carry the title and a page number, but the author's name must be deleted to facilitate fair, anonymous judging.

Entries submitted electronically must be double-spaced and must include the title and page number on each page, but not the author's name. Electronic submissions will separately include the author's legal name, pen name if applicable, address, telephone number, email address, and approximate word count.

7. Manuscripts will be returned after judging only if the author has provided return postage on a self-addressed envelope.

8. We accept only entries that do not require a delivery signature for us to receive them.

9. There shall be three cash prizes in each quarter: a First Prize of $1,000, a Second Prize of $750, and a Third Prize of $500, in US dollars. In addition, at the end of the year the First Place winners will have their entries judged by a panel of judges, and a Grand Prize winner shall be determined and receive an additional $5,000. All winners will also receive trophies. The Grand Prize winner shall be announced and awarded, along with the trophies to winners, at the L. Ron Hubbard awards ceremony held in the following year or when it is able to be held due to government regulations.

10. The Contest has four quarters, beginning on October 1, January 1, April 1, and July 1. The year will end on September 30. To be eligible for judging in its quarter, an entry must be postmarked or received electronically no later than midnight on the last day of the quarter. Late entries will be included in the following quarter and the Contest Administration will so notify the entrant.

11. Each entrant may submit only one manuscript per quarter. Winners are ineligible to make further entries in the Contest.

12. All entries for each quarter are final. No revisions are accepted.

13. Entries will be judged by professional authors. The decisions of the judges are entirely their own, and are final and binding.

14. Winners in each quarter will be individually notified of the results by phone, mail, or email.

15. This Contest is void where prohibited by law.

16. To send your entry electronically, go to:
www.writersofthefuture.com/enter-writer-contest
and follow the instructions.
To send your entry in hard copy, mail it to:
L. Ron Hubbard's Writers of the Future Contest
7051 Hollywood Blvd., Los Angeles, California 90028

17. Visit the website for any Contest rules update at:
www.writersofthefuture.com

L. Ron Hubbard's
Illustrators of the Future Contest

The most enduring and influential
contest in the history of SF and Fantasy

Open to new and amateur SF & Fantasy artists

$1,500 in prizes each quarter
Quarterly winners compete for $5,000
additional annual prize!

ALL JUDGING DONE BY
PROFESSIONAL ARTISTS ONLY

No entry fee is required

Entrants retain all rights

Don't delay! Send your entry now!

To submit your entry electronically go to:
   www.writersofthefuture.com/enter-the-illustrator-contest

Email: contests@authorservicesinc.com

To submit your entry via mail send to:
   L. Ron Hubbard's Illustrators of the Future Contest
   7051 Hollywood Blvd.
   Los Angeles, California 90028

1. The Contest is open to entrants from all nations. (However, entrants should provide themselves with some means for written communication in English.) All themes of science fiction and fantasy illustrations are welcome: every entry is judged on its own merits only. No entry fee is required and all rights to the entry remain the property of the artist.

2. By submitting to the Contest, the entrant agrees to abide by all Contest rules.

3. The Contest is open to new and amateur artists who have not been professionally published and paid for more than three black-and-white story illustrations, or more than one process-color painting, in media distributed broadly to the general public. The ultimate eligibility criterion, however, is defined by the word "amateur"—in other words, the artist has not been paid for his artwork. If you are not sure of your eligibility, please write a letter to the Contest Administration with details regarding your publication history. Include a self-addressed and stamped envelope for the reply. You may also send your questions to the Contest Administration via email.

4. Each entrant may submit only one set of illustrations in each Contest quarter. The entry must be original to the entrant and previously unpublished. Plagiarism, infringement of the rights of others, or other violations of the Contest rules will result in disqualification. Winners in previous quarters are not eligible to make further entries.

5. The entry shall consist of three illustrations done by the entrant in a color or black-and-white medium created from the artist's imagination. Use of gray scale in illustrations

and mixed media, photo and design software, and the use of photography in the illustrations are accepted. Art generated using programs such as artificial intelligence, or similar programs will be disqualified. Source and reference imagery may be requested at any time to ensure all rules have been met. Each illustration must represent a subject different from the other two.

6. Electronic submissions will separately include the artist's legal name, address, telephone number, email address which will identify each of three pieces of art and the artist's signature on the art should be deleted. Only .jpg, .jpeg, and .png files will be accepted, a maximum file size of 10 MB.

7. HARD COPY ENTRIES SHOULD NOT BE THE ORIGINAL DRAWINGS, but should be color or black-and-white reproductions of the originals, of a quality satisfactory to the entrant. Entries must be submitted unfolded and flat, in an envelope no larger than 9 inches by 12 inches. Images submitted electronically must be a minimum of 300 dpi, a minimum of 5 x 7 inches and a maximum of 8.5 x 11 inches.

All hard copy entries must be accompanied by a self-addressed return envelope of the appropriate size, with the correct US postage affixed. (Non-US entrants should enclose international postage reply coupons.) If the entrant does not want the reproductions returned, the entry should be clearly marked DISPOSABLE COPIES: DO NOT RETURN. A business-size self-addressed envelope with correct postage (or valid email address) should be included so that the judging results may be returned to the entrant. We only accept entries that do not require a delivery signature for us to receive them.

To facilitate anonymous judging, each of the three photocopies must be accompanied by a removable cover sheet bearing the artist's name, address, telephone number, email address, and an identifying title for that work. The reproduction of the work should carry the same identifying title on the front of the illustration and the artist's signature should be deleted. The Contest Administration will remove and file the cover sheets, and forward only the anonymous entry to the judges.

8. There will be three cowinners in each quarter. Each winner will receive a cash prize of US $500 and will be awarded a trophy. Winners will also receive eligibility to compete for the annual Grand Prize of $5,000 together with the annual Grand Prize trophy.

9. For the annual Grand Prize Contest, the quarterly winners will be furnished with a specification sheet and a winning story from the Writers of the Future Contest to illustrate. In order to retain eligibility for the Grand Prize, each winner shall send to the Contest address his/her illustration of the assigned story within thirty (30) days of receipt of the story assignment.

    The yearly Grand Prize winner shall be determined by a panel of judges on the following basis only: Each Grand Prize judge's personal opinion on the extent to which it makes the judge want to read the story it illustrates.

    The Grand Prize winner shall be announced and awarded, along with the trophies to the winners, at the L. Ron Hubbard awards ceremony held in the following year or when it is able to be held due to government regulations.

10. The Contest has four quarters, beginning on October 1, January 1, April 1, and July 1. The year will end on September 30. To be eligible for judging in its quarter, an entry must be postmarked or received electronically no later than midnight

on the last day of the quarter. Late entries will be included in the following quarter and the Contest Administration will so notify the entrant.

11. Entries will be judged by professional artists only. Each quarterly judging and the Grand Prize judging may have different panels of judges. The decisions of the judges are entirely their own and are final and binding.

12. Winners in each quarter will be individually notified of the results by phone, mail, or email.

13. This Contest is void where prohibited by law.

14. To send your entry electronically, go to: www.writersofthefuture.com/enter-the-illustrator-contest and follow the instructions.
    To send your entry via mail send it to:
    L. Ron Hubbard's Illustrators of the Future Contest
    7051 Hollywood Blvd., Los Angeles, California 90028

15. Visit the website for any Contest rules update at: www.illustratorsofthefuture.com

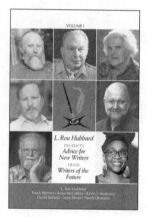

Writers of the Future
10-Book Package and Slipcase

Since Volume 30, the annual anthology has been published as a handsome trade paperback.

In addition to the Writers' Contest winning stories and hard-won tips from Contest judges, each volume features an impressive full-color 16-page art gallery. Additionally each includes three stories from bestselling authors. All this makes for a captivating book to read, treasure, and discover the best new writers and artists each year.

$15.95, 432 pgs $15.95, 496 pgs $15.95, 432 pgs $15.95, 400 pgs $15.95, 470 pgs

$15.95, 440 pgs $15.95, 472 pgs $15.95, 448 pgs $22.95, 496 pgs $22.95, 528 pgs

The slipcase features full-color artwork from Volume 33 by Larry Elmore, Volume 35 by Bob Eggleton, Volume 36 by Echo Chernik, and Volume 39 by Tom Wood.

$22.95, 506 pgs

Get the slipcase free by completing your collection with a minimum order of $50.

ANY 10 FOR $125 $183.50 (SAVE $53.50)

To order call toll-free 877-842-5299 or visit GalaxyPress.com

7051 Hollywood Boulevard Los Angeles, CA 90028